MW01277913

PRAISE FOR REPLACEMENT CHILDREN

"The relationship between limo driver Charlie Woods and matriarchal Vivien Granville may initially remind readers of Driving Miss Daisy. But not for long. Author Rick Maloy has other catfish to fry. Atmospheric and character-driven, *Replacement Children* is a skillfully woven tale of greed, lust, tragedy – and unlikely redemption – in the rural South. St. Paul allegedly said that it was better to marry than to burn. He might rethink that after reading this fine book."

> —Lawrence De Maria, author of eight novels, is a former *New York Times* senior editor and currently a board member of the Washington Independent Review of Books.

"Readers in search of a great story, populated by fascinating characters, should try Rick Maloy's *Replacement Children*. Set in small town Georgia, this collision of two families - one wealthy, the other constantly on the brink of ruin - is a blend of humor and pathos. Greed, conflicting family loyalties, and Internet-age sexuality power both clans toward their fates in this page-turner. Surprising, funny, touching, and well written. "

> —Nancy Nickolas, former editor of best sellers at Simon & Schuster,

"*Replacement Children* throws hard punches. Maloy knows his refreshingly mature characters, and is not afraid to send them down rough roads. Real people make for scarier horror stories than do vampires and werewolves. Charlie "Dense" Woods and Vivien Granville are lost in a forest full of shadows cast by their own ravenous kin. Here's a dark look at the institutions of marriage, family, and money that you cannot easily dismiss."

> —Sohrab Homi Fracis, author of *Ticket to Minto: Stories of India and America* (Iowa Short Fiction Award)

"Rick Maloy's *Replacement Children* brilliantly explores how the pull of money can affect people no matter where they started, whether it's the wealthy, entitled Granville family or the sad but ambitious Desiree Woods. Maloy's characters squander their emotional and mental energy trying to find the next angle, with no regard to those they're manipulating. But he does a masterful job of showing where every machination eventually leads, and the tragic consequences of greed come through in frightening ways with every twist in this fascinating plot. With *Replacement Children*, Maloy has produced a fabulous debut novel"

> —Russell Roland, author of *High and Inside, In Open Spaces, the Watershed Years*

"Faulkner meets Honey Boo-Boo in the Southern-fried reality show that is Rick Maloy's *Replacement Children*. Much like the morbid attraction of a roadside wreck, the clash of culture and class in Maloy's debut novel shines a spotlight on the human condition with a cast of characters readers will remember long after the last page is turned."

—Parker Francis, author of the Quint Mitchell Mystery series

REPLACEMENT CHILDREN

a novel by

RICK MALOY

REPLACEMENT CHILDREN

Published by Seward House.

Copyright © 2013 by Rick Maloy
www.rickmaloy.com

Author services by Pedernales Publishing, LLC.
www.pedernalespublishing.com

Library of Congress Control Number: 2013913569

ISBN 978-0-9896239-0-2 Paperback Edition
ISBN 978-0-9896239-1-9 Hardcover Edition
ISBN 978-0-9896239-2-6 Digital Edition

Printed in the United States of America

To Curly, ever there in spite of me.

ACKNOWLEDGMENTS

My biggest debt is to Steve Lipsitz. This saint has endured from my earliest pages to the present. He was friend enough to trash the inaugural efforts and supportive enough to stuff my nose into books of true merit.

Workshop gurus Lynn Skapyak Harlin and Frank Green deserve credit for any "craft" that has found its way into my books. Each emphasized short fiction as the path to disciplined writing, and both turned weak efforts into learning opportunities.

My wife, Ann Marie, and one-time school marm, Pasley Mansfield, were my test lab. Each waded through the slow stream of chapters, unearthing the bright spots and flaws. If this book is a pleasant reading experience, it's because of their countless hours and invaluable feedback.

A bow to Jose Ramirez and Barbara Rainess at Pedernales Publishing for their professionalism and patience, particularly through the process of cover design.

Special thanks to authors Lawrence De Maria, Sohrab Fracis, Parker Francis, and Russell Rowland for reading the final product and offering their publishable praise. Same for editor Nancy Nicholas's input and kind words.

I even offer a nod to Jeff Kleinman, the agent who ultimately rejected an early version of the book but offered excellent advice on how to improve it.

Apologies to all those I've missed.

REPLACEMENT CHILDREN

CHAPTER ONE

MEN WHO'VE BEEN to war sleep differently. Not so much because of dreams raging with what they've done or seen, but from knowing that time unaware is the most dangerous.

Noise knocked Charlie Woods awake. A band of light glowed under the door, killing enough dark that he could make out the water stain on his ceiling. He was home, in the bedroom of his single-wide, not in a tent or Marine barracks, and like every morning since they mustered him out, his first duty of the day was to beat back disappointment.

Silverware clanged onto Formica in the kitchen.

He laid an arm over his eyes and assessed the situation on the bright side of the door.

"I said get up," Desiree shouted.

Didn't take a genius to know his wife was still mad from last night. Even worse, with her already out of bed, makeup sex before his trip was looking like a long shot.

...happy wife, happy life...

"GranDelia," he whispered toward the panels sagging above his face, "let a man wake up, for heaven sake." Older he got, the less he welcomed his departed grandmother's advice, that nugget in particular. In his three years as a husband, hardly a day had gone by he didn't hear *happy wife, happy life* at least once.

"On my way," he called to Desiree. Whiffs of bacon and coffee pulled his head off the pillow. Quick peek at the clock showed 5:04. He flipped the covers off and dropped his feet onto the spiky indoor-outdoor, so cold it felt wet. Must have gone below freezing again overnight. His toes stroked the floor. "Please don't, honey."

Plumbing in the mobile home was nearing its final reward, and the thought of burrowing underneath to fix another break, like last week, brought a shiver. Garbage bag poncho, bellying through ice and mud, navigating around mystery turds so big he made sure to sweep the flashlight into every cranny before going any deeper. He'd wrapped each pipe after fixing the busted one, but if this cold snap didn't lift soon, no telling how long before another blew. "Hot-lanta, my butt." He ripped the blanket from the bed and draped it around his shoulders.

Careful to support the bedroom's accordion door in its track, he pulled it aside far enough to lean his face through. "Mornin', Baby Girl. Smells—Aw, c'mon." Quitting smoking had been Desiree's wedding present to him.

"Don't start, Charlie."

"You promised."

His old *Greensboro Volunteer Fire Dept.* jacket hung over her flannel nightgown like a cape. "You promised," she said, her voice going all high and whiny. She shot a glance at the blanket he was gripping at his throat. "And you're a big help. Who's making the bed today?" Plate of food in hand, she kicked her skinny leg forward and caught up with the good one. At the table, she dropped into a chair across from his plate and stared at it.

Her usual prettiness took on some ugly. Might have been because he was mad about her smoking, but the overhead light wasn't doing her any favors either. Glare from two bare fluorescents showed every day of the seven years she had on him. Skin for sure, but her home-colored hair suffered, too. Brown ripples with a hint of purple, at least the side she kept long.

Her eyes stayed on his food. "I got up in the middle of the damn night. Eat."

He decided to let the smoking go, for now. "Baby Girl, I'm freezing, and I don't have time to get dressed twice. Lay a paper towel over it. Two minutes."

Without looking his way, she stood, parked the cigarette between her teeth, and limped his bacon and eggs to a counter next to the sink. One yank on an upright roll of paper towels ripped out an arm's length. She bunched it into a ball and swiped his breakfast into an open garbage bag under the sink.

"Hey!" He took a long step toward her.

"Said you was late. Just making time."

"Gotta stop this." He stabbed a finger at her. "Only a few days, and the money's great. I have to go." No sex, no breakfast, and he still got pulled back into the scrap.

One last drag before she darted the cigarette into a half empty coffee, a cup that already had a soggy butt floating in it. "Bull. You *want* to go."

"You're right. So what? Going crazy here doing next to nothing, and we need the money." These would be their first-ever days apart, and he didn't want to go with them mad at each other. "C'mon, Baby Girl," he said, edging closer.

"Stop calling me that!" She whirled toward him. "Going through the damn change. Feels ridiculous you calling me that." Tears swelled and shined in her eyes, but she swept them away before any made it down her cheeks.

He didn't know "the change" was happening. Could have explained why everything he did lately was wrong or "stupid," a needle that never missed the nerve. "Coulda told me." He reached for her.

"No." She shoved her palms at him. "Want to go? Get on with it. Go take up with some bit of whatnot."

Turning things lighter felt worth a try. "You mean like a pretty little hotel maid?" Grinning, he inched forward.

"That ain't funny." She bounced a finger at him. "Good lookin' man like you on the road. Think I don't see what happens?"

He snorted a laugh. "Right. That Ritz Carlton must be a regular Sodom and Gomorrah."

"Nobody knows better the maid, Charlie, and rich or poor, men turn into pigs in hotels."

This was a conversation with no chance of a quick wrap-up. "I gotta go."

She blocked his path to the shower. "I see it, dammit. Every day. Something about hotels. People think they're, I dunno, invisible or something. But those rooms tell stories."

"You got too much imagination. Step aside."

"They don't even try to hide it." She knocked his hand off her arm. "Wastebaskets piled with liquor bottles and beer cans. Charge card receipts from whore services. Used—"

"Hang on. Says 'whore service' on the ticket?"

"Gotta spell everything out," she said, rolling her eyes. "Charlie, can one man eat three hundred dollars of takeout from Asian Delights?" Her fingers notched the air with quotation marks. "Oh, and there's worse. Used rubbers, right there on top of the trash, like they're bragging to me. Last week? Found one tucked in a Bible like a book mark. The *Bible*, Charlie," she said, leaning toward him, eyes big. "Could've used the Book of Mormon, but no. I threw it out. God forgive me, I threw out a Bible."

Gossipy as she was, hearing this now made him wonder how much was outrage and how much was a delaying tactic. "Y'know, I need to hear more about this." He nudged her sideways. "After my shower."

She whacked his hand away. "You don't care."

"Truth be told, I don't. None of my business what goes on there. Yours neither. Just do your work and keep your dang head down."

She hobbled to the sink and cranked both faucets. "G'won," she said, twisting a dishtowel into a mug like wringing a chicken's neck, "can't keep her highness waiting. But you remember what'll happen if you come home and gimme something."

Early on, he'd learned that talking to her back was a waste of time, so he slipped into the tiny bathroom for a shower, unhappy about accepting this driving assignment no matter how good the pay. Limo jobs had never taken him away for even one overnight much less five, and yesterday, when he told Desiree about the job and mentioned the client was a Mrs. Granville, she stayed deaf to the part about the woman being over eighty. Said if he came home and gave her an STD, she'd blow his "non-existent brains out," a real possibility since she slept with a .38 under the mattress.

"How do I look?" He stepped into the kitchen in his driver's uniform: blue blazer, white shirt, black tie, charcoal slacks, and black shoes.

"Dangerous." Arms wide, she hobbled to him. Her face nuzzled his chest. Fingers swirled soft circles on his back. "Tell me I'm being crazy."

"Loopy as a deer eating fermented apples." He whisked her slender body off the floor, one hand around her back, the other under her knees. "Dump you at the nut factory in Milledgeville if it was on my way. Pin a note on you saying this Baby Girl needs five nights in their finest padded room."

"I'm serious, Charlie," she said, ducking his try for a kiss, "time you stopped calling me that. Last Friday at the VFW, I saw Wanda Dunphy's boy cover his mouth when you said that."

"What do you care what a pimply teenager thinks? So what do I call you?"

"How about …?" She shook her head. "Was gonna say GranDesiree, but a woman what never was Momma can't be a Gran."

"Shh." He bounced her one time. "Baby Girl, please be done with that."

She smiled but didn't look at him. "Have to admit, I do love when you call me that, but there's times I think it's because, y'know."

"Hush. Told you, if the Lord had blessed us that way, fine. He didn't. That's fine, too." That was as close to a lie as he was willing to tell her. "And what happens in the end with kids?" He jiggled her until she looked at him. "They're yours for awhile, then they're gone. And what's left after that?" Having someone else look confused for a change pleased him. "What's left is what we had in the first place. You and me."

She smacked a loud kiss on his cheek.

"That's better." He swung her feet to the floor and reached into the door-less closet for his trench coat.

Her arms lashed around his ribs. "Don't go."

"Desiree, stop," he said, pulling at her arms. "I've quit my last job for you. Y'hear me? Selling cars, landscaping, Comcast, for heaven sake." Other than being a Marine, installing for Comcast was the happiest work he ever did, but she made him quit after overhearing his friend Spuv, another installer, lying at the VFW about all the sex he was getting from drunk housewives.

"This is different." She hugged tighter. "This is hotels. Something's gonna happen."

"Two thousand dollars is what's gonna happen. That's it." If he did well on this Granville assignment, the work might come steadier. Him and Desiree both working at the same time, they might even get ahead a little.

"Sugar," she said, almost like singing, "don't you even know what today is?"

He clicked through birthdays and anniversaries but came up empty. "Got no time for guessing games."

"You surprise me sometimes. It's Charlie stays in bed and Desiree does anything he asks day." She bumped her hips into him. "Starting right now."

Sex as a weapon. Made him more angry than horny. He held her away, hands firm on her shoulders. "I'll call you every chance I get." He dug his dress-up leather gloves from the pockets of the coat. "Gonna kiss me goodbye?" he said, hand paused on the knob of the outside door.

"Y'know, maybe I ain't gonna be here when you phone," she said, eyes wandering and sparkly. "Maybe …" Hands on her hips, chin up, she shifted from one foot to the other. "Maybe I'll just take up with one of the guests. First one that flirts, and don't think they don't, wins a night with yours truly. What do you think of that?"

"Don't let me leave like this."

"Maybe I'll charge for it. Cripple might bring extra." Hands clamped over her mouth, she scouted the little room for an escape hole.

Hearing "cripple" told him this was way worse than he'd thought. He cornered her by the cooktop and pinned her arms under a tight hug. "Shh," he said until she quit squirming. "What's really going on? Be straight."

Her shoulder pushed into him. "Just go."

"C'mon now." Like his grandmother, Desiree talked plain, at least some of the time. One of the reasons he'd come to love her.

"You grew up here." The side of her face rolled on his chest. "Y'ain't gonna get it."

"Talking about Greensboro or the house?"

"Everything."

"That's a bit too much territory right now." He pushed on her shoulders, but she hung tight.

"Want to know why I talk so little about The Ritz?"

At least that narrowed the topic some. "Gimme the short version."

She let out a long, slow breath. "Breaks my heart is why. Thought about quitting, but a person can't stop knowing what they know."

"This don't sound like the short version."

"It's a damn paradise, Charlie. Can't describe it any different. Takes my breath sometimes. Seen stuff that grand on TV, but I've touched it now, wandered around in it. It's real, and it's never gonna be for me."

Seemed like it wasn't okay anymore to do your best and enjoy the fruits. Anybody else had more, you were supposed to feel cheated for some reason. Seeing symptoms of that disease in Desiree hit him worse than her smoking. "Everyone has their own life. Leave it go."

"I ain't explaining right. It's like … Okay, yesterday I was doing up a corner suite. Those always get, y'know, the fanciest people. Anyway, in the bathroom I could smell cinnamon and lemon from scented candles along the back of the jet tub." She pulled him closer. "Know what I did?"

"Baby Girl, I have to go. Call me in the car." He loosened his arms, but she didn't.

"I climbed into that tub, laid back, and closed my eyes. Imagined I was relaxing under a steamy blanket of bubbles."

"Sounds like fun. Now let go."

"Shoulda known." She shook her head. "Charlie, I couldn't keep from crying." Her face slipped lower on his chest. "And then I come back here. A breaking down woman in a falling down trailer."

"Careful now," he said, swaying her in the hug. "No one bad-mouths my wife or my sacred birthplace."

"I'm serious, Charlie. Me and this trailer, both caving in on ourselves, like Nature's bent on fixing two mistakes at once. And then you being in hotels with that rich woman. You're gonna come back feeling the same."

"Let's do this," he said. "While I'm gone, you make a list of things that need doing around here. We'll put the whole two thousand into turning this place into a palace."

"Already done it." She held up one finger. "Light a candle and set it on the shelf in the bedroom closet." A second finger popped up. "Close every window and door." A third finger. "Blow out the pilot and turn on the burners and the oven." Her pinkie flipped up.

"Wow," he said. "You've given this some thought." A little too much, far as he was concerned.

"Not done, and this here's the big one." She tapped the pinkie to her thumb. "Run like you stole something."

A joke. Not a good one, but enough to signal she was settling down. "You okay now?" He kissed her on top of the head. "Already gonna be late, and they told me Mrs. Granville tends toward the cranky."

She hooked her hands behind his neck, pulled their faces close, and planted a trail of soft kisses from his mouth to his ear. "Charlie," she whispered, her warm breath buzzing his whole body, "don't let me get lost."

Relaxing his hug, he tipped backward. "Course not," he said, seeing a chance to wrap this up.

A tiny smile pulled at the corners of her mouth. "Still love me?"

"Now and forever, Baby Girl."

Backing the Dependable Car Service limo out of his driveway, he wondered if the fifteen minute ride to Reynolds Plantation would be enough time to figure out what "lost" meant.

CHAPTER TWO

DRESSED AND PACKED, Vivien Granville returned her house to darkness and waited at the bay window of the dining room. Outside, distant streetlamps dusted her landscaping a pale orange, last color before the grays of dawn. Bygone stirrings quickened her breaths. During the juicy years, this tail end of night had always titillated, aroused notions of traffickers in the shadows, those who caused floor creaks, not shrank from them. Often, her beloved Marshall awoke at this hour to find her spooned against him, breath on his neck, hand rubbing his thigh. Six children, all conceived pre-dawn.

Headlights penetrated into the circular driveway and grew larger until the limo centered between the columns of her portico. The chauffeur eased from the vehicle, killed the headlights, and shut the door far enough to douse the dome light. He stood to full height behind the vehicle, hands resting on the roof. Steam from his nose and mouth puffed into the chill.

"Neanderthal," she said on her way to the foyer, "keep your lips shut." She flicked the carriage lights once and opened the door before his steps reached the bell. "Good morning," she said from the dark threshold, doing her best to sound imperious. Like everyone nowadays, the man seemed quite tall.

"And g'morning to you, ma'am," the silhouette said, his deep drawl commercially cheerful. "Dependable Car Service." He held out a business card scissored between two gloved fingers. "Name's Charlie Woods. Call me Charlie. And at this hour, I sure do hope you're Mrs. Granville."

"You reek." Arms folded, she left the business card untaken. "I specifically said non-smoker."

"Huh?" He re-pocketed the card, sniffed his sleeve, and shrugged. "I don't, ma'am. Promise. Must be on my clothes from the wife. She's trying real hard to quit, but, y'know … So," he said, gloves muffling a clap, "you about ready?"

"You'll need to fetch my bags." She waved him into the foyer and closed the door. "Follow me." As a younger woman she had a magnificent figure, and this procession was one she relished. Shoulders back. Slow the stride. Lengthen it slightly. Give whomever it was, male or female, sufficient opportunity to appreciate the proportion and grace, to regret they would never have her or be her. No point now. The shoulders didn't lift what they used to, and her peach had pancaked ages ago.

"Don't you want some lights on?" he said as they passed through the foyer and started down a long hallway to the kitchen.

"Almost there." At the far wall, past the granite island and wall of stainless steel appliances, she pushed open the door to a small bedroom and stepped to the side. "Those." She pointed at two large suitcases beside the bed.

Crouching between the bags, Charlie grabbed the handles. He stood and jiggled the one containing nothing but her Depends. "Left one mostly empty, huh? Bringing back presents for the family?"

"Oh," she said, covering her first laugh since the news about poor Devon. "A little grab bag for each of them. That *would* be fun." As they passed through the kitchen, she dragged her oversized tote off the island.

Charlie helped her into the warmth of the Town Car's rear seat, stowed the luggage, and settled behind the wheel. "Okay, just wanna make sure I got this right. We're going to Key West, right?"

"I gave all this to the girl over the phone."

He pulled a paper from his shirt pocket and unfolded it. "I know, but let me just make sure. Overnights in Ocala and Key Largo. Then Key West by noon on Saturday. That right?"

"Correct. The noon arrival part is quite important."

"Okay, that's what I got. None of my business, Mrs. Granville," he said, refolding the paper, "but wouldn't it be a lot easier to fly?"

"Correct again."

"Then how come you're driving?"

"I meant you were correct that it's none of your business." In the rearview, she saw him wince. A poor start to six days together, but he had no need to know that she no longer considered airplane toilets manageable, that she refused to risk extended time in the air or on the runway, chafing in her unpredictable outflows. She'd considered explaining this to the children so one of them might offer to drive to the funeral, but long-term risks dwarfed the one-time benefit. A plot was afoot, and any admission of creeping infirmity would only have stoked their treachery. Better to remain "difficult" or "impossible" until she conceived countermeasures.

The chauffeur's frequent checks of the rearview betrayed his discomfort.

"Forgive me, Charlie. Senior crabbiness. One of the few percs of surviving too long."

His face broke into a smile. "Hey, no problem. The wife's always saying my nose is too long."

She found the switch to a goose-neck reading light and clicked it on. Her hand tunneled through three of the disposables she'd tucked into her carryall. Out came a hardcover *East of Eden*. "Have you read this?" She steadied the book for his glance in the mirror.

"Ma'am, take me a dang year to read something that big."

"It's quite riveting." Experience taught her that a meaty book, with a classic title, was the secret to privacy while traveling. The book's spine cracked. She spread her hands across the pages and left them covering the print. Eyes to the window, she watched her winter-dead garden crawl by.

SITTING BEHIND a tall coffee, Charlie rose part way from his seat and smiled as she approached from the Ladies room. Her first face-on look at him in strong light. She decided he was quite handsome. Dark complexion, outdoorsy. Tight, angular face, almost military. Early thirties, but youthful, particularly the smile. Impish, not yet weary. Dense brown hair, parted high. He'd never be bald like her four sons. Three sons. Naturally, all of them blamed maternal genes, as if it was more evidence of her power, her malice. As bizarre members of that confederacy, even her two daughters seemed to agree.

"Get you something?" He pointed to the menu board. "Egg and bacon on a biscuit? The wife loves those."

She stopped short of the molded plastic booth and shook her head. "No, nothing, and our arrangement is that I provide all food and lodging."

"Cup of coffee won't break me. Tea? Bottled water?"

Small steps brought her next to the table. She bent toward him. "So that we don't go through this vaudeville at each stop, I'll be clear. When I say 'nothing,' that's what I mean. It's not an invitation to be coaxed. Now," she said to his stony face, "you may either dump that coffee or bring it to the car."

"Mrs. Granville?" he called to her back.

She pretended not to hear. Broad hands on her shoulders startled her.

"Something on your shoe, ma'am," Charlie whispered, lips so close his breath warmed her ear.

A peek behind her heels showed his gleaming black oxford planted on the kite-tail of toilet paper she'd been dragging.

"Okay," he said.

Face pointed at the door, she tugged her eyes to the side and fixed briefly on his smile. Head back, she marched to the exit, shielding her eyes from the new sun.

"Ma'am," he said after setting his coffee into the Town Car's cup holder, "we gonna be stopping every hour, give or take?" He clicked his seat belt.

"Your point?"

"Well, nothing," he said, starting the engine, "but we have to cover about three hundred fifty miles today. Barely got to Macon. Y'know, maybe sixty miles."

"Hot date waiting for you in Ocala, Charlie?" Pheromonal as he was, it would not have shocked her to find he had ready companionship scattered throughout the south.

"No, ma'am." Head shaking slowly, he laughed. "All my hot dates are with the wife. Married to a great woman. Feisty, like you." He bumped the limo off the curb-cut and headed for the entrance to I-75.

His intelligence jumped a notch for recognizing the difference between feisty and difficult. "Enlighten me about the stops then."

"It's the gas. I usually fill up at these pit stops." The car accelerated up the entry ramp. "If we're gonna make a bunch of them, I won't bother."

"Hourly would probably be the most comfortable," she said. "Yes, hourly. Let's do that."

"Smart." They merged into light traffic. "My wife likes to stop a lot, too. Stretch those legs. Most people go too long."

"Charlie, it appears your wife is going to be a recurring visitor during our little sojourn. Has she a name?"

"Desiree." His beaming face caught her in the rearview. "Name's Desiree."

"Is she a stripper?"

The smile left him. His eyes returned to the road.

"Sorry. Clumsy attempt at humor."

"Mrs. Granville, how could you say something like that about a man's wife?"

"One apology per infraction, Charlie." She shifted her hips in the seat, made a show of opening the book, and dropped her eyes to the pages.

EVEN THROUGH DARK GLASSES, the lowering sun made Vivien squint as she neared Charlie's poolside table. A waitress clad in tight white shorts and a cinched tropical shirt stood in front of him, exchanging a new bottle of beer for his empty. Back straight, the young woman bent from the waist, one of those, "And what's your name?" bend-overs women use when speaking to a strange toddler. Clever girl, Vivien thought. Front and back at the same time.

"Hang on a sec," Charlie said into his cell phone. He covered the mouthpiece. "Well, thank you," he said to the server.

"My pleasure, honey. I'll keep checking on you." Their smiles lingered. His eyes followed the rolling shorts to their next delivery.

Vivien thumped her straw carryall onto the table.

"Hey, there you are," Charlie said to her, pushing to his feet, the phone still pressed to his chest. "Getting a touch worried."

"And a touch frisky, I see." She lowered into a webbed, plastic chair.

"I'm gonna go," he said into his phone. "Mrs. Granville just joined me. Bye ... Now and forever, Baby Girl." He snapped the phone shut and sat. "Thought we were meeting at five?"

"Had to make myself beautiful for our date, dear boy."

She was late because of poor Devon. He'd been hovering since Charlie got her settled in the room and left. After a much-needed soak in the tub and some fresh underwear, she'd slipped into bed. Without any more distractions, she could no longer avoid her last-born. Always so needy. Maddeningly defenseless. Too many tugs on the skirt to redress injustices. Too theatrical, too delicate. A sixth child should have eventually understood that reservoirs of affection and patience weren't limitless, especially a child whose very existence divided a husband and wife.

She must have cried herself to sleep. If not for rolling a cheek onto a blot of cold wetness, she would have stayed in bed while Charlie enjoyed the shapely bodies parading in front of his sunglasses. "I'm curious, Charlie. Would ogling that girl's posterior bring out the 'feisty' in your wife?"

"Caught me, huh?" His eyes found the waitress again. "Just killing time. Couple beers. Sunny day. Pretty girl." He shook his head slowly. "But I'd never do that if Desiree was here."

"Short leash, eh?"

"Not that." He shifted toward her. "See, Desiree's got this bum leg, from when she was a baby. Not just skinny, it's a couple inches shorter than the other one. Makes her limp. She forgets about it most of the time, but a place like this, women in bathing suits and whatnot." He crinkled his nose. "I'd never do something to make her think it matters, because it don't. I mean doesn't."

"Ah, true love. So rare these days."

His lips thinned. "You throwing off on me and her again?"

"Not at all. In fact, I commend you. Sensitive to people's dignity."

"I just care about her."

"Untrue. You even did it for me. The toilet tissue, at the rest stop. You could have left it on my shoe. Had a laugh at my expense. I know my children would have." She removed her sunglasses and set them on the table. "Small kindnesses reveal a great deal, Charlie."

"You okay?" He leaned toward her.

She backed away. "Why?"

"Your eyes." He pointed a finger and spun it in a tight circle near her face. "They're all red. The edges and everything. Nose, too. You been crying?"

"And now we have it, the quintessential nosey parker question."

He smiled. "I can guess what that means. Sorry."

"Must be allergies." She donned the shades again. "Isn't it fascinating how changes can occur so dramatically in one day's car ride? Probably all sorts of things I'll have to get used to."

"Couple of times in the mirror today. Thought I saw you—"

"Charlie." Her open hand pushed at him. "Don't be dull. Allergies. In fact," she said, rising to her feet, "I've decided to dine in my room tonight, allow the air conditioning to work its magic." She hoisted the straw bag and hung it from her elbow. "I presume you have a charge card of some kind?"

His answer was something between a shrug and a nod.

"Well, if you leave the property for dinner, or for," she cleared her throat, "killing time, save the receipts. I'll reimburse you in the morning."

"Ma'am, what's in Key West?"

She stared briefly at him before walking away. "That beer should probably be your last," she said without turning. "I'll see you in the lobby tomorrow morning. Six o'clock sharp."

CHAPTER THREE

A NARROW BEACH fronted the Casa Marina Resort in Key West. Cell phone pressed to his ear, Dr. Ward Granville paced the dry edge of the waterline's lazy ebbs and rushes. "Where the hell are you?" he snapped at his sister, Lauren, as soon as she picked up the call.

"I know, brother dear, I should have called. Tomorrow. We'll be there tomorrow."

"Well, that's just great." Time with Lauren would have been the only upside to this whole debacle.

"I'm sorry," she said. "So, tell me about Devon and this morning. Was it—"

"Hold it. *We'll* be there? Is Mother coming with you?"

"She already left. That idiotic limo? Remember?"

"Then who's 'we'? And you better not mean that motorcycle mechanic." Last week, she emailed him a picture of her latest dalliance, a spike-haired twenty-something, his arms and neck an explosion of multicolored ink.

"Be nice," she said. "Justin's sitting right next to me, and he can hear you. And why shouldn't I be with someone? You're there with Philippa."

Ward winced at the notion his wife could be a comfort. "Yes, there is that."

"I'm sad about poor Devon," Lauren said, "and I may need a shoulder to cry on." She giggled. "Yes, and that," she said to the person in the car.

"Laurie, I'm not the one who needs to be careful."

"You're not the boss of me. And you didn't answer. How bad was it this morning?"

This time her question dragged up the image of their youngest brother, rigid and grotesque on a morgue tray. "What do you think?"

"You're a rock. None of us could have done it. Did he look bad?"

"So many years since I'd seen him, it took a few seconds to add back a full head of hair and knock off fifty pounds, but it was Devon. Once I confirmed that to the Medical Examiner, he pulled the sheet up and slid him back into the cooler. I signed a few things, and it was over. In and out in ten minutes."

"Could you see the rope marks and everything?"

"Let's change the subject," he said, reliving the first-glimpse queasiness from seeing Devon's blood-bloated lips and tongue, purplish flesh, and distended eyes. "Was I wrong about you flying in this morning?"

"That was Plan A, but then Justin arranged a few days off, so we're heading down in the Ferrari first thing in the morning."

"Jesus Christ, Laurie. How about some boundaries?"

"I'm coming to say goodbye to a tortured soul, and I won't apologize for myself, to you or anyone. Should we hang up?"

"No." A bad conversation with Lauren was better than no conversation. "I, uh, just don't want Mother upset by anything unnecessary. So," he said after a long, calming exhale, "you said she left yesterday. Has she phoned you? Because I've heard nothing."

"*Nada*, m'dear. And you know she never turns her cell on, so don't waste your time there."

"I know. She's becoming a bigger pain in the ass by the day."

"That, um, other matter. Did you bring the brochures and everything?"

"We'll go over them at dinner tomorrow, not that I give two shits what any of you think. If I'm left with the work, I'm going to decide where she ends up."

Lauren laughed. "That old feline may not be as easy to herd

as you think, brother dear, but I'm with you. See you at dinner tomorrow night."

"Come solo." He hung up before she could object.

He waded ankle deep into the gentle wave wash. The cool blues and greens spreading in front of him tamped down his irritability but not his disappointment. He'd been counting on a day with Lauren before the rest of their siblings showed up. Time with a beautiful, spontaneous woman. The anti-Philippa. His wife had already instructed him to exclude her from everything non-essential, so it would have been just him and Lauren at lunch and dinner today. Possibly some bar-hopping in Old Town.

Now he and his wife would find reasons to stay resort-bound. They'd share two more low-intensity meals, made all the more tedious by knowing that while he faked interest in Philippa's fish, Lauren would be with her man-child, devouring life, extracting joy from the ordinary, risking extremes. Or, like his nightly Internet favorites, gasping and moaning through a marathon of pleasure.

Air whooshed in and out of his nostrils. Lauren's generous sensuality, always wasted, this time on a tattooed mechanic nearly half her age. Hands bunched inside the front pockets of his Bermuda shorts, he kicked out of the surf and went in search of Philippa.

CHAPTER FOUR

VIVIEN FINISHED her routine in the gas station's rest room and pushed into a blast of stifling air and harsh sunlight. Wearing the wide-brimmed straw hat she'd just bought, she strode toward the broad canopy where Charlie was filling the Lincoln, the only car in the station. Behind him, a casino in the Miccosukee reservation rose from a sea of feeble palm trees. "Ghastly, don't you think?" she said, pointing to the industrial-looking gaming hall.

"Probably better than what used to be here," he said after a glance over his shoulder. "Nice hat, by the way."

"Thank you. I can add it to the twenty I have at home." She hitched and twisted the waistband of her slacks, dipped her knees, and smoothed hands across her backside. "Where, by the way, is 'here'?"

"Everglades somewhere. Not real far from Ft. Lauderdale." He returned the nozzle to the cradle. "You know," he said, a smile playing on his lips, "starting in the middle of the night like we do, we got buckets of time. How about a little exploring?"

She elbowed the tote bag around to her back, leaned forward, and scanned both directions of the curveless highway. "What a perfectly nauseating idea."

"Saw a bunch of signs for airboat rides. Ever do that?"

"*Gawd*. Hardly."

"Me neither. C'mon, my treat. Got no money, but you can clip it off the bill."

Pleasure in the moment, with someone enthusiastic about

such a simple lark, made the suggestion almost seductive. "Let's get you out of the heat. You're delirious."

"Little excitement might cheer you up," he said. A tiny grin showed he was undeterred.

"You're not in charge of my attitude." The fact she was even participating in this impertinent banter surprised her.

"Ma'am, barely past 11:00. What're we gonna do in Key Largo all afternoon?"

"The door, Charlie?" She swept her hand at it.

"We'd just be sitting. Like being in the car, kinda, but fun. Probably only take about an hour."

"We've already had this conversation. No means no." She opened the door, but left it ajar after sitting. Carryall centered on her lap, she stared forward.

He ambled closer, stopping just short of the door. "Birds, alligators, wind in your face. Bet you'd love it. Seems to me you need a little something."

"You're not very quick on the uptake." She tilted out of the car and pulled the handle. The door rocked in, then out, tugging her with it. "Charlie!" Back-first, she dropped toward the concrete, eyes squeezed shut, her body braced for impact. The landing was soft. He was underneath, holding her in a basket of arms and chest. Contents of the tote washed across her and onto the pavement.

"You okay?" he said.

"Get me up," she said, both hands securing the hat.

"Hang on a sec. Gotta …" He hefted and jostled her as he repositioned his legs. "Okay." Holding her like a bride, he stood, limped into the shade, and set her on her feet. A breathy groan seeped through his bared teeth as he flexed his legs, one at a time. Ragged, red-ringed holes in the knees of his slacks framed raw flesh. "Dang, that was close. Y'alright?"

"I think so." Last time she'd been held like that was her trip across the threshold nearly sixty years ago, but she'd become such a shrunken bundle, Charlie's ease in handling her recalled her father, not Marshall. Her eyes flicked between him and the personal items arrayed on the ground.

"I'll collect all that," he said. "First; let's get you into the car. Crank up that AC."

"Don't herd me." She recoiled from his hand on her shoulder. Again, she glanced to her scattered belongings. "And I don't want you pawing through my things."

"Ma'am," he said, his voice soft, "my grandmother raised me until she got real sick and died. I know what those packets are, and I know why we stop so often. So what? I mean, who cares?"

Pitied by the chauffeur. Life continued its descent. Trembling lips and burning nostrils told her what was lurking, but a squeaky whimper horrified her. Stoicism in the face of her decline had colored this private slide to the inevitable as heroic, almost desirable. At the very worst, acceptable. Charlie glimpsing behind the curtain, however well intentioned, held the equivalent humiliation of standing before him naked. She covered her mouth and coughed, but another appalling yelp escaped.

"Aw, don't. C'mon, now." He stroked lightly on her arm. "I'm thinking it's something else. Something in Key West."

Warmth rose in her face. "What business is it—Why do you care?" Head lowered, she squeezed her eyes shut. "It's a funeral, if you must know. My youngest son. My poor Devon. He killed himself. There. Satisfied?" Those infuriating tears returned.

"Oh," floated out of him on a long exhale. He inched next to her, rested a hand on her shoulder, and pulled gently until her face touched his chest. "I truly am sorry, ma'am."

Much as hiding in this breach-of-protocol embrace had some appeal, she pushed out of it, nodded, and fluttered a hand toward her things. "There should be some tissues, if you don't mind."

He slid the straw bag from her arm, scooped everything back inside, and handed it to her along with a mini-pack of Kleenex. "Let's get you into the car," he said, his hand light against her elbow. At the rear door, he paused. "Y'know, been told I'm a pretty good listener. If you want to talk, sitting up front would make it easier."

She dabbed a clump of tissues to her eyes and blew her nose. "No questions?"

"You want to say something? Fine. You don't? That's fine too."

Knowing he'd been spying in the rearview, the front seat seemed the lesser evil, and he did have an engaging spark. "Thank you. I believe I will."

He helped her into the car and circled the front bumper on unbending legs.

When the driver's door opened, she shook a twenty dollar bill at him. "I'm sure they have things inside. Get a bottle of water, paper towels, sterile pads, surgical tape, and some Bactine or something."

"My knees?" He waved his hand and stuck a leg into the car. "I'm good."

"Do as I say. God knows what filth you've got in there."

He returned from the Speedy-Mart swinging a plastic bag from his hand. "No bandages or tape," he said through the open rear door, "just Band-Aids. And like me, they never heard of Bactine. Change is in the bag with the receipt." The sack thumped onto the floor behind the driver's seat.

"No," she said. "We'll do it now. Get in back there and shut the door." She joined him and inched toward the middle of the seat, a position she hadn't occupied since drive-in movie days. "Okay," she said, "back against the door." She patted her thighs. "Legs here."

"Ma'am, I'm dirty."

"Don't squander this, Charlie." She draped layers of paper towels on her lap. "Pants legs to the knees. Let's go."

He raised his cuffs over the scrapes, pivoted on the seat, and lowered a leg onto hers.

Hands on his hairy calf, she squinted at the damaged flesh. "I suspect you'll live." A moistened paper towel swabbed away grit, blood, and tiny swatches of torn skin. "Brings back memories. I've done this for all my children at some point. Skating, bicycles, general idiocy. Tell me if I'm doing it too hard."

"No. Feels good."

She froze, stared at nothing. "You know, I can't remember

doing this for poor Devon." Her attention returned to the knee. "Then again, he was the only one to puncture himself with a sewing machine." She blew on the angry gash. "Just letting that one fly by?"

"I promised no questions, but since you asked."

"Have you and Desiree any children?"

He shook his head.

"If that day ever comes, perhaps you'll be equally flabbergasted how they turn out. Virtually identical circumstances for each upbringing, but …" She shrugged. "And the variations happen quite early. Poor Devon, for instance. Virile father. Athletic older brothers. Well, one, anyway. But from the beginning Devon was fascinated by women's things. Jewelry, makeup, high heels, all of it. Always commented on how his sisters and I looked in our outfits, whether the belts, or shoes, or scarves were right."

Charlie's mouth pulled into a wide frown.

She laddered three Band-Aids over the red pulp. "Of course, my husband and I agreed the die was cast when he asked for—no, *pleaded* for—a sewing machine for his twelfth birthday. Hence, the finger. To this day I have no idea how he did it."

"Could've told him no."

"If you do have children, get yourself fixed after two." She patted his thigh. "Other leg, dear. You see," she said, wetting another paper towel, "each child is a separate battlefront, and the parents' will to fight wanes over time."

His leg muscles tensed at her touch to the second knee.

"Sorry. Out of practice." She flicked the damp towel across the redness. "How's that?"

"Real good."

"Of course, as they mature, their tactics improve, particularly when the opposing force contracts by half. They band together. It's not just your authority that erodes. Eventually it becomes, oh, I don't know, retribution or something. Then that escalates, overwhelms your ability to conduct your own life. You're no longer entitled to choices. You become 'difficult,' possibly a simpleton. They hint at consignment. Pressure you to sign things."

The paper towel stopped mid-swipe. "And then, one fall in the tub and you're moved from the master to the maid's room because it's on the ground floor and has a shower. The house has an elevator, but still the upstairs becomes off limits. Sheets, like shrouds, are spread over your lovely things. What *they* determine to be your needs invalidates your wants." Pooling tears shimmied her vision. "But what if the bed you shared is where you're most content? What if a luxurious hot bath is the last physical delight left to you? And who says you couldn't fall in a shower? Who are they to tell you anything? *They're* the children." She threw the bloody towel to the floor, ripped a fresh one from the roll, and pressed it to her face.

"Ma'am?" Charlie said after some seconds.

She glanced at him when he touched her hand.

"Where'd the maid go?"

"Pardon?" The paper towel slid to her chin. "The maid?"

He nodded.

She blew her nose and laughed. "Oh, Charlie, Charlie, Charlie. You are a tonic. Thank you." After a deep breath, another small laugh popped out of her. "Let's finish you." She pinched a Band-Aid from the box.

"I don't see the joke, ma'am. If you're in her room, she had to go somewhere."

"Frequently, Charlie, wealthy people build homes that include servant's quarters, even if they never employ any. Good for resale, I suppose."

"Never was a maid?"

"Nannies when my husband and I traveled, and some day help, of course. Oh, and we had a cook when the children were home, but that's it." She pasted on the last Band-Aid, patted and shook his legs. "All done. Fix yourself. We'll get you some new slacks in Key Largo. Something smart."

"Do you want one? A maid, I mean."

"To be robbed blind? No, thank you."

"Desiree. That's what she does. A maid. Works like a demon, and the only thing she'd steal is your heart."

Sappy clichés normally tagged people as idiots, but coming from him they had an endearing cornball innocence. She turned narrowed eyes toward him. "I'm starting to believe you actually speak this way."

He smiled and shrugged.

"Well, rather pointless now." Head tilted back, she closed her eyes. "I believe an ambush has been planned for after the funeral. Lots of oblique references lately, from all of them. Too much house. Too dangerous to be alone. No friends. No activities. Things along that line. It's my suspicion mother's about to be warehoused. There's too many to fight, Charlie," she said, unable to stop her voice from rising to a high, shaky whisper, "and I'm tired."

"Sad, too," he said. "That can smack a person down." He patted her fingers. "Gonna take some time."

She squeezed his hand, straightened in her seat, and blotted her eyes and nose with a fresh paper towel.

"Ma'am, why you letting them do this? Nothing wrong with you I can see."

"From your lips to God's ears."

He twisted toward her. "Got no idea what that means, but heck, even in just a couple days I can see you're fine. Get around pretty good. Smart. Feisty, like I said. Going through your boy's suicide and whatnot. I think you're managing great, all things considered. Don't know if I'd do any better."

She searched for guile in his slate blue eyes and found none. His reassuring words both soothed and angered. Encouragement and support should have been the province of her children, not this hayseed charmer.

"Look," he said, "you already know I stick my nose where it doesn't belong, but if it was me, I'd tell them all to go to h-e-double hockey sticks."

"Where do you live?" she said. "What town?"

"About fifteen miles from you, just outside Greensboro."

"Own or rent?"

He looked puzzled. "Got a single-wide on a pretty acre. Free and clear."

"Would you sell it?"

"Why on earth would I do that?"

"Well, because ..." She broke into laughter. "I have no idea. How odd. I suppose we should go." Enjoying an inexplicable giddiness, she settled deeper in the seat. The children would not win, at least not in Key West. There would be no discussion of anything except poor Devon. If they insisted on more, she'd have Charlie drive her somewhere. Perhaps she'd take him on that ridiculous airboat ride. He'd earned a treat.

CHAPTER FIVE

ASKING MRS. GRANVILLE to ride up front didn't work like Charlie hoped. The whole way to Key Largo, she sat next to him in an eyes-open coma. First time she even changed position was when the Town Car crawled to a stop under the Ocean Reef Club's entry canopy. She sat taller when two uniformed employees hurried toward them, one for each front door.

"Welcome to Ocean Reef Club," a smiling young man said to him through the open window. "Would you mind popping the trunk, sir? And will this be valet?"

Charlie glanced at Mrs. Granville and shrugged. In Ocala, they stayed in a real nice Marriott Courtyard, but nobody came running. Ocean Reef Club must have been more like the Ritz Carlton where Desiree worked, not that he'd ever been anywhere but the Employee Entrance.

"Valet," she said, leaning to speak through the driver's window. "Charlie, the trunk?"

Having no idea how things were done in these fancy situations, he was more than happy to have her take charge. Outside the car he hung at the fringe of the bustling and watched her direct the staff. After a bellman loaded their luggage onto a cart, Charlie trailed behind and drank in the swanky lobby while she checked them in.

Being so outnumbered, with everyone doing and saying alien things, his defenses lit up. Eyes swept but never stopped. His ears tuned for clicks, voices, or footsteps that didn't fit. Street patrol uneasiness, nervous about the interpreter. Guiding him to a target or into an ambush?

But no M16's here. This crowd fought with polished manners and lawyers. A life that scared him. A life that wasn't built on anything he could understand. Too many playmates with too much money and time. Too few demands. The inside track for a person to lose their way and their honor. Knowing that Desiree wanted to join this party slipped her into the shadows with Mrs. Granville and the rest of them.

...think hard before you promise, then never think about it again...

"I know," he said to GranDelia under his breath. "Better or worse. Richer or poorer." Would have been simple to brush aside his concern if Desiree hadn't gone back to smoking yesterday. Breaking promises had to be like killing. After the first, didn't much matter anymore, and he knew that one for sure.

Wondering what else might be unraveling back home was pointless, so he searched for a distraction. With their conversation from yesterday morning still fresh in his head, he eyeballed the guests, watching to see if they really were all that different from her and him.

No question Desiree was right about the younger women. Each one who strolled past looked "put together," like she said. Had a confidence, too. And a distance. If his eyes met theirs, a few twitched back a nothing smile, but most treated him like a pane of glass, like they knew he couldn't add to what they had.

"If you can tear yourself away, Charlie," Mrs. Granville said, "our rooms are ready. And PINK, by the way, is the name of a clothing company."

"Excuse me?" He trotted to catch up with her and the bellman who was pushing a luggage cart.

"Based on your fixation," she said, "I thought perhaps you were having trouble understanding why that young woman had a sparkly PINK across the front of her yellow top."

"Ma'am, you don't miss much, do you?"

"All part of nature's delicious perversion, dear boy. You may have the wand, but we have the magic. Bellman," she said, shaking a ten dollar bill at the end of her outstretched arm, "the duffel bag goes to three-twenty-nine. The rest go to my suite. We'll take our keys, thank you." She handed Charlie his key folder and pointed down a long corridor. "Pants await. The golf shop will have the best selection." She hooked a hand onto his elbow. "I don't suppose you golf, do you?"

Might as well have been on Mars.

CHAPTER SIX

WITH MRS. GRANVILLE down for the night, Charlie took his first easy breaths of the day. He lifted his feet onto the chair she'd sat in for their poolside dinner. After straightening the crease in his new tan slacks, he fished out his phone. Waiting for Desiree to pick up back home, he tilted toward the table and grabbed a sweaty bottle of beer from next to his empty pie plate. Wasn't going to have any dessert, but he didn't want the peaceful pleasantness to end, so he let the young waitress flirt him into a wedge of key lime pie.

"Hey," Desiree said. Hardly past 8:30, but her voice had the heaviness of someone who'd been asleep.

Disappointing. He wanted her fresh for his updates on the trip, and about Mrs. Granville switching back and forth between entertaining and obnoxious. "Did I wake you, Baby Girl? I'm sorry."

"No," she said, still no zip in her voice, "Too early for bed." This time she sounded sniffly.

"You getting sick?"

She broke out crying. "Charlie, I did something."

He kicked his feet off the chair and sat straight. "Y'okay?"

"I got fired. That Mrs. Jackson, she fired me."

Flutters hit his stomach.

"Swear to God, Charlie," she said, some hiss in her voice, "gonna shoot that black bitch. I am."

"You know you're not." He heard a *boink,* like wet suction after a sip from a bottle. "So what happened?"

"Couldn't miss that prize hog with my eyes shut."

"Desiree, why were you fired?"

"Feel like such a jerk. I was … Y'all are gonna kill me."

"Just spit it out."

"Alright! I was trying on a guest's clothes, and she caught me."

She'd gone crazy, and him five hundred miles away. Soon as they got off the phone, he'd call his friend, Spuv, and put a reliable pair of eyes on her until he got home. "Why in God's name would you do such a thing?"

"You won't get it."

"How 'bout you keep trying until I do?"

"Like I was telling you before you left. Tired of being me. Okay?"

"Nope. Keep trying."

She blew her nose a couple times. "Alright, was like this. I was doing up a corner suite. Opened the closet in the master bedroom so I could vacuum the floor, and there was this pale blue dress. I mean to tell you, it was *beautiful*. Anyway, I took it off the hanger, but only so's I could hold it against me at a long mirror. Fabric was so light, Charlie, felt like I had hold of a breeze. Length was perfect, and blue being a good color for me, I couldn't stop wondering how I'd look in it. How I'd, y'know, feel in something that classy. Wasn't like I was fixing to steal it."

Not that he ever would, but if he was going to do something that reckless, he would have done it in a locked bathroom. "How'd you get caught?"

"Don't know if that porch-butt bitch knocked or said anything, but next I knew, her reflection slid next to me in the mirror. Scared the stink outta me. 'What in the *hell* are you doing?' she said, all growly and pig-faced. With my uniform laying on the bed, nothing I could do but admit it. She waited for me to change and walked me right to Human Resources."

"God in heaven," he said softly, a hand covering his eyes.

"Someone's gotta pound a stake through that bitch's heart. May as well be me."

"Calm down. Done is done." While he was pinching at the flesh between his eyes, he heard another *boink*. "What're you drinking?"

"Me? Nothin'. Wish you was here, sugar. Could use a hug. Still love me?"

Felt like she was lying about the drinking, but accusing her would have only widened the ruckus. "Now and forever, Baby Girl."

Soon as they hung up, he dialed Spuv's cell, hooked a finger around the neck of his beer, and headed for the beach. Phone rang so many times he expected voicemail.

"Well, I'll be," Spuv shouted over crowd noise and music. "If it ain't Charlie dense Woods. Talk fast, son, I'm the only bartender tonight."

Their fourth grade teacher, Mr. Coburn, called him "dense Woods" once as a joke. Least that's what the man told GranDelia when she lit into him on parent's night. Of all the old classmates he saw around town, no one but Spuv ever called him that anymore. Only a great friend can cram love into an insult. "Need a favor, Spuv. I'm on my trip, and I want you to swing by the house tomorrow night and keep Desiree company. Bring Belinda so Desiree don't think an oversized hound like you is there for something else. Can you do that?"

"NFW, hoss. For one, Belinda's history. Woman on the rag still has responsibilities. Know what I'm saying? But more important, tomorrow night's Bingo, and I got the bar again."

Finally, something good coming out of this trip besides the money. He'd rather pull hairs out of his nose than go to Bingo, but Desiree loved it. She wouldn't drive at night, so he had to take her. "Perfect. Swing by and pick her up."

"Dude, how does she get home? I'm still working here two hours after the—Woody," Spuv shouted, "other side of the bar. No, right now ... Charlie, I gotta go. Woody's been here since lunch. Want me to call you after I close?"

"That'll be too late. Catch you tomorrow." He'd reached the water's edge. Being in his business shoes, he was mindful to stay clear of the wave wash. With the resort glowing at his back, he zoned out on the endlessness in front. A quarter moon fired hypnotizing sparkles off the ripples. Light breezes carried that peculiar smell of the ocean, mixing decay with renewal. Peaceful, but tending toward the sad.

Chilly water washed over his shoes, soaking his ankles. "Dammit." He back-stepped to higher ground. Now he'd have to polish them while they were wet. He tipped a spill of beer into his mouth and spit it out. Been standing there so long it had gone warm.

He started the squishy-footed trek back to the lobby, still troubled about Desiree. Full of surprises lately and none of them good. He'd heard "the change" could be tough on a woman, but could it change her character? Make her threaten to shoot someone? And he'd never heard her talk against black people. Marines of every color got him home in one piece. She ever did that again, he'd set her straight.

...think hard before you promise, then never think about it again...

"There you go again," he said to GranDelia, searching into the deep night. "See, I don't know what you mean sometimes. You telling me I should deal with what is, or I didn't do enough thinking in the first place?" Silence stretched out long enough he went inside without an explanation.

CHAPTER SEVEN

BUZZING STARTLED Ward Granville into a sitting position in the lounge chair. Instead of a menacing hornet on his hotel balcony, as he first thought, the threat came from his iPhone, vibrating on a plastic table. He stood and turned his back to the Key West sun. Hooding the tiny screen, he read a text from his brother, Luke, the only member of the immediate family still unaccounted for.

Unwell. Apologies and love to all. Mother knows.

"Bastard," he said through clenched teeth.

Out of his four surviving siblings, Luke would have been the most useful today. Mother's favorite, and she made no pretense of it. Ward suspected Luke's most-favored-nation status was the bi-product of his ten years as the baby, a rank he somehow maintained even after Devon's surprise arrival. At last night's dinner, the family all joked about Luke, the only light moment in an otherwise weighty evening. They all agreed that the moment he arrived he'd be handcuffed to Mother. If any of them could blunt the horror of Devon's stunning departure, he was the man.

Luke. Just the reminder of him produced a faint but persistent tension. Even before his two successful screenplays, Mother accorded him celebrity status. Since those, she was a saucer-eyed groupie, hanging on his words, laughing on cue. During his rare visits from Malibu, she beamed and boasted when introducing him to friends, acquaintances, and surprised strangers. For Luke to risk her disfavor—and continuing cash flow—meant only one thing: Betty Ford again.

Mother knows. Had the sonovabitch told her by text, as well? Ward sagged at seeing his funeral role doubled. First-born responsibilities, which his parents drilled into him from earliest memory, had already sent him to the morgue to identify Devon's body. Now with Luke out of the program, he'd have the added task of consoler-in-chief, a position both he and Mother would find awkward after fifty-six years of polite distance.

Lone positive element of the deteriorating situation was that her limo wasn't due until lunchtime. That left nearly two hours of quiet time on the suite's balcony. Two hours to stare at the blue-green water, hide from them all, and manufacture feelings for poor Devon, the brother born after Ward had already gone off to Johns Hopkins. The brother who hadn't appeared at a family gathering in over ten years. Who never phoned, or emailed, or texted, or sent a card. Whose discolored, swollen face on the morgue tray elicited no sense of loss, no disquieting awareness of a family transitioning from is to was.

The suite's sliding glass door opened a crack, tumbling cool air across his bare shins and sandaled feet.

Philippa, dressed in a one piece navy bathing suit, poked her face through the gap. Always a woman of close-cropped hair, no makeup, and curveless form, lately his wife's bland appearance smacked of intentional withdrawal, as if she'd discovered his growing fascination with Internet exhibitionists and was relieved to pass him off to them.

"Luke's not coming," he said.

"God, your mother's going to implode." She fanned her face. "Aren't you dying out here?"

"Did I hear you on the phone just now?"

She folded her arms and leaned a shoulder against the doorjamb. "Are you aware Lauren has brought a *date* to the funeral?"

Questions like that, as if she was still an assistant prosecutor, never failed to knot his jaw muscles. "I believe Justin is my sister's latest boyfriend. And you care because?" He rolled a hand at her.

"So you did know." Satisfaction lived briefly on her face before indignation replaced it. "I'm told he's in his twenties."

"Envious?"

"We're here for Devon, not more of Lauren's disgusting flamboyance. Thank God she had the good sense not to bring him to the viewing or to dinner last night."

"You sound suspiciously like dear sister Sophia. Is that who you were on the phone with?"

"Thirty-five years as a rebellious teen is more than bizarre, Ward. It's obscene. Your mother's coming here to bury her baby. This is a horrible slap, to her and poor Devon."

"That answers my Sophia question." He couldn't remember exactly when or why, but his mother had begun referring to Devon as "poor Devon" many years ago. Hearing it from a blood relative was a shared joke, but from a spouse or significant other, it smacked of presumption and self promotion. He sat forward and sniffed. "Any of that coffee left?"

Philippa shrugged, her attention focused on retying the white coverup she'd draped around her minimal hips. "Tell Lauren to keep him hidden. She listens to you for some reason. I'll be at the pool." The rolling door banged shut, followed by the thud of the door out of their suite.

Two more days as ringmaster for this bunch offered the same joy as a mass on a CAT scan, but as the senior sibling, he knew his duty. Inside the suite, he dialed Lauren's room. While the phone rang, he tipped a room service carafe. "Naturally," he said as the few remaining drops dribbled into a cup.

"Yeah?" a man growled into the phone.

"Is this Lauren Granville's room?"

"It's for you," the man said. "Take it in the bathroom, and shut the fuckin' door."

"Hi." Lauren sounded like she'd cupped a hand around the mouthpiece. "Who's this?"

"Laurie, it's Ward." He heard a door click shut. "You let him talk to you like that?"

"Oh, c'mon. Who wakes up happy to a ringing phone?"

"This is pretty strange, Laurie, even for you."

"Y'know, I think the lines just got crossed. Someone's saying things that are none of their fucking business."

"Laurie, this should be for family."

"Blah, blah, blah. So, tell me, handsome, have you and Philippa had breakfast yet? I'm *ravenous*, and I'm sensing Justin would prefer to sleep in this morning."

He brightened at the unexpected opportunity for a one-on-one. "Philippa's at the pool, but I'll have coffee with you. How much time do you need?"

"Ten minutes, and eat something, you scrawny shit. You're going to make me look like the sow I am."

"I prefer 'wiry', and you're hardly a pig. You're *zaftig*." No one-word description did justice to a woman who quieted every room she entered.

"*Zaftig*. What a sweet word for obese. You always say the right thing."

"How about we meet at the inside restaurant?" If they ate outside, Philippa might see them. Convincing Lauren to hide Justin would be hard enough without Philippa joining them and volunteering opinions. "And come alone."

"I will not sit for a lecture, Ward."

"Just a few ground rules. Mother's putting up a brave front, but this has to be killing her."

"Poor Devon, always so far away."

"I know. Downstairs in ten."

Sipping his second refill of decaf, Ward spotted Lauren entering the restaurant with their brother, Archer. "So much for alone," he muttered, standing to greet them.

Not merely stunning, Lauren glowed. Even today, in spite of the grim theme, she'd swaddled her head in a floral scarf, leaving a sweep of soft brown hair to spill over her shoulders. A sleeveless white turtleneck showcased her considerable breasts. Snug dark slacks tapered to her recently tattooed ankle and wedge sandals. As always, a look that was earthy, exotic, and approachable. A woman of appetites and pleasures. "Alone? And ten minutes?" he said to her, tapping his watch.

"Elevator door opened," she said, "and there was Archer. He hasn't eaten yet either." She pulled Ward into a hug, kissed each cheek, and sat. "Sorry about the tardiness. Something came up."

"Mr. Idiot's member, no doubt," Archer said, eyes scanning the room. "And good morning to you too, Ward." Archer ran a knuckle across each side of an unruly, silver Fu Manchu. "Lauren tells me you've summoned her. Am I welcome at this caning?"

Despite being two years apart, he and Archer had often been mistaken for twins in their teens. The only physical similarity anymore was a bald head, and even there the difference was pronounced. He kept his scalp buzzed to a shadow, but Archer braided the remains of his into a salt and pepper rope that trailed halfway down today's red, purple and gold tunic. Years on the Navajo Reservation had absorbed him utterly.

"It's not a caning, Archer," he said, disappointed at having to share Lauren. "I just want to wring a few promises before Mother gets here. And Mr. Idiot would be Justin?"

Eyes on Ward, Lauren raised her middle finger in front of Archer's face. "Frightfully witty, isn't he? Justin? Justin Idiot? Apparently, he and dear sister Sophia have decided that sobriquet is beyond hilarious." She turned a smile Archer's way. "You know, Justin may look like a chiseled beast, but he has a wonderful sense of humor. Try that on him if you meet later. Please. For me."

"I see," Archer said, nodding slowly. "A woman, terrified of aging, indulges a bi-sexual's Oedipal fantasies, and I should be beaten for it. Interesting." He pushed higher in the chair and searched the room. "Ward, which one is ours?"

"Oh, 'bi-sexual.'" She wiggled a finger at Archer. "That's very good. Make sure you include that."

"Shut up," Ward said. "Both of you." At any other time, revisiting the dining-table warfare of his childhood might have been amusing, even weirdly endearing. "Archer, I know we haven't seen you for …" He shrugged.

"Sixteen years," Archer said, "and you'd like me to leave."

"Five minutes."

A smile widened Archer's mustache. He snorted as he stood. "And you all wondered why I fled." His napkin floated to the vacated chair. "Or perhaps you didn't."

"Archer," he called after his brother, "for godsake."

"Let him go," Lauren said, patting his hand.

Ward checked his watch. Mother would be there within the hour. She'd be expecting a tidy brood, coalesced around common sorrow, a huddle of sympathy for a fallen brother. But none of them seemed to know or care very much about Devon. "What's wrong with us, Laurie?"

"Please, he's always been an asshole."

"I mean all of us. Three days ago Devon hung himself. Why does nobody talk about that? Or anything else about him?" Other than agreeing forty-year-old Devon looked like a bald adolescent in the casket, the only mention of him at their post-viewing dinner came from Sophia. She wondered which of the men in the scant crowd might have been his partners.

Lauren's eyes darted to his and dropped to the table. "When, um, was the last time you spoke to him?"

"This is terrible, but I don't even remember. A lot of years, I know that."

"Well, we all know who to blame there. She threw him away. Daddy should have stopped her."

"The Darlington School?"

"Ward, who boards a first-grader? And ten miles from home. I don't care how often she visited, or said she did. It was barbaric. Poor kid never had a chance." She shifted her hips in the seat and sat tall. "Well, let's see how *she* likes it. Payback's a bitch, honey."

He recoiled from this glimpse of venom. "Laurie, don't you be the one to start that conversation. I'll know when the time is right."

"But you said it last night. Except for shithead Luke, we're all together for the first time since Daddy died. She can't hold out against a unified front."

"Listen to me," he said. "We are burying our brother, without incident, which brings me to why we need to talk. No Justin when Mother's around." Protecting a dead brother and establishing family protocols restored his sense of the natural order.

"You think Archer and Sophia, or darling Philippa for that matter, are going to be quiet about him?"

"I'll handle them. All I ask is that you do your part. Send him out on a jet ski, or his Hot Wheels."

"Very funny." Smiling, she stood and scanned the uncrowded dining room. "Since the waitstaff believes we're invisible, I'm going to head up and get ready for the *en famille* luncheon. You said an hour?"

"No Justin?"

"Promise."

"Okay. Poolside at 12:30. And thanks, Laurie. Love you." More eyes than his followed her exit.

" ... *a woman, terrified of aging* ..." Ward had no doubts about Archer being an asshole, but he had to agree the day was near when Lauren would have to graduate from cougar to bawdy senior, mistress of the double entendre and knowing laugh. Failing to cross that threshold with grace held two potentials for her, both bad. Bitterness was one, but even worse, she could become submissive, grateful for any attention and willing to do the necessary to keep it coming. Her new tattoo and echoes of Justin's hostility on the phone made him wonder if the latter hadn't already begun.

CHAPTER EIGHT

ONE DEADLINE on the whole trip, and they missed it. The dashboard clock showed 12:41 as Charlie swung his Town Car into the driveway of the Casa Marina Resort.

Traffic on Rte. 1 had been terrible, bunching and stretching like a worm the whole way from Islamorada. Bathroom stops complicated their progress, too. Not a lot of chain restaurants on that highway, so Mrs. Granville made them stop every time he saw the golden arches. Only hit three of them, but at most traffic lights, even if they were green, she had him slow down and scope out both directions of the cross street. Got a lot of horn blasts and a couple middle fingers, but she didn't seem to care, not even when he warned her about the time.

"Ah." She pointed to a man under the Casa Marina's broad entrance canopy. "Ward, my eldest son. Always on that ridiculous phone. How can a periodontist be so tethered to a phone?"

The man she'd pointed out was a short guy with a shaved head. Even in his tan suit, he had a lot of boney angles, like a marathoner or a coyote. He was yammering into the cellphone while he paced, his free hand flipping every which way. Soon as he spotted his mother in the car, he stopped walking, spread his arms and legs, and shook his head.

Young bellmen hurried to the car, but her son got to the passenger door first and opened it. "Why are you in the front?"

"Such a tender greeting," she said, laboring out of the car.

"I was just leaving you a message," he said. "Mother, *please* stop turning off your phone." He pecked a kiss to her cheek. "How you holding up?" he said, pulling her toward the entry doors. "Y'okay? Everyone's waiting at the table. Leave your things here. The driver can check you in."

"For heaven sake, Ward." She swiped his hand away. "Take a breath, darling." Smiling, she turned back to the car. "I want you to meet Charlie, driver *par excellence* and my guardian angel."

Still planted in the driver's seat, Charlie leaned across to the open passenger door and reached out a hand. "Charlie Woods, Mr. Granville. Real sorry about your brother."

"Charlie," she said, "it's Dr. Granville. Periodontist, remember?"

Looking puzzled and frazzled, Ward nodded at him but left the offer of a handshake hanging.

"Ward." Mrs. Granville tilted her head toward Charlie's still-outstretched hand. "Manners."

Shoulders sagging, Ward reached into the car and squeezed the tips of Charlie's fingers. "Pleasure," he said without making eye contact. Returning to his mother, he slid an arm around her shoulder. "We are *so* late. Restroom is on our way if you need it."

"Wait for Charlie," she said. "He's joining us."

That news surprised Charlie. Her son, too, based on the tight-faced glare he shot Charlie's way. That look recalled the start of nearly every brawl Charlie had ever been in, and there'd been a few. "Ma'am," he said. "you just go to your family. I'll take care of things out here and grab something after."

"You," she said to the nearest bellman. "Would it be possible to arrange Mr. Woods's room and my suite, and then deliver the luggage? Mine all have tags marked Mrs. Vivien Granville."

"Actually, Mrs. Granville," the bellman said, "you're a little early for check-in, but what I can do is put your things in the store room, park the car, and bring the claim checks to your table. Sound good?"

"There you have it," she said, a smile for all involved. "It's settled."

"Anything," Ward said. "Let's just go." He fluttered a hand at Charlie. "I'm sorry. Things are nuts. Your name again?"

"Charlie's fine." He fell in line on the other side of Mrs. Granville.

She hooked each man's arm and headed into the lobby. "Charlie's been my Galahad these past two days, Ward, with a dash of Sigmund Freud. An absolute rock. Ah, the facilities," she said, pointing to *Ladies*, "and none too soon. You two get acquainted while I'm gone."

Even before the swinging door closed, Ward turned his back. He wandered in silence, both hands rubbing his scalp. "You're leaving," he said, eyes finding Charlie, thumb pumping toward the front doors. "Already have one uninvited problem. Nothing personal, but take off."

Dependable Car Service wasn't going to like hearing this. First chance at steady work he'd had in months, and he was enjoying it, at least some of the time. "Dr. Granville," he said, "if this is for being late—"

"Stop," Ward said, hands waving. "Just go. We'll take her from here. I'll see you're paid."

One thing a man gets from the military is respect for chain of command, and Ward Granville was not in charge. "All due respect, sir," he said, extra slowly, "your mother is my employer, not you."

That comment drew another challenging squint.

Clearing houses in Kandahar, one rat's nest at a time, made unarmed confrontations—like this might turn into—sort of a joke, but a bantam rooster like Dr. Granville could dish out punishment in a hurry if a man was fool enough to concede him the first shot. Arm hairs tingling, Charlie angled his shoulders and readied his hands.

"Business card." Ward snapped the fingers of his reaching hand.

Careful to stay out of range, he fished one from the breast pocket of his blazer.

Mrs. Granville exited the restroom and pointed to the card Charlie held out. "Well, you two seem to have bonded. Use him, Ward. He's wonderful."

"Mother, Charlie's leaving."

45

"Excuse me?" She stopped cold, her mouth turned down at the corners. "Charlie?" she said with a shrug.

"Mother, you don't need him anymore. Your family is here. We'll take care of you. Funeral, ride home, all of it. Now, can we *please* join the others?"

"Charlie?" Her open hands reached toward him.

The panic on her face touched and confused him. They'd spent maybe twenty waking hours together. That shouldn't have been enough time for this level of obligation, but leaving her felt wrong. His words wouldn't line up right, so a bounce of the shoulders was all he could come up with to show he wasn't in on the change of plans.

"I see," she said. Lips pressed flat, she turned an angry face toward her son. "You listen to me. I will make my own decisions, thank you very much. Charlie's staying. He's taking his meals with us, and after we've buried poor Devon, he's driving me home." Rising taller, she offered Charlie her elbow. "We seem to be holding up the program. Come, I want to introduce you to the rest of the family."

"Don't unpack," Ward said to him, flapping the Dependable Car Service card like he was drying it.

Out in the damp heat, the three of them, with Mrs. Granville shuffling in the middle, followed Ward's guidance along the paths, past the pools and tiki bar, toward a loose formation of green umbrellas.

Casa Marina's terraces reminded Charlie of the Ocean Reef Club in Key Largo, only smaller. A grid of stone slabs made up the walkways and seating areas. Bushes with red or yellow flowers separated walkers from the swimmers and eaters. Same smells of sea and grilled food. Same sounds of gulls, reggae, and happy vacationers, but finding himself as a draftee in a family war soured any enjoyment.

A pudgy bald man with a braided pony tail stood as they approached his table. He swiped a napkin across a droopy white mustache and stood beside his chair. "Hello, Mother."

"Archer, love, you came." She wrapped him in a hug he didn't seem to want. "We weren't sure. Thank you. Our poor Devon."

Others at the table, all women, rose and formed a line in front of Mrs. Granville. Last woman in the line wasn't young, but younger than the rest. Killer pretty, with an awesome body. She caught his eye and held it. When she smiled, the tingle in his chest and elsewhere made him force his eyes to the other grievers.

Watching the family get tender with each other turned him from battle-ready to orphan-lonely. Growing up with just GranDelia in the house, he'd never been part of a scene like this, and he never would be, not with Desiree being barren. He'd keep lying to her about wanting kids, but being a daddy would have been the cherry on his life. Seeing how even hard cases like the Granvilles benefitted from being part of a clan only stabbed the regret deeper.

Ward drifted away from the huddle around his mother. He stood next to Charlie, but kept his eyes forward. "Time to go, friend," he said in a soft voice.

Charlie didn't want an open disagreement, but until Dependable or Mrs. Granville called him off the job, his duty was to stay. "Already told you, sir, I can't."

Mrs. Granville snapped her face toward them. "Charlie, there you are. All," she said, raising her voice, "I want you to meet someone. This is Charlie … Charlie …" She patted her leg. "It'll come to me. Anyway, he's not only endured my ill temper for the past two days, but he saved my life. Literally. I'll tell you all about it while we eat."

"No last names." The pretty woman smiled and flicked her gaze between Mrs. Granville and him. "Mother, how modern of you."

"Woods." Mrs. Granville tapped a finger to her temple. "Charlie Woods." Nose crinkled, she bowed at Ward, who was punching keys on his cellphone. "Not completely senile, darling. And would you please stay off that ridiculous phone."

"One second." Ward slipped Charlie's business card into his shirt pocket and turned away from the family. "Charlie, stay close," he said. "They may want to speak with you."

Charlie took a step to join Ward, but a small hand pulled at his arm from behind.

Sweeping past surprisingly fast, Mrs. Granville darted in front of Ward, snatched his phone, and bounced it into one of the lighted reflecting pools that lined the walkways.

"Hey!" Ward raised an open hand for an instant before dropping it to his side.

"You will not do this," she said, trembling, her face inches from her son's.

"Have you lost your mind completely?" Ward pointed to his drowned phone.

"I invited Charlie," she said, her voice hushed. "It is for me to un-invite him, and I will not. If that doesn't suit you, leave."

Retrieving his dead phone, Ward trained slits of eyes on Charlie. The man's flared nostrils, tight-pressed lips, and slight nod told him this wasn't over.

"Darling," she said, pulling a reluctant Ward into a hug, "of course you know I don't want you to leave. You're senior man in the family. I need you here. We all do. Just stop making me angry." Still holding his shoulders, she tilted her head back. "Am I forgiven?"

Arms at his side, Ward shut his eyes and nodded.

"And I'll replace your phone, naturally." Latching onto Ward's elbow, she leaned toward the table and the collection of startled eyes. "Shall we eat now?"

Unsmiling, Ward nodded again. "We need to be done by 2:00," he said. "Limos are picking us up for the final viewing at 2:30." He bobbed his head toward Charlie. "Is he taking you, or are you riding with Philippa and me?"

"You, of course, dear." She hugged her son's arm as they headed for the table. "Come along, Charlie," she called over her shoulder. "Ward, I've just had the most wonderful idea. Charlie will follow us. That way, if things become too much for me, none of you will have to miss the services on my account."

"Mrs. Granville?" Charlie said. "Hang on a sec." The more time he spent in this family's free-fire zone, the less chance he had of surviving the assignment, and with Desiree canned, he was the only income for a while. "If I'm gonna be backup, instead of following, it'd be better if I went on ahead. Y'know, see what's what. You have my number, so just enjoy your time together." He shuffled backward toward the lobby. "And I'll be in town, ready if you need me."

"But you haven't had a morsel, dear."

Ward positioned himself between her and Charlie. "Mother, sit. His plan sounds very practical. Thank you, Charlie," he said, raising his voice but not turning. He mumbled something else that made the Fu Manchu brother laugh.

Guesses about Ward's snotty comment picked at Charlie on his way up the walk. Given different circumstances, spreading that pint-size dentist's nose across his face would have been kinda fun. He pulled the lobby door open and calmed the instant a rush of cool air hit him.

Still had over a half hour before he had to leave, so he set off on a slow roam of the comfortable main floor. Strolling past the front desk, he pulled the collar of his shirt away from his neck and whistled out a long breath.

"Got hot early this year," said a tall blond woman from behind a Concierge sign. "Anything I can help you with?"

"Do you rent weapons?" He smiled extra wide after realizing not everyone would think that was a joke.

"Oh," she said, a grin brightening her face, "it's not that bad."

Her inviting attitude drew him closer to the counter. "You know, ma'am, I do have a question. You're probably familiar with driving around Old Town. Is it tricky?" He glanced at her name tag. Crystal.

"It's not something I do for fun. Where you going?"

Stomach pressed against the counter, he dug the itinerary paper from his shirt pocket and turned it right-side up for her. "Those last two places, the handwritten ones."

"Aw." Sadness took her face. "You're here for a funeral. I'm so sorry."

Every now and then he'd meet a person he liked right off. This woman was one. Spending three days with nothing but Granvilles probably gave her a leg up, but his first reaction was how lucky her friends were. "Thank you," he said, "but it's no kin of mine. I'm just driving."

Her nose crinkled. "Still … So," she said, slapping both hands on the counter, "let's get you a map."

According to her, Evergreen Mortuary had good parking, but the little lot at St Paul's Episcopal Church could be a problem. Armed with her turn-by-turn directions for circling the church, if it came to that, he headed outside to get the car. With no idea how to duck dinner the way he had lunch, he suspected the next couple hours were going to be the day's most relaxed until his head hit the pillow.

CHAPTER NINE

GRANVILLES OCCUPIED the entire front pew of St. Paul's Episcopal Church. Waiting for the celebrant to take the altar, Ward beat back disgust. Not for the stranger who would eulogize Devon, but for himself, for his Granville-esque detachment from emotion. Only his sister Lauren had managed to reconfigure that part of the family's DNA. Earlier, while the rest milled about the funeral home, stayed silent, and checked their watches, she alone leaned over the edge of the coffin to kiss Devon's forehead and whisper a private goodbye. No hysteria, just a tender final outreach. Only she dropped a tear at the casket closing. At least their brother would head off to cremation and the afterlife with one loving gesture.

Mother, in particular, had irritated him at the viewing. Her impassive face while she sat in front of the casket made him want to scream in her ear, rouse her from self-absorption, release any long-buried generosity of spirit. Even now, in the church, he glimpsed her stoic profile and wanted to shake her by the neck until she acknowledged feeling something, anything.

Aware of Ward's eyes on her, Vivien shot him a short glance and returned her attention to the church's interior. St. Paul's was adequate, but a mere side chapel compared to the Cathedral of Saint Philip in Buckhead, where she and Marshall had worshipped for more than forty years. Even so, St. Paul's appeared gargantuan relative to the paucity of mourners. Two dozen at most, all seated alone, scattered throughout the pews on either side of a broad center aisle. "Ward," she whispered, "he doesn't seem to have had many friends or co-workers."

Even dead, Devon was diminished, trivialized. "His note was specific." Ward did his best to filter annoyance from his tone. "No religious services. I'm guessing his circle was aware of that, and more willing to abide by his wishes than you."

"Tell me again why your boy couldn't come?"

"Boy? Tyler. His name," he said, more softly after faces turned toward them, "is Tyler. How hard is it to remember the name of your only grandson?"

"Don't scold. This is all very difficult for me. So where is he?"

"I told you. Singapore. Had Devon shared his plan with us, I'm sure Tyler would have postponed the trip. And he's not a 'boy'. He's twenty-seven."

"Of course, darling." Her eyes roamed the walls and ceiling. "Isn't it sad poor Luke couldn't come?"

So now Luke had become "poor." Apparently, Devon had a successor, unless each of them became "poor" fill-in-the-blank when theirs was the empty chair.

"Out of all you," she said, "he and Devon were closest, and he would have loved the stained glass in here. Color and light—"

"Are his great inspirations." Ward flipped the backs of his fingers at her. "I know. We all know. He's a genius."

"You're being small, dear." Perfect word for how he was acting. Small. Even Charlie was on the receiving end, and that delightful man had been nothing but a boon during this entire ordeal. Adding him to events may have nipped at the ankles of tradition, but poor Devon would have understood, just as he would have agreed that once dead, his right to decisions ended. The living had to be allowed to deal with the aftermath. If that required the solace of an Episcopal rite, as all deceased Granvilles had received since the 1730's, so be it.

A cassocked, middle-aged celebrant—not the one Ward had made the arrangements with—strolled slowly from a side door near the altar, hands pressed together like a toddler learning to pray. "Welcome," he said after he reached the center and faced them with arms spread. "We gather today in both sorrow and joy.

Sorrow at losing beloved DeVon at such a young age, and joy at him beginning his eternal—"

"Hold it." Lauren rose to her feet. "DeVon? De*Von*? It's Devon." She side-stepped past family knees on her way to the middle aisle. "What the hell is wrong with everyone?" she shouted, her back to the altar, face oscillating in front of the assemblage.

"Madame," the priest said, "I am so sorry."

"Did any of you even know him?" Lauren's extended arms swept back and forth at the sprinkling of attendees. "You jokers just in here for the air-conditioning? Is that it?"

"Laurie, please." Still seated, Ward fanned a hand toward her empty seat.

"Mother," Lauren said, "is Charlie waiting outside?" The delay in getting a reply must have gone too long. "Answer me!"

Ward couldn't decide if his mother's face flushed pink from fury or fear, but she barely nodded her answer.

"I'm borrowing him," Lauren said. Eyes on Ward, she stabbed a finger toward their mother. "She's yours."

He watched the bump and swing of her cream knit dress for the entire, unhurried exit, and didn't turn back to the altar until the huge wooden door had drawn a slow curtain on the fleeing light.

"Poor Laurie," his mother said, her head tilted toward him. "Every little pang needing a voice. Little wonder her men disappear so quickly. Must be exhausting."

To Ward, Charlie lurking outside the church became sinister. Lauren would be alone with another unworthy man, another who had the athletic good looks she seemed weak for, and young enough based on her current preferences. The creeping desperation he feared for her this morning sparked images he couldn't banish. Charlie, luring her to someplace secluded, into the back seat, and out of her clothes. Taking her from the front. From behind. Fistfuls of hair guiding her head to the finish—a vision quite like his favorite Internet videos on Philippa's yoga nights.

He shifted his hips in the pew, grabbed a hymn book from the rack and laid it open on his lap. Disgusted again by his feeble involvement in Devon's funeral, he swallowed away dryness and focused on the flustered cleric, now blathering from notes on an index card.

Charlie floated back into his mind. This time Ward's fantasies turned to spin kicks, snapped taekwondo punches, and a bloody-faced redneck in a blue blazer unconscious on the pavement next to a limo.

CHAPTER TEN

STRETCH LIMOS in the No Parking zone in front of St. Paul's Episcopal Church told Charlie the family had arrived for the funeral. Annoyed that he wasn't included in that arrangement, he began the loop he'd drive until the service ended, or until Mrs. Granville fired a rescue flare. Pretty simple route. Straight on Duval, left onto Truman, left onto Simonton, left onto Greene, and then left onto Duval again.

He got even more irritated when the first circling took less than five minutes. On top of the prospect of a whole bunch of loops, visibility to the church's entry from Duval Street was so poor he'd have only two or three seconds on each pass to check for the black dress and broad black hat Mrs. Granville said she'd be wearing.

Second time around the block, he didn't see that black outfit, but a pair of special breasts caught his eye. They bounced and swayed inside a beige turtleneck dress as the woman hurried down St. Paul's few steps. She waved an arm over her head as she ran down the walk. Surprised the heck out of him when he heard her call his name. Weaving and dodging in the thick traffic, she'd nearly reached the car before he recognized her, the Granville daughter who looked so good at the luncheon. Ripping open the front passenger door the way she did, he was afraid something terrible had happened.

She hopped in, shut the door, and pointed forward. "Go."

"Something wrong with your mother?"

"She's fine. I'm not. Drive. I don't care where." Fingertips to her forehead, she closed her eyes and started crying, the soft kind that comes from way down and goes on for as long as it has to.

A horn honked behind him. "Ma'am," he said, pressing lightly on the accelerator, "I feel for you. I do, but once a Marine, always a Marine. My orders are to circle this church, and that's what I'm doing. You're welcome to ride along."

In no more than a block, crying that started as a sniffling trickle raced to a full meltdown. She slipped out of the shoulder harness, bent over double, and howled into her hands.

He slid his thumb to the phone button on the steering wheel, but took it away. An out-loud conversation in front of her would have been cold. Besides, a breakdown this strong couldn't last much longer. Eyes flipping between her and the frequent brake lights, he swung left onto Truman.

"He called me," the daughter said, her words sounding like she was being strangled. She took a breath big enough to blow out fifty birthday candles and stunned him with a scream.

Every sense perked up. Night patrols. Kicking in doors. Shrieking Afghan women crouched along walls, glowing green in his goggles. Arms reaching, as if palms could stop M16 rounds. Scanning the room for wrong movement, wrong shadows, lumps in wrong places. Listening for metal clicks and running feet. Sniffing for tobacco and man sweat. First muzzle to flash announcing the winner.

Mercifully, her screech lasted for only a single breath. She settled back into shaky sobs, allowing him to stand down, swallow away some cotton. A post-skirmish shiver rattled through him in the middle of the turn onto Simonton.

"He called me." She sat taller but was still crying hard. "He called me!" Screaming again, her arms windmilled, legs bicycled, elbows and fists rebounded off everything within reach, including him.

Already fight-primed, he shoved a hand through the whirling arms and sunk his thumb into the soft depression behind her collarbone.

She collapsed like a puppet that had its strings cut. "Ah! Stop. Stop." Her trembling hand rose like a white flag. "Please."

Might have been his training, or adrenaline, but he gouged the thumb a little deeper before letting go. *Make sure they know it coulda been worse*, his drill sergeant always said.

Her breathy cry from the last jab could have come from a woman enjoying sex. The fact he could recognize the similarity, that he could cause both, horrified him. She'd left him no choice, but dishing out that extra bit of hurt made him want to sweep her into a hug and tell her how sorry he was. Let her cry everything out until it was gone.

She sat up straight. Short gasps and pants puffed from her open mouth. Fingers dabbed at the new sore spot.

Brake lights out of the corner of his eye were the only reason he peeked back at the traffic. "Ma'am, y'okay?"

Tears dripped past her curled-down mouth. Pain grabbed her face when she bent to pick her purse off the floor.

"Didn't know what else to do," he said. "That's going to hurt awhile, I'm afraid."

"I have to talk to someone." She dug a clump of tissues from the glittery black handbag. "And I need a drink. Take me someplace for a drink." She patted the wad to her eyes and blew her nose.

"Ma'am, my instructions are to stay close to your mother, and that's what I'm doing."

"That thing you did," said, sounding distracted as she watched the fingers of her left hand open and close, "is it a trick, or would someone need hands as strong as yours? And it's Laurie."

"No first names, ma'am. Company rules. Only thing I don't know is whether to call you Ms. Granville, or Mrs. something else." Not that he'd ever step out on Desiree, but he wanted to hear Missus.

"Granville, not that I'm proud of it. Oh my *God*." Elbow out, she rolled her shoulder. "Could you have killed me doing that?" She poked a finger into his shoulder. "I mean, all that crap about killing with a finger. Is it true?"

As he did with everyone who asked that kind of question, he turned dead eyes to her, held the stare, and looked away. Letting civilians wonder about a Marine's deadly potential was one of the rewards of service.

"You're full of shit," she said. "And when you get to Duval, make a right. That should take us to the Ocean Key Resort. I saw an ad for it in a magazine in the room. There's a pier with umbrella tables and a view of boats and islands. Looked amazing. That's where we'll go."

"Ma'am," he said, eyes on the road, "I can't. That's it."

"Please, I have to talk about this, and sometimes a stranger's the best person." Sounded like the crying was coming back.

He turned left onto Duval. "Y'know, like most husbands, I get a lot of practice listening." Dropping his marital status into the conversation struck him as a bit of cleverness. "I'd be happy to do it in the car if you're okay with that. Or you can just ride along and be quiet. Or, I can leave you off at the church if that's what you want. It's coming up in another block."

"So, you're married. Children?"

"Sorry to say, no." He regretted saying it that way. Desiree popped into his head, her finger pointing at him. *I knew it! Liar!*

"Me neither," she said. "Brothers and sisters?"

"No, ma'am."

"Lucky. Parents living?"

"They're gone." He always used those exact words. It stopped most people from going further, and the answer was true. His mother was dead for sure. GranDelia even took him to her grave every now and then. Wasn't until he was thirteen he learned she'd died of an overdose in some alley in Atlanta when he was two months old. He had no idea about his father. If his grandmother ever knew, she never said, so the best explanation was "gone."

"You're young" she said. "How'd they die?"

"Thought you had something on your mind." He glanced at her before turning onto Truman.

"I'm not sure." Her eyes searched left and right. "Promise it doesn't leave this car?"

"Yes, ma'am." Of all the Granvilles, she seemed the easiest to like. If he could help her offload some sadness while he killed time, no skin off him.

Her head flopped back against the restraint. Sniffling came back. "He called me. My brother, Devon. Had to be just before he hung himself. First time I'd heard from him in, God, like eight or nine years. He didn't start with, 'How are you?' or 'What have you been up to?' Just went right into a speech. Said he'd already rewritten the note as often as he was going to, but he wanted me to know the part about him being unloved and invisible his whole life didn't include me. And then, click. Other than 'hello', I never got to say a word."

"Hope you're not thinking you could've stopped him." He checked her during the turn onto Simonton.

Her head slumped forward, fingers massaging between her eyes. "Worse. My first reaction … I can't believe I'm telling you this … My first reaction was relief. His call frightened me, but whatever was going on with him, it wasn't my fault. How pathetic is that?" She blew her nose into a new bunch of tissues. "After he hung up, I should have called him back. Called someone. Sent the police or something. But I had no idea where he even lived. If anyone knew, it was Mother, but I didn't call her either. Why didn't I?"

That had the feel of a Desiree question, and he handled it the same way: a shrug and shake of the head. Let her keep burning the trash without him adding more by mistake. Worked most of the time.

"No one else has said anything about Devon phoning them, so I don't know if he did, and they're ashamed like me. But how do I ask without telling them about my call? And if it was only me, I'm never going to know if it was because he thought I cared enough to stop him. Or maybe it was like, I dunno, a test or something. He called to see *if* I cared enough to stop him." Her voice climbed to that high pitch again. "I mean, what if, in that closet, he's strangling, dying. His last thought is to hate me, even more than the rest. Me," she said, the word coming out like a fiddle screech. "I was the one who played Colorforms with him for hours. Not them. I watched the Smurfs, and Sesame, and that *Barney* thing. Not them. And I'm his final betrayal? Don't you see?"

They'd already turned down Greene, and he could see Duval ahead. Learning the Old Town map as well as he had, he knew the hotel she'd mentioned was nearby. If they went, and Mrs. Granville phoned, he could be back in front of the church in three minutes. "Still want that drink?"

"What? Really?" She faced him and pressed the tissues to her eyes. "Omigod, you have no idea. Thank you, but drive slowly. I need some repairs. Jeeezus," she said after flipping down the visor and opening the lighted mirror. "Sunglasses will have to do." She dug them from her purse, along with a hair brush. "God *almighty.*" She hoisted the brush like it was made of lead. "How long is this going to hurt?"

"Day or so. Maybe a little more. Sorry."

On the lookout for Ocean Key Resort, he enjoyed the sound of the brush scraping through her shoulder-length brown hair. Like a lot of things, it reminded him of sex. Last thing most women did before slipping between the sheets was fix their hair, and soon as it was over, they went straight for the brush. He was disappointed when the sound stopped.

"Presentable?" She angled toward him for inspection, arms wide.

He struggled to keep his eyes from dropping to the breasts she was pushing out.

...think hard before you promise, then never think about it again...

GranDelia's whisper flicked a devil off his shoulder. "You look just fine," he said.

At Ocean Key's dead end, he u-turned and stopped in front of the resort's entrance. "Dropping off," he said to the attendant who opened the passenger door.

"You're what?" Miss Granville said, half out of the car. "I'm not going in alone."

"Ma'am, here's the plain truth. My wife wouldn't like me being in there with any woman, and sure as heck not one pretty as you. I'll wait out here for you."

"Sorry," she said to the young man holding the car door, "change of plans." As they drove away, she reached over and shook Charlie's knee. "You, mister, have just made yourself irresistible. I hope your wife knows what she's got. And as for me," she said, checking the visor mirror one more time, "I should get back to the church. One crisis passed. Let's go for two."

He dropped her off and waited until she'd made it across the street and into St. Paul's. That rolling caboose of hers was as good a show as the front, and the short pause gave him a chance to make sure Mrs. Granville hadn't come outside looking for him.

The car phone rang as he accelerated slowly up Duval. *Home* showed on the dash display. "Hey, Baby Girl," he said to the hands-free, "let me call you back. I gotta keep the line clear."

"Charlie, wait. Y'all talk to Spuv today?"

"Desiree, really, I gotta go."

"Case him or anyone else calls, nothing happened. Want you to know that right off."

"Nothing happened about what?" he said, his hands tight on the wheel for the left onto Truman. "And make it quick."

"Well, last night, Brandi Wade come by with a cousin, Darrell somebody. He's a Marine, heading to Afghanistan on Tuesday, and she thought you might have some tips for him. Anyway, they showed up with a case of beer. Not a big fan of Brandi, as you know, but I was so lonesome I 'bout dragged them in. We had a couple. Ordered a pizza. Had a few more. Next I know, Spuv's hauling me out of Darrell's car and carrying me inside. Woke up this morning on our bed next to Brandi. Her cousin was gone, so I drove her home. And that's it."

Felt like a ladder got kicked out from under him. "Why were you in his car?"

"Charlie, I have no idea. Didn't even know I was in there 'til Spuv."

"Was, uh, this Darrell in the car, too?"

"Maybe. Not sure. Way Brandi was looking at me all sly and everything this mornin', I guess he musta been."

"How you sure nothing happened?"

"Trust me, a woman knows."

He wondered if that included her being on the giving end. Just the idea of asking made his guts clench. "Why was Spuv there?" He slammed on the brakes halfway through a red light at Greene.

"I dunno. Maybe he saw cars and pulled in."

His life just got smaller. Private business was private business, and Spuv's peek inside theirs would put new distance between them. "What am I supposed to say?"

"It was dumb. I know it. And now Brandi's gonna shoot her damn mouth off."

Her problem was having too much time with nothing to do. "Girl, you need a job. Been doing any looking?"

"A job. Really. Now why didn't I think of that?"

He knew that tone. "Back off."

"Tell me, Einstein, what do I put on the application about leaving my previous employer? After three whole weeks no less. And what's The Ritz gonna say when someone checks? Y'know, saying stuff just to say stuff makes you sound stupid, Charlie. You can have the line back now." She hung up.

Early on, he'd asked her not to call him stupid. Big mistake, especially from a man with military training. Exposing a weakness invited attacks to that very spot. She had no call lashing out, but he did have to agree that "untrustworthy" would be a death sentence on a job application. Her best hope would be to get work where reference checking wasn't done real good.

A picture floated into his head. Second-story rooms in Mrs. Granville's mansion, sheets covering "her lovely things." He still had two days left to pitch Desiree for day work. Even if the woman was right about her kids wanting to stick her into a home, that wouldn't happen tomorrow. If Desiree could log a month or two working there, she could leave with a good recommendation. At worst, she'd be too busy to be a devil's workshop.

CHAPTER ELEVEN

ELBOWS ON THE BEACHSIDE railing, Vivien rolled a cool glass of Chardonnay against her lips. Dots to her right grew into a passing chain of pelicans, modern pterodactyls that shank back into specks and disappeared. Wave tips glittered in the blue green Florida Straits. Sky and sea in a single view. Infinity squared. Ideal for contemplating existence, her own and those to whom she'd given life, including a son who may no longer be part of anything. But that truth, one which was losing its terror, would reveal itself soon enough.

She hadn't wanted any wine. The flavor no longer lived up to the bouquet, and her tolerance had become less predictable over the years. Loss of mass, she presumed. Nearly two inches and thirty pounds in the too-many years since turning sixty. But Ward insisted she have some, handed the glass to her before she'd reached the table by the pool. Except for Charlie, who hadn't arrived yet, everyone else held a goblet or tumbler of something. She assumed that meant a toast, but each had greeted her with a small kiss and hug and drifted away, content to keep their thoughts private and allow her the same consideration.

She let a small sip of the wine spill back into her glass. Metallic and sour, another unsatisfactory element in the ghastly day. If a toast was planned, she would fake it.

"I saw that," Lauren said, smiling as she joined her at the rail. She mirrored Vivien's pose, their shoulders nearly touching. "How old are you? Two?"

"Don't you look lovely." Vivien brushed Lauren's bangs to

one side. "That's better. Another turtleneck, darling? You must be roasting. How fortunate your arms haven't gotten too big for a sleeveless yet."

Face tilted toward the twilight sky, Lauren shook her head and laughed softly.

No surprise Lauren appeared so content based on her late afternoon. Eager to de-ruffle feathers after their church fiasco, she'd gone to Lauren's room. Finger poised at the suite's doorbell, she was sent tiptoeing away by rhythmic grunts and moans from inside. "So," she said, forcing a smile, "where's your new man?"

Lauren turned a stunned face to her. "How do you know about that?"

Her daughter's proficiency at musical beds both intrigued and appalled, as did the ring of dolphins tattooed around her ankle, but Lauren adding Charlie to the scalps on her lodge pole smacked of molestation. "Disappointing really." Vivien's eyes returned to the horizon, "I rather liked believing a man that good looking could be a devoted husband. But few have been a match for you, dear." She patted Lauren's wrist.

"What are you talking about?"

"Laurie, I went to your room around 4:30. I heard you, let's just say, *entertaining* Charlie in there?"

"*Gawd*, mortifying." Lauren covered her eyes. "But why would you think Charlie? Not that I'd turn him down." She checked over both shoulders. "His name is Justin, and you can't say anything. Ward would be furious with me."

Charlie's rehabilitation lifted a weight, only to have it replaced by an image of her daughter pulling a salesman into her suite by the necktie. "Laurie, I do hope you're being careful, disease-wise. This city." She rocked her hand and crinkled her nose.

"Mother, I'm thirty-five years beyond this conversation, and please, promise you won't mention Justin to Ward."

"Why would Ward be miffed?"

"He thinks you'll be upset, that Devon is enough for you to deal with right now."

"Is Justin black or something? If so, I could care less." Saying that was mandatory these days, but it felt like an honest opinion. Children were no longer a potential, and as long as the man wore his hat straight and pants at the waist, she could wait out Lauren's fickleness.

"He's white and twenty-eight, Mother. Okay? Twenty-eight. Sophia, Archer, and dear Philippa think I'm a degenerate. So go ahead." She backed away, arms wide. "Take your shot."

"Oh, Laurie." Open confrontation always spiraled Lauren farther beyond the pale, but a lover of twenty-eight wasn't just a naughty diversion. It was surrender, to narcissists nourishing themselves on silly women's anxieties, and more often than not, their wealth. "Darling," she said, reaching for her daughter, "if today has a lesson, if poor Devon was telling us something—"

"No you don't." Lauren retreated, her finger aimed at Vivien's face. "Don't talk to me about Devon. Not you." Feet sliding backward, accusing finger still bobbing, she bumped into Ward, who gripped her by the elbows.

"Don't do this," he sing-songed through clenched teeth.

"She knows about Justin," Lauren said, loud enough to silence the conversation between Sophia and Philippa standing poolside. "She was eavesdropping outside our door while we were screwing this afternoon."

"Enough," he said, catching the grimaces on his wife and sister before they turned their backs. Behind Lauren, he saw his mother inching toward them.

Lauren kept jabbing her finger at their mother. "She thought I had Charlie in my room. What was I supposed to say?"

"Nothing," Ward said, "like you promised." Every mention of that chauffeur was a pebble in his shoe.

Behind Lauren, the pace of his mother's advance and the set of her face portended an escalation.

"I was hardly eavesdropping, Laurie," she said.

"Why don't we all sit?" He beckoned to the waitress who'd been assigned to their party.

66

Vivien checked her watch. "But I told Charlie 7:30. If we're pushing up the program, I need to let him know. Dear," she said to the server, "please phone room two-one-seven and tell Mr. Woods we're waiting for him."

"Mother, no." Ward realized how much that sounded like a demand. "I mean, please, just the family tonight."

She only had to get through this dinner and tomorrow's breakfast. With Charlie in attendance, her future would not become a table topic, and now that he'd been restored to her high opinion, she also hoped Charlie's good-nature and simple decency might be contagious. "Ward, he's been invited. That's it." Her twiddling fingers shooed the server on her errand. "And," Vivien hooked a hand on Ward's arm for the stroll to their seats, "he may be what we need right now. A change. An energy. Something's wrong with everyone. Don't you feel it, too?"

"Why do I even open my mouth?" he said, allowing her to pull him toward the table.

Seeing Charlie amble down the walkway from the lobby, Vivien waved until he nodded. "Waitress," she called after the server.

"It's Monique, ma'am."

"Of course." Vivien smiled as she lowered onto the chair Ward held for her. "Forget the call, dear. The man in the blue blazer and tan slacks who's coming this way. Please see what he'd like to drink. There's a good girl. And Sophia, darling," she said sweeping a hand sideways, "Charlie will sit between you and Philippa. He's a delight, and you two need a break."

Philippa's flint-eyed glance told Ward either he should say something, or she might. He rose to his feet. "While it's still just family, I want us to toast Devon, to assure him one last time that he was loved and will be missed." He rotated his raised glass around the table. "To Devon, may he finally know peace."

"Devon," returned to him in a muddied murmur.

"That was sweet, Ward," Lauren said. "Let's keep it going. I know, let's go around the table and each one say what they most admired about Devon. I'll start." Both hands fumbled at the back of her collar. "He didn't judge." Releasing the dress clasp drooped her breasts. She folded the fabric and tucked it into her cleavage. "You were right, Mother, much cooler." Throat bare, she leaned forward and ran a finger under a tattoo of an Asian symbol. "This is Chinese for love, and Devon would have found it beautiful. Your turn, Philippa."

"Oh, Laurie," Vivien said into cupped hands.

"You need professional help," Philippa said in a soft voice, head shaking.

Lauren beamed at her sister-in-law. "And you, my pet, need to fuck more." She turned a broad smile to her sister. "Your turn, Sophia."

"Stop right now," Ward shoved a palm at Lauren. "I'm serious." His gaze panned from Mother's horror, to Archer's grin, to his wife's seething, to Sophia, bracing for her moment in Lauren's crosshairs.

Lauren dropped a wave in Ward's direction, swept her hair behind both shoulders, and tilted toward Sophia. "Sister dear, say something nice about Devon."

Tears swelled in Sophia's eyes. "You're pathetic. That poor man can't have five seconds of attention without you demanding the spotlight."

Still smiling, Lauren shook her head. "Not me. Devon. Say something nice about Devon. You still have four seconds. Go."

Moist gaze leveled at Ward, Sophia pointed at their mother. "You encourage her. Both of you, and I've never understood why. I can see Mother wanting to keep us babies, Ward, but what do you get from it? Your affection. Your tolerance. It's always mystified me." She scrapped her chair away from the table, stood, and dropped her re-folded napkin onto the table. "And I've always wondered why you could never spare any for me."

"Freak show," Archer muttered, twisting in his chair to watch Sophia's exit. Barefoot and spacey when he'd arrived for pre-dinner cocktails, Archer downed what was at least his fourth glass of red and faced the family. "Okay, my turn."

"No more turns," Ward said. "Sophia, wait." He jogged after her, but paused in front of Charlie, blocking the chauffeur's path to the table. "Are you brain dead?" he said in a gruff whisper. "This is for family. Get lost."

"Dr. Granville," Charlie said, resisting the urge to get in the little man's face, "you and I know that. But for some reason, your mother insisted I come." He had a pretty good idea why, and that suited both of them for the time being. "Looks like I'm not gonna be able to please both of you," he said, scratching his head, "but she's got the whip hand, so here I am."

Chest out, Ward inched forward. "Listen to me."

"Your family is disgusting." Philippa stormed past without a glance at him or Charlie.

"Shit," Ward said under his breath. Pointing at their table, he backpedalled after his wife. "Don't be there when I come back."

"Charlie," Mrs. Granville called to him, "come sit between Lauren and me." She smiled and patted the empty cushion. "Charlie Woods," she said as he neared the table, "I'd like to present my son, Archer Granville, PhD. Archer dear, say hello and take Ward's place next to me until they come back. No need shouting across the table."

With some difficulty, Archer stood. He grabbed the roll from his bread plate and wobbled to his assigned place. "Nobody's coming back," he said, flopping into the chair. He stuffed half the roll into his mouth and leaned across his mother. "Pleasure." He extended a hand toward Charlie.

"Real sorry about your brother, sir," he said, gripping Archer's disinterested mitt. He nodded a greeting to Lauren as he sat. The silence reminded him of the quiet after a mortar thump, but he sure as heck wasn't going to be the one to speak first.

"If you're curious about my son's appearance, Charlie, he's been living on a Navajo reservation in Utah for many years now. Teaches English. He quite loves it." She lifted and dropped her son's braid. "Don't you, dear?"

Staring forward, Archer tipped away and fanned a hand as if shooing a bug.

"Even took a Navajo bride," Vivien said. "Has three little girls whom I'd enjoy meeting some day. I wouldn't wait much longer, darling," she said, rubbing his back.

"No." He tilted away from her touch.

Unwilling to sit through what looked like another family skirmish, Charlie slid forward in his chair and rested his forearms on the table. "Maybe you can help me, Mr. Granville."

"Archer's a doctor, dear," Mrs. Granville said. "PhD's are doctors, too."

"Okay," Charlie said, tired of being schooled on the unimportant. "So, Doctor, a good buddy of mine in Afghanistan was Navajo. Not Utah, though. New Mexico. I promise you that boy was one special Marine. Name was William MacDougal, but he liked being called *Ahiga*."

"Means 'he fights,'" Archer said, eyes forward, head nodding.

"That's right," Charlie said, "and he called me *Hastiin*. Y'know, I answered to that name for eight months without knowing what it meant. Then one day an IED took Ahiga's leg, arm, and eye. They shipped him home without him ever telling me."

"A compliment." Archer continued the slow nodding. "Means 'man', someone deserving respect." His head fell back, mouth hung slack "What the hell you doing here?" he said softly. Without looking at any of them, he rose and steadied himself.

"For godsake, Archer," Lauren said, "sit down before you fall down."

"Have to ..." Archer's finger doodled in the direction of the hotel. Cautious strides carried him in a semi-circle around the table. Cradling the rolls he harvested from the unattended bread plates, he weaved up the path to the lobby.

The server arrived with Charlie's bottle of beer and a frosty mug. "Everybody else okay?" she said, pointing at their glasses.

Lauren leaned closer. "Mother, do you want anything?"

The words spilled into Vivien's head as if called into a cave, the speaker faceless and distant. Life compressed and swelled at the same time. Glimpses of a larger understanding flitted in a din of noiseless echoes, racing just beyond her grasp. Competing energies ignited a brilliant static. A hand shook her arm, rocking her enough to know she'd wet herself. She also knew Archer was lost, as were his little girls.

Lauren came into focus, her hand rocking Vivien's arm. "Mother, would you like an iced tea or something?"

"I'm thinking," she said, fingers drumming on the table while she reoriented. "Nothing, thank you. In fact, I'm going to bed. Charlie?" She held out her hand. "If you wouldn't mind?"

"I'll do it," Lauren said. "Poor man hasn't even touched his beer."

"No," Vivien said. A meltdown lurked, and Charlie had already soothed her through more than one. Lauren might do as capably, but the tale would spread. "Someone has to be here to explain things when the others come back."

Lauren rose and pushed her chair in. "Sit here alone? I don't think so. They'll figure it out."

Something had rattled Mrs. Granville. Charlie could feel it in the way she hung heavier on his elbow, by her stiff shuffling steps and thousand-yard stare. A day as sad as this had to catch up with her at some point, but the change happened in a blink. Seemed like forever before he and Lauren got her into the lobby, and he was relieved they made it without running into Ward. Last thing that woman needed right then was to be the wishbone again.

"Goodnight, darling," Mrs. Granville said to Lauren after Charlie lit the Up button. "Not much of a send-off was it? Poor Devon."

Lauren pulled her into a tight hug and dissolved into tears. "Mother, I'm sorry. I am so sorry."

"We all are, I dare say." Being the comforter restored Vivien, at least until she could be safe in her suite. "Do something for me, will you?" She leaned away and swiped tears from Lauren's cheeks with her thumbs. "We're none of us perfect, darling. Don't let Archer or Luke get away, too."

Lauren's puzzled expression changed to slit-eyed anger. "What do you mean, 'too'?" She seized Vivien's wrists. "Did he call you?"

"Did who call?" Vivien said, failing to tug her hands free. "What's wrong with you?"

"Of course he did. He must have."

Her daughter's face crowded nearer, close enough that Vivien could smell more alcohol than one glass of wine could produce.

"You hateful witch," Lauren said. "Why didn't you do something?"

Fear and confusion on the old woman's face sent Charlie into rescue mode. "Miss Granville, that's enough." He wedged between the women and added his hands to the tangle.

Lauren released one of her mother's wrists and slapped at his arm. "Stay out of this."

Taking advantage of the partial freedom, Vivien ducked behind Charlie, slid her hand under his blazer, and gripped the waistband of his slacks. Pressed against the sanctuary of his broad back, she felt like a bullied child, spared by a grownup's miraculous intervention.

"Miss Granville," he said, "let go. Now."

"Or what? You'll hurt me again?"

The grip on Vivien's wrist weakened.

"If I have to," Charlie said, his voice calm.

Shock joined Vivien's relief when Lauren released her arm. Lives had been colliding in secret, right under her nose. When did Charlie have the opportunity to hurt Lauren? And how? Perhaps it really was these two she heard having it off this afternoon. If so, why fabricate a Justin? She tried to step from behind Charlie's shield, but his arm hooked backward and pinned her.

He scanned the hallway and lobby. A few guests and staff stood motionless, eyes drawn to the raised voices and mini-scuffle at the elevators. "It'd be best if you took off, ma'am. I'll tend to your mother."

"Back off, pal. This is family."

"Please," he said, "just let today end."

Two chimes announced the arrival of an elevator.

"G'won," he said. "We'll get the next one."

72

Lauren circled him far enough that the two women could see each other. "Don't you leave tomorrow before Ward talks to you," she said, backing into the elevator. "Pleasant dreams, you evil—" Closing doors muffled the end of the insult.

CHAPTER TWELVE

LAUREN'S ATTACK prepared Charlie to do some listening while he escorted Mrs. Granville to her suite, but she plodded next to him in a trance. Other than "goodnight," a word that sounded like it might be her last on earth, that old lady didn't utter a peep. Never answered when he asked if she was okay. Just stared into his eyes and eased the door closed in his face.

Didn't take a genius to know that woman was in for another tough night, but sympathetic as he was to her situation, her closing that door opened one for him. His duties were over until morning, and he still had a lot of evening left. Getting away from the Casa Marina, and the dark moods of the Granvilles, took on the urgency of a mission.

In the lobby he spotted Crystal, the concierge who'd helped him with directions. She stood behind her counter, smiling for any passing guest who made eye contact. "Evening, ma'am." He laid both forearms on her counter. "Don't know if you remember me."

"Absolutely. The funeral."

Surprised him how such a sorrowful word could lose its sting when delivered through a generous smile. "Yes, ma'am. Just wanted to thank you. Saved me a pack of trouble."

"That's why we're here, and it's Crystal." She tapped the name tag parked at a steep angle over her heart. "Anything else I can do for you?" Her head turned and tilted a bit, eyebrows rose, smile stayed put.

Her being flirty, if that's what she was doing, didn't set

right. Turned her from nice person to available woman, with all the confusion and tensions he was glad to be rid of. He could see Desiree's point about people feeling invisible in hotels. Opportunity just might exist here. Opportunity he needed to get away from. Not that he would, but if he got Crystal or any other woman up to his room for a little of this and that, wasn't a chance in hell he'd get caught.

Knowing things like this, stuff like "*What happens in Vegas stays in Vegas*" disappointed him in humanity. Shouldn't be an industry that encouraged people to break promises and lose honor, to wake up worth less than the night before, and for nothing more than a wink and a high five from the devil.

Crystal pointed to a rack of brochures. "Directions? Restaurants?" Still smiling, she rocked her hips and shoulders through a dance step. "Entertainment?"

What he needed was to get out of there. Get his butt onto a barstool and watch sports on TV. "Thanks, but I was thinking more of a place to go native for a few hours." A joint like the Greensboro VFW would have been perfect. Women and men enjoying time together without sniffing each others' crotches all night.

"Then stay away from Old Town," she said, reaching for a map. "The Green Parrot. That's what you want."

"Good food?" Playing referee at Granville free-for-alls, plus doing his real job, had knocked both lunch and dinner off his plate today, and right now eating held more appeal than sex, mostly because one was going to happen and the other wasn't.

"Grab something here at the hotel," she said. "We have the best food on the island. If it were me, I'd have a sandwich or burger at the tiki bar and then go. You'll really enjoy the Green Parrot. Big drinks, amazing live music. Fantastic. Like a party. My friends and I go there all the time. Might even go tonight after I get done here. Probably around ten."

He slapped the counter and backed away. "Thank you. I'm gonna do just that."

"The bellman can get you a cab. Just ask out front."

"I believe I'll take my own car, but thanks." He continued to shuffle backward, toward the exit to the tiki bar.

"Then give me your valet receipt." Arms folded, she smiled and leaned onto the counter. "I'll have the car brought around for you. Say … forty-five minutes?"

"Know what?" He dug the ticket from his wallet on the way back to her. "You made it sound so good," he said, handing it to her, "let's just do it now."

Her fingertips ran down the length of his hand as she took the ticket. "Your name?" She lifted the receiver to her ear.

"Charlie."

"No, last name."

"Oh, sorry. Woods. No, wait." He didn't remember giving his name to the valet. "Could be Granville."

YELLOW BRIGHTNESS from Casa Marina's entry canopy, windows, and rooftop glowed in the Town Car's rearview. Reminded Charlie of a burning building, and if it really had been on fire, fine with him. A quick left dropped the hotel from the mirror altogether, making his trip to the busy part of town feel more like going than escaping. Didn't have any idea where he'd end up, but he knew for sure one place he wouldn't. The Green Parrot. He'd never fall, but if Crystal was making herself available, he'd make sure that temptation was off the table.

Tomorrow being getaway day, filling the tank before rush hour seemed like a smart idea. At a Hess station on A1A, he locked the flow lever in place and fished out his phone. Calling Desiree crossed his mind, but when they spoke right before the funeral dinner, everything he said as encouragement flew back into his face. Felt more like a goalie than a cheerleader. He punched in Spuv's number.

"Charlie," Spuv said, "you at home, dude?"

"Hi Charlie," a woman sang into Spuv's phone. "It's Candy."

"Hey, Candy," he said, even though he doubted she could hear him.

"Charlie," Spuv cut in, "can you hear she's naked?"

Candy's "Woohoo!" confirmed she not only was, but Spuv was probably getting an up-close reminder, too.

"Big man, go back to your company. I'll call you later."

"Don't worry about it," Spuv said. "Just setting in my hot tub. Hairy-ass naked. Drinking some Jack. She's gonna blow me while I talk to you."

"Shut up," Candy shouted, laughing.

"So tell me, son," Spuv said. "You queer yet?"

"What?"

"Key West. As if you didn't know, you sweet thing." Spuv smacked a kiss into the phone.

"Tell Candy I said bye."

"Charlie," Spuv said, his voice low and serious, "listen good, son. You get lucky in a bar down there, check around the package area real good before sealing the deal. Know what I'm saying?"

"Later." He hung up on Spuv and Candy's laughter. His energy for a night on the town flagged a touch. Imagining himself in a bar, wondering which of the women might not be, added a complication he was in no mood to deal with. Hotels probably offered less of that mystery, but other than the Casa Marina—which he was glad to be away from—the only other spot he knew was Ocean Key Resort, the place Lauren Granville wanted to go for a drink during the funeral.

Took less than fifteen minutes before he'd turned the Town Car over to a parking valet at Ocean Key and was sitting at an outside table on the long pier. Music from a two-man combo mixed with the smells of shallow sea and his two favorite foods: charcoaled flesh and fried anything.

Soon as the waitress left with his beer order, he tallied his cash. Forty-six dollars. On the first day of the trip, he kinda let Mrs. Granville think he had a charge card, but only to stop any questions about why he didn't. Running his finger down the right side of the plastic menu, he put together possible combinations. Best he came up with was fish and chips and two more domestic beers.

Waiting for his order, he noticed how small the crowd was, especially for such a comfortable Saturday night. Being among the few made him lonely enough to risk another fuss with Desiree.

"Hi, sugar," was how she answered the phone. "Was hoping you'd call." Sounded the way she spoke with a cigarette in her mouth. "Didn't want to go to sleep with us mad at each other."

Of course, she had no problem doing that very thing on the night before this trip. "Me, too, Baby Girl. Let's never do that again."

"I promise."

"A real promise. Not like the smoking." He winced even before the last word got past his lips.

"For godsake, Charlie. Thought women were supposed to be the naggers."

He caught sight of a man and a familiar woman waiting at the hostess stand. The woman's face turned his way as he twisted his back to them.

"My bad, Baby Girl," he said, hoping he'd ducked in time. "I know you'll get back to it."

"Don't pretend you didn't see me," Lauren Granville said from close behind him. "We're joining this gentleman," she said to the hostess.

"Who's that?" Desiree said.

"The hell we are," Miss Granville's companion said.

"That's Mrs. Granville's daughter," Charlie told Desiree. "I'm just getting around to eating, and she was passing by my table."

"Never said nothing about a daughter."

"I did," he said. "Yesterday. All Mrs. Granville's kids are here. Look, I'll call you right back. Two minutes." He ended the call as Miss Granville flipped her purse onto the table and dropped into the seat across from him.

The man with her stayed standing, glaring at her.

She'd already confided to Charlie about having no kids, but if she did, the man with her would have been about the right age. The guy reminded Charlie of a TV heavy. Tall and thin. Popped

78

veins running down stringy muscles. Spiky dark hair. Oversized, metal-rimmed holes punched through the bottom of each ear. A few days of stubble, plus a thicker tuft under his lower lip. Tattoo sleeves growing out of his black Key West t-shirt. Ratty jeans and biker boots.

"Get up," the man said to her without even glancing Charlie's way.

"I need to eat," she said, "or I'm going to pass out." One hand covering her eyes, she bounced a finger between the men. "Justin, Charlie. Charlie, Justin."

Manners called for Charlie to stand and offer a hand.

"Who are you?" Justin said to him, the question sounding a lot like a challenge.

"Charlie Woods." He withdrew the hand Justin left hanging and sat back down. "I drove Miss Granville's mother down here for the funeral."

Justin snapped his fingers in front of Lauren's face. "C'mon, up. Place is a morgue."

"You said we could get something to eat." She sounded whipped. "I need to eat."

"Whoa, I got it." Justin aimed both index fingers at Charlie. "Limo guy, you eaten yet?"

"Name's Charlie, and I've ordered, but it hasn't come."

"Perfect." Justin reached onto the table and opened her purse. "You two have a little dinner," he said, poking through whatever she had in there. "Get to know each other." He slid a credit card from her wallet. "Then you drive her back to the Casa Marina, and I'll see you later, or whenever. Thanks, babe," he said, wiggling the gold plastic.

Looking puzzled, she let her eyes drift from Justin, to the charge card, to the table top.

Charlie bobbed his chin toward the little pocketbook. "Sir, maybe you should put that back."

"Fuck off, Jack."

"What does 'whenever' mean?" Miss Granville said.

Rising slowly, Charlie risk-assessed his target. "Brother," he said so softly Justin leaned closer, "name's Charlie. And you are putting that card back."

Eyes big and busy, Justin leaned away. "I'm telling you, dude, she doesn't mind."

He inched into the spaces Justin kept leaving. Something bigger than this lone maggot made him itch for the moment to explode. Like he was in front of everything wrong in the world. All the things he'd hoped to change as a Marine stood within range.

"Charlie," she said, "mind your own business."

And right there was his disappointment. Those he thought needed help didn't seem to want it.

"See?" Justin sidestepped around him to the table and rubbed Miss Granville's back. "This is how me and her roll." He bent, lifted her chin, and pecked a kiss on her dead lips. "Behave. Understand?"

He watched Justin strut down the pier and into the night. Turning his eyes back to her, Charlie noticed the tattoo below her throat for the first time. Looked new. None of his business, but it bothered him. All tattoos bothered him, thanks to GranDelia. According to her, no matter what a tattoo looked like, it was nothing more than a billboard advertising a fool. If Lauren Granville got hers to please Justin, that made her a double fool. "Ma'am, sorry for butting in. Just felt wrong to me."

"Relax." She slid a cell phone from her handbag. "There are better ways." After punching in a three digit number, she held the phone to her ear. "Yes, American Express please." Unrolling a set-up, she wiped her lips with the napkin. "Um, cardholder services, I guess."

Took only a couple minutes for the person on the other end to locate her account and cancel the card.

"Sure that was smart?" Charlie said after she hung up.

She leaned toward him and patted the back of his hand. "So, what did you order? Doesn't matter. We're splitting it."

"You gonna be safe tonight?"

"*Gawd*, I need food." Frowning, she rubbed a hand across her forehead. "Did my mother get you a suite?"

The way Desiree described suites, the little sitting area near his TV didn't strike him as fancy enough. "Just a room, pretty sure."

"I can tell by the number. What is it?"

"Two-seventeen."

"We're in two-thirty-two. Thought maybe if you were next door. Two-seventeen, two-seventeen. No. Doesn't really tell me anything."

"Ma'am, that boy's gonna be plenty mad. Would he hurt you?"

She shrugged. "Maybe he'll be arrested. How long ago did you order?" she said, craning her neck toward the main building.

"But what if he—"

"Stop. Just … stop." Elbows on the table, she fanned a hand in the direction of the kitchen. "You're the man. Hunt. Bring food."

A quiet, uncomfortable few minutes passed before his order showed up. Hungry as he was, he made the mistake of using his fork to lift a piece of fried fish from the plastic basket and set it on his plate. Miss Granville picked out pieces with her fingers and bit off steaming chunks. She panted through an open mouth between bites or snatched swigs of his beer. Seeing slivers of fish wash back into the bottle not only killed his thirst, but his appetite. He dropped back in the chair and watched until the last French fry disappeared. Wasn't happy, but he wouldn't starve. According to the commercial that ran every time he turned on the hotel TV, Casa Marina's room service operated twenty-four/seven.

"Greasy food," she said, digging a long fingernail at a back tooth, "was put on earth to save the over-served." Her eyes rose to the heavens. "Thank you, Jesus. Thank you, Lord."

"If you're ready to go, ma'am, I'll get the check."

She brushed crumbs off her breasts. "Don't really need a napkin on my lap, do I?" Smiling at him, she flipped that pretty brown hair of hers behind her bare shoulders. "Why don't you like me?"

"Not my place to judge people, ma'am." Truth was, physically he liked her way too much.

"Pity there's so much light out here." She leaned back in the plastic seat, turned her face to the night sky. "I bet the stars would be glorious." Shimmying deeper into the chair, she laced fingers on her stomach and closed her eyes. "Tell me about your wife."

"You look tired. Let me get the check and take you home." Based on his cash, they had no other option, anyway.

She stayed silent and still, except for her nostrils. The pulsing reminded him of a rabbit. Little snorts came next, along with twitchy breathing and a turned down mouth. One big tear started a shiny run toward her ear. "So stupid," she said, hardly above a whisper.

Abuse from a client was one thing, but she wasn't the client. He stood and threw his napkin on the table. "Y'know, I'm about fed up with you people."

Her expression slowly changed from startled to amused. "Not you." She ticked a finger from him to herself. "Me. I'm the stupid one. Please sit."

Same lesson as always, especially with women. Open his mouth and eat a shoe. Still wanting out of there, he lowered into his chair anyway. "Sorry."

"Not your fault." Sitting forward, she dabbed at her eyes with the napkin, pinched her nose with it and looked inside. She folded it and blotted one more time. "We've dropped most of our veils in front of you. You'd be stupid *not* to be repulsed."

"How about we get going?"

"Not yet. Please. So pleasant here." Her gaze roamed the pier. "Really, tell me about your wife."

Felt dangerous opening any window to a Granville, except maybe the mother. "Ma'am, please, let's just go. We could both use some rack time."

"Tell me how you first met. Maybe it's something I haven't tried."

Short-and-sweet might get him out of there. "At a wedding."

Her nose crinkled. "Fertile ground, but nothing new. What was your pickup line?"

82

"Nothing like that," he said, laughing at the notion he could be slick. "Had on my Marine dress blues. If she hadn't walked over to thank me for my service, probably still be single." Reliving Desiree's pretty face coming his way, and all that followed, laid a terrible loneliness on him. If duties weren't holding him there, he'd have scrammed back to her that second.

"And then you danced, and it was all over. Right?"

"How'd you know that?"

Her smile said she not only knew the answer, but he wouldn't understand if she told him. "Charlie, why do you think women love weddings?"

"Happy for the new couple, I guess."

"Wrong." She crossed her legs, twisted sideways in the chair, and smoothed that beautiful hair behind her ears. "Sex, pure and simple. Think about it. Ceremony ends, and the bride and groom just want to go someplace and screw. But they don't. They delay it to have a party. Group foreplay. *Hours* of it," she said, leaning toward him. "And since that's what women like best, they go nuts. Tight clothes. Lots of skin and cleavage. Hooker makeup and heels. But where are they going to use all these weapons? Sitting at tables talking to each other?"

She'd stopped and was staring at him, so he figured she wanted an answer. He shrugged.

"Dancing. All of it's a setup for dancing. With a husband or boyfriend it says, 'Wait 'til we get home, big boy.' For the unattached, it's a no risk chance to advertise how they'd be in bed."

Down the pier, the little combo started playing *Mustang Sally*.

Still sitting, she started her head, shoulders, and hips rolling to the music. Fingers ran up her neck until both hands held hair on top of her head. "Everything works the message." Her eyelids dropped to half-staff, lips puckered. "Eyes need some leer, some promise of the ecstasy to come. Pouty smile says I'm ready for pleasure. Hair touching is brilliant. Shows abandon, and raising the arms slims the body, hikes those boobs."

His eyes went right to her big beauties. Wasn't sure if the tingle in his face came from getting excited, which he was, or because he'd let her push a button just to make a jerk out of him.

She rocked her butt more aggressively. "But hips close the deal. Get the men to want, to imagine how sex would feel with those motions." She let go of her hair and flapped a hand at him. "Utterly primal. Check it out at next wedding."

More proof to him that this world had all kinds. "Wasn't like that for me and Desiree. Not even close."

"No? Then how?"

He'd never told anyone the real story, but he didn't like leaving Miss Granville with the idea Desiree was cagey and slutty the way she'd had been describing. Besides, the woman probably wasn't going to remember eating his dinner much less hearing how he fell in love. "My Desiree, she's got—"

"Ooo, Desiree. I like that. Sounds exotic. Pretty?"

"You bet." He leaned closer. "Anyway, like I said, she's got this short leg from when she was a baby. Noticed it when she limped toward me to thank me for my service. Pretty as she was, that leg didn't bother me a lick. Just like that," he said, snapping his fingers, "I knew I wanted to spend the rest of the party with her."

"Was she the only woman there?"

"Huh?"

"Never mind. Continue."

"Well, dancing would have been the normal way to keep things going, but I didn't want her to misunderstand. Y'know, like I was some smartass about her being lame. So I got us each three beers and we sat in chairs as far from the dance floor as we could be."

"Thought you said you were a victim of dancing?"

"I'm getting to it. Anyway, we must've talked for an hour or more. Real comfortable and fun. But every now and then, I'd see her good foot bouncing to the music. 'Would you care to dance?' I said when the DJ put on *Georgia*. That's a nice slow one, in case you're not familiar."

"I live in Atlanta. And on planet Earth. I know the song."

"Fair enough. So, I could see she was thinking about it, but then she shook her head. 'Not built for dancing, I'm afraid,' and then she patted her skinny leg. Well, to the side of us, I saw this walk-in coat closet. Being June, nobody was using it. 'How about this then?' I said to her. 'You ride with me while I take a spin.' Could've been the extra beers, but before she could say yes or no, I hooked a hand under her knees and scooped her off the chair. Saw shock on her face, but a happy kind. Twirled us in little circles until we were in that dark closet."

Miss Granville sat up straight, eyes big. "Well done," she said clapping slowly. "What happened? Fuck or suck?"

"We're done here." He bounced his chair away from the table.

"Oh, lighten up." Reaching an arm to slap at his knee, she nearly tumbled out of the chair. "I'm sorry. You love her. It's a very sweet story, and I want to hear it. All of it. Really, I'm totally sorry. So you're in the dark closet. Then what?"

"I do love her."

"No more of my crap. Promise." She drew an X on her heart. "Just an ugly way to cover envy. Finish your story. Please."

"Ma'am, we connected. I felt it. Never happened like that with another human being. Not once in my life, except maybe my grandmother."

"She's very lucky, Charlie, and I'm sorry. If you'd like to keep telling me, I'd like to hear."

The apology felt genuine, and he enjoyed remembering that day. "Okay, so being in the closet, nobody could see us. I slowed the whirling until we were moving more normal. Small steps, just keeping time, both of us quiet. Didn't take but a few seconds before her arms were around my neck. Loose at first, then a little tighter. Her cheek brushed mine and slid down so her face rested against my neck. And then she started shaking. Not a sound out of her, but I knew she was crying. Hadn't a clue what I'd done, but I told her I was sorry and went to put her down. She locked a hug on me, wouldn't let me do it. So I went back to rocking and swaying 'til the end of the song, her crying and me kicking myself for messing up."

"Omigod. She'd never danced before."

"That's it, exactly," he said, aware of a change in her expression from when he'd started the story. No sass around the eyes. No smile of any kind. She'd shared a peek into her better part, and he liked her for it. "How could you know that?"

"Charlie," she said after a long quiet, her attention far off in the water, "be careful with us. Mother especially."

"Ma'am, you got nothing to worry about there."

"You misunderstand." Her head swiveled side to side, the pier's torches sparkling in her damp eyes. "She's up to something. You're not safe."

If anyone was up to something, it was him—trying to get Desiree hired—and he wasn't real proud of it. "I appreciate your concern, ma'am."

"Ah, the polite brush off." She rose and steadied herself against the edge of the table. "Shall we then?"

She hugged his elbow for the slow walk down the pier, and hard as he tried to avoid it, her breast bumped against him every couple steps. With the hot dancing in the chair, and all the talk about sex, he had to make his mind land on a whole different topic. Disassembling, cleaning, and reassembling an M16 occupied him until he was behind the wheel and heading for the safety of his room.

CHAPTER THIRTEEN

WARD RETURNED to the poolside table, but without Philippa. Not one family backside occupied a chair. Everything he'd hoped for after Devon's funeral had been shot to hell. While he never expected to be thanked for handling the minutia of the surprise funeral, he had hoped for some positive fallout. Maybe some recollected pranks or family excursions. Overdue admissions of pride in another's accomplishments. Hooting and laughter at exaggerations. Mostly, he'd wanted the others to publicly love and miss Devon, to create a sentiment so endearing it snared him as well. The only bonding he detected so far was between Sophia and Philippa, unlikely BFF's allied against Lauren.

Every face he recalled from the evening sparked an angry memory. Jittery fists rapped against his legs as he ambled toward the piped-in reggae music at the tiki bar. Parked at a small table, he ordered Luke's cure for the shakes: vodka on the rocks, "mumble soup" as Luke called it.

The first drink only boiled his blood higher. Halfway through the second, he visited the evening's offenders in his mind, one at a time. Red belt holder in taekwondo, he imagined spin-kick knockouts for each one stupid enough to answer the door. Everyone, man or woman, made his smash-mouth list, and that irksome Charlie earned multiple knockouts.

He sipped and replayed the satisfying mayhem until nature's call sent him back to the hotel. Instability during the short trip cautioned him that even though his mission was to get hammered, a return to the tiki bar might end in public embarrassment.

Back in his suite, he tiptoed past a snoring Philippa and the glow of a muted TV. He plucked two dinky vodkas from the mini-bar and slipped out onto the balcony.

Nipping at the first midget bottle, he marveled at the geniuses who ran hotels. Bastards knew their clientele cold. Guests were never more than a few steps from extortion-priced liquor and porn. Guiltless goodies for closet drinkers and masturbators, for nervous hookups who needed one last drink or the titillation of an HD erection to lose those panties. Everything private. Everything a secret. Brilliant, but he doubted the marketing wizards had a sliver on their pie chart for men who needed to get wasted after their wives stormed away from a brother's funeral dinner.

His first grab for the edge of the lounge chair came up empty, but the next slap latched on. He pulled himself forward far enough to peer through the glass door and sheer curtain. Images flipping on TV lit the room like an electrical storm. In bed, covers to her chin and mouth open, Philippa looked the same as when he'd slipped into the room. Dead. Hospital-bed dead.

His wife of thirty-two years. The only woman he'd ever had sex with. Tyler's mother. Some day he might see Philippa like he was now, and she would be dead, same as Devon on the morgue tray, except he'd feel something for her. At least he hoped so. Hadn't been a good night for the ties that bind.

A belch gurgled fire into his throat. He set the little bottle on the table.

She should have come back to the table with him. A dead brother, for crissake. Tonight wasn't like huffing out on a Christmas or Thanksgiving dinner. So what if Lauren told her to fuck more? Might have been the perfect advice. If she went back to screwing, instead of beating him off, maybe her vagina would remember how to get slippery again. And yes, his brother Archer was an asshole, but an asshole who showed up every sixteen years. No way that should trump a dead brother. Maybe everyone did beat on sister Sophia a little too casually, but she'd had fifty-one years to learn how to cope. Her boo-hoo'ing was pocket change next to a dead brother.

He wiped at cold sweat on his lip and forehead, gagged back another incendiary burp.

Philippa had the whole thing cockeyed. The only sibling she hadn't spit on was Luke, and he deserved it. At least everyone else showed up and suffered through the burial and their mother's senile antics. Luke hid out in celebrity de-tox, if that's where he really was. Palm Springs, cucumber slices on his eyes, witty banter with fawning therapists. Spending Mother's money, then dumping her on him. Son of a bitch.

And Mother. Still clever at times, but if she thought her Charlie ploy was working, tomorrow was going to include a shock. He'd brought brochures from three first-rate assisted living centers. At breakfast she'd have choices. Scrambled or poached, Earl Grey or English Breakfast, southern or eastern exposure. Wouldn't be pleasant, but that was his lot as the first-born.

The whirling in his head expanded to his guts. He yanked the sliding door open, banging it hard enough to pop a wide-eyed Philippa onto her elbows. Stumbling past the TV and into the bathroom, he slapped the light on and dropped to all fours. Sinus-scorching vomit splashed onto the marble floor.

"Dear God," came from behind him.

He knee-walked to the door, shut and locked it. His mouth and nose burned bitter. And the stink. Enough to roll him onto his hands and knees for another ejection.

"Why did you lock it?" Her voice had a reverb, like her forehead was touching the door.

"Leave me," he said. Sweat plastered his shirt to his back. A shiver rattled through him. Maybe it was food poisoning.

She jiggled the handle. "Ward, open the door."

"Go to bed. I got it." Blurry vision cleared enough to see the lake of pea soup he'd yakked up, and how much work there'd be.

"Please let me in."

Been a long time, but he knew that tone. Tenderness. If he opened the door, she'd comfort him. She was the good spouse, the spouse who didn't picture the other one dead and then felt so little about it. Shame replaced his anger. Not just toward her, but every target of his raging evening. All of them, except that smirky limo driver, sensed his remorse and lined up to accept an apology. Even Devon, who hadn't been one of the punch-outs, showed up in the queue, delighted to be included in any generosity from his most distant brother.

He stripped a towel from the nearest rack and buried his face in it. Dry heaves, apologies, and sobs lost themselves in soft terry.

"Still with us in there?" The handle rattled again.

He patted his eyes with the towel. Blowing his nose into it refreshed the vile taste. Chilled, woozy, and fighting wretches, he dragged his hips to the door and unlocked it.

Philippa paused in the doorway, groaned, and covered her nose. The sweep of her gaze found him last. Shaking her head, she squatted next to him and slid hands under his shoulders. "Okay. Up."

On his feet, legs wide, he leaned into her for the wobbly trip to the sink. "Vodka, Phil." She didn't like her name clipped, but speaking had become surprisingly difficult. "Too much maybe."

"No."

"I'm really, really, so sorry," he said, close to tears again.

"We're here. Hands on the counter." She wet a washcloth and swabbed his face and arms. The tossed cloth slapped against a wall of the Jacuzzi tub. "Probably going to need every towel in here," she muttered.

"Could be, y'know, food poisoning," he said, fighting for balance. "Might have a fever."

Eyes rolling, she draped his arm over her shoulder. "Ready?" She led him on a stagger to the bed. "Wastebasket will be on the floor next to you. Please use it."

"Think I'm done." He eased onto the pillow and closed his eyes. "God, my head."

She lifted his feet onto the bed and pulled the covers to his chest. "I'll be in the bathroom. Call if you need me."

"Philippa?" This time tears did sneak down his cheeks. "I don't want you to die."

"Go to sleep, and don't forget the wastebasket."

"I will. I mean I won't." He added the hotel maid to his list of sorries, but in her case, an extra twenty on the nightstand would have to do the talking. He'd make sure they checked out long before she got to know who they were.

CHAPTER FOURTEEN

CHARLIE SAID GOODNIGHT to Lauren outside her suite and hustled past the four doors to his. For the first time since this trip began, his room was more than just a place to crash. It was cover from rooftops full of sniping Granvilles. Inside his personal "green zone," he stayed dressed for what he hoped would be the best part of this nutty day: room service.

Impatient for his two beers and grilled cheese with bacon, he paced the room. TV on. TV off. He opened and closed doors. Same with drawers. The one in the nightstand held The Book of Mormon and The Bible side by side, at peace in the same spot. He imagined slipping a Koran in there and shutting the drawer. Three seconds later, explosion flashes and small arms fire, black smoke pouring from the edges. Seemed a perfect solution. The books caused the trouble, let them fight it out.

GranDelia had brought him up Christian, but without any love for holy books. She said anyone who needed that many pages to learn right from wrong never would. But he liked them. Not to read so much, but to see, to hold. Rich and important looking. Leather covers, gold lettering, pages shiny around the edges when they were closed. He ran a finger over the sunken letters on The Bible and remembered Desiree telling him how she'd found a condom as a bookmark in one at the Ritz.

"Oh," he whispered, dropping backward onto the bed. Desiree. He hadn't called her back after Lauren showed up at dinner, his almost dinner. "...*two minutes*..." must have turned into two hours by now. Late as it was, he dug out his phone and dialed her.

"Having fun?" was how she answered.

"Baby Girl, before you start, I'm sorry. I said I'd call, and I forgot. But there's a good reason."

"Oh, don't I know."

"Got it all wrong. Miss Granville's boyfriend was with her. They got to fussing. He took off, and I got stuck with her. She was in a state, and I let her talk it out. She went on for so long, I just forgot to call. That's it."

"They fighting about you?"

"Desiree, getting tired of this. I forgot. I love you. I'm sorry. That's it." So much quiet happened he checked the face of his phone. Looked normal, so he put it back to his ear. "Still there?"

"I'm sorry too, sugar, but two hours? What am I supposed to think?"

"Nothing, or I forgot."

A knock hit his door, along with what sounded like flat-hand slaps. "C'mon, c'mon," someone whispered out in the hall, like maybe the tray was getting too heavy.

"Baby Girl," he said, taking long strides toward the door, "I'm gonna go. Room Service just showed up."

"Room Service," she said, her laugh relaxing him. "Well, la-di-da. Bring me home a toothpick, Prince Charlie."

"Gonna get something a lot bigger than a toothpick, I promise you." He pulled the door open wide. "Whoa!" His hand slapped over the phone's mouthpiece.

Dressed in a white bathrobe and holding an ice bucket, Lauren Granville rushed past him into the room. "Shut the door," she whispered, then ducked into the bathroom and turned the lock.

"What happened?" Desiree said.

Only the clunk of an ice bucket on the bathroom counter made him believe someone was really in there.

"Charlie, y'okay?" Desiree said.

"Real good. Right as rain. The, uh, the room service guy, he darn near lost my tray." He leaned into the hallway, checked both directions, and eased the door closed. "Yes, sir, over there's fine," he said in a raised voice. "Hang on a sec, Baby Girl. Gotta take care of the paperwork."

Heart hammering, phone pressed to his chest, he walked through everything that would have been happening. *Server gives him the check. He asks where to sign. Wrinkles his brow to figure the tip. Scribbles at the desk. Hands back the stub and walks the guy out.*

He opened the door and took his hand off the phone. "You too. Thanks again." He slammed the door hard enough that Desiree had to hear. "I'm back," he said to her. Shaky fingers rubbed his forehead. "Baby Girl, I'm gonna go. Nothing worse than cold grilled cheese and bacon."

"Aw, don't. Talk to me while you eat. All I did today was watch TV, and I'm lonesome."

The bathroom door opened. Nodding her head and pressing a shushing finger to her lips, Miss Granville slid small steps into the room and sat on the bed. Her pretty green eyes left his and stared at the floor. Both hands grabbed the robe closed, one hand at her throat, the other at the knees.

"I'd sure like that, too," he said, "but, y'know, probably get grease all over my phone. Stuff like that. And I'm dogged. Just want to eat quick and get some sleep. Long drive tomorrow."

"Two more days. Wish you was here now. Still love me, sugar?"

"Now and forever, Baby Girl." He hung up and tossed his phone onto the desk. "What in *hell* are you doing?" he said.

"I need to sleep here." Her gaze stayed to the floor.

"Oh no. No no no," he said, head shaking, arms waving.

"Charlie, it's Justin. He's not …" She tapped her forehead.

"Ma'am, that doesn't concern me, and you're leaving."

"Please listen." She tucked smaller and turned misty eyes his way.

This woman scared him like no one since he got married. Each side she showed him had some appeal. "Make it quick, and then you're going."

"He got back here before us, in the room."

"That's not so." Thinking of her as a liar turned his burners down some. "I said goodnight to you at your open door. No one was in there."

"He was in the bathroom, with the light off. When I dropped my purse on the desk, I saw some empty mini-bar bottles that I didn't remember being there. Then from behind me I heard, 'Canceling the Amex. You are fucking hilarious.' Scared the crap out of me. I turned, and he was walking toward me, big smile, arms wide. 'Crazy bitch,' he said. 'No wonder I love you.' But his eyes, Charlie." Her head shook slowly.

"Well, you're out now, and this whole building's full of your kin. Pick one and go." He started for the door. "I'll walk you if you're afraid."

"Charlie, no. Please. How do I face them? Any of them."

If the teary-eyed defeat on her face was an act, it was a good one. But maybe that's what she was best at. The way she'd gotten him to say his room number at the pier bothered him now. Could have been part of a game. Maybe she could tell how he was for her and decided it'd be fun to make a fool out of him. Got together with that maggot, Justin, and set up the whole thing so they could take down a man who's trying his best. All of it just to prove everyone's slime like them.

Longer he checked her, the less his suspicions made sense. She looked like a kid whose dog just got run over, or who found out her parents were getting a divorce. A confused sadness, one she may have had a hand in but couldn't fix. He'd caught her in some good moments, too. Things she couldn't have faked. Caring so much about her dead brother. Understanding how Desiree got overcome by her first dance. Still, things weren't lining up. "Ma'am, what's the ice bucket for?"

"Are you going to make me go?" She patted a sleeve of her robe to each eye.

"Answer my question." He hoped the explanation sounded fishy enough that he could toss her without feeling guilty.

"Like I said, he came toward me with his arms open.

We hugged and kissed a little. I even felt bad about embarrassing him. Only took a few minutes before we were on the bed, naked."

"I don't need every detail."

"Thought you might be curious why I'm wearing the robe."

Last thing he needed was confirmation about what she wasn't wearing under that terrycloth. "The ice bucket?"

"So, we were getting busy, and he starting kissing my neck." She pulled a shoulder of the robe to the side, showing the bruise Charlie had given her in the limo. "He asked where this came from. When I told him you did it, he snatched my hair and twisted my head. 'You fuckin' him?' he said."

Charlie flinched. "When would we have had the chance?"

"I know, right? So, I told him why you did it, but he kept accusing me and bent my neck even more. Felt like he was going to break it if I kept denying, so I said I was sorry."

He wondered what he was doing, or how he was acting, that everyone could see his attraction so easily.

"Charlie, I'm sorry, but I didn't know what else to do. For some reason, admitting it got him to ease off a little. But he still had me by the hair, our faces maybe an inch apart. He was growling low in his chest, snorting breaths, staring. I only knew I was okay when he said, 'Get some ice.'" She glanced at him. "Y'know, for …" She pumped a tubed fist at her open mouth.

"Ma'am!" He shoved both palms at her, but that didn't drive away the picture.

She shrugged. "Anyway, the ice bucket was my ticket out, and yours was the closest room."

"At the pier, you went to some trouble finding out my room number. You settin' me up? That was this is?"

"You scared me, asking if Justin would hurt me for canceling the card." Eyes shut, she shook her head. "I could see he was afraid of you. If things went south, I wanted to be able to phone your room without having to go through the hotel operator. Maybe even bang on your door if need be."

"What about your brothers? Archer looks pretty useless, no offense, but Ward acts like he isn't afraid to mix it up."

"I can't." Twitches and tugs of crying started to take her face, but she waited them out. "Charlie, my whole life I've had a special place in the family. The free spirit. Dancing on the knife's edge. I've always done what they'd love to, but haven't got the gonads. They're dying to see me crash and burn."

Like with Desiree at times, he was going to have to nudge her back to the topic. "Archer's here alone. He'd let you stay in his suite. Call him."

"I can't face this tonight, not with family. Tomorrow maybe, but not tonight. Please. You won't even know I'm here. I'll sleep in the tub. Please?" She pressed praying hands against her lips, but those shiny green eyes kept pleading.

Granville women. They had his number for sure. One sad face, one whiff they might be in danger, and he was okay to take a bullet. Kin were supposed to do that. "Ma'am, you can't sleep in the tub."

"The floor then. I wouldn't mind."

"You can't sleep in the tub because I may have to use the bathroom." Teeth clenched, he banged a fist against his leg. "Take the damn bed."

"Charlie," she said, rushing to him, "you're a prince. You won't be sorry." A knock on the door froze her mid-stride.

Tingles took his body, like the first incoming round in an ambush. Only good turn this nonsense could take was if Justin was out there, unaware he was five seconds from a rearranged smile.

"Room Service," a man said, knocking once more.

Charlie wondered if everyone on the staff knew how many people were supposed to be in each room. "Get in the bathroom," he whispered to her on his way to the door.

She flapped a hand at him, sat on the bed, and crossed her legs. The robe fell open in a way that showed a good bit of thigh.

So much for gratitude. "C'mon in." Charlie opened the door to a smiling young man with a tray held above his shoulder.

"Evening, Mr. Woods. Evening, ma'am." The server's attention

97

hung on Lauren long enough that if she had been his wife, Charlie wouldn't have been real happy. "Where would you like this?" the young man said, dragging his smile away from hers.

"Desk is fine," Charlie said. "And I'll take the check." By the time he'd penciled in the total and turned his head, she was fussing with the edges of her robe, and the server was looking at the ceiling.

"Here you go," Charlie handed the check to the red-faced kid.

"Have a good night," the server said, skating backward, his hand feeling for the door. He avoided looking at Lauren like he'd turn to salt. "Thanks. Goodnight."

"Something happen?" he said to her after the door closed.

"That boy will be the hit of the kitchen tonight." She smiled and stretched her neck to see the tray. "What'd you get us this time?"

He'd never smacked a woman, but she was working hard to be the first. "Ma'am, I'm gonna tell you this but once." He jabbed a finger at her face. "Stain yourself any way you like, but leave me out."

"C'mon. Just a little fun."

"Tell me you understand, or you're out of here right now."

"I'm sorry."

She'd done it again. Popped his anger like a soap bubble. That wounded little girl face, the one that made him want to hug her, and more. Being close to that mischief for a whole night was going to be a chore.

CHAPTER FIFTEEN

GETTING HER HAIR right after a pre-dawn bath had taken a good bit of time and effort. Little wonder, thin as Vivien's tresses had become these past few years. More evidence of life's progressive abandonment, from the withering surface to the very engines of continued existence buried beneath. The seen and unseen, in cahoots, requiring ceaseless actions against the irreversible. Lacquer spray for the top, disposables for the bottom. Should the day ever come when she'd agree to leave her home, a first rate salon on the premises would be her highest priority.

That day would not be today. Lauren's inebriated threat last night confirmed the worst, and Vivien had been packed and ready since 4:30 AM.

Her plan was to wake Charlie at 5:45, so she still had a good bit of time to kill. Sitting on her suite's dark balcony, she observed Key West in pre-dawn arousal. Kitchen bangs and gongs. Smells of coffee, and trash, and low tide. Screams of invisible gulls, in lust, or combat, or both. Distant, illuminated marinas tended by silhouettes. Boat lights streaming toward the horizon for purposes unknown. Myriad lives aboard each one, important to themselves, yet if one of the vessels never returned, few would know or care. Like poor Devon and soon, her.

Only the looming battle to preserve her speck of planet in Reynolds Plantation kept her from another comfortable depression. She returned to the room and peeked at the clock. 5:33. Close enough. Reading glasses on, she punched in his number on the room phone.

"Hello?" a groggy-sounding woman said after a single ring.

"What are you doing?" a man said in the background. He sounded furious.

"Oh dear," Vivien said, "what an abysmal time for a wrong number. I am so sorry."

"Mother, it's Laurie."

"Laurie?" She squinted at the phone's keypad. Without her finger touching the keys, she redialed the number she was certain she'd entered.

"Give it here," the man said.

Charlie's voice, without question, and it chilled her. He and Lauren. She'd caught the liars for sure this time. Fabricating a Justin wouldn't work twice. That they'd even gone through such a deception made no sense. Her slut daughter had never bothered with secrecy in the past. Justin, Charlie, fill-in-the-blank. No one would have cared. Unless Charlie was one of the plotters. She already knew the whole family was in on it, but Charlie, too? If so, his treachery astounded. She'd succumbed like a dreamy schoolgirl. A man that handsome. Dripping sex appeal, yet devoted to a cripple. Victorian eyewash. And Desiree, of all the cartoon names to concoct.

"Ma'am, please. This is not what you think."

"You're fired." She slammed the phone. The glow of empowerment fizzled the instant she realized she'd just torched her only bridge to freedom.

CHAPTER SIXTEEN

LAUREN COVERED her head and scrambled all the way across the huge bed. Her fearful escape surprised Charlie, until he realized he was holding the receiver like a raised club. Another shocker was a clear view of her bare backside and a new-looking tramp stamp. Green vines with red and blue flowers grew from the top of her butt crack and spread sideways.

She pulled the sheet over herself and twisted toward him. "Take it easy," she said, shielding her face with an open hand. "Phone rings when you're asleep, you pick it up. I'm sorry."

He banged the receiver down and locked a tight grip on the bedcovers. "You're out of here."

"Don't!"

One teeth-clenched yank snapped the sheet from her hand. The cloth floated over the bottom of the bed like a parachute landing.

Last night, she'd gone to bed with the robe on, but that was gone. Breasts swelled inside her hugging arms. A bent leg blocked his view to her privates.

"Tried to warn you." She sounded bored. "May I have a towel or something?"

Second thing to catch his eye was a small blot of blood in the center of the bottom sheet.

She glanced at the stain and shrugged. "My friend has no schedule anymore. The robe caught most of it. Are you getting me a—Oh, for godsake." She swung her feet to the floor and stood.

Shoulders back, she fluffed and finger-combed her hair on a jiggly march into the bathroom.

Through the door she'd left ajar, he heard her pee and flush, followed by rushing tap water in the sink. Being early like it was, he didn't want to be loud. Quiet steps brought him to the bathroom door. Anger drifted away as he watched her, bent over the sink comfortable as can be, brushing her teeth with his brush, her hips and breasts swaying to the motion.

For the tiniest moment, Desiree was a horrible mistake. A woman like Lauren Granville would have suited him better. Whole and curvy and free. With her, this was how mornings would be. He'd lose his clothes and join her. Share a smile, a new-day "g'morning," and a kiss. Hug her from behind and run his hands over every part he could reach. Get a giggle for his effort, not a "quit it!" Coax her back to bed for whispers, and laughs, and heavy breathing. Slip inside and pound with her until he heard the same cry-out as when he'd hurt her in the car. Enjoy the rest of this and every day for a long, long time.

"Making me uncomfortable," she said, her words garbled. "C'mon in if you want. Nothing you haven't seen already."

He was afraid going in might turn into what he'd been enjoying in his mind, so he stayed outside after pushing the door wider.

She spat white foam into the sink and angled toward him, his toothbrush dripping over the basin. "Hope you don't mind. Morning mouth. Yuk."

Appeared to him like she was posing, inviting inspection. So he did. And if he was ever going to drag up this memory again, he wanted the details right. He started at the creepy Chinese tattoo below her throat and paused at her breasts. A little droopy, but still great, white where the sun hadn't tanned. Past the soft swell below her belly button he spotted another tattoo, real small, setting dead next to her shaved privates. Took a second, but he made out a fat tongue sticking out of cherry lips.

"I was going to get that on both sides," she said, brushing a finger on it, "but you wouldn't believe how much it hurt. Quite the hoot, though, don't you think? Justin's a freak for the Rolling Stones. Let's hope the next one is too. Oh well … Hey, up here." She snapped her fingers over her head. "Still mad at me about the phone?"

Starting at her tattooed ankle, his eyes crawled north one last time. Up those long, sexy legs to her tattooed privates, to her tapered waist and awesome breasts, to the Chinese tattoo below her throat, and finally to her beautiful green eyes. "What?" croaked out of his dry throat.

"The phone. Are you still mad?"

He swallowed away fur and forced himself to focus on her nose. "Just got fired. How should I feel? And cover your damn self."

Smiling, she grabbed a towel. "Don't worry about Mother. I'll call her."

He was so cranked up it took a second or two before her bad idea got through. "You're doing no such thing. Good chance I'm fired because of being with you. Makes me an enemy, too."

"Don't be dramatic." Towel draped over a shoulder, she inspected her reflection. "The old witch won't remember last night." She leaned closer to the mirror, giving him a better view of that tramp stamp. "Good *Gawd*," she said, pulling at her forehead and cheeks, "speaking of witches."

No mother could forget that kind of cruelty, especially on the day she'd buried her son. "You are not calling her, but there is something you are gonna do. You're getting the blood out of the robe and the sheet."

"Don't be stupid. They have people for—"

His first long step made her jump. The others drove her backward until she flattened against a glass wall of the shower.

"You *will* clean that blood," he said, his face close enough to feel the warmth of her breath, smell the minty toothpaste. Trapping her, all pretty and naked, raced his heart, like he'd finally caught her after a chase, one they'd both been playing at. Her nervous, searching eyes said the same. She dropped her lids half closed and tilted her chin up. His eyes closed. Lips touched, soft and first-kiss electric. Mouths opened. Tongues found each other. She slipped fingers into his back pockets and pulled. His hands found her hips, pulled a hardening pecker into the gap at the top of her legs. Her moan buzzed through his whole body.

He broke from the kiss and snatched her wrists. "No!" he said, trembling. "The blood. You have to clean the blood."

"Hey. Hey. Honey, relax." Her voice had a soothing lure to it. "We'll go slower if you want."

"Not going anywhere." He struggled not to crush her bones.

"You did something very sweet last night," she said, breathy and low, that pretty smile of hers making the words sound reasonable. Her leg curled behind his, stroked his calf. "Let me thank you. I know, why don't you go get some ice?"

"Stop it! The blood. Clean the blood. Nothing else. Do you understand? Nothing."

"Okay," she said softly, her face a mix of patience and disappointment. "But if you ever want—"

"I won't." He shook her wrists. "I'm getting out of here, and you're doing what I asked."

"Why? You're not doing what I want."

"You owe me!" He grabbed tighter and zoomed close to her startled face. "And call that maggot while I go see your mother. Tell him to slide both room keys under this door, then disappear. If he doesn't, I'm gonna find him. You tell him that." A good fight right now wouldn't burn all his fuel, but it would sure help.

"Umm, you should probably brush your teeth before talking to Mother." She shook free of his grip and headed for the bedroom.

Seeing her once more as a smart-ass, overgrown teenager cooled some fever, blew away the fantasy of happy mornings. So did splashes of water on his face and neck while he brushed his teeth. He'd been crazy stupid to fly so close to that flame, and was grateful he'd stopped at a striptease and a kiss. "I know, I know," he told GranDelia when she showed up in his head, one eye closed, a scolding finger wagging in his direction.

"Mrs. Granville," he said, tapping a finger on the door of her suite. "It's Charlie."

"What do you want?" Her voice sounded like her face was an inch from the jamb, which was good because they could keep talking quietly.

"Ma'am, can I ask for two minutes to explain?"

Her side of the door stayed quiet.

He tapped again. "Ma'am?"

"I'm timing you."

Now he wished he'd prepared something. "Well, first, your daughter did stay in my room last night, but we didn't sleep together. I'm married and glad of it." He waited a bit in case she wanted to say something. "And second ... Actually, there isn't any second. I'm married. That's it."

The door opened until the sliding latch caught. Her shoulder and a narrow slice of face appeared in the gap. "I don't believe you." Even her one-eyed stare held a lot of power.

"Ma'am, I've never cheated on Desiree, not with your daughter or anyone else. You want to fire me, I can't stop you, but if I'm going to lose my job, I'd sure as heck like it be for the right reason."

Her face stayed still, that probing eye of hers never leaving him. "I'm not a fool, Mr. Woods, and I have no delusions about my daughter."

"Looks bad, I know, but what happened was, she and that Justin had some trouble, and she didn't feel safe. Mine was the closest room, and I probably shouldn't have, but I let her in. I slept on the floor, and she got the bed. Like brother and sister. That's it, so help me." Her eye going squinty told him she was puzzling things. Went on so long he wondered if she was waiting for him to say something else, but after the truth, wasn't any more to tell.

"Are you ready to leave now?" she said.

"Guess I am." He stepped backward, panicky over how he was going to explain all this to Mr. Carter at Dependable Car Service. "Thanks for listening."

"No, I mean back home."

Sunshine through the clouds, but he'd misunderstood her before. "Need about twenty minutes. Ma'am, just want to make sure, I'm not fired?"

"Oh, hardly." She glanced away. "It's 5:58. Get the car and meet me out front at 6:15. Tell no one, especially Laurie." The part of her mouth he could see turned up at the corner. "And they think I'm in for a surprise this morning."

The whole way back to his room he tried to come up with what he was going to tell Lauren as he packed. Still had nothing solid, even as he slid the key in and opened the door.

She was gone. Bloody sheet still on the bed. Bloody robe lying where she'd left it on the bathroom floor, but no her. He wasn't sorry, but it did make him wonder where she'd gone, and why she couldn't have gone there last night.

CHAPTER SEVENTEEN

PUSHING A LOADED luggage cart, a Casa Marina bellman approached Charlie at the Town Car's open trunk. "No one else here," the man said when he got close, "so you must be Charlie."

"Guilty," he said, leaning against the car. "Is Mrs. Granville in the lobby?"

The bellman shook his head. "She said you should go to her room."

That wasn't what he wanted to hear. "She okay?"

"Looked fine to me." The man hefted a suitcase into the trunk.

"Was she alone?" If not, he wanted to be ready.

"Far as I could tell." The bellman stowed another bag and squinted at him. "You an off-duty cop or something?"

"Just nosey." He hurried inside to the elevators, eyes sweeping the lobby and hallways. Had no idea what he'd do if he encountered a Granville, but anything would be a slap fight next to what he'd survived in Afghanistan. He reached her door without spotting any unfriendlies. "It's Charlie, Mrs. Granville," he said after a fingertip knock.

The door opened to the limit of the safety latch. "Are you alone?" she said, one eye checking the hallway behind him.

"Yes, ma'am. Y'alright?"

She jiggered the latch and opened the door. Wearing sunglasses and a wide straw hat pulled low, she lifted her tote bag onto an elbow and pointed to the hall. "Let's go, and be quick."

"Who we running from?" he said at the elevator. "Lauren?" The way her daughter treated her last night made that the reasonable guess.

"All of them. You heard her. They're springing something on me this morning." She scanned the hall and batted her thumb on the already lit *Down* button. "Should we take the stairs, you think?"

"I hear one coming." He wanted to sound calm, but she'd made him jumpy enough that when the car arrived, he shielded her from anyone who might have been in there. Relief at seeing it empty made him smile. Plain foolishness to let a Granville feud put him on edge.

Elevator doors opened at the lobby. Only life there was two clerks behind the faraway check-in counters, and Ward Granville who popped upright in a wing chair. Reminded Charlie of a prairie dog spotting danger.

Ward sprang from the chair and trotted toward them.

Mrs. Granville hooked tight onto Charlie's elbow for a moment, but let go, stood straight, and waited. "Ward, darling," she said as her son slowed to a stop between her and the front doors. "I'm so glad you're up." She offered her cheek. "You can kiss me goodbye. We've decided to beat the traffic."

"Mother, you're not leaving. We have to talk." His eyes found Charlie's. "Family only."

Head shaking, she started around her son. "I'm still too distraught about poor Devon. Whatever it is will have to wait."

"Mother, no." Ward hopped in front of her. "The whole family's here, and we're concerned about you."

"If it really is a family discussion," she said, beginning another flanking maneuver, "then Luke should be included. Poor dear still isn't well."

"No." Ward knocked her wobbly by grabbing her arm. "Now."

"Whoa." Charlie rushed to them and steadied her by holding the other arm. "Sir, take it easy."

"Listen carefully," Ward said, his shaky finger inches from Charlie's nose. "Stay. The fuck. Out of this."

"Ward, language." She shook her elbow. "And let go of me."

"We'll do this in my suite," Ward kept his grip on the arm she was trying to tug free. "I'll have a nice breakfast sent up, then we'll show you a few things I know you going to love."

"Sir," Charlie said, leaning in, "your mother asked you to remove your hand."

Ward flinched, but held his ground. "Last time," he said, a catch in his voice. "Get lost."

"Stop it," she said. "Both of you. Couple of children."

"Sir, I won't tell you again." Charlie said. "Take—" A crisp jab caught him in the solar plexus. He dropped to his knees. A blow he never saw nailed him on the bridge of the nose. He toppled backward. His head bounced off the hard floor. Swirling. Floating. Pain swelled in his head, front and back. Choking blood in his throat. Rust-flavored.

"Ward!"

Mrs. Granville's shout pulled Charlie back to Key West, shocked to realize he just got his butt kicked by a middle-aged dentist. He rolled onto his side and turned his head so blood would drip on the floor instead of down his throat.

"Have you lost your mind?" she shouted. "Help him up."

Charlie's breaths began to come back, shallow and achy, but enough to cough away the gagging blood. Through a watery-eyed blur he caught sight of Ward, posing like a Ninja, skittering on the balls of his feet just out of range. He struggled to all fours, causing new zaps of pain, this time his knees. Kneeling crushed the scabs he'd got from saving Mrs. Granville two days earlier.

"You poor man," she said, putting herself between him and Ward. "Mind your tie, dear."

An opened packet of Kleenex appeared in front of his eyes.

"Use these," she said. "*Gawd*, how awful."

Lights popped behind his eyelids as he squeezed the broken cartilage back in place. Head hanging, he twisted Kleenex into each nostril.

Heavy, trotting footsteps clicked closer. "Problem here?" a man said. A walkie-talkie crackled. "Elevators, main lobby," the man said. "Mop and pail."

"Roger," returned to him through the static.

"This man assaulted me, officer," Ward said, "and I defended myself."

The man's hand pushed down lightly on Charlie's back, keeping him from standing. "Sir, do you need medical attention?"

Charlie shook his head.

"No need, officer," Mrs. Granville said. "A family tiff gone awry. One of those boys will be boys things, and since this gentleman and I have already checked out, there won't be any recurrences. Thank you so much for your concern, though." She patted Charlie's shoulder. "Will you be able to drive after a bit of cleanup?"

He nodded and stood. Each move set his face throbbing.

"And you might want to …" She wiggled a finger toward his nose. "Quite a bit of paper hanging."

He replayed the past hour as he headed for the men's room. Between Lauren, Ward, and their mother, Granvilles had produced quite a morning.

"Sir, not you," the guard said when Ward must have started to follow. "You wait here with me. When they leave, then you're on your own."

Charlie disappeared around a corner and leaned against the wall to let a rush of dizziness pass. Half of him eavesdropped, and the other half itched to go back and stomp that scrawny runt into red paste.

"Officer," Ward said, "this is crazy. She's crazy."

"Ward Granville, how dare you. And stand still for heaven sake."

"Officer, I'm her son. That guy's a limo driver, and he's taking her away when the whole family wants her to stay. It's like kidnapping. No, it is kidnapping."

"So," the guard said, "do you want me to call the police? Are you the legal guardian?"

"He most certainly is not. What an insulting question."

"Ma'am, I apologize. The way this gentleman was speaking I thought—"

"I have court papers, Mother."

"Only for the Foundation."

"We'll see."

"Ward, I'm leaving with Charlie, and that's that."

"Sir," the guard said after some quiet, "sounds like we're about done here. I'm going to wait for the other gentleman to come back. Then I'm going to walk him and this lady to their car. If you want anything more than that, I suggest you take it up with Key West's finest."

"Unbelievable," Ward said, so low Charlie barely heard it.

He headed for the Restrooms sign with a smile on his face. That old lady just got his nose busted, but he couldn't help admire the Marine in her. Low on ammo, but still firing.

CHAPTER EIGHTEEN

THE FIRST-AID ITEMS they'd bought for his skinned knees were still in the back seat of the limo. After Charlie got Mrs. Granville settled in the front, he slipped two Band-aids from the box, sat behind the wheel, and used the rearview to stick them over the break in his nose. Hurt like heck, but at least they were headed home. He took a last peek at the Casa Marina. Behind the arms-folded security guard, he caught sight of Ward, watching them through a glass panel next to the revolving door. No question they saw each other because Ward nodded.

Mrs. Granville fumbled in her tote bag as they drove down the hotel's driveway. "Why am I even bothering? I barely know how to turn it on." She shoved the bag to the floor. "Charlie," she said, tapping the dash, "the phone thingee in there. Can you call people? Oh, your poor face." She patted the hand he had on the wheel. "You really are a dear man. Thank you for the continuing gallantry. I must say, though, I am a bit shocked Ward could do that."

"Leave it go." He pushed his palm at her. A society lady like her had no idea how a surprise attack could overwhelm superior force.

"Excuse me?" She batted his hand down. "How dare you?"

Two more nights, he reminded himself, and he was the only paycheck for awhile. "Sorry. I just meant you know nothing about combat, so no point heading down that road."

"Still. I mean, really. Dented machismo is no excuse for rudeness."

"Understood, ma'am." He blew out a slow breath. "So, who we calling?"

"Calling?"

"You wanted to know if I could use the car phone for something."

"Ah, thank you. Hotels. I think we should change our way back. Oh," she said, fanning a hand in front of his face, "and we'll get home a day early. He won't expect that."

Only good thing on this whole trip so far was hearing they were lopping off a day. "You think he's gonna chase us?"

"Better safe than sorry. So, can you arrange all that without plunging off a bridge?"

"Why don't we just pull over? Do everything over a hot breakfast somewhere."

"No no. If he does follow, he might see the car, and then what? Another donnybrook? Unthinkable. You're damaged enough."

He knew pride goeth before the fall, but she was digging at a pretty raw nerve. "Ma'am, I promise you, if there is a next time, your concern should be for your son. Marines are trained—"

"Of course." She backhanded his arm. "You have military training. We should think of this as a campaign. Strategies, trickery, that sort of thing."

First bit of trickery was going to be getting her to agree to a breakfast stop. "Makes sense." He rubbed his chin. "Okay, so let's say we're being chased. Route 1 is the only way off these islands, and that runs over a hundred miles, two lanes for most of it. If he was going to catch us, his best shot would be in that stretch."

"Or at our hotel. Don't forget that. He knows my itinerary."

"Right." That impressed him, to the point of wondering once again how the Granville kids thought she was going simple. "I say we get him lost."

"Excellent." She'd turned her shoulders toward him and lost the sunglasses. Excitement on her face made her seem younger. "How?"

"Well, if he is coming after us, he'd most likely start right away. Probably be on the road no more than thirty minutes after we left. Sound about right?" He glanced at her.

She nodded, rolled her hand.

"So, if we got off Route 1 for about an hour, he'd shoot right by and never know it. Might end up driving all the way to the hotel." He tipped toward her and forced a smile. "The one we *won't* be staying at."

"Ooo, I like that," she said, rubbing her hands together. "This is fun. Don't you think?"

Fun and a throbbing broken nose weren't pairing up in his achy head. He twisted the bloody tissues from his nostrils and tossed them out the window. "Need some ice for this." He dabbed above the Band-aids. "A restaurant, that's where we'll go. We can get ice, eat something, and call around to change hotels. All at the same time."

"You, dear boy, are brilliant. Onward," she said, flapping the back of her hand at the windshield.

He knew she was wrong about him being smart, but that crumb tasted pretty good.

CHAPTER NINETEEN

WARD MADE NO EFFORT to be quiet entering their suite. "Philippa, get up." He swung a suitcase onto his side of the king-sized bed. "Be ready to leave in ten minutes." Still pulsing from post-fight adrenaline, he ripped open two dresser drawers and flipped clothes over his shoulder with each hand. Hearing nothing, he paused and glanced at her.

"Leaving?" She rose onto one elbow, blinked her eyes. "Time is it?"

"Six-thirty." He went back to emptying the dresser. "C'mon, get up."

"But I thought this morning was the big powwow."

"She's gone. Took off with that goddam chauffeur a few minutes ago. If you can believe it, I actually got into a fight with that troglodyte. I mean, a real fight." He turned to her, assumed the stance, and snapped off two lightening punches. "Pretty sure I broke his nose. Hot shot Marine, and I'm hung over." Years of schooling, training, and mental preparation, and today was the payoff. He'd dropped an experienced fighter. The fact it was someone who menaced the entire family only made the triumph sweeter.

"You hit that man?" She sat up, braced on stiff arms. Her eyes livened, lips parted.

She's impressed, he thought. Might even be turned on. Maybe Lauren's advice to screw more required some rumination time, and this was the trigger. A few extra minutes wouldn't compromise running down his mother.

"You make your living with your hands," she said, "and you're punching people?"

Yet another misread in their thirty-two year union, and her concern about his income was a straw man. Both knew his trust fund threw off triple the money he made from his practice.

"How stupid can you be?" she said. "Are you cut?"

It amazed him how quickly his fantasy of passionate coupling could reconstitute as a giddy strangling. "Catch a ride back with Sophia. I'm going after them."

"To do what, for godsake? Run them off the road?"

Her sensible question only doubled his frustration. There'd been a plan, a reasonable one that he'd spent considerable time putting in place. The fragile quorum, votes he'd cultivated despite some reluctance, would disappear within hours. "I have to finish this thing. We're all here now. It's time."

"She won't agree to anything without her precious Luke. You should know that."

His wife's savvy about family internals cracked open a tiny willingness to include her in deciding the next move. "Well, you're right there. That's exactly what she said."

"Then let her go." She glanced down and hoisted the neckline of her nightie. "What does a few days mean?"

He trudged to her side of the bed, sat on the edge, and lowered his face into his hands. "I'm tired of this, Philippa. They want me to be the glue for everything."

"I'm not sure they do." She inched closer. "I think they want you to handle things and not bother them. All goes well? Hooray. If not, as long as the checks keep coming, it's 'Oh, well'. Has anyone even thanked you for handling Devon's funeral?"

"Not even you."

"You're right."

He braced for the jab. Wanted it. Another simmering score to settle.

"I made things worse," she said, "and I'm sorry."

As with last night, drunk and sick on the bathroom floor, he regretted his readiness to raise the battle flag with her.

"You did fine," she said, "in spite of everyone. I'm sure wherever Devon is, he's very grateful." She flipped the covers back. "You've had a tough few hours. Come back in here."

He undressed quickly while she watched the ceiling. Down to his briefs, he snapped the waistband.

She glanced over, closed her eyes, and nodded.

"Want a piece of the conqueror, huh?" Mentioning the fight reflated his exhilaration. Naked and ready, he stood at the edge of the bed, wanting her to feel as differently about him as he did. He pressed his hips forward. "Philippa?"

She cringed at seeing what he was wagging at her.

"Say aah."

"That's disgusting."

"Then how about?" He circled two fingers and pumped his index finger through the center.

"You know it hurts me." Her eyes closed. "Do you want me to or not?"

He crawled under the covers, fluffed the pillow, and fell back onto it.

"Thought so." She threw the sheet to his knees and wriggled down the bed far enough to slip an arm under the small of his back. Cheek on his naval, she set her free hand to the task. Their routine now for almost two years.

He understood her not wanting to do something painful, but today he'd fought, for her and all of them. If she was ever to expand her repertoire to include something he couldn't do for himself, this was the time. His hands moved from her neck and shoulders to the back of her head. A gentle shove met resistance.

"Do that again, and I'm stopping."

Another downside to monogamy. Experiences expanded no further than the wife's willingness. He ached for the Internet's vast menu of pleasures. New-age women. Women delighted to present luscious swells and curves and cavities. Skilled, eager performers, unfazed by observation. Women who blurted nasty praise and preened at hearing it fired right back. Women consumed in the moment. Women like Lauren.

Obviously, Philippa knew he had needs, but the robotic milking didn't merely drain off accumulated pressure, each session added another coating of disappointment and self-conscious distance. The only worse option was doing it himself, so he rode out her diligence until the never-changing, "There you go." More like a toilet training success.

She used the sheet to wipe her hand and mop his groin. Never looking his way, she crawled over his legs to the edge of the bed, swung her feet to the floor, and disappeared into the bathroom. The door closed. Water rushed in the shower.

Drowsy, he pulled the sheet up. Cold wetness zapped his chest, prodding him sideways until the blot no longer touched skin. Clear of the evidence, he nestled deep into a pillow. Now that chasing his mother was off the schedule, they wouldn't check out until after ten. Plenty of time for some extra winks, and the sheet would dry long before the maid could tell what had happened. Even he'd nearly forgotten already. His swimming thoughts had diverted to replays of dropping that halfwit Marine.

CHAPTER TWENTY

"YOU CAN'T be serious," Vivien said when Charlie slowed the Town Car and turned into the parking lot of Big Pine Restaurant.

His dining choice appeared as derelict as the Route 1 locals who'd appalled her throughout their morning drive. Everywhere, lumpy women dragging lumpy children, a fast food pacifier in every mitt. Potbellied, dull-eyed men, sporting tattoos and hygiene-suspect hair. Apprentice, teenage prostitutes smoking unaffordable cigarettes, yakking into unaffordable cellphones, their precocious breasts and rumps showcased in spray-painted outfits. Young men, future inmates, sauntering nowhere or leaning against whatever was handy. Hats askew, pants drooping, unaffordably tattooed like daddy, assuming they had a clue who he was. Each new mile piled on more evidence of humanity's race to the bottom, provided more reasons not to fear death.

"Looks like they have parking in the back," Charlie said. "If not, we'll leave."

"If so, we'll leave. I doubt I've had the proper shots." Visions of a mounded toilet in a door-less stall sent a quiver through her.

"Ma'am, I need ice, and I'm hungry." He turned a pained expression toward her. "C'mon, gimme something here."

She studied the swollen nose and creeping discoloration around his eyes. "Alright, but you have to promise, if the bathroom fails inspection, we leave. Fair?"

"Actually, it isn't. I need ice. Right now." He pulled the limo into a shielded space behind the building. "I need ice because of you," he said, turning off the engine, "and for the first time, at least with me, a Granville is gonna honor a debt." He popped his door half open. "Staying or coming?"

Erring on the side of caution, they added an extra ten minutes in the delightful restaurant. Not only was the bathroom spotless, but they poached her egg to exact specifications. Even the tea water was piping. Charlie appeared satisfied as well, holding a poultice of ice to his nose while he shoveled down pancakes, scrambled eggs, and sausage links, all doused in amber goo. Nauseating, to the point she rarely glanced at his plate until he'd finished.

Dishes cleared, she allowed him access to her grossly misnamed "smart phone." Another example of Ward's bullying. She'd invested four years mastering a flip-phone, and he made her "upgrade."

Took Charlie a few minutes and a "damn" or two, but he stumbled onto the Internet.

Sipping tea refills, an indulgence she knew would mandate additional rest room stops, they mapped the trip home. According to Charlie, Orlando cut the trip into roughly equal halves, each taking a shade under eight hours, the same duration as her last flight to Rome. Riding that long was a cringing prospect, but superior to entombment in assisted living, and Charlie's pleasant company would no doubt continue to lighten the monotony. For their overnight, she had him reserve a suite and a room at the Grand Bohemian, a property operated by the same company as the Casa Marina. Her family may have been horrid at poor Devon's sendoff, but the accommodations were first rate.

Having no more unfinished details, she paid the check and hooked an arm on Charlie's elbow for the short walk through the parking lot. "Perhaps I should get in the back," she said at the door he held open. "If he turns around, both of us being in the front would be easier to spot."

"He won't turn around. Longer he doesn't find us, faster he'll go."

How he could possibly know that didn't matter. His confidence did. It bolstered her in a way she hadn't experienced since her husband died. Charlie possessed nothing akin to Marshall's intellect, but he had similar stability, and the more time she spent under his umbrella, the more often foolish possibilities sneaked into her thoughts. Flash musings of him being there for, "What if today we did such and such?" or, "Guess who I saw today?"or, "Oh, look at that lovely whatever." Nothing as inane as a romance, but genial companionship. His Tonto to her Lone Ranger. In rare versions, even Desiree gained admission. A faceless shadow, industrious and silent.

She backed onto the front seat, gripped her dress at the knees, and pulled both legs into the car. Once he got behind the wheel, she twisted deeper into the cushion. "The view is better from up here, and really, what can he do?"

To Charlie, getting home a day early sounded as good as a death-row pardon. He smiled at the idea of keeping it a secret from Desiree when they talked on the phone later. Saw himself busting in tomorrow night. He'd sweep her up the way she liked, toss her onto the bed, and give her the payoff Lauren had boiled up in him. A good night's sleep and they'd set about finding Desiree some new work. Him too. Staying at Dependable Car Service meant he'd risk another Granville assignment, and that wasn't happening.

CHAPTER TWENTY-ONE

CUTTING THE TRIP by a day suited Charlie, but adding three hours to the daily drive might have been a mistake for Mrs. Granville. Her enthusiasm flattened as soon as they got back on the road after breakfast. She spent most of the trip with her chin bouncing on her chest. Every now and then her head would snap up. She'd rub her neck, maybe ask how much longer or where they were, but then a couple minutes later, down again. If it wasn't for stretching her legs at Wendy's, and the three bathroom stops, she'd have frozen into a question mark by the time they got to the hotel, just short of 4:00.

Being in the Florida home of Mickey Mouse, Charlie thought the Grand Bohemian hotel would be a zoo. Overexcited kids screaming and pin-balling around the lobby and halls. Wasn't like that at all. A few kids, but mostly older folks and business people, so checking in went quick and quiet. He got Mrs. Granville settled in her suite, swung by the ice machine for his achy face, and stretched out in front of ESPN, all by 4:20. Soon as he saw two talking heads on the TV instead of a game, he hit the mute button and dialed Desiree.

"Hey, sugar," she said. "Didn't think I'd hear from you 'til after dinner."

"I'm in the hotel now. Just watching TV, missing you. Wanted to hear your voice."

"Same here. Even more, maybe. Got nothing else to look forward to."

"Yeah? Well guess what?" He caught himself. As a little kid, he'd get so excited each year about the Christmas present he bought

GranDelia, wasn't one year he made it to Jesus's actual birthday without telling her what it was. Rushing Desiree's happy scream tempted him like that now, but he knew seeing her face at the same time would double the fun. "I, uh, got my nose broke today."

"Omigod! In the car?"

"Worse. One of Mrs. Granville's sons. Little dude surprised me with some pretty slick taekwondo. I'm near twice his—"

"Charlie, no. You get fired?"

"Nothing like that."

"So, why'd he do that?"

"Sort of complicated, but the man flat don't like me."

"Was it over that sister? The one who made you forget to call me?"

"God in heaven, Desiree, would you get off that horse?" Good thing this conversation wasn't face to face because he felt his go warm. "Want you to promise me, no more about her. Ever. Hear me?" Bad at lying as he was, that would be the safest way to bury that bone.

"Then why'd he smack you?"

"Short and sweet, he thinks I'm sticking myself into family business, which is foolishness."

"And why would he think that?"

"Look, I'm gonna be home tomorrow. We'll talk then."

"You mean Tuesday."

"What'd I say? Tomorrow?" He whacked a fist against his leg. "Little puke must have hit me harder than I thought. I meant Tuesday." More warmth rose to his forehead and cheeks while he waited out her silence.

"Does it hurt much?" she said.

Her change of tone relaxed him some. "Just a boo-boo needing a kiss."

"Oh, count on that. He, uh, hurt you anywhere else needing a special kiss?"

He knew what her giggles meant. "Change the subject or I'm not gonna be able to sleep."

"Lordy, five days. Guess I'm in for it."

"It's been eight, and yes you are. Baby Girl, I am never going away again."

"Wish you was here, Charlie. Miss you something crazy. I'm no good when it's just me."

The way her voice went high told him she'd started to cry. "C'mon now." Again, he considered spilling the good news about getting home tomorrow. "Couple of minor setbacks is all. Like they say, what doesn't kill you makes you stronger. Right?"

"Well then I'm about ready for the damn Olympics."

Her small laugh told him it'd be okay to postpone the surprise. "That's more like it. How about I call you later. Want to shower the road off me before supper."

"I guess. And don't let some hoochie make you forget this time."

Lauren Granville's naked posing flashed in his head, like she was showing Desiree what the competition looked like. "Course not," he said.

"Still love me, sugar?"

"Now and forever, Baby Girl."

DINNER WASN'T MUCH livelier than the day's car ride. Mrs. Granville barely touched her Cobb salad, and before he got halfway through his steak, she'd already signed the check, so no dessert. He told her she didn't have to hang around on his account, but she did anyway, staring at the candle on their table, chin in her hands, elbows on the table—something she'd told him to stop doing today at Wendy's. Looking done-in the way she did, he figured she must've hung around to get some help back to her suite, so he finished quick and half-walked, half-dragged her up there.

"Charlie," she said before closing her door, "people have been noticing your face. Should anyone be rude enough to ask, you tripped in the dark and fell against a table in your room. Understood?"

Being wupped by a hundred and fifty pound, middle-aged

dentist wasn't something he wanted to advertise, but the truth didn't require a good memory or any embarrassing backtracks. "Why am I supposed to lie about it?"

"Ward is a highly respected professional."

Her stare told him he'd heard the whole reason. Reminded him again how quick he wanted to be out of her world. "G'night, ma'am."

CHAPTER TWENTY-TWO

VIVIEN LIFTED her head in painful stages. Through the Town Car's windows, the unchanging greenery on Interstate 75 whizzed by, same as every other time she roused from a spine-wrenching snooze. She chided herself for not remembering to bring that inflatable neck ring she carried during her air travel days. It would have prevented a good deal of agony, and more importantly, she wouldn't have drooled in front of Charlie, twice yesterday and once today. Nothing bespoke nursing home more eloquently than a harnessed octogenarian, seated and unconscious, a string of saliva connecting lip to lap. The plan she'd been noodling these past two days would be harder to sell if Charlie believed her personal needs commanded more attention than domestic chores.

Macon 4 mi. on the green roadside billboard warned her of the shrinking portal of opportunity. "Charlie," she said, patting fingertips on his forearm until he glanced at her, "I have something to say."

His expressionless peek offered no encouragement.

"You've helped me through a very difficult patch, and at a painful cost. Thank you. You're a good man." That last line may have penetrated. She detected a hint of softening around his eyes and mouth.

"Pleased I could help, ma'am."

Not a syllable of reciprocity. Hardly the keep-going response she wanted. "Funerals … Such a terrible reason to gather family. Reminds us how easily we lose touch." She checked from the corner of her eye. He could have been deaf based on the lack of reaction. "Do you know I hadn't seen Archer for sixteen years?"

"That's a long time."

He claimed to be nosey. Where was that now, she wondered. "Pity he spent so little time with us at the dinner Laurie ruined. You two seemed to be hitting it off. Swapping Navajo mumbo jumbo and all that."

"Seemed an interesting sort."

"Oh, beyond interesting, dear boy. He has two doctorates. Not sure in what exactly. Russian literature, comparative religions, things of that sort. Useless egghead gobbledygook in my opinion, but two degrees is quite impressive. Don't you think?"

He nodded, his eyes forward.

"A voracious student, Archer. In fact, he lived at home and did nothing but attend school until he was past thirty. Took meals in his room and tapped non-stop at his infernal computer. Then Marshall died." She touched Charlie on the shoulder. "That was my husband's name. Not sure if I ever mentioned that. Anyway, the night of Marshall's funeral, after I'd gone to bed, Archer packed his car and left, lickety-split. Four days later, he phoned from Utah. 'Mother,' he said, 'I've found my destiny.' Of course, I was stunned. Other than Brigham Young, whose destiny could possibly be in Utah?"

"I don't know that name, ma'am."

"Not important." She sensed a modicum of expansiveness in the response. "What is important is that my son now has a family out there, and I've never met any of them. Wife, three little girls, in-laws of some sort for all I know."

His brow wrinkled. "You didn't go to the wedding?"

Progress at last. "Never knew there'd been one. You see, he only phoned on my birthday, and several years ago he was late by a day. When I scolded him, he told me his daughter's appendectomy had taken precedence. As you can imagine, I was floored."

"You wanted him to ignore a sick kid because it was your birthday?"

"Of course not. In fact, I was quite pleased he'd come to care about anyone. But why keep it a secret? 'You have a daughter?' I asked. 'Three', he told me, 'and a wife'. Well, I'm afraid I took his little news blackout rather badly. Voices rose. Words were said that shouldn't have been, at least from Archer. The birthday calls stopped after that. No one was even sure if he was coming to poor Devon's funeral. Oh, my heart broke and soared at the same time when he greeted me at the luncheon."

Charlie chewed his lower lip, making her think he wasn't recalling the event. She touched his arm. "We'd just arrived? Ward began his unwarranted dislike for you?"

"I remember," he said, nodding slowly.

"Okay." She angled toward him. "So, here's what I've been thinking. I'm going to ask Archer and his family to move east and live in my home with me. Is that madness?"

He raised his eyebrows and blew out a slow breath. "Depends. How bad would it hurt if he said no?"

"Charlie, you've seen the house. What parent would deny their children a life like that?"

"Ma'am, I'm wrong a lot, but I think a kid can be happy in a cardboard box, and miserable in a castle. Ain't—Isn't the building."

His smile telegraphed he wouldn't admit to being wrong in this instance. Combining that with his indifference to the advantages of her home, she put the balance of her presentation on hold. Relocation decisions were the province of the wife, anyway. "Charlie, we're so close, would you indulge me before dropping me home?"

"Sounds like a favor."

"Precisely. I'd very much like to meet your Desiree."

SHOULD HAVE SAID NO, but Mrs. Granville's request knocked him sideways so sudden, anything other than "okay" would have required an insult or a lie. But no matter what, he was going through with the surprise of getting home a day early. "This is us," he said in a hushed voice as they turned into his driveway cut.

"Oh," she said, so softly he almost missed it. "Tell me, why are we whispering?"

"Desiree still thinks I'm getting home tomorrow. Don't spoil it." Keeping the tires on trimmed weeds instead of gravel, he rolled the Town Car ahead until it stopped next to the carport. His gray pickup stood under the rippled roof, glowing pale green from afternoon sun passing through the fiberglass.

"And you live here?" she said.

"Except for the Marines, every day of my life. Okay," he said, scanning the house for signs that Desiree might have spotted them. He removed the ignition key to keep the car from gonging when he opened the door. "You stay here, and I'll bring her out. And ma'am, please be quiet."

Eyes still on the house, she turned a make-believe key in her lips.

He got out and eased the door mostly shut. On tiptoes, house key in hand, he ducked under the front window, where he heard voices from the TV. At the pressure-treated front steps, he tested for creaks. Safe on the small landing, he mouthed a count of three, shoved the key in, and shouldered into the house. "Surprise!"

Dressed in a black bra and panties, which he'd never seen on her, Desiree yelped, covered her ears, and jumped up from her chair at the kitchen table.

"Baby Girl, I'm sorry," he said, laughing. Cigarette clouds in the room knocked some of the fun out of his mood.

Without looking at him, hands still clamped over her ears, she darted toward the bathroom. Second step, she fell hard on her side. Never put her hands out to break the fall.

"Desiree! It's me." He rushed to help her, but she hopped to her feet, lurched into the bathroom and locked the door. "Baby Girl, it's me," he said, hands and cheek pressed to the door. "You okay?"

"You crazy?" she hollered. "Scared the stink outta me. Cut my damn self, idiot."

"Wanted to surprise you. I'm sorry. Open up. Let's have a look." He wondered why she let herself take that fall so hard.

"Gimme a minute." Water rushed into the sink. "Why didn't you tell me?"

"Guess I should've." After turning off the TV, he noticed a coffee cup full of soggy cigarette butts and four empty beer bottles on the kitchen table, everything within reach of a mirror on a stand. Closer look showed a price sticker on the mirror's base. $11.89. Pretty penny for something they didn't need. Rolling it with one finger, he twitched at a double-sized image of his swollen nose and black-ringed eyes. No wonder she didn't know it was him.

Water in the bathroom stopped, and the door opened. Eyes darting every which way, Desiree inched into the main room holding a wad of toilet paper to her elbow. Had on nothing but a towel wrapped around her like a skirt. Her face was all made up like when they went to a wedding. She couldn't have done that in the little time she'd been in there. "Oh, sugar," she said, her busy eyes stopping on him, "look what he did to you. Okay to kiss it?"

Arms wide, he reached her in two steps. "You start," he said, not knowing if a hug or a swoop off the floor would hurt her.

Rising onto her toes, she puckered for him but kept her hand on the clump of tissues, so no hug, and the kiss ended before tongues joined the party. "Glad you're home," she said, her shiny eyes still acting unsure where to land. "Been crazy without you."

Wasn't exactly prime time to ask, but seeing the underwear, beers, cigarettes, and mirror felt almost like he'd gone into someone else's house. "So that explains …?" Arms loose around her slim back, he bobbed his head toward the table.

"Practicing, is all."

"Y'already know how to smoke, so practicing what? Drinking in the afternoon?" Bad start for a hot and happy reunion, but concern had drawn neck-and-neck with horny.

"You don't know what it's been like." She looked more hurt than mad. "Getting fired. All alone. And, y'know, things you been making me think. Needed something 'til you got back." Her eyes stayed on him this time, lips pulled into a smile. "And now you're here." She inched closer until their legs touched. "Still love me, sugar?"

She was playing him, and he didn't mind a bit. "Now and forever, Baby Girl." Pulling her close, he rubbed and patted her back. "So, what *were* you practicing?"

"My new look." Head tilted back, she grabbed the long side of her hair. "Gonna cut off this horse tail. Do my face up more often." She turned her head this way and that. "Like it?"

"I do," he said. "But I promise you, I had no problem with the old you." He lowered his attention to her breasts, about half the size of those he'd been treated to that morning. "And being mostly naked never hurts."

She batted away the hand trying to loosen her towel. One more peck on his lips and she pushed a finger into his chest. "Wait out here until I call. Okay?"

"Aw, c'mon. Nothing I haven't seen before." That echo of Lauren Granville's words popped her into his head. Pretty, curvy, naked, available. Heat rushed to his face.

"Why Charlie Woods, you're blushing" Desiree grinned and pushed her finger harder into his chest. "Could just eat you up." She backed into the bedroom and winked at him. "Hold that thought."

Seconds after she tugged and shimmied the accordion door shut, he heard drawers open and close. Same with the closet door, and then things went quiet. "Come and get it," she said, followed by a giggle.

A knock hit the front door. "Helloooo," Mrs. Granville called from the other side. "Everything alright in there?"

"Losing my damn mind," he whispered. "Yes, ma'am," he said, voice raised, fist shaking in her direction. "Be there in one second."

"Who you talking to, Charlie?" Desiree said.

He hurried to the bedroom door and opened it a crack. "Mrs. Granville's here. Forgot I left her out there in the car. Get dressed. She wants to meet you."

"Now?" Still wearing the towel, she crawled across the bed toward the mirrored closet door. Near the bed's edge, she froze like an animal coming face to face with trouble. "Omigod." She gaped at her reflection. One hand slapped and pulled at the long side of her hair. "Why'd you say yes?" She swung her legs to the floor, slid the closet door aside, and stared at her clothes. "Tell her to go away. Tell her I'm sick."

Even in the dim light, he could tell neither of her elbows was even red, much less bleeding. Puzzled him why she'd been holding that ball of tissues and telling him she'd cut herself. "You're fine. Throw on a dress and come out when you're ready."

Her startled face snapped his way. "A dress? We going out?" She dropped to her knees, stretched an arm under the bed, and dragged out a store bag. "Dammit, Charlie, why do you just, y'know, do stuff?"

"Relax. A quick hello. I drive her home. Then back here for some bed-rocking. You take your time. I'm going to let her in." He closed the door before she could launch the next objection.

"Charlie?" Mrs. Granville said, along with some new knocking.

"Be right there, ma'am." He detoured to the table. Soggy cigarette butts hit the open trash bag. He rinsed out the coffee cup and beer bottles and left them in the basin. Room still stunk from smoking, so he raised the little window over the sink. With nothing more to fix, he opened the door to see Mrs. Granville's tight face and folded arms. "Ma'am, I apologize. Surprising Desiree like I did shocked her so bad she took a spill. Had to do a little first aid." He backed away from the door. "C'mon in. She'll be with us directly."

Stepping as if the house was mined, Mrs. Granville eased indoors. Her gaze swept the room, one of her hands climbing until it covered her nose and mouth.

"It'll clear out in a minute." He twisted Desiree's chair away from the table. "She's trying to quit. Real hard for some people."

"I'll stand, thank you." She stared like he'd tricked her and she caught him.

Hadn't done anything, but he looked away just the same. His eyes fell on an inch of coffee left in the pot. "Can I offer you some?" he said, pointing to it.

132

"It's 'may', and you just did," she said, words muffled by the hand over her lower face. "Besides, you know I drink tea." She tilted her head to one side and paused. Turned it in a new direction and waited again. "Was she rendered unconscious?"

"You about ready, Baby Girl?" he called to the bedroom.

The door folded in its track, and Desiree came out looking fantastic. Light blue sweater and long white skirt, neither that he remembered. All the new stuff he'd seen in the last few minutes clicked through his head. Black underwear, mirror, sweater, skirt. Only price he knew was the mirror, but the rest had to be more, maybe a lot more. Wasn't like beer and cigarettes were cheap either. Soon as he got back from taking Mrs. Granville home, he and the wife were going to have themselves a money talk.

"How do, Mrs. Granville," Desiree said. "Sorry I was so long. You see—"

"I heard," Mrs. Granville said. She pointed to the front door. "Everyone, outside." At the front door, she waited until Charlie reached around her and opened it. "*Gawd*, my hair," she muttered before turning sideways on the landing to clomp down the three stairs one at a time.

"Charlie," Desiree whispered, hand tugging at the back of his blazer, "cold out there. She nuts?"

"Nor deaf, young lady," Mrs. Granville said, facing them as they exited. "And you are correct. It is chilly, so let's get right to it, shall we?" She tilted her head sideways and fanned a hand at Desiree. "Come out from behind there, dear. Being accused of lunacy no longer offends me, and this concerns you as much as Charlie."

Alarms clanged in his head.

"Desiree," she said, "you're quite fortunate to have paired with this man. During our few days together, I benefitted almost hourly from his decency. Up to an including …" She wiggled a finger at his broken nose and shiners.

Desiree hugged his arm and smiled up at him. "Don't gotta tell me, ma'am."

Mrs. Granville blinked and shook her head. "Let's hope that's fixable."

"Ma'am," he said, feeling Desiree shivering, "she's not dressed right for out here. Mind if we finish this in the house?"

"In fact, I do. Cigarettes killed my husband. They will not kill me. I've already endured enough exposure to merit a discarded outfit and an hour at the salon. Desiree," she said, narrow eyes turned her way, "be truthful, could you quit?"

"I really don't smoke now, ma'am. Slipped back into it with Charlie gone. Kind of a crutch, y'know? He's back now, so that's done."

"Well." Mrs. Granville clasped her hands and smiled at each of them. "The last domino, far as I'm concerned. Say yes, and we'll celebrate with old fashioneds and an early dinner."

"Yes to what?" Soon as the question left Charlie's mouth, he was sorry. Anything that included celebration or another meal with her had to be bad.

"Desiree," she said, covering a chuckle, "you may have been right about the dementia. Forgive me. I'm offering you jobs, of course. Both of you."

"Oh no." Charlie waved his free arm. "Thank you, but I got a job, and Desiree will, too."

"What's the pay?" Desiree said.

"That really don't matter," he said, shocked by Desiree's question. "We're fine as is." GranDelia would roll in her grave if he ever took a government food card, but he'd do that before going to work for Mrs. Granville.

Shaking her head, Desiree crinkled her nose at him. "I think we should listen." She turned her eyes to Mrs. Granville. "Ma'am, please come in out of the cold for just a minute. My husband needs to see something before saying no."

"Show me when I get back." He offered an arm to Mrs. Granville. "Mind your step."

"Wait." Mrs. Granville said. "Let's do this. You start the car. I'll stay warm in there while you go inside and discuss whatever it is."

"Ma'am," he said, "nothing to go over."

"Charlie, stop," Desiree said. "The mail while you was gone." She shook her head. "Not good."

CHAPTER TWENTY-THREE

THEY WERE LOSING the house. Simple as that.

Elbow on the kitchen table, hand rubbing his hair, Charlie took a third run at the letter. Nothing changed. In thirty days Greensboro was taking the house for three years of unpaid taxes. Sixty-seven hundred dollars. May as well have asked for a sixty-seven million.

"Well?" Desiree said from behind his chair. "Say something."

His head felt like a hundred pounds. He rested it in his palms. "Why didn't I know before now?"

"Kept hoping we'd get ahead a little, and I'd catch up. Charlie, they can't want this house. I mean, c'mon, who the hell would?"

Whole time they'd been married, she did the bills, so he mostly lost track of what came in and out, but even with as little as they earned, it should have been enough. "What happened to the money?"

"I dunno. Just kinda goes. Food, gas, y'know, stuff."

"God almighty," he whispered into his hands. He'd lost GranDelia's house.

"Charlie," Desiree said like sharing a secret, "that old woman. Talking about jobs. Right out of the blue like that. Almost like heaven sent her."

"So now you're God-fearing?" While he and Desiree courted, they attended Antioch Baptist every Sunday. Since their wedding day, he went alone. Remembering that now had the same feel as her going back to smoking.

"Should at least listen to her," she said, her voice a little closer.

"Desiree, you got any idea how much we'd have to make to clear sixty-seven hundred in thirty days?"

"No." Her fingers crawled onto his shoulders, squeezing and stroking.

"Me either, but a heck of a lot, I promise you."

"What if it don't have to be paid that quick?" she said. Her fingers worked his neck the way GranDelia readied dough for a pie, like she was doing it without even knowing. "We could say we'll pay over time."

"With what? You got yourself fired, and I only got two grand coming for this ride." He waved the town's letter. "That ship's sailed."

Her hands slowed and stopped. Arms circled his neck. Her hair swept soft on his ear. "Sugar, don't hate me." Body shaking, she tightened her hold, nuzzled warm tears across his cheek.

"Hey now." He stood and pulled her close. "C'mon. We'll figure something."

"I don't think so." She tipped her head back, black streaks leaking down her cheeks. "Charlie, that old woman's throwing us a rope. Won't cost nothing to listen."

Lose the house or work for Mrs. Granville. Felt like having to pick between two doors, knowing each was booby-trapped.

THE SUN had dropped low enough that Charlie's limo sat in shadows. Foot tapping, Vivien lowered the window every few seconds as defense against carbon monoxide poisoning and to listen for Charlie's and Desiree's footsteps or voices. Each time she returned the car to quiet, her clumsy job offers echoed like canned voices in a funhouse. She imagined the two of them inside, conferring as to which mental health agency should come and collect her.

Charlie emerged from the hovel first, still attired in his blazer and the tan slacks she'd bought him in Key Largo. Her role in his well-tailored appearance produced a proud parent satisfaction.

Holding the front door, Charlie stood aside for Desiree, who'd thrown on a hooded sweatshirt. She'd also swapped her white skirt for black slacks. Pants made her up-down gait more pronounced, raising Charlie's stock even higher for his commitment to the damaged creature. How hard it must have been, she thought, to resist a beautiful, accomplished slut like her daughter for an entire night—assuming he'd been truthful about that.

He circled in front of the car to get to the driver's side.

Desiree opened the front passenger door. "Oh," she said, looking puzzled.

"Yes, dear?" Vivien said.

"Nothing, I guess." Desiree closed the door, got in the back, and slid to the middle of the seat. "This'll be fine. Be able to hear all y'all from here."

She found Desiree attractive, in a peculiar way, but her role in the house would have to be non-speaking in the presence of guests, few as there were these days.

Charlie settled behind the wheel, shut the door, and rested his back against it.

"Before either of you utter a word," Vivien said, "I must apologize for my artless presentation earlier. Pretend you heard nothing. Here's what I meant to say." She turned sideways and smiled at each of them. "I've reached a point in my life where I could use bits of assistance now and then to keep things, you know, humming along. The house, the grounds, transportation, things of that sort."

Desiree nodded.

Poker-faced, Charlie flipped glances between the two women.

"I've been reluctant to employ the extra help out of fear. Actually, fear is too strong. Distrust is more accurate. You see, the optimum arrangement in my opinion is live-in staff, preferably a husband and wife. But turning one's safety and comfort over to fanciful resumes is, well …" She checked the two faces. Blanks. "My point, Charlie dear, is that I am utterly comfortable with you. I'm also confident that you would choose a spouse as decent and diligent as yourself."

Beaming, Desiree shoved the arm Charlie had draped over his seat.

He didn't smile back.

"Desiree," she said, twisting more toward her, "I mentioned to Charlie that I'm thinking of bringing my son and his family east to live with me. Huge house. Perfect for them. Pool, lake, boat, jet skis, lovely grounds for the children to play." Desiree's lean forward encouraged Vivien to add more details, particularly those of interest to a housekeeper. "Exquisite kitchen, all stainless steel and granite. Laundry on both floors, central vacuum, and charming details throughout. Broad hallways, hardwood and marble floors, high ceilings, most of them coffered."

That last feature brought a crease to Desiree's brow, and a wrap-up to the sales pitch. "Anyway, I'm sure they'll love it, but I want it ready before inviting them. Charlie tells me you're an experienced maid, which is exactly what I need for the inside. Oh, and can you cook?"

"No one's died yet."

Vivien returned Desiree's smile and extended an open hand to Charlie. "The rest will be yours. Driving mostly, but some handyman things from time to time." The dilapidation of his trailer flew in the face of his maintenance skills, but that had no bearing on her offer. "So, what say you?" She pivoted her most encouraging smile to each.

Arms folded, Desiree fell back in the seat. "Ain't said how much?"

"Ah, right to it," Vivien said. "I like that. How much would you find adequate?" Marshall would have been proud. He always said the first person to name a price in a negotiation lost.

One eye closed, Charlie pulled at his chin. "What about this? You advance us seven thousand dollars now, and—"

"Ten." Desiree snatched Charlie's wrist. "Ten thousand."

"Ten thousand," Charlie said, casting a puzzled look at his wife, "and we work it off over two months."

Not that it would crimp, and she had no idea what the market called for, but sixty thousand per year, plus free room and board, seemed exorbitant. "Three months." Vivien hoped she'd sounded unreceptive to a counteroffer.

"Baby Girl?" He shrugged at his wife.

Tears welling in her eyes, Desiree clapped both hands over her mouth and nodded.

"Excellent," Vivien said. "Oh, I can't tell you how pleased I am." She'd beaten the plotters to the castle, and tomorrow she'd raise the drawbridge. "I'll wait here while you pack."

"Now?" he said. "Ma'am, we got loose ends. Can't just up and leave."

"Charlie, we can." Desiree ran a fingertip under each eye and checked it. "We gotta get the truck up there anyway. You take Mrs. Granville now. I'll pack and drive it up when I'm done. "

"But I gotta give the car back. How about I come back for you, and we do it together?"

"Sugar, no," Desiree said. "Putting too much into one night. They ain't expecting you 'til tomorrow, right? That's soon enough."

His head and shoulders sagged. "Could help you with the packing."

"I'll be fine," she said. "Ain't like we got much. C'mon now. Won't be long."

Vivien detected a sultry promise in the woman's inflection and smile. Were she not a widow north of eighty, her flash of resentment for Desiree might have been misinterpreted as jealousy, rather than its bloodless twin, envy.

CHAPTER TWENTY-FOUR

WARD FORCED himself to ease back on the accelerator. First day back in the office after Devon's funeral, and he had to cancel his afternoon appointments, drive an hour, and undo Mother's latest flight of mental infirmity.

He'd phoned her house during lunch to leave a message, but a woman answered the phone. "Granville residence," was how she answered, her drawl more appropriate for hog calling than domestic service. A few questions unearthed that his mother was out, and this woman had been hired as a live-in maid—yesterday, which was improbable. Based on his mother's itinerary, she would have had to hire the maid while still out of town.

On the likelihood this woman was an intruder, he'd called Reynolds Plantation security and asked them to swing by the house to check on things, and if Mother wasn't there, to have the maid produce identification and something to show she was authorized to be there, perhaps a key or knowledge of the alarm code. They'd called him with a "no problem" ten minutes later, but the situation still made no sense.

He parked under his mother's front portico and sprang up the four porch steps two at a time. His key didn't fit. Nothing fit, he thought as he rang the bell.

Uneven but rhythmic steps approached the door from inside the house.

The woman who answered surprised him. Her elocution on the phone, coupled with the sound of her pronounced limp, prepped him for a hag. The woman barring his entry into the foyer bordered on pretty. Low-budget from head to toe, but attractive, despite a chill in her stare. "Mrs. Granville's not to home, sir."

"I'm her son, Dr. Ward Granville. I believe we spoke on the phone earlier."

Hand still on the doorknob, she scuttled sideways and blocked his attempt to enter. "How do I know that?" she said.

At least the woman was protective. He slipped a business card from a gold, monogrammed holder. "And you would be?" he said, handing it to her.

"Desiree." Reading what appeared to be every letter on the card, she wobbled backward and widened the path. "Don't know when your momma'll be back. She's on some errands."

"God, tell me she didn't drive," he said. No longer licensed, she nevertheless insisted on keeping a vehicle for Luke's rare visits from California, an extravagance made even more idiotic by an annual upgrade to BMW's most expensive model. He pinched away a smile as he imagined a fender-bender, one little smashup that produced two home runs: mother needing assisted living, and Luke cruising around Reynolds Plantation in a rented Smart Car.

"She went with my husband, in the pickup."

"Your husband?" He pictured his mother belted into the front seat of a balloon-tired mud buggy.

Her wary eyes studied him for a few seconds. "Might've met him if you was at the funeral. Charlie Woods?"

"Jesus Christ!" he screamed at the ceiling.

Desiree inspected him again, this time running her eyes down and up. "Well, I'll be." The merest suggestion of a smile tugged at her lips. "*You* busted his nose?"

Subtle but unmistakable. That she would dare telegraph ridicule conveyed dominion. While he and his siblings bickered and dithered, Charlie and this woman had Trojan-horsed into his mother's life. He kicked himself for dragging his feet on Philippa's suggestion to have Mother declared incompetent. Tomorrow for sure, but first he had to rid the house of these parasites. "I'm getting you a cab." He slipped a phone from his pants pocket. "Collect your things. You're leaving."

"Hell I am." Arms folded, she stood with her good leg forward.

"C'mon, move. You can leave a note."

"Your momma told me if any of y'all phoned or showed up giving orders, I'm to tell you to take it up with her, so, take it up with her." Her look was that of a child convinced she'd just delivered the killer of all comebacks.

He re-pocketed his phone. "Well, I'm going to do just that."

An appliance in the kitchen beeped.

"That'd be my coffee." She hobbled toward the sound. "Made plenty if you want some."

"No." Except more information couldn't hurt. "Um, actually, I will."

Footsteps toward the coffee clicked on the foyer's marble floor, rushed up the wainscoted stairway, and echoed back as if to say, "Nope. No one up here either."

The time had more than come. Mother was a flea in this palace, a residence that couldn't possibly have any emotional attachments for her. Other than Archer's brief hermitage in a back bedroom, not one of them had spent a formative day here. His father lived less than a year after the last slap of paint dried. She should have been eager to leave, not lash herself to the mast.

Before starting down the hallway to the kitchen, he paused at a railing of the sunken great room and soaked in the panorama that would soon belong to someone else. Spreading across a two-story expanse of glass, blue sky capped Lake Oconee's rolling greenery. French doors led to landscaped terraces and sloping lawns. Staged below that, the pool and cabana house. To one side, tucked behind a winter skeleton of crepe myrtles, a stone stairway to the boat house and shoreline. On the other boundary, a nearly secret entrance to a hedge-lined gravel path, wandering in privacy until it found a koi pond and waterfront gazebo. Magnificent in architectural concept, but the entryway began with a three stair hazard. Case closed.

Standing next to him, Desiree swirled a finger at the mass of glass. "Told your momma I didn't think I could do them big windows, but she said a service handles that. I'm only in charge of the upstairs and kitchen, anyway. The Monday-Wednesday-Friday girl—think her name is Marisol—she's got down here. Guess I'll meet her tomorrow." She shrugged and continued toward the coffee.

Had she heard nothing? It didn't matter if a service did the windows, and no one was meeting anyone. She and that devious husband of hers were leaving. Today. He followed her into the kitchen without argument and dropped into a chair in the breakfast nook, a glass-wrapped rotunda with views to the grounds and lake.

"Yes or no," she said, taking two mugs from a cupboard. "Was it you busted my Charlie's nose?"

"Man has a right to defend himself."

"That so?" Mugs filled, she opened and closed drawers under the granite counter until coming up with two spoons. "See, that don't set right. My Charlie, I'm told he can fight, and no offense, but you're a touch small and old for him to bother with."

Speaking with this trailer trash was a waste of time. Only a face to face with his mother would fix things.

Coffees held far in front, Desiree hobbled to the table and placed one in front of him. To his surprise, she sat in the chair next to him. "Something real bad must've happened." Her gaze stayed forward.

"Why I hit him?"

She nodded.

He'd revisited his victory often over the past two days. One more time, to a new and interested audience, had appeal. "I don't expect you to understand, but plans have been gelling for some time on a matter concerning my mother. With all of us together at the funeral, the time was right to present it." He glanced to see if her expression betrayed complicity in Charlie's conniving. Instead, she'd tightened as if awaiting a blow. "But whenever the moment was ripe, your husband would materialize, as if by magic, and ruin it. His final interference included a threat, and he paid for it."

Eyes wide, she laughed into her hands.

More ridicule. Woman or not, he would have delighted in turning her face into a bookend of her husband's.

"Sorry." Head shaking, she fanned a hand at him. "Whole time, I was afraid it was about your sister. Y'know, Charlie messing with y'all's sister. Oh my lord," she said, laughing again. "It's your momma. She's took a shine to him."

While he could accept Desiree's need to denigrate any man who'd humiliated hers, inferring he was Mother's lap dog pressed the attack beyond her means. Charlie discovered the peril of underestimating him, and so would she.

"Of course, I have no idea what your husband did with Lauren the times they were together. And I'd be in no position to object, anyway. Single woman can do as she pleases." Seeing Desiree's face harden told him he'd deployed the right weapon, one he could re-use.

Jaw muscles flexing, she lifted her full cup and headed for the sink. "Some big family, you Granvilles." She dumped out the coffee. "I see pictures of all y'all when I vacuum the front stairs. Y'all got what, two sisters?" She turned toward him and dried her hands on a dishtowel.

He added a dash of smirk to his nod.

"You said 'single', so I'm guessing Lauren's the one in the strapless, not the wedding dress."

"Beautiful woman, don't you think?"

Her nose wrinkled and relaxed. "Hair says that picture's got some years. She the oldest?"

"Hardly, and if she walked in here this second, you'd think she was thirty-five, tops." Desiree lowering her eyes to the floor spurred him on. "And the picture being a portrait, you can't tell the half of it. She has the figure of a Vegas showgirl." He smiled and shrugged. "Brothers probably shouldn't notice those things, but we always had a pool, and she's never been bashful."

Lips pressed flat, Desiree threw the towel into the sink. "Got work to do," she said, hobbling toward the great room. "Be obliged if you stayed out of my way."

"If you're still here," he called after her, "maybe you and Laurie will become friends. She spends a lot of time here, especially in the warmer months." The hesitation in her step let him know his sister had landed on Desiree's imagination. Perhaps sunbathing at the pool. Predator eyes unseen behind sunglasses, following Charlie as he labors in shrinking circles around her lounge chair. Arching her back and stretching. Fingertips of both hands pinching the top of her swimsuit, tugging up and side to side. Re-crossing her long legs during a shared smile. An invitation? Or worse, a reminder of past visits.

It was also possible that, like his mother, Desiree was nothing more than another fool for Charlie. If so, introducing an ominous shadow like Lauren had been cruel. But dupe or not, she'd chosen the wrong side of the barricades, and war is hell.

DISAPPOINTED that the bank and grocery trip took so little time, Charlie turned Mrs. Granville's BMW Alpina into her driveway. Finest vehicle he'd ever seen, much less driven. Quitting his job at Dependable Car Service meant he wouldn't be driving those classy Town Cars anymore, but that wasn't going to bother him for another ninety days. Eighty-nine, come this evening. "Got company," he said to Mrs. Granville after spotting a silver coupe under the portico.

She sat taller in the passenger seat. "It begins."

Her getting ready like that meant only one thing. "Which one? Ward?"

She nodded. "Bad luck we were out. I read somewhere that animal trainers survive because they're already in the cage when the beasts are let in. Gives them an enormous advantage. Territorial dominance or some such. So," she said, scanning the house and grounds, "how do we turn him into a timid lion?"

The way she talked had a smart sound to it, but he missed half of it. If she'd just say what she meant, like GranDelia used to, things would have been more comfortable. "You mean get him out of the house?"

"Precisely."

He wheeled the BMW toward the garages on the side of the house. "Ma'am, your family's a pure puzzle to me. What'd be wrong with going into your own dang house and saying something like, 'I appreciate your concern, but I'm fine. How about a beer'?"

"How about a beer, indeed." A laugh puffed out of her nose, but without a smile. Drooping forward, eyes closed, she looked asleep. "Dear dear Charlie." Her tender tone surprised him. "Have you ever heard the expression, 'Once bitten, twice shy'?"

"Ma'am, if you're worried about me gettin' whipped again, he was just lucky."

She laughed again, more genuine this time. "You really are priceless." She rose straighter in the seat. "The children—and by children I mean Ward—have challenged me once before, and won. Two years ago I was invited off the board of The Vivien and Marshall Granville Foundation. Isn't that astounding? Lawyers can actually remove a person from their own organization."

"What'd you do? Steal a pen?"

"Nothing funny about this," she said after a good long glare. "I did nothing improper. Marshall and I created that Foundation. Twenty-five million expressly to support the arts, and my son, Luke, is an artist."

Luke's name had been dropped a few times last weekend. At least now he knew who that was. "If you don't mind me asking," he said, "why'd he miss the funeral?"

"Ah, a commitment he couldn't get out of, I'm afraid. Poor darling. A genius, my Luke. Award winning screenwriter." She wiggled a two-finger vee. "Golden Globes, if I'm not mistaken. Anyway, he was halfway through a documentary about … something or other, but couldn't scare up funding to complete it. Ward must have been unavailable, so I may have signed his name to a check. *Well*, when the auditors discovered it, I was treated like a criminal. Summarily cashiered for sending *my* money to an artist who by pure happenstance was my son. Oh," she said, tipping closer, "and the lawyers weren't satisfied just sacking me. I had to repay the five hundred thousand, plus, mind you, their exorbitant fees."

They'd arrived at the garages, and he reached for the button to raise the door.

"Not yet." She gripped the sleeve of his windbreaker.

He couldn't get his head around people living like this. Nutty old lady. Nice in a way, but hard. Money to burn. At war with even nuttier kids who were almost old themselves. Here she was, trying to trick one of them out of her palace so she could fire at him from the high ground. If he could have been anywhere else, he would, but this morning she transferred ten thousand into his new account. That made her the boss for the next ninety days, but a million more wouldn't get her a ninety-first.

Wrinkles on her forehead told him she was thinking hard about something.

"You figuring how to get Ward out of the house?" he said.

She nodded. "Any ideas?"

"Yup. Go in and tell him to leave. What's he gonna do?"

She tapped the heel of her hand against her forehead. "Charlie, was my Foundation story too subtle for you? He's in there with an ultimatum. I either consent to assisted living, or he'll unleash the lawyers."

"How do you know that for sure?"

She fell against the seat back and closed her eyes. "Then I'll need lawyers. Both sides will make me go through humiliating tests. I'm not sure how anyone proves they're not senile, but I'll have to." She fished through junk in her tote bag and hauled out a packet of tissues. "And my children … No matter where I land," she whispered, a clump of Kleenex blotting her eyes and nose, "I'll hate them."

"And you can't just say that? Sure as heck worked on me."

"They're not you, I'm afraid." Her small smile looked forced. "The Granville way includes some level of gamesmanship, always, and I've about lost all of my chips." She stared off into nothing until a bit energy came back to her face. Tote bag on her lap, shoulders back, she pointed toward the garage door. "Ah well, such is life. Once more into the breach."

He guessed that meant they were going into the house.

CHAPTER TWENTY-FIVE

CHARLIE HAD ALMOST forgotten how slow and careful Mrs. Granville stepped when she wasn't holding his elbow. Plastic bags hanging from every finger, he inched behind her down the hall from her garage. For the first time since they took the job, he realized that her being fragile like she was, bad things could happen on their watch. Marines had taught him some first-aid, but after that, 911 would be it. Worst would be if something happened that left her unconscious, and she couldn't tell her crazy family that he and Desiree weren't to blame. He'd keep his fingers and toes crossed. They only had to make it through eighty-nine more days, come bedtime tonight.

Before they got halfway to the kitchen, Ward Granville strutted into their line of sight. "Well, well," he said, hands held away from his sides like a ready gunfighter, "the spider and the fly."

She raised a palm to him. "Ward, if you're here to be unpleasant, leave now. Charlie," she said over a shoulder, "put the sacks on the island for the time being. I have to show Desiree where I like everything."

Ward's gaze stayed on Charlie. "Mother, why are they here?"

"Oh, you were all so concerned." She hauled her tote bag onto the island, "I wanted to put your minds at ease, so I've employed this wonderful couple to keep me and the house ship-shape."

"Did he tell you to change the locks?"

"Completely my idea. I read somewhere you should do that every so often. Keys floating about hither and thither. Who knows where they end up or if they've been copied?"

Charlie had no idea when she called them, but locksmiths were already working when he came downstairs in the morning. Switched over the whole shebang. Main building, pool and boat houses, garage door keypad. They even synced the door-lifter button in the BMW.

"I'll need one," Ward said, hand extended.

"Not anymore, dear. That would be like me having one to your house. Why?"

"You're not letting them do this." Ward tracked Charlie's progress to the island. "For all you know, they're just out of prison."

"Excellent point," she said. "Why don't you go check on that and get back to me? So, how about a beer?"

The smile she tossed Charlie made the chauffeur chuckle.

"Oh, so we're sharing jokes now?" Ward's eyes darted between his mother and Charlie, stopping on him. "You don't think I'm onto you?" he said. "You and your little wife?"

Desiree appeared at the foyer end of the long hallway. She leaned a shoulder against the wall and returned Charlie's nod.

Ward's eyes pulled hard to the side, like he'd heard something but didn't want to look.

Head shaking slowly, Mrs. Granville positioned herself between the men, her back to the foyer. "He's not up to anything, darling. In fact, he took quite a bit of convincing."

"Mother, unfortunately I know why you're blind to it, but trust me, he's been playing us from the beginning. You, me, Laurie."

"How on earth are you being 'played'? And Laurie? He protected Laurie, for heaven sake."

"How do you know?" Ward said, voice raised, eyes pulled to the side again. "All the times they were together, you think he was *protecting* her? Is that what they call it these days?"

"I believe him," his mother said, "and we're not discussing this. I've paid them for three months. That's it."

"Hold on." Ward stepped toward her. "In advance? David Miller allowed that?"

"David's my advisor, dear. I don't need his permission."

"So you *did* pay the whole thing?"

Doubt joined the stubbornness on her face. "That is our arrangement. Yes."

"How much?"

"That's none of your business."

Ward flashed her a big fake smile. "Well, at least I won't have to go to court to get *them* out. Soon as they have what they want, they'll sneak out of here while you're asleep. Or after they kill you."

"Hey!" Desiree ran toward the kitchen, one hand sliding along the wall. "You got no call." The effort, plus being angry, had her snorting by the time she reached everyone. "Charlie, stand up for heaven sake."

"Baby Girl, don't." He waved her to join him. Marines had taught him when to attack, and when to withdraw. He realized they'd been outmaneuvered. Crafty old woman had lined up a couple of human shields, and he knew first-hand from Afghanistan, not many ended up good.

Glaring at Ward as she passed, Desiree slipped under Charlie's waiting arm and wrapped her arms around his waist.

"It's been lovely to see you, darling," Mrs. Granville said to her son as she headed for the hall. "I'll walk you out. Come again when you've rediscovered your manners."

"You're forcing my hand, Mother," he said, checking over his shoulder as he followed her.

She spun toward him. "How? How do you even have a hand? Stop bullying me."

"I'm trying to protect you."

"You're the one I need protection from."

"It's not just me. We're all worried."

"Stop it," she shouted into Ward's face, tipping him backward. "*My* life." Both her hands slapped hard on her chest. "Mine." Trembling, she shuffled tiny steps to the wall and braced a hand against it.

Ward did nothing but watch her, so Charlie readied for

a catch. Turned out not to be necessary, but only after some worrisome seconds.

"Ward." She took a big breath and let her hand slide off the wall. "I don't want another Foundation war, but whatever time is left, I'm spending it as I see fit." She fanned a hand toward the kitchen. "I've hired these two capable people, as is my right. They will help me until no one can. When that day comes, you will be the second to know." She pointed to herself. "I shall be the first."

"Wasting my time," Ward said, stepping around her. He backpedalled toward the foyer, finger rocking between Charlie and Desiree. "Don't get comfortable."

As if there'd ever been a chance of that.

"SOUNDS LIKE you're calling from the car." Lauren said to Ward. "Out buying me a birthday present?"

"Heading back from Mother's, and sister dear, we have a problem. She's hired that limo driver, Charlie. Full time. His wife, too."

"Christ. As what?"

"Live-in help. She's the maid, and I'm not sure what he's doing. Pumicing her calluses for all I know. He got her to change the locks, though."

"Wow. Old bitch still has a few tricks left. How do you get her out now?"

Hearing Lauren say "you" added unwarranted weight to his mother's accusation that he alone had the agenda. "Not me, Laurie. *We* are hiring Gardner Culpepper again. He already has lots of ammunition from that Foundation fiasco with Luke. Getting her declared incompetent after this latest idiocy should be child's play."

"*Gawd*, lawyers. How are you going to get the Foundation to pay?"

"Uh-uh. This one's on us."

"No no," she said, laughing. "Not all of us make side fortunes from gingivitis, honey. I'll kick in for a hit man, but not a lawyer.

And I can't imagine the others will either, so if that's what you're thinking, better think again."

"Really. Then think about this. That guy and his missus may have just wedged themselves between us and the checkbook. If we don't all—and I mean all—do something, those two cons could get away with a lot more than Gardner Culpepper's fees."

"Well, how about this then? Give us all raises from the Foundation."

"Would, but can't. According to the auditors, we're max'ed, and I've been holding back some potential bad news. They also told me we may have to reimburse some of last year's Cannes expenses."

"For godsake, Ward, grow a pair. Our money bankrolled that film. We had every right to be there."

"As the bean counters delight in reminding me, it isn't our money. It's the Foundation's. And yes, they agree the trustees had the right to attend, but you stayed in Monaco."

"Forty-five minutes. Big fucking deal."

"Laurie, they showed me the limo bills. Nine thousand in seven days?"

"Was I supposed to hitch? And what about you and Philippa staying an extra week?"

"They challenged that, too. *And* Sophia's spa sessions. *And* Randy's air fare and meals."

"Omigod," she said. "Randy? Wouldn't that be the ultimate kick in the crack? Sophia got dermabrasion and new tits for that geek, and he flew home after what, two nights?"

"Not sure I'm supposed to share this, but do you know she had a chapel picked out?"

"Please. It's way worse. I got daily phone updates for weeks. Personal trainer. Lost twenty pounds. Randy's been so sweet. Still loves her. Had a few nooners. Blah blah, blah. And—God, she'd kill me for this—she even brought the nightgown from their wedding night."

"God almighty. Now there's a 'B' movie."

"I know, right? Like it was so lucky the first time. Poor Sophia. Crazy as the rest of us."

"Well, poor Sophia's going to be a little poorer unless I can talk the auditors out of a few things."

"Pencil dicks. What do they know about promoting the arts?"

"And we do?"

"It's in our DNA, brother dear. Granvilles have soul. At least some of us. Me, Luke, even Devon. He was very creative."

"Laurie, our entry at the Festival. What was the title?"

"Um, wait. I got this. *Martian … Daydreams.*"

Upset as he was, that made him laugh. "*Martial Delusions.* Nice try, though."

"Ward, I don't care if it was *The Agony of the Friggin' Christ, Part II.* I'm not paying. Not for Monaco and not Culpepper. When you figure it out, call me. And in case you forgot, my birthday is next Wednesday. Bye, sweetie."

"Laurie, wait." She'd nearly diverted him from the real reason he phoned.

"Forgot my sizes?"

"This Charlie thing with Mother, it has to end, and you may be able to help. His wife—Desiree, if you please—feels threatened by a 'sister'. She didn't mention you by name, but it's unlikely she meant Sophia. Without being indelicate, what happened between you and him?

"Forget it."

"His wife suspects. Can't be much of a secret."

"Then ask her."

"They're going to clean Mother out, Laurie. Maybe hurt her."

"Oh, please. I see what you're up to. That man didn't do anything, and you're not hurting him by whoring me out." She hung up.

None of them, not even Lauren, were going to leave everything to him and then set the rules. More specifics about what might have happened between her and Charlie would have made things easier, but he'd heard enough, and if necessary, he'd become a creative Granville, too.

CHAPTER TWENTY-SIX

CHARLIE COULDN'T REMEMBER seeing Desiree this happy. Shame it had to end. Sitting in the breakfast nook, he smiled back at her as she placed bowls of beef barley soup in front of him and Mrs. Granville.

"Desiree," Mrs. Granville said, spreading a napkin on her lap, "this soup smells divine. I've been manufacturing reasons all morning to putter in here."

"Wait for me now." Desiree hobbled to the counter for her bowl.

Only their third day and his wife had taken to life in the mansion like she came with the deed. Part of the happiness had to be the awesome new hairdo she got at Mrs. Granville's salon yesterday, but mostly, it was just being there.

He knew that for sure. With nothing much to do, he'd been dogging after her as she did chores. Every room, she'd find a reason to sit on all the seat cushions or the bed. Dust a table or shelf. Inspect a little statue or brightly colored bowl. Reposition a lamp, or book, or picture frame, always working her way to the windows. Reaching those was like a reward, like she'd earned a good long look at the beautiful view. After a spell, she'd take a big breath, run fingertips across the sill or the drapes, and move on. Never lost that tiny smile.

Nights suited her, too. Bedroom as big as their house. Long sessions in the attached bathroom, jet tub churning warm bubbles, almost drowning the sounds of her purrs and sighs. The terry robe she found on a hanger in the closet. Her own sink in the jumbo bathroom, fussing with her hair at her mirror. Humming, smiling.

Nightgown from the dresser, folded and laid at the end of the bed, for after.

Just couldn't bring himself to remind Cinderella they were in the countdown. Eighty-seven more days of smoking this crack. But happy wife, happy life, and he hadn't enjoyed a stretch of nights like the last three since their honeymoon. "Ma'am," he said, stirring his steamy lunch and struggling for words that wouldn't light up Desiree's radar, "could we go over again what I'm supposed to be doing for my wages?"

"I told you, dear boy, driving, plus a pinch of this, a dash of that." She reached for another napkin from the holder in the middle of the table. "I adore soup, but it makes my nose run. Aren't I simply a joy?" She patted her nose and laughed.

Desiree smiled at both of them, bent down to a spoonful, and blew on it.

"I know what you told me, ma'am," he said, "but I've been out of both 'this' and 'that' since we got the master and our room set up first night."

"About that," Mrs. Granville said. "I've been hesitant to ask." She leaned close enough to lay a hand on Desiree's. "Vicious liars have accused me of snoring. Does being next door bother you?"

"Not a lick," she said. "Hope we're as quiet."

"I hear a little." Mrs. Granville winked at her. "But nothing unpleasant."

His face warmed. Their bed stood against the wall of Mrs. Granville's closet. Last three nights, some fine fun had thunked the headboard against the wall a time or two. On top of that, when Desiree was in the mood, and they got the rhythm right, that little woman could throw off some sounds. Tonight, if his luck held, they'd face the dresser.

"Blushing," Mrs. Granville said, smiling and leaning to a spoonful of broth. "Charlie, you are beyond precious."

"About my chores, ma'am," he said. "Since there doesn't seem to be much, I was wondering if it'd be okay to put my name back in at Dependable Car Service?"

"Charlie, no." Desiree's face looked like he'd just volunteered to be a lab animal.

"She's right," Mrs. Granville said. "You're bought and paid for, dear boy. Lay back and enjoy."

His guts clenched. "Is that a fact? Well, eighty-seven days from now, you're gonna need yourself a couple new whores."

Mrs. Granville flinched. Desiree's spoon splashed into her bowl.

...think first, speak second... Surprised him how often he heard GranDelia's advice after it was too late.

"Ma'am," Desiree said, eyes pleading, "we ain't—I mean, we *aren't* outta here at the end of our pay, are we?"

"Of course you're not, and as for you, Charlie Woods," she said, frowning and wagging a finger at him, "whether it's one day or a thousand, mind how you speak to me." Her expression relaxed. "And stop being such a tot. We're in a lull. That's all. Bulb flowers are up. Azaleas in a week or so. There'll be oodles on your plate after that."

"Such as?" Arms folded, he fell back in his chair.

"Stop sulking." Vivien imitated his pose until he sat forward and laid his arms on the table. "That's better. So, you want to know 'such as.'" Her fingers drummed on the table. "Well, there's opening the pool, for one. Then the pool house and boat house have to be made ready for company. After that you'll have to service the boat and jet skis."

Last part wasn't something he knew how to do, but learning might be good for getting a job afterward.

"Who's the 'company'?" Desiree said. "Oh, right, the son from out west."

Mrs. Granville's face crinkled. "Is Luke coming?"

Desiree shrugged. "Not sure you ever mentioned his name. He the one with the kids?"

"Oh, *Archer.* Yes yes yes," Mrs. Granville said, spanking her forehead. "Precisely. And assuming you continue being competent, as I'm sure you will," she said, big eyes locked on Charlie, "the timing will be perfect. End of school year and all that. I'll need you both more than ever."

He couldn't see any reason to jump into this nonsense. Eighty-seven days from now, he and Desiree were in the truck and back to Greensboro. Soup had cooled enough to eat without blistering the roof of his mouth, so he decided to eat rather than fire up an argument. They'd have that in private soon enough.

"Ma'am," Desiree said, eyes on her lunch, "if this son comes, will other family, y'know, be around a lot?"

"Based on the certified letter I received yesterday, I doubt we'll see much of Ward, but the others perhaps. I shouldn't worry about them creating a lot of extra work if that's your concern."

"Hardly got enough now. More interested if you got anyone else in the clan like Dr. Granville. Someone, and I mean no disrespect, we gotta be careful of." She shot Charlie a quick glance.

Mrs. Granville patted her lips and nose with the napkin. "Ah, the combatants. Reasonable question, I suppose." Head tipped back, she squinted one eye. "I would say the only other candidate at the moment is Lauren. We had a bizarre disagreement after Devon's funeral. She became furious with me. Came after me physically, if you can believe it. And I still have no idea why." She bobbed her chin at him. "Charlie, my champion, you rescued me yet again. But wasn't that astonishing? Out of the blue like that?"

He knew Lauren got mad because she thought her mother could have stopped Devon's suicide but didn't—something he was almost sure wasn't true—but no one at this table needed to know that. "Sad day. Too much to drink." He shrugged. "Stuff happens."

"You there for the drinking part, sugar?"

"Oh, the poor man," Mrs. Granville said. "Dinner disintegrated so quickly I doubt he had a single sip of his beer." Head shaking, she fell against the cushioned seat back. "Laurie and turmoil. Hand and glove, I'm afraid. But, we've had a complicated relationship since puberty. For all I know, she'll breeze in this evening at cocktails and act as if nothing happened."

"I see her picture every time I go up and down the front staircase." Desiree's eyes followed her spoon as it plowed along the bottom of her bowl. "Right pretty woman. So pretty Charlie's been afraid to mention it." Smiling at him, she slipped a full spoonful into her mouth.

"C'mon, Baby Girl. Woman had her boyfriend there. Pretty's got nothing to do with nothing." That was close enough to a lie that his faced warmed.

"And a rather disreputable beau at that, as I understand it. Your husband merely intervened."

"Mrs. Granville, excuse me," he said, "but can you spare me for a couple hours? I'd like to take care of a few things at my home. Cut the grass, check the mail, stuff like that." First time he realized a hideout existed only a few minutes away. Felt like high-fiving himself.

"Running from something, honey?" Eyebrows raised and still smiling, Desiree shoved in another mouthful of soup.

"You're free as a bird, dear boy. I suspect there's a lovely nap in my future after this feast. I can't tell you how wonderful it is to be back upstairs in my room. Naps and baths on my whim. Nirvana."

He rolled his chair away from the table.

"Take Luke's car," Mrs. Granville said. "Desiree can lay me in the back of your pickup if an emergency strikes."

Desiree lifted her eyes to his for only a second. "That anything like laying someone in the back of a limo, sugar?"

Looking confused for a second, Mrs. Granville chirped a laugh into her napkin.

Mighty clever of Desiree, sniping from behind Mrs. Granville. She'd dropped into a mood over Lauren, and was picking at him with a smile. That way, if he got mad, he'd be in the wrong. A little time apart right now suited him just fine. He shook his head and stood.

"Oh, c'mon," Desiree said. "Just funnin'."

"Call if you need something," he said on his trudge to the garage.

The next eighty-seven days stretched in front of him like a mined road. Lauren's name would come up, and he'd blush, or be afraid Mrs. Granville would slip about the night Lauren spent in his room. If that happened, Desiree would refuse to believe his side. She'd explode like a normal wife. Their lives would change, and for next to nothing. No more than a kiss or two. And some tongue. And his hands pressed onto that woman's fine backside. Her hands jammed into his back pockets. Both of them tugging, grinding the pieces together. But he stopped in time. Nothing to be guilty about.

Even right then, backing that awesome BMW into the cool sunshine, Lauren occupied too much of his mind. All women did. Spent so much time around skirts lately, next pair of panties he got into might be his own. Needed to be around a little spitting and scratching. Still in the driveway, he threw the lever to Park and fished out his phone. Felt wrong loading his info into someone else's hands-free, but that'd be better than getting distracted and smashing up a ba-jillion dollar vehicle.

After a bunch of minutes of Owner's Manual frustration, hollering "Call Spuv" at the female inside the dashboard finally worked.

"Charlie dense Woods, been thinking about you, old son. Where the hell are you?"

"Gonna be at my house in a few minutes, Spuv. Drag your fat butt over. Gotta show you the awesome Beemer I'm driving."

"Bull crap."

"You show up, then say that."

"Dude, I'm at work, but no lie? You really stole—I mean bought—a Beemer?"

"Long story. Tell you the whole thing when I see you. Got a naked woman in it and everything."

"The car?"

"The story, butthead." Seemed like Mrs. Granville's daily routine included a long nap after lunch, so he should be free any afternoon. "How about you come over Saturday, about one o'clock. Spuv, I promise you, you gotta see this thing."

"The naked woman?"

"And I'm the stupid one. Later."

Arriving at his house, he stopped at the mailbox. No check. Disappointed and a little angry, he slowed the BMW to a stop halfway up the driveway. Couldn't decide whether to pull into the carport or leave it in the open. Roof on the carport needed some attention, and he imagined it giving way soon as he pulled underneath and turned off the engine. But if he left it in the driveway, the mower might kick up a stone. Should have taken the pickup. Even the good had turned bad.

...never own something you're afraid to lose...

"I don't own it," he said to GranDelia. And he didn't really want to own it. That Beemer was a danger he wasn't trained to handle.

Still might not be too late to get away, he thought. Deal's a deal, but maybe Mrs. Granville would agree to a new one. So far, they'd only dipped into the advance to pay the taxes. Maybe she'd let them give back the rest and cut their time by a month. His two thousand from Dependable Car Service would hold them for awhile. Soon as that lifeline showed up, he'd talk to her. Should have been there by now. If it wasn't there Saturday when he came over to meet Spuv, he might have to do something.

CHAPTER TWENTY-SEVEN

VIVIEN HAD SUFFICIENT experience with domestic help to know that private matters in the house were anything but. Yesterday morning's FedEx envelope from Ward's attorney, while not a huge surprise, must have been upsetting enough that she let it show. Wherever she settled after reading it and phoning the family's attorney, scant minutes passed before Desiree found a chore needing attention in that exact zone, or had a question about this or that, always followed by, "Ma'am, y'okay?" or "Ma'am, can I get you something?"

She thought the attorney had mollified her concerns, but this morning's flurry of phone calls with him resuscitated it. Desiree managed to hover within earshot of each conversation. Humming, dusting, fluffing pillows, anything but vacuuming. On the rare moments Charlie tore himself away from Luke's BMW and appeared in the house, he and Desiree shared whispers in passing.

The doorbell rang precisely at ten.

Desiree hobbled to a front-facing window in the dining room. "They're here," she said, loud enough to be heard in the farthest bedroom.

"And who would '*they*' be, dear?" she said, standing only feet behind Desiree.

Desiree twitched, but didn't turn. "Uh, guess I should find out." Still faced away, she hurried to the front door. "Ma'am, you in or out?"

"Desiree," she said, unwilling to continue the charade, "you know very well I'm expecting my attorneys. Now, wait for me to leave before letting them in, then offer coffee and bring them to the office. It's the mahogany—"

"Ma'am, I wasn't listening."

"The mahogany door," she said, hand raised, "next to the fireplace in the great room. I'll join them shortly." Small steps brought her toward the elevator near the kitchen.

Guests, rare as Yeti sightings these days, deserved a freshened hostess. During the ride upstairs she pictured the unpleasant regimen awaiting her in the bathroom. Of all the ghastly aspects in the life Ward intended for her, shift-work strangers assisting in her personal hygiene topped the list. Hiring Charlie and Desiree held the potential of postponing that curse indefinitely, particularly if Desiree could be eased into the most delicate tasks. She chided herself for accusing the woman of eavesdropping just now. Not the brightest bond-building tactic, but fixable.

WITH HER BUSINESS concluded, Vivien opened the office door to find Desiree polishing a conveniently located burlwood table. Poor thing should have known how distinctive her gait sounded when she tried to run.

"Thank you for coming, Bartram, and all of you." She shook hands with each of the three lawyers as they left. "Desiree, dear, please show these people out, then join me in the kitchen. There's a good girl."

"Sad business, Vivien." Bartram bent to kiss her cheek. "Especially on the heels of Devon. I doubt we'll have trouble squashing this, but still … sad." Briefcase in one hand, he patted her shoulder. "Hold a good thought. As I said, we'll contact Ward's attorney to let them know they're to deal with us going forward. In the meantime, avoid all contact. Calls, visits, even emails or texts. And if any mail or packages do come, let me know. We'll handle everything."

"You're a good friend, Bartram." She hooked onto his arm for the trek across the great room. "Marshall would be comforted knowing you're still manning the castle walls." Caution rose as she approached the meager three-stair climb to the foyer. Recurrent whispers questioned the wisdom of resisting Ward. The cost in dollars and scars, to gain nothing more than a deferment. But the battle had been joined, and if nothing else, Granvilles fight. "Thank you, again," she said, diverting toward the kitchen as Desiree led the lawyers to the front door.

Seated at the breakfast table, she waited for Desiree's clip-clop to reach the center island. "We need to talk, dear." She patted the cushion of the chair next to her.

Desiree froze mid-stride. "Please. I swear I wasn't listening."

"It's alright. Come and sit."

"Ma'am, voices …" Eyes large and fearful, Desiree lowered onto her assigned chair. "Sounds just carry sometimes. Y'know, big empty hallways and—"

"Stop." She smiled. "I don't care that you were listening. In your position, I'd do the same. If I'm kicked out, you're out. I get it, and I'm not angry. Understood?"

"Yes, ma'am." Desiree began to stand.

"Sit, child. That's not what I wanted to discuss with you." She waited for Desiree to settle in again. "I'll be blunt. You and Charlie are my last throw of the dice, and our relationship hasn't the luxury of time. I need to trust you. Today. This minute. Eavesdropping, for example. I don't object to you listening. I mind you denying it. There can be no more of that. Do we understand each other?"

Nodding slowly, Desiree studied her. She repositioned her hips and shoulders back in the chair. "This go both ways? This trust thing?"

"Naturally." She found Desiree's steady dark eyes unnerving.

"So, if I asked you if my Charlie, y'know, *misbehaved* in Florida, you'd tell me the truth?"

"I would, and he didn't." She hoped Desiree hadn't detected the atom of suspicion she still harbored about Charlie's night with Lauren.

"Okay." Desiree's slow nodding and inscrutable stare continued. "Okay. Good talk, ma'am. Thank you. And we're going to help you win this thing. I promise you. Don't want to leave here. Not ever."

"Excellent. Then I suggest you get cracking on Charlie. He seems to be of a different mind."

Grinning, Desiree tapped the edge of her new, blond-streaked wedge cut. "Oh, I got me a plan going already." She giggled into her hand. "Wall's gonna tell you how good it's working."

"Speaking of work, dear, I'm afraid we left the office in need of some attention. Thank you." Both offered smiles in parting. Hers lingered as she watched Desiree hobble from the room. Once a pawn, now an ally, and committed to recruiting Charlie. Momentum in her favor, and the house hadn't been this tidy in years.

CHAPTER TWENTY-EIGHT

AT HIS OWN HOUSE for the first time in days, Charlie turned the front door key and bumped it open with his shoulder. Stink knocked him backward. From the landing he could see into the kitchen. Flies were zooming everywhere, but mostly around an open garbage bag under the sink. Desiree told him the last thing she'd done before locking up was turn the thermostat to fifty. Should have been the second to last thing.

Gagging into his hand, he rushed inside to the sink. So many flies, their buzzing made a steady hum. Darting around the walls, ceilings, and counters, dive-bombing his eyes and ears. He needed both hands to unstick the window over the sink, so his nostrils became two new targets. Holding his breath, he dashed for the front door, arms whirling around his head. On the landing he paused only long enough to reach back inside and click on the paddle fan.

He prized himself on being a man slow to anger, but his teeth clenched at the possibility she left the garbage on purpose. Looking back at the house from his scraggy lawn, he called up what he'd seen between swatting flies and getting the heck out. Dirty dishes in the sink. On the kitchen table, beer bottles and a plateful of stubbed cigarettes. Desiree said she'd spent three hours packing that night, but at least part of the time went for something else.

The phone in his pocket jangled. Display showed 12:48, and it was Spuv on the line. "Hey big man. I'm already here, but if you're comin' now—"

"Dude, don't get pissed."

"Lemme guess. You're not coming." That'd be no surprise, the way this day was going.

"Not my fault. Here's what happened. I'm in my car, all set to back out, and Candy pulls in behind me."

"Thought you two were done."

"Surprised hell outta me, I promise you. So, I jump out y'know, all primed for a brawl, but she's all smiley and pretty. And Charlie, she is dressed *hot*. Anyway, next I know, she reaches through her car window and pulls out a goddam steamer pack of Krystals sliders. I mean, c'mon, man. Krystals? Pussy? Krystals?"

His bad day just dropped another rung. No paycheck in the mailbox from Dependable, a polluted house, and now he was gonna miss the knucklehead afternoon he'd been waiting two days to enjoy. "What about tomorrow?"

"Oh, abso-damn-lutely, son. One o'clock, Candy or not. Gotta see that Beemer. Hear your story about the naked chick. Hang on a sec. Candy's at the window. What the hell is she—Whoa, *nasty*," he said laughing. "Tomorrow." The call ended.

Dragging his legs up the slope to the house, he realized his mending nose ached. Must've nicked it on one of his fly swats. He pinched it and inspected his fingers. No blood. Least that was good. And maybe a little swelling would block some stink.

Back inside, it looked like a good bunch of flies had taken the hint. He'd deal with the stubborn ones after closing down their chow line. He twisted the garbage bag shut and hugged it to his middle for the short sprint to the trash can beside the carport. The whole way there he had to snort and puff flies away from his face. Felt as dirty as a third day on desert patrol.

Instead of going straight back inside, he dropped his butt onto the front steps. Hands shoved into his jacket pockets, he shrunk deeper into the collar. Sitting a spell would give the flies more time to realize their restaurant had closed, and the stiff March breeze was clearing out some stench.

Daylight had moved enough to draw a shadow over the stairs, adding to the chill and matching his mood. His Georgia life hadn't changed fast like this since GranDelia died. Today even had the same feel as the day he buried her. Things going on, and then they weren't. Church service, burial, folks back to the house. Ladies from the congregation filling the place with food and tenderness. Hugs and handshakes all done by the end of lunchtime. Spuv and a few friends wanted to hang, but he sent them home. Eighteen, and not a blood relative left on this earth. He just wanted to cry it out one last time in private. Did it on these very steps. Turkey leg in one hand, dish towel in the other.

Duty called. He pushed to his feet and braved the indoors. Bad, but not as bad as it had been. Swinging a plastic placemat, he spooked flies into the air and herded them to the window or door. Got rid of a boatload, and with nothing left on the menu, the ones he missed would most likely be legs-up and ready for the vacuum tomorrow.

Still inside, he closed the house up, cranked the heat to sixty, and warmed his hands in front of a rusty register. First time he remembered seeing the rust. He'd have to paint or replace it. Maybe others too, but he didn't bother scouting because none of that would happen until Dependable came across with his pay. Should have been there two days ago.

...best way to get something done is do it...

"You're right," he said to the ceiling, "like always." He dug out his phone. Pacing and swatting at stragglers, he listened until voicemail at Dependable asked him to leave a message. "Afternoon, Mr. Carter. Charlie Woods here. Just calling to let you know I haven't got my check yet. Tell you what, it's Saturday now. I'm gonna see if it shows up Monday, but if it doesn't, I'd like to swing by the office and pick up a replacement. Call me if that's not okay. Thanks."

Taking action improved his attitude. He decided to spend the rest of his time straightening the place. A new trash bag got the beer bottle and cigarette butts. He washed and dried the few dishes. Vacuuming tomorrow would get the dust balls and, hopefully, a bumper crop of dead flies. That only left the bedroom.

Bad as she'd left the kitchen, the bedroom had been picked clean. Looking as different as it did, the thought crossed his mind that someone could have broken in and taken stuff. He headed straight for the headboard on Desiree's side of the bed and slid a hand under the mattress. His fingers bumped the handle of her pistol. "Ah, home is where the gun is," he said, smiling.

As he backed out of the driveway, he felt a little sheepish about being so quick to blame Desiree for the garbage. Anyone can make a mistake. And all her talk about staying at Mrs. Granville's. They'd get past that. Down deep she knew this was home, and eighty-five days from now, they'd be back here, kick-starting their happy life, right on top of that peacemaker.

CHAPTER TWENTY-NINE

SPUV WASN'T DUE until 1:00, but Charlie got to his house on Sunday at 12:30. He popped a Dr. Pepper and waited by the front window.

Around 1:10, Spuv called to say he'd be over soon as he could. Didn't take a genius to figure out Candy hadn't left yet. The call at 1:45 had Spuv just out of the shower. Wasn't until 2:20 that his black Corvette rolled up the driveway. It grumbled to a stop a few feet short of Mrs. Granville's BMW.

Spying from the edge of the front window, Charlie watched as Spuv tried the Beemer's locked driver door, then peer inside through cupped hands. Big as Spuv was, he reminded Charlie of a grizzly at a national park, terrorizing trapped tourists. Except grizzlies didn't shave their heads or have Van Dyck beards, and they sure as hell wouldn't be out in the cold wearing t-shirts, plaid shorts, and flip-flops.

"Walk away from the vehicle, sir," Charlie said after stepping onto the front landing. "Hands where I can see 'em."

"Dude, where the damn hell you get this?" Grinning, Spuv trotted toward the steps, hand open. "Keys." He stopped dead, jaw hanging. "Nice face, son. Who give you that?"

"Little puke of a dentist actually. Tell you about it inside."

"Bullshit. I want to drive this thing." Spuv bounced the open hand. "What's a mouth-breather like you doing with this space shuttle."

"Aren't you cold? Bring it in here. Give you all the details over a beer." He went back inside and waited. "Smell anything?" he said as Spuv passed him and headed for the fridge.

"Why? You do something?" Spuv bent low to look inside the under-counter refrigerator. He checked the label and shut the door. "I can't drink that piss. Y'all really this poor?"

"Serious. What's it smell like in here?"

"I dunno. Old trailer, I guess. Why?"

"Not garbage?"

"Hey, Martha Stewart, shut up about the damn smell. For all I know it's still in my beard." Spuv grinned and sat back against the sink counter. "On that subject, let's hear about the naked woman in the Beemer."

"Wasn't in the car. My hotel room, actually."

"Holy shit." Spuv grabbed his gut and busted out laughing. "Extracurricular ass? You? Never thought I'd—"

"No. You know better."

"So, what then? Blowjob? Blowjob's not cheating. Everyone knows that."

"Nothing. No sex. Long story short, my passenger was an old lady. Her daughter was afraid of her boyfriend and hid in my room. She slept naked, and I saw her when she got up in the morning. That's it." Telling the story that way made him feel more innocent.

"Leave it to you to waste a perfectly good woman. At least tell me she was fat and ugly."

"Just the opposite." Sharing details with Spuv about Lauren Granville's shape and tattoos was a mistake. The more he spilled, the more Spuv pressed, and Charlie needed her less on his mind, not more. Only way he could think of to change the subject was toss Spuv the BMW fob. "You need some air."

Spuv zapped the fob like a frog and a bug. "Let's do this thing."

"VFW," Charlie said. "And I'm going straight back to Reynolds after we're done, so I'll drive your Vette."

"Got me a better idea. We're going to *Who Cares* over in Eatonton."

Charlie had kept a hundred cash when he deposited Mrs. Granvilles' advance—fifty each for him and Desiree. Spending his anywhere but the bargain-priced VFW didn't set right. "Kinda light on funds, and we don't even know anyone over there."

"Won't need money."

"Take me now, Lord," Charlie said, eyes raised to heaven. "*You're* buying?"

"Got my ways, son. Let's roll."

ENJOYING A DROWSY afternoon in the solarium, Vivien heard the phone ring several times before Desiree answered, far enough away that her part of the conversation drifted in as gobbledygook. She readied for an imminent intrusion, but seconds stretched enough that she nestled deeper into the lounge chair, closed her eyes, and surrendered anew to the serenity and cozy warmth.

Phone-ringing repeated twice more, the second one dead on the heels of the first.

"Desiree," she called out, flipping back the afghan and laboring to sit on the edge of the lounger, "what on earth is going on?"

"Won't happen again, ma'am." Desiree hobbled into the room and stood in front of her. "Can I get you anything?"

"Most annoying. Who was that?"

Wrinkling her nose, Desiree waved a hand like shooing a pest. She pointed at a wrought iron bistro table along the glass wall. "Y'know, it's just coming onto four, and right there's so pretty, how about I set you up with a nice cup of tea? Right there."

Spring sunshine sparkled on the lake and electrified the tips of her budding trees and shrubs. Reds and yellows, blues and greens. Warm and cool at the same time. Desiree appeared to have the artistic eye Vivien admired in her favorite children. "What a splendid idea. I would like that. Thank you." She reached for the hand being offered. "Who was on the phone?"

"Y'know, might be a touch chilly by that glass. We'll just bring this blanket for your shoulders." Afghan over her forearm, Desiree took Vivien by the hand. "Ma'am, if you have a better view than this one, I sure ain't—Oops, I sure *haven't* seen it."

"Bravo." Desiree's good natured acceptance of correction, coupled with her industry and energy, made the blind luck of finding her all the more delicious. "We'll work on 'y'all' next."

"Y'all are gonna have a time with that one," Desiree said with a wink and smile. "All set?" She held tight to the hand until Vivien sat and relaxed her grip. "Ma'am, I noticed a tin of English cookies in the pantry. How about I add a couple of those?"

"Oh, get thee behind me, Satan." Smiling, Vivien leaned closer. "Or," she held up one finger, "you could bring two cups and four cookies, and we'll let the doctor figure out who had what?"

"Well, you are just the dickens. Ma'am, that is so nice. I believe I will. Back in a jiffy."

WARD LET HIS WIFE answer the incoming call. His one sports passion was the NCAA men's basketball tournament, and Philippa knew better than to interrupt.

Hand covering the mouthpiece, she appeared in the doorway of his den. "It's Lauren."

"I'll call her back."

She inched closer to the recliner. "I think something's wrong."

Lauren, his former ally. By refusing to support the competency action, or provide ammunition about what happened between her and Charlie, she'd signed on with the rest of the apathetic siblings. If this call was anything but a change of heart, it would be a short one. He lowered the TV volume, took the phone from Philippa, and pointed her out of the room. "Yes, sister dear," he said, spellbound by a slo-mo replay of a monster dunk.

"Did you start Mother's competency thing?"

"What's wrong with your voice? Sounds like you're eating peanut butter. And yes, I started it Thursday. Why?"

"Thought so. She won't take my calls. Is Bartram Winfield representing her?"

"Who else?" The topic of this conversation put him on guard.

As a disinterested sister, Lauren held no peril. As an opponent, she could cause real trouble. "Why are you trying to reach her?"

"I thought she'd like to know I'm in Piedmont Hospital."

He kicked the recliner upright. "What happened? Are you alright?"

"I'll live."

"But what happened?"

"Broken jaw. A parting gift from Justin last Friday night."

He choked back a told-you-so. "For godsake, why?"

"My guess is he was miffed I marooned him in Key West."

"Laurie, tell me you're okay."

"Peachy."

"I'm coming over. You said Piedmont?"

"Don't bother, unless you want to watch me sleep. Ward, I may get beaten up every week. The friggin' drugs are *awesome*."

"Where'd this happen?"

"My apartment. Around eight someone knocked on the door. Security desk never called, so I figured it was someone from the building. I looked through the peephole, and there he was."

"He doesn't have a key?"

"Haven't made *that* mistake in years, m'dear. Anyway, I saw him grinning and wiggling his fingers. Kinda silly and fun, y'know? Fooled me, that's for sure. I remember opening the door, then waking up in a pond of blood. Everything hurt so much, and all the blood, I thought," her voice shook. "Ward, I thought he shot me. Right in the face."

"So what was it? A punch?"

"I guess. Fractured jaw, top and bottom on my left side."

"God." Her beautiful face, the free pass for her entire life. When those "awesome" drugs wore off, she was going to be one unhappy woman. "Did they operate?"

"Two hours, sweetie. Pins, wires, fifty-one stitches, temporary bridge."

"Is he under arrest?"

"Still looking for him, far as I know."

"Don't leave me helpless, Laurie. What can I do?"

"You've already done it. Mother's new maid, Desiree. Name's a hoot, right? Anyway, that backwater bitch is screening Mother's calls. Now that I know Bartram Winfield's involved, that's how I'll slip past her. And Ward, a favor. Don't call anyone else. If you have to tell Philippa, I tripped in the dark and went face-first into a doorjamb. Okay?"

"When do they say you'll be discharged?"

"Could be tomorrow, which is why I want to speak to Mother. Going to have to swallow a super-sized portion of crow—puréed of course—but I want to hide at her place until my Frankenstein phase is over. I'll also feel better once they catch Justin, and I know he's afraid of Charlie."

"Not a bad idea. Security is pretty good." An upside dawned on him. "Laurie, you know that I'm sorry this happened, but it could be a blessing. You'll be on the inside. You can feed me anything that might help the case."

"Wow. Ward, and I say this out of love, sometimes you're a total dick." She hung up.

A dick. Besides him, no one had any interest in saving their mother, from herself or Mr. and Mrs. Con Artist, but he was the dick. Because it suited her, Lauren would feign remorse, raise false joy in a woman regressing to childhood, but he was the dick. The others set their hollow fangs into Mother years ago, content to gorge and leave him blameworthy and unthanked, but he was the dick.

So be it. Even without supplying actionable intelligence, Lauren would help by merely strutting her irrepressible allure in front of Charlie, juxtaposing her perfection against Desiree's scratches and dents. Doses of this, day upon day, would foment unrest. And if Desiree happened to answer the phone when he called, and he managed to lob in a few flaming bottles of innuendo, that might be just the thing to blow a hole in the earthworks.

"HOPE CHARLIE EATS something with Spuv," Desiree said as she arranged tea dishes on the tray. "Not hungry after those cookies." She sat back, blew out her cheeks, and patted her tummy.

"Spuv," Vivien said. "He's actually gone through life as Spuv?"

"Ma'am, you do know that's a nickname."

"I rather thought so, dear. Short for something, I suppose."

"Spenser Upton Vaughn." Desiree's finger bounced in the air at the start of each word. "Spuv," she said, big smile on her face, arms spread.

One of the more pleasant afternoons in Vivien's recent memory. As with Charlie, Desiree's homespun simplicity disarmed and warmed her. The Spuv explanation reminded her of a little girl showing a parent she now understood something which heretofore had eluded her. The future, with its promise of more moments like these, brought an unexpected glisten to her eyes.

Desiree stood and took a test step to make sure the dishes were steady on the tray. "Get you anything else, ma'am?"

Shaking her head, she puffed her cheeks as Desiree had done, eliciting a burst of giggles from both.

The phone rang.

"Be right back," Desiree said, hurrying toward the kitchen. She returned with the handset pressed to her ribs. "Someone from the lawyer's office," she whispered. "I'll just ..." She wagged a finger toward the kitchen.

Vivien pointed at Desiree's chair and smiled. "You'll be listening anyway." She raised the phone to her ear as Desiree sat. "This is Mrs. Granville."

"Mother, finally."

"Laurie?"

Eyes wide, Desiree snapped tall in the chair.

"Quite a goalie you've got there, Mother. Hung up on me three times. I had to disguise my voice and say I was one of Bartram Winfield's lawyers."

Vivien covered the mouthpiece. "You hung up on my daughter?"

"Ma'am, I can explain."

"Don't you go anywhere." Glowering at Desiree, she returned to the call. "We're still ironing out the protocols, darling, but frankly, I might have done the same. Your disgraceful behavior after the funeral. I'm surprised you're calling. Why are you?"

"To apologize. Sometimes bad things have to happen to people to remind them who's important. These last two days in the hospital have taught me a lot."

"Well, I should think—Hospital?"

"Afraid so. Broke my jaw Friday night during a midnight stroll to the bathroom. I rolled a foot on a misplaced shoe and dove face-first into the doorjamb. Ambulance, surgery, the works."

"My word." If Lauren acquired the slightest disfigurement, her future and the future of any unfortunates who shared it would be unbearable. "What sort of surgery, darling?"

"Quite a lot. Wired jaw, temporary bridge for a few teeth, stitches in my cheek. Plastic surgery later, possibly. They won't know until the stitches are out and the swelling goes down. Looks pretty gruesome, though."

"Which hospital, darling? I'll have Charlie bring me this minute."

"Actually, I'd rather you didn't. Sleep's the best thing for me. Pretty sure I'm getting discharged tomorrow, but I'm not focusing very well yet."

"Then you're not ready. Tell them to keep you."

"I wish. Apparently, anyone who can eat, pee, and poop gets the heave-ho."

"But how will you manage?"

"Haven't quite figured that out. Eating will certainly be tough, but I'm more nervous about getting around. I have the concussion, and the pain meds make me dopier than usual." Her little laugh sounded feeble. "Can you spare that snippy maid for a week or two?"

Lips pressed flat, Desiree shook her head.

"Well, no," Vivien said, "but hiring someone is a wonderful idea. A nurse or something."

"Mother, that's sort of why I called. Not for a nurse, but for a place to be around people until I'm not so shaky."

"You mean stay here?"

Desiree's change of expression, both stony and seething, registered her opinion.

"Well, yes," Lauren said. "I wouldn't blame you if you said no."

"How could a mother say no?" Not that she didn't want to. "So it's settled. Tomorrow, the next day, whenever. Charlie will come for you."

"I know I don't deserve this, Mother. Thank you."

"Get your rest, darling. And call whenever you like. I'll see that Desiree moves you to the 'approved' list. Sweet dreams." She hung up and handed the phone to Desiree. "You said you can explain, dear." Hands folded on her lap, she sat back. "Begin."

"Ma'am," Desiree said, chin held high, "lawyers said if anyone from their side contacted you, turn it over to them, and that's what I told her. Twice. Hung up on her the last time because nobody calls me a stupid cunt."

"Desiree! *Gawd*. You needn't have repeated it."

"Not how I talk either, ma'am. I apologize, but, y'know." She shrugged and held eye contact.

Lauren and Desiree would be challenging housemates. More than most, her daughter craved attention. When beauty failed, she created chaos. Unknown days of compromised attractiveness would certainly stoke Lauren's boiler past the red line, but she was in need, and maternal duties trumped the delightful cocoon Desiree had spun this past week. She accepted Desiree's apology with a nod. "Continuing our promise of being direct, dear, I detect you would prefer that Laurie not come. Is this correct?"

"Your house. Your rules."

"That answers my question, but may I ask why?"

"Don't matter why. Daughters outrank maids. I'll do whatever you say. Not getting myself kicked out over her."

"That's the spirit. We'll soldier on, you and I. Two shakes of the lamb's tail and she'll be back in Atlanta, doing whatever it is she does. And then it's back to normal for us." Defeat in Desiree's expression showed she wasn't reassured. "Desiree," she said, extending her open hands, "you're safe, dear."

Desiree accepted the hands, but dropped her gaze. "If you say so, ma'am."

She bounced their joined hands and offered her gentlest smile. "You know, I think we're beyond 'ma'am'. I'd be very pleased if you called me Miss Vivien." Desiree's beaming face told her she'd saved the moment. More challenges to come no doubt, and one battle seldom won the war, but a victory was a victory.

CHAPTER THIRTY

SOON AS THE BARMAID at *Who Cares* saw Spuv and Charlie come through the door, her smile turned real. "Take that one, baby," she said to Spuv, pointing to a high-top near the bar. "The usual?"

Spuv nodded, held up two fingers, and leaned toward Charlie. "I'm tapping that."

Should have known Spuv wanted *Who Cares* instead of the VFW because of a woman. A girl, really. Pretty as a new penny, and shaped like a Victoria's Secret model, but way too young. "You trolling school bus stops now?" Charlie said without smiling. He grabbed a stool with a view to the basketball game on TV.

"Twenty-two, dude. Street legal and cra-zy for my unit." Spuv's eyes stayed on her as he climbed onto a stool. "Name's Lexie. I told you about her. Drove the drink cart at Cuscowilla last summer. Slipped me a napkin with her number on it. Remember now?"

Charlie had stopped listening years ago. Partly because the list got so long, but mostly to avoid hearing details. Spuv shared every one, and Charlie didn't want a headful of pornographic images of the women he'd be likely to bump into at Moon's Supermarket or Hunter's Drug Store. "I recall you taking up golf for a couple weeks. Not sure about the rest."

Spuv shrugged. "Anyway, that's her." His little smile grew wider. "God all *mighty* we had us a time before she went back to college. Knocked me on my butt when I come in here last week and seen her behind the bar."

After a quick introduction, Charlie saw right off how Lexie was for Spuv. With each beer delivery or unnecessary swipe of the table, she angled her back, leaned on an elbow, and swapped soft talk with Spuv. Busy as the bar was, their conversations had to stay short, but all had something to do with them hooking up after she got off at six. Charlie couldn't decide if she featured herself Spuv's girlfriend, but one thing was pretty certain, they weren't getting charged for the beers. Each one she brought came with a wink and a pat on the table.

The deeper they got into the afternoon, the less he felt part of it. "Gonna take off," he told Spuv just past five. "How much I owe?" Even if he was wrong about the beers being free, the two he'd nursed couldn't have been much.

"Bullshit." Spuv sprang across the little table and hooked a beefy arm around Charlie's neck. "Not going anywhere, you good lookin' rascal." Roaring out a laugh, he scraped knuckles across the crown of Charlie's head. "Friends don't let friends drink alone. Ain't that what they say?"

Being extra careful of his tender nose, he squeezed out of Spuv's headlock. "Who says you have to drink?" His hair was too short to get mussed, but he smoothed it anyway, even the new sore spot. "Drink sweet tea and watch the damn game." Spuv wasn't drunk, but he was on the way, and Charlie wasn't hanging around to find out was if it was fun drunk or fighting drunk. "Told you at the house, Desiree's expecting me."

"Check your sack, dude. Your nuts may be missing. No, hang on. I'll get Lexie to do it."

He yanked down the arm Spuv was waving toward the bar. "Don't go embarrassing that girl. And me. I'm leaving. Period."

Spuv wrapped his huge hand around Charlie's neck and rocked it. "Dude, shake a tree and out falls a woman. Home at six. Home at ten. Who gives a shit? Live your damn life, son. She don't like it, find one who does."

The night Spuv yanked Desiree out of Brandi's cousin's car popped into Charlie's mind. Spuv had never said a word about it. Made him wonder if Spuv caught her in the middle of something, something making him hint that maybe she wasn't a choice worth sticking with.

"Miss you, man," Spuv said, still swaying him by the neck. "Quit Comcast. Quit the fire company. Softball, hunting, fishing. Like she's got you in one of them baby harnesses with a leash."

"Get married, then tell me how things are done." He smacked Spuv's arm away. "Have fun playing Barbies." He backed toward the door. "Call you tomorrow."

Everything lately pried another finger away from his grip on the familiar, and now he was driving back to that cursed mansion, dropping deeper into the nightmare, to a bedazzled wife who might need a two-by-four across the forehead to snap out of it. And the damn Granvilles. His life and Desiree's knocked off kilter because he brushed against a diseased family. Should have been easy to fix, but every move he tried so far only stuck him tighter to the flypaper.

His disappointing day with Spuv made going through the automatic gate at Reynolds more depressing than usual. Even after dropping to fifteen miles an hour, he got to the house too fast. Inside the garage, engine off and door down, he stayed in the car so long the overhead light timed off. Still hadn't budged when Desiree opened the door from the house. He started to get out, but she shoved an open hand at him and eased the house door shut.

She got in the passenger side and tugged the door until it clicked shut. "Have fun?" she said, staring forward.

He knew that wasn't a real question. "Not late."

Her face got hard and tight. "She's coming here. Tomorrow. Maybe Monday."

"Who is?"

"Sneaky bitch!" She backhanded her fist against the side window. "Shoulda recognized her damn voice." She lit into the glass like killing a snake, a yelp and grunt with each whack.

"Stop!" He grabbed her arms. "Gonna break it. What's wrong with you?"

Took some seconds, but she quit struggling. Eyes forward, she rubbed the side of her smacking hand.

"Okay," he said, still holding loosely around her wrists. "So, who's coming?"

"That Lauren."

His head tingled. "Daughter can't see her momma?" He'd make sure to be running errands.

"Ain't like that. Not even close. Seems your little friend busted her face. Got it busted is more like it. And she wants to stay here 'til it's healed."

Last thing he wanted to hear. "Stop calling her my 'little friend'. Helped her out of a jam. Period." He waited for her to look his way, but she wouldn't. "So," he said, trying to sound casual, "got any idea for how long?"

"We had her." Desiree started rocking, kept a steady gaze out the windshield. "Told me we were her last throw of the dice. Her exact words. Last throw of the dice." Still rocking, she shook her head. "Had to keep 'em away a little longer. Just a little."

"Desiree, talk plain."

"Me and her. We had tea this afternoon. Talking like a couple of old friends, enjoying the view, guessing if the azaleas were gonna bloom by April Fool."

"That's upsetting?"

"Told me to call her Miss Vivien." She peeked at him, went back to staring forward and rocking. "Something, huh? One week. 'Miss Vivien' in a week. Telling you, we had her."

"Had what? Come the end of June, we're done."

"Shut up!" Fists trembled in front of her chin. "Shut up about days, and June. Not leaving here. I'm not. That's it." She rocked harder, noisy breaths rushing in and out of her nose. "Got to get rid of her."

"Hang on. Get rid of who?"

"Heard her three damn times yesterday. Shoulda recognized that whore voice."

"You lost me." Was like trying to talk to someone wearing three hats and pushing a shopping cart full of cardboard.

"Useless!" She hunkered into a tuck and yanked at her hair. Shoulders quaking, she broke out crying into her hands.

Not knowing what else to do, he leaned across the console and pulled her close, rubbed her back and shoulders, waited it out.

"Who has tea with her tomorrow, Charlie?" she said after a good long while. "Not me."

"You might could. I mean, why not?"

"Any of them's around," she said, her head rolling side to side, "I'm the maid. The snippy maid. That's what that bitch called me. Woman's gonna get me kicked to the curb. I know it." She sat tall and patted a sleeve to her eyes. "Gotta get rid of her."

He doubted she'd ever hurt someone, but talk like that made him glad he left the .38 under the mattress back home, and come the end of June, even if he had to drug her into a coma, she'd be sleeping on it again.

CHAPTER THIRTY-ONE

VIVIEN SAW her opening. With Desiree upstairs readying Lauren's room, Charlie was alone, finishing his Cheerios at the breakfast table. She brought her tea, sat next to him, and gazed out the rotunda's wide windows. "Rain all day, I'm afraid."

"So I hear."

"Some people are terribly affected by weather. Sunny, happy. Cloudy, sad. Is Desiree that way? Or have the last two days been a coincidence?"

He focused on capturing the remaining soggy rings with his spoon. "She'll be fine."

"If it's the extra work with Laurie coming, I could probably get Marisol back."

"I don't think it's that."

"I wouldn't have let Marisol go in the first place, but Desiree assured me she could handle everything."

"Ma'am," he said, holding up an open hand, "fretting over nothing. It'll pass."

"I hope so. We've been getting along so well. I'd hate to think I've done something to flatten the soufflé."

He paused, blinked, and went back to his cereal.

"Could it be something else?" She knew for certain Desiree's ill humor involved Lauren. Being forewarned of specific friction points during their brief overlap would be valuable, but that required she know the truth. "Has she an inkling about the night you and Laurie spent together?"

"Whoa." Eyes wide, he jumped from his chair and hurried into the kitchen on tiptoes. At the island sink, he ran water and checked the hallways every few seconds. "Ma'am," he said in a hush when he returned to his chair, "I am *begging* you, do not say that in front of her."

"So you have been lying." The slump of his shoulders girded her for a confession.

"I am so sick of this," he said, eyes closed.

"You're still saying nothing happened?"

"Ma'am," he said, hands flat on the table, "I'm done talking about this, and I mean forever."

"I'm sorry, but Desiree knows something. At least tell me what you told her so we don't cross wires."

"Nothing. Told her nothing."

"Charlie," she said, leaning closer and lowering her voice, "three times yesterday, our dear Desiree refused to put Lauren's calls through. My daughter had to disguise her voice and claim to be calling from my attorney's office. Desiree had a semi-valid excuse, but I sense more. How does she even know Laurie exists?"

He kept a constant eye to the hallway leading to the foyer. "Couple of times in Key West, Lauren was around when I was on the phone with Desiree. Somehow, she's paired us up in her head. Been slow work setting her straight, and tell you the truth, I'm glad she's coming. Gives me the chance to show Desiree your daughter don't mean spit to me, no offense."

Knowing her daughter as she did, if Lauren had set her cap for him, Charlie could be in deep trouble. "Of course," she said, reaching to pat his hand, "I'll help in any way I can. You're such a rare couple. That wife of yours, Charlie. My God, if I had children that tender and considerate, I'd never have had the chance to meet her. She'd still be a maid at … Where did she work?"

"Y'know, hotels." He picked up the cereal bowl and stood. "Ma'am, would you excuse me? I'm gonna see if she needs any help."

"Charlie, be honest, are you happy here?" Dangerous question, but the answer might improve her strategy going forward.

"Beautiful place, gotta say that. Comfortable as all get-out. Beemer's been a lot of fun." He shrugged. "Not the worst place to kill three months."

"And after that?" She didn't like his pained expression as he sat again.

His eyes flicked between her and the empty bowl, stopping on the bowl. "Not a question of happy or unhappy." Frowning, he fidgeted in the chair. "I don't belong here. I don't *want* to belong here. Don't want Desiree to either, but she does."

"She's blossoming, Charlie. I've seen it in a week. Why take that from her?"

He scratched his neck. "Blossoming into what, exactly? Liked her fine before, y'know, all this." His finger wandered in every direction. "And it's gonna end sometime. What then? Longer she sees this as real life, harder it's gonna be to become a civilian again."

Rather perceptive for a man claiming to be less than clever. "Not sure I like hearing about the end," she said, smiling, "but you may be overthinking, dear boy. What doesn't end? And when it does, life goes on in a new way. Let it happen." She squeezed his wrist. "Charlie, as I've already told Desiree, I haven't time for a protracted mating dance, so I'll just say it. I would be enormously pleased if both of you became a permanent part of my life." That might have been laid on a touch thick, but the moment felt crisis-like.

"Wow." He nodded for an agonizing length of time. "That's a great compliment, and I thank you." He stood, no hint of reaction on his face. "Ma'am, if you'll excuse me?"

"Charlie, I don't know if Desiree mentioned it, but I've asked her to shelve the ma'am's and call me Miss Vivien."

"Well ma'am, we're still here on the ninety-first day?" He snapped his fingers and aimed one at her. "You're gonna be Miss Vivien, I promise you." He headed toward the foyer.

"Charlie, please."

He stopped, but didn't turn.

"Would it cost that much? Play nice."

His head and shoulders drooped. "Miss Vivien it is." He resumed his escape.

That went poorly, and with her daughter about to flit about the house for God knew how long, private conversations to further the cause would be nearly impossible. Each day Charlie saw the end of the tunnel grow brighter would be another day closer to losing Desiree, and most likely the war with Ward.

Her daughter hadn't even arrived, but suffering or not, Lauren had to go.

CHAPTER THIRTY-TWO

BASED ON WHAT Charlie learned on their trip to Key West, the more people Miss Vivien was likely to run into, the fancier the getup. This morning he had a straight view to the elevator door from his seat in the breakfast nook. When the door opened, her broad white hat, string of pearls, dark blue dress, and white shoes told him fetching Lauren from the hospital was a big deal. "Well, look at you," he said.

The compliment fired up a smile on her face. "My hunting outfit." She clicked her white purse open and took out a pair of white gloves. "All those handsome doctors to dazzle. Who knows? Perhaps you'll have a new father by nightfall. Darling," she said, squinting into the handbag, "be a lamb and get my fox coat from the hall closet, would you?"

"What?" He knew what she'd said, but he wanted to know if she did.

"Not 'what', dear. Either 'excuse me' or 'pardon'. And I asked if you'd please get my fox jacket from the hall closet. Not the mink, the fox. Thank you. I'll wait here." She set her purse on the kitchen island. Smiling at him, she wriggled fingers into a glove. "Off you go then."

Like most times when he wasn't sure if saying something would be good or bad, he stayed quiet about "father," but it was still working on him at the hall closet. Crossed his mind to rush upstairs to where Desiree was finishing up Lauren's room and ask her if the same thing had ever happened with her, but Miss Vivien was ready to go, and being short-timers like they were, it didn't really matter.

He must've guessed right on the fox because she held her arm out straight soon as he reached the kitchen. She held a piece of paper in her fingers.

"This is Laurie's address." She flapped the note at him. "Plug it into the gizmo in the car, but don't lose it. Her apartment number and the doorman's name are on it. She asked if we'd swing by and pick up a fresh outfit before going to the hospital. Only clothes the poor darling has are the ones when they admitted her." Coat on, she smiled and tugged on the second glove. "This is all rather exciting. I've never been to her place."

"Is it new?"

"I have no idea. Shall we?" She hooked onto his elbow.

THE DOORMAN stepped aside after opening the door to Lauren's apartment. "It'll lock on its own when you leave," he said, "and please tell Ms. Granville we're all looking forward to seeing her back here real soon. She's a huge favorite. Staff, other residents, everybody."

"Tell me," Miss Vivien said as she passed the doorman, "were you the one who let the thug into the building?"

The doorman flinched."Excuse me?"

"Well, the lawyers usually sort those details. Thank you for everything." She shut the door in the man's startled face.

Charlie didn't know what she was talking about either.

"Isn't this charming?" She dropped her gloves and purse onto a round table that reminded him of a traffic circle. Living room exit at twelve o'clock, hallways at three and nine. "Let's try this way," she said, pointing toward nine o'clock.

At the end of the hall, she opened a door and peeked in. "Oh my," she said, shuffling into a giant bedroom with windows wrapping along two walls. "Must be the master. Wonderful space. Remind me of this next time she asks for money. Come." She tugged his arm toward a sink and mirror they could see through an open door. "I absolutely must see the bathroom."

Her hand tightened on his arm at the stall shower. "Good lord."

The glass door reminded him of cloudy ice, but with a tall, clear oval in the center. Etched smack in the middle, there was Lauren, naked and standing in a giant seashell, hair blowing sideways, an arm crossed over her breasts, and a hand over her privates. A little thinner and younger, but scratch on a few tattoos and it was pretty much what he remembered from Key West.

"Stop it." Miss Vivien jostled his elbow. "You're making me uncomfortable."

"Sorry." Felt like the time he was doing homework at the kitchen table, and GranDelia slapped a hidden Penthouse next to his algebra.

Standing aside, she waved him by. "Go. Shoo. Get a cool drink in the kitchen or something. Shouldn't take me long to cobble together her outfit."

While Miss Vivien poked through the bedroom for Lauren's clothes, he roamed more of the classy layout. City views from the living room caught him first. Being on an upper floor, the lights had to be awesome at night. Next, he nosed around her stuff. Furniture, wall pictures, table junk. Loads of framed photos, almost all of her someplace tropical. Different man in each. Her wearing a bathing suit in a bunch of them. None newer than ten years, if he had to guess.

Miss Vivien scuffed out of the bedroom and set down a small suitcase. "I'm sure everything in here will be wrong, but I tried. No doubt she'll pack ten times this amount when we swing back here later." Nose wrinkled, she tilted her head, "You know, a precautionary visit wouldn't be completely foolish."

"Saw one right there." He pointed to a door next to a four-stool bar.

Purse under her arm, she flipped on the light and fan in the powder room and shut the door.

Usually took her a few minutes, so he followed the scent back to the shower door. Same as in Key West, his eyes drifted over all of her. Always another part he needed to see more than where he was looking. Something blood-boiling about that woman. An energy he wanted to join. If his life wasn't how it was, he'd jump into that volcano without a second thought.

"Why am I not shocked?" Miss Vivien said from the doorway.

"That was quick." He rubbed his warm forehead. "All set?"

She stared at him a good long time, her expression softening from angry to tender. "Don't overestimate yourself, dear. Laurie's drowning. Keep clear, or she'll take you with her."

WAS PAST FOUR by the time they got back to Reynolds Plantation and he'd lugged Lauren's three suitcases upstairs. Off to Publix after that for her prescriptions and the baby monitor she wanted. Getting back to the mansion a touch past five left enough time for a mail run to his house, but Lauren was acting so wounded, he wanted to stay available if they had to take her someplace quick. Also gave him a chance to put in some work on Desiree's sour mood.

One-word and no-word answers in the kitchen let him know he wasn't a welcome spectator at the chopping and cooking, so he parked in front of a TV in the breakfast nook. Close enough and far enough.

"Supper's ready," she called to him at six-thirty. "Go fetch everyone, if y'ain't too damn busy. Last I heard out of this thing," she said, tapping a carving knife on the baby monitor, "they were both in her room. Been a while, though. Maybe she's dead. Now wouldn't that be a damn shame."

"Baby Girl, you best hope that squawk box don't work both ways." He turned off the TV and headed past where she was slicing pot roast. "One too many," he said tapping a finger next to a stack of four plates. "She can't eat that."

"You seem to know a lot."

He u-turned and stopped inches from her. "Her mouth's wired shut," he said, voice kept low. "You really need someone to tell you pot roast don't work? And I saw Miss Vivien give you a piece of paper about her food. C'mon now."

"Not making something special for that bitch. Starve for all I care."

"Desiree," he said, putting on a pretend stern look, "don't you make me go for the strap." He swatted her lightly on the backside.

"Don't you touch—" Teeth bared, she jumped sideways and cocked the knife.

"Hey!" He hopped out of range, the way his drill sergeant had trained him. *Keep clear of a knife. Rush a gun.*

Shaking, she ran her eyes from him to the smeared blade and back to him. The knife clattered into the sink. Hands rubbing her thighs, she took a step away from him. "What, uh, what about Miss Vivien?" she said, still rubbing her legs. "Think I should make up a tray or something?" She licked her lips and swallowed. "Whadaya think about a tray?"

"What I think is, you need to get outta here. *We* need to get out."

"Wanna go?" she said, her face mashed small and tight. "Then git. I'll pack your damn bag."

He'd never taken the Beemer without asking, but he snatched the fob from the counter and headed for the garage.

"Charlie?"

If he'd heard her footsteps, he would have stopped.

LOTS OF FLIERS and a thick packet of coupons at the house, but no check from Dependable Car Service. He screamed high into the cold dark and stomped a dent into their rusty mailbox.

...act in haste, repent in leisure...

"Not now!" he shouted at GranDelia. Thrown mail fluttered out of the starry night. Pacing until he calmed a bit, he called Mr. Carter to let him know the check still hadn't shown up. Got voicemail again, but this time instead of being asked to record a message, he heard, "Mailbox full."

Leaving the litter where it landed, he jumped into the car and skidded a turn on the soggy crabgrass. The Beemer grabbed pavement on East Street and sped toward Madison. Unlikely, but maybe Mr. Carter was at the limo yard.

Nearly there, the hands-free phone rang. Dashboard displayed *Spuv*. Not much in the mood, but he popped a thumb on the talk button. "Make it fast, big man."

"Sounds like you're in a car. Driving my Beemer?"

"Whadaya want, Spuv?"

"Two things, you testy little shit. First, sorry for being such a tool on Sunday. Should've just gone to the VFW like you said. Shot some pool and caught up. That whole thing."

"Sounds like whats-her-name showed you the door."

"Lexie? Hell no. Up, down, and sideways, dude. Ask me about flavored lotions some time. But the second thing is fishing. Trout season opened yesterday, so the Atlanta dickheads are probably bored already. How about it? Want to run up to Dukes Creek on Thursday?"

Was like listening to a conversation from the past, or from someone else's life. Fishing happened when slates were clean, and he still had eighty-three days left. Fifty-three if Miss Vivien let them pay down the third month, but that meant he had to get this Dependable thing squared away. "Gonna take a pass, but thanks."

"You got any fun left in you, son?"

"Got work on Thursday. And now that I think of it, why don't you?"

Spuv coughed and sniffed. "Spending so much time naked lately, think I caught a chill. Come Thursday, good chance I'm gonna need a recuperation day."

"And that's not stealing?"

"Hey, reverend, someone gives you sick days, you get sick. Can't tempt you? Supposed to be sunny and near seventy."

"Already told you, I'm out of commission 'til the end of June. Maybe a little earlier if things break right."

He'd reached Dependable's lot and knew right off the ride had been for nothing, maybe worse. The office shack being dark didn't concern him, but what he saw behind the building did. All five of

Mr. Carter's limos sat inside a chain-link corral topped with razor wire. Usually just the stretch was in there, or at the most, two other cars. "Hang on a sec." Rolling past the building, he noticed a sign stuck on the glass door at a sloppy angle.

"Thinking it over?"

"Just hang on." Quick backup trained headlights on the sign. NOTICE OF SHERIFF'S SALE.

"Talk to me, dude."

"Gotta go." He turned off the engine and stared at the Notice until his headlights clicked off.

Unfair things in his life, big and little, stacked one on the other. Parents who dropped him like a gum wrapper. Little League strikes that were high. A childhood as "dense" Woods. Elbows in the face with no ref whistle. GranDelia dying eleven days after graduation. The Marines refusing him a third tour. Each one made the load harder to balance. His head filled with air and lights and a want to hurt someone.

CHAPTER THIRTY-THREE

WAITING IN A CHAIR by Lauren's bed, Vivien listened to rips, snips, and soft "ow's" floating from the *en suite* bathroom.

Lauren opened the door, her fresh bandage concealed by a beige cashmere scarf that left only her nose and eyes visible. The robe she'd been wearing hung over an arm, leaving her dressed in a filmy nightgown.

"I certainly hope you plan on wearing the robe for guests," Vivien said, averting her gaze.

Lauren tossed the robe onto the bed, crawled onto the spread, and slapped pillows into a ramp. "Hot enough to grow orchids in here." Reading device in hand, she eased back. "And what guests? Charlie's peg-leg pity bride?" Her eyes squeezed shut. A gasp puffed out the scarf where it covered her mouth.

"There, you see? God punished you. Be nice. She's been an enormous help and a delight."

Book thingamabob on her lap, eyes still shut, Lauren ran fingertips softly over the stitched area of her jaw.

"You know, darling, I could have done the bandage for you." The nurse at Piedmont Hospital insisted she observe how to change the dressing on Lauren's cheek, just in case. That single glimpse of the wound confirmed her suspicion about a beating. Damage from smashing into a doorjamb would have been vertical.

"I'm a big girl." Lauren eyes settled on the little display screen in her hand. "You don't have to stay."

"No bother really, and it's dinnertime. I thought we'd have it together. Up here if you like."

"I wouldn't."

"Meaning what, dear? Eating together, or dining up here?"

"Not hungry, and if you don't mind, I'd like to finish this book." She jostled her hips and shoulders to angle away from Vivien.

Maternal duty had deposited Lauren in the house and disrupted the idyll Vivien had been engineering, but that obligation would not include playing the fool or ceding preeminence. "You know, darling, I should think good manners would require you at least pretend to be grateful."

"I'll leave if you want," Lauren said, sounding bored, her eyes still down.

"Morning's soon enough." She patted the mattress and pointed to the baby monitor on the nightstand. "In the meantime you've got that doohickey if you need anything. Sweet dreams," she said, hands on her knees to stand.

"Mother, wait." Lauren's eyes betrayed fear. She flipped the tiny computer onto the bed. Head back, she beat flat hands softly on the spread. "Why do you always do this?"

"Let's see," Vivien said. "You assault me at Devon's funeral, fake remorse, upset my household, spit on my generosity, and somehow *I've* committed the crime. Much as I love you, darling, I can't deal with this anymore."

"Generosity." Lauren snorted and gazed at the ceiling through dewy eyes. "It's not generosity when you demand tribute."

"And silence isn't appreciation." Vivien rose to her feet to deliver what she'd been itching to say for ages. "Laurie, you're a rude, angry, selfish brat. All of you are. Baby birds in the nest." Both hands pinched the air. "Gimme gimme gimme. Heaven forbid one of you say 'thank you' for anything. No," she said raising a finger, "actually, that's not fair. For all his shortcomings, at least when poor Devon cut the cord, he sliced it clean."

"So, we're going to play truth or dare now?" Lauren winced and dabbed at her jaw. "How about this? I know Devon called you the day he killed himself, and you did nothing to stop him."

"Rubbish." Suspects lined up in Vivien's mind, without any of them becoming likely. "Who told you that?"

"You did, at the funeral. You said don't lose Luke and Archer, too."

"How could you possibly interpret that to mean Devon called me?" She wondered if pain medication was making Lauren delusional.

"You said 'too', like I knew what Devon was planning, and did nothing. The only way you could know that was if he told you."

Throughout Lauren's illogical explanation, Vivien shook her head slowly, both in denial and amazement.

Drops shimmered on Lauren's lower lids and dropped into the cashmere. "Please say he called you," she said, barely audible.

"I'm sorry, darling." She sat, stretched her hand to Lauren's and squeezed. "How awful for you. What did he say?"

"He doesn't blame me."

"For what?"

"He hated everyone. Just not me, I guess."

"Poor Devon."

Lauren ripped her hand free. "Stop saying that!" Her eyes squeezed shut throughout a slow groan. "I could choke you when you say that. You treated him like a disease. You and Daddy. I never understood."

Vivien glanced away and filtered words until they felt appropriate. "I suppose it can't hurt now," she said, more to herself than Lauren. "You may have always known this, but your father was my everything. Most women lavish love on their children. What's left goes to the husband. That was never me. It still isn't. I adore him to this day. Whatever I do, I try to do what I think would please him."

Her daughter's stare conveyed neither condemnation nor acceptance.

"Anyway, when I became pregnant with Devon, your father was less than thrilled. Not that he was home much, but ten years with no baby in the house suited him quite nicely. I don't know if his, let's say, lack of enthusiasm affected me as well, but when the nurse handed Devon to me in the hospital, I gave him right back. Claimed I had back pain. Try as I might, the feeling never changed. Never. I don't know why, but I couldn't love him. I'm sorry. And you needn't look at me like that."

"You didn't have that luxury."

"Have a baby, darling. Then tell me how it should be done."

"I'd have done it a helluva lot better than you."

"Famous last words, but I suppose based on my scorecard, you're probably right. Good night." She rose and left, relieved her confessions of maternal deficiency hadn't expanded beyond poor Devon.

CHARLIE SHUT THE DOOR from Miss Vivien's garage and slogged up the hallway toward the kitchen, still unsure what he'd have done if Mr. Carter had been home. Under-counter lights glowed on the dark granite and lighted his path. He laid the Beemer fob next to the phone.

"Where you been?"

Desiree's question from the dimly lit breakfast nook gave him a start. "Thought everyone was in bed." He wished they were.

"Gone near three hours. Catch up with Spuv somewhere?"

"Just setting at the house. Thinking." He left out that the "house" was Mr. Carter's in Madison, and he was "thinking" about doing the man some serious bodily harm.

"This here's a house, sugar. You were at a shack." She sipped from a coffee mug.

"If we're just gonna fight, I'm going to bed." He started for the foyer.

"Charlie, wait." She caught him at the end of the counters and slid her arms around his waist. Smiling, she pressed her hips into him and swayed, like to music. "That feel like I'm looking for a fight?"

Wasn't beer, but her breath smelled of some kind of alcohol.

Sort of overnight she'd added drinking to his basket of worries. Passed-out drunk with Brandi Wade's cousin. Drinking alone the day he got back from Key West. Drinking alone here. When else that he didn't catch her, he wondered. "What's in that cup?"

"Charlie, you gotta taste this." She wobbled a zigzag back to the breakfast table and bent for something on the floor. Came up holding a dark bottle by the neck. "Label says Jordan mer-lot. Must be religious wine," she said, giggling. "Cause I'm sure enjoying the hell out of it."

"Where'd you get that?"

"Y'know that big bar in the great room?" Swinging the bottle in that direction knocked her a touch off balance. "Charlie, it is so *cool*. There's this door in the way back. Always figured it was a closet. Well, this afternoon I found out it ain't. Opens to a curvy set of stone stairs. Down to like a dungeon, but with wine in it. Rack after rack. Hundreds of bottles."

"You swiped that?" He checked toward the foyer on his way to her.

"Don't gotta ask for nothing, sugar pants. 'It's here, it's yours.' That's what Miss Vivien told me." She held the bottle toward the counter lights and squinted through it. "Still got plenty. Grab yourself a mug. We'll toast something. The future. Or a miracle recovery for that slut bitch." She poured some more for herself.

"You're done." He snatched the cup and held it away from her grasping hand.

"Gimme that."

"And the future don't look real toastable at the moment."

"Give it here. Y'ain't my keeper."

"Baby Girl, just listen." He deflected her lunges like a sword fighter. "We been stiffed. Dependable's out of business."

"You don't give me that, I'm gonna do something. I am."

"Did you hear?" He set the cup on the table and blocked her reaches with his body. "The two thousand. It's not coming."

She hooked a roundhouse at his crotch, but he ducked enough that she missed high. Next swing headed at his face. He slapped it away, shoved her onto a wheeled chair, and chased it all the way to the windows. "Out of your damn mind?" he said, doing his best not to shout.

"I don't owe you nothing." She tucked tight, arms crossed in front of her face.

"What are you talking about?" He backed away so she'd know he wasn't fixing to smack her. "Dependable screwed us. Wanted you to stop drinking long enough to understand."

"I got it." She uncoiled some. "Ain't stupid, like some people."

"Drunk. Stupid. Hard to tell the difference most times."

"Stupid's worse." She pushed out of the chair, steadied herself with a hand on the window. "You just don't get it. Dependable's a hundred years ago, Charlie. A million. Pay, no pay. Means nothing. Two thousand?" She smiled and shook her head. "Probably her electric bill each month."

"You're the one who don't get it. Dependable, or something like it, is our future. Not here."

"Well sir, that there's a problem. Big, big problem." She limped past him, snagged the neck of the wine bottle, and flopped into a chair within reach of her mug. "Don't wait up."

They needed to talk more, but not in her condition. On his way out of the kitchen, a moan or sigh from the baby monitor stopped him. "What if she needed something while I was gone?" If Desiree messed up because she was drunk, they could be out the door by morning, and still be up to their noses in debt.

"Y'all want someone really stupid?" she said, pumping a finger toward the ceiling. "There's your champ. She don't know, or maybe don't care, but I can hear everything she and Miss Vivien says." Cup paused near her lips, she nodded. "And that whore should care. 'Cause if I get my chance …" She clicked out of the side of her mouth, like people did around horses.

He lifted and inspected the monitor. "This thing is kinda over the top. Not like her leg's busted."

Desiree banged a fist on the table. "That's what I told Miss Vivien, but she said it's 'cause the bitch don't want to be seen. Both times I was summoned," she scratched quotation marks in the air, "her head was all wrapped in a scarf. Spooky, seeing nothing but those witch eyes following every move I made."

Her eyes were green, and way more than spooky. Every time he remembered something personal about Lauren, guilt chewed at him. "Baby Girl, let's not have the night end like this. Leave that and come up with me."

Hands empty, arms wide, she stood and wobbled to him. "I'm not just a bit of sympathy, am I?"

"What's that mean?" he said, folding a hug around her.

"Nothing ... Drunk talk." She drew on his back with her finger. "Still love me, sugar?"

"Now and forever, Baby Girl."

Nuzzling her cheek against his chest, she slid a hand under his fly and played. "Sorry about, y'know. This hurt?"

"I'll let you know." He dropped his hands to her backside.

She reached behind, pulled his hand off her smaller cheek, and set it on her breast.

"Before we get too, uh, too distracted," he said, "please tell me you understand about here."

"Sugar," she set both hands to the task, "I may just have too much man on my mind right now to concentrate on that."

He twisted away from the fingers pulling down his zipper. "G'won up," he said. "I'll be there directly."

"Gonna start alone if you don't hurry," she sing-songed from the hallway.

Miss Vivien probably did tell Desiree she could take whatever she wanted, but on the chance Desiree heard wrong, he washed the mug, poured out the rest of the bottle, and brought it to the recycling bin in the garage. With no chores left, he headed to sex knowing he'd lost ground on every front today, but Desiree the most. *Don't let me get lost* didn't mean anything when she said that on the day he left for Key West, but now he could see the change, like a peg that needed whittling to fit in its hole again.

CHAPTER THIRTY-FOUR

WARD GRANVILLE shielded his personal life from the office staff as if his dental practice was cover for the CIA. On the remote possibility any of the employees knew Gardner Culpepper was one of Atlanta's premier attorneys, he'd instructed the lawyer to call only his house, and only in the evening. Should the need arise for workday contact, as apparently just happened, Culpepper was to call personally, no secretaries or assistants, and say the gardener needed to speak with him.

He took the handset his receptionist had brought into the examining room. "Excuse me," he said to a patient in no position to voice an objection. Closing the office door behind him, he cupped a hand around the mouthpiece. "Make it quick," he said softly.

"We're wasting our time," Culpepper said.

"Explain." He paced, fingers snapping.

"Bartram Winfield runs a very good practice. I couldn't even get us an order for a medical evaluation."

"You said this would be a breeze."

"No. I said I'd have it done quickly."

"You know people. Find a better judge."

"What I need to find are better grounds. To recap Bartram's presentation, you're the only family member petitioning the court. She takes no cognitive drugs. Fear of flying is a common phobia, not dementia. There's been the occasional trip to the emergency room, but no hospitalizations. No traffic accidents or citations. Even her credit score is perfect."

"What about hiring that limo driver and his wife?"

"Not for competency, but there may be *some* potential in that one. The wife has two shoplifting convictions from a long time ago. No time served, so that's pretty much nothing, but then a few days ago she left a job after only three weeks. That smacks of termination. Problem is, it's within the normal probationary period, so without sending someone in to sneak a look at the personnel file, we'll never know if it was because she performed poorly, or something more serious."

"Do it."

"No." Culpepper dragged out the word as if speaking to an imbecile. "And even if it was 'for cause', your mother merely exercised poor hiring judgment. If that were grounds for legal incompetency, every corporate manager in the country would be in assisted living."

"So, what's plan B?"

"Takes time, but a private investigator might turn over the right rock, and I do have a top man. Six hundred a day, plus expenses, if you want to go that route."

"Let's see. You want to know if I'll pay a detective *per diem* what you charge for an hour? Of course I'll pay, but I want daily reports. None of this run-the-meter crap that you pull."

"I'm one for one with you, Doctor. You get your money's worth."

"Let's say this snoop comes up cold, too. Then what?"

"Stay vigilant, especially about what she spends."

"I don't get to see that. My father set her up with a business manager when he was dying. David Miller. Know him?"

"Miller, wow. I play racquetball with him. Your father knew quality. Miller's one smart rascal, but even better for you, he's reasonable. Let him know your concerns. If he sees erratic spending patterns, he'll tell you. Of course, the bad part is that a good bit of money could disappear first."

"I pay you to prevent that, for crissake. And by the way, this call could have waited until tonight. You made me leave a patient just to tell me you're a bad lawyer."

"That's unfair. When I can't even get a medical evaluation, c'mon. Ever consider you might be wrong?"

"About you." He banged his thumb onto the Off button and sat at his desk. Mrs. Aronstein's gums could wait a few more seconds. She wouldn't want him gouging in this mood, anyway.

The detective could strike gold, but failing that, a quick sifting of options left only one: make peace with Mother and defeat her from inside the walls, and with Lauren in residence, the big gun was already in position.

CHAPTER THIRTY-FIVE

PALE BLUE SCARF wrapped around most of her head, Lauren shuffled barefoot into the kitchen. Besides the pretty headgear, Charlie took notice of her white t-shirt and blue nylon running shorts, split high on the sides. He tried not to watch, but caught enough sway and jiggle to fire up memories of how she looked wearing even less. The way Desiree was glaring at him, her cereal spoon paused mid-bite, he must not have tried hard enough.

"Good God," Lauren said, rinsing out a plastic glass that had a permanent straw through the cap, "why the hell is everyone up at this hour?"

"Sleep well, darling?" Miss Vivien said from her chair next to Desiree. "Would you like a little something before you leave?"

Like she'd heard a distant gunshot, Desiree cocked an ear toward the sink.

Lauren sagged forward. Bending the way she did, flowers in her tramp-stamp showed above the elastic of her shorts. "Mother, may I speak to you alone?"

"If you wouldn't mind, dears?" Vivien said to Desiree and Charlie. She watched them troop toward the foyer.

As Desiree passed her daughter, still drooping into the basin, she tapped Charlie's arm and wiggled a finger at the horrifying bit of tattoo visible above Lauren's waistband.

The subtlety impressed Vivien. Desiree would never have directed Charlie's eyes that way unless it was to ensure that the doddering mother noticed, as well.

Their footsteps in the hallway and foyer faded to silence.

Lauren straightened and ran water onto a paper towel. Blotting her eyes, she turned and rested her hips against the counter. "We aren't friends," she said. "I know that. But I have nowhere to go, and I'm afraid. Please. I won't be a problem. I promise."

"I don't understand, darling. You have a lovely apartment, with security."

"I didn't fall. Okay? Justin did this, and he hasn't been caught. I just want to get a little better and not be looking over my shoulder all the time."

"So, at least you told the police the truth."

Lauren nodded. "He's probably in Barbados or Oregon by now, but I have no way of knowing. Mother, you won't even see me. Please, just 'til he's caught."

"Have you no friends? Oh, I know. What about Sophia? No, forget I said that." She clapped her hands. "Luke. He'll be in Betty Ford a few more weeks. California might be just the place for you right now."

"Other than the Luke part, that's not a bad idea, but I can't fly yet. Would it be okay to stay until I'm cleared to fly?"

"The train," Vivien said, hands clasped to her heart. "Ooo, I used to love the trains in Europe. It could be such a pleasant adventure for you."

Lauren loosened the scarf and pulled the edges away from face. "The doctors aren't finished with this." On her cheek, a cloud of white gauze floated on marbleized blues, purples, and a sickly yellow. Puffiness had improved, but the bruising continued to expand like a building storm.

"I'm doing my best, darling. Now you come up with something, because I'm sorry, but you can't stay."

"Then why—" Lauren flinched and stroked lightly over the wound. "Why did you let me come at all?"

"Well, we're all susceptible to plucks on the heartstring. A dash of false hope too, I suppose. An opportunity to witness your rise from the ashes a wiser woman. But no. You're addicted to drama, Laurie, and I'm weary of the production."

"Or another needy child to turn your back on."

"You're hardly a 'child', darling. And a word of advice. Tattoos don't stop the clock. For a woman in your circumstances, they're a cry for help, and frankly, an embarrassment."

"Really. And exactly how does a needle in me hurt you? Or does it show I'm not frou-frou enough to be a proper Granville?"

"At times, dear, you're not a proper anyone. This morning, for example. You traipse into my kitchen nearly naked. And why? So Charlie can desire you in front of his poor wife. It's not only cringingly inappropriate, it's sadistic. I won't have it."

"Mother, you keep the damn house over eighty. And I couldn't know he'd be in here."

"Laurie, please. We know each other too well. You're entirely too enamored of your form to keep it covered for long. He survived your insecurity in Key West. One trial by fire for the poor man is quite enough."

With her back turned toward the breakfast table, Laurie filled the plastic glass with coffee and screwed the cap on. She moaned through a short sip. "I'll stay in my room the whole time. I promise."

"Laurie, I'm sorry."

"Mother!" Laurie slammed the cup on the granite. "Oooh," leaked out on a long breath. Her head slowly pivoted side to side. "I'm afraid … Okay? I'll do it however you want, but I need to stay."

Hope for her daughter's rehabilitation revived anew, alongside a hefty rush of guilt. "In your room? No exceptions?"

"There'll be doctor appointments." Lauren turned to her, eyes glistening. "I'll have to leave for those."

"Naturally."

"Do you think Charlie could drive me?"

"Absolutely not."

"What about that wife?"

"Out of the question." Those two women unsupervised would be an invitation to disaster. "Borrow Luke's car or take cabs."

"Luke's car," Lauren said softly. "No, I won't be taking Luke's car. A cab would be best. Then when I'm okay to drive, I could bring the Ferrari back. Would you be okay with that?"

"An excellent solution." House arrest would bore Lauren so quickly an escape vehicle at the ready would accelerate her departure.

"Are we done?"

"Don't make me regret this, darling."

Head lowered, Lauren trudged from the kitchen, hand raised like taking an oath.

She watched until her daughter disappeared. Whether through superior genes, cosmetic surgery, hormone therapy, or some sorcerer's blend of all three, she had to admit Lauren retained an excellent figure. Pity her life never filled out the way her body had. But where there's breath, there's hope. Perhaps a few more days of quiet contemplation as a battered woman would work a miracle, although she doubted it.

WARD USED lunch hour to catch up on phone messages. iPhone set on *Speaker*, he uncapped the Tupperware bowl holding his dry arugula salad, same lunch he'd made for years. He pressed the number next to Lauren's *missed call* and ran a paper towel over ivory chopsticks until she picked up.

"Ward, thank God. A human."

"Sometimes. Thought I'd hear from you last night. So, how are things at Mother's?"

"Didn't you listen to my fucking message?" Along with the odd pronunciation because of her wired jaw, Lauren sounded drunk.

"Give it to me now." He pinched a single salad leaf and laid in on his tongue. First bite was always the most bitter.

"I'm in time-out, if you can believe it."

"Hostilities that fast, huh? Use the wrong fork?"

"My accursed beauty, apparently. Mother thinks I incite destructive passions in the staff. It was either confinement in my room or she was kicking me out."

Once more, his mother was a step ahead. "Why would she think that? What'd you do?"

"She found my coffee-fetching outfit a bit too risqué for Charlie's baby blues, which is laughable since he's seen me in the altogether."

He bent closer to the phone. "He's seen you naked? When?"

"I shouldn't talk to people right after my pain meds. Shit's amazing. So, tell me about the competency whatever. Is she out of here soon?"

"You have a little time yet. Laurie, that other thing. When would Charlie have seen you naked?"

"That morning you brought the robe to me? That was Charlie's room. I spent the night there."

"Well well. And I presume the two of you became one, as they say?"

"Think I'd like to change the subject. This is kind of, um, icky for brother-sister talk."

He didn't need more. "Sorry. I'm just worried about you down there, trapped with that bunch."

"Well, that's very sweet, brother dear, but I'm fine. Everyone's fine. Just fucking ducky."

"You're including Mother?"

"Sweetie, I know you want me to say she's wearing her underwear on the outside, but far as I can tell, she's doing great. Still a colossal pain in the *derriere*, but her redneck toadies seem to be just the ticket."

"Laurie, they're cons. The wife's a thief. Arrests and everything."

"Wow," Lauren said, dragging out the word. "Does Mother know?"

"I've been trying to warn all of you. She's low-hanging fruit for sleazebags like them. You have to help me get rid of them." Lauren had already given him new ammo, but direct assistance would be even better.

"Ward, all I want is to hear Justin's been arrested, so I can blow this popsicle stand. Although, seeing that gimpy little twat get the ax wouldn't spoil my day."

"Let's make that happen." At least he sensed some progress. "Okay, sister dear, I have some more calls to make. We'll talk."

OPENING THE PANTRY DOOR on a lunch hunt, Charlie was surprised to find Desiree in there. Her too, based on the way she jumped and tucked a hand behind her back. "Sorry," he said. "What's that you got?" He pointed behind her.

Desiree brought the baby monitor out of hiding and rocked it at him. "Always knew I could never keep you, Charlie, but her?" Eyes shiny, she shook her head.

Only person she could have meant was Lauren. His face turned hot. "What are you talking about?"

"Heard with my own ears." Again, she wiggled the monitor at him. "Your night with her in Key West."

Not knowing exactly what she'd heard, he figured the skimpiest truth might clear him. "Okay, probably should've told you." He pushed his damp plums at her. "But here's the all of it. Her boyfriend threatened her. My room was closest. She knocked and asked to hide there. Should've said no, but I didn't. She got the bed. I got the floor. In the morning she popped out of bed with nothing on, and I saw her go into the bathroom. I left while she was still in there. No sex. End of report."

"Charlie," she said, wobbling closer, "I ain't a fool. Woman don't get naked for a man for no reason."

"Desiree, I didn't do anything."

"Bull."

"I didn't do anything."

She squinted at him. "You let her do anything to you?"

"Nothing like that. And you're making me mad. I don't break promises, and I don't lie." He'd have a hard time keeping to that last part if the conversation kept going. "You gotta stop this, and I mean now."

"Told you not to go." She pushed a hand into his chest as she limped out of the pantry. "Just knew it."

He reached for her. "C'mon, Baby—"

"Don't touch me!" She lurched backwards into the kitchen.

"Desiree, no." He chased after her, snapped her into a hug that pinned her arms. "I didn't," he said over and over until her storm blew itself out. She dropped into crying, and he held tight until that slowed, too.

"I see how you look at her," she said, her breaths hitching.

"Desiree, you're my wife. That's it."

She shook her head slowly. "I was a man, I'd want her. 'Specially compared to me."

He kissed her on the hair. "Don't. You're my now-and-forever woman, and I'm glad of it."

"She make a try for you?"

"Leave it go. Nothing happened." He wished she'd stop making him recall how Lauren looked that morning. "I got an idea. Such a pretty day, let's go for a drive."

"Can't both go," she said, running a finger under each eye. "Ain't just the bitch. Got Miss Vivien, too."

"Then you go. Don't remember you having a minute to yourself since we been here. Maybe you could go to the house and check the mail or something. G'won."

"I suppose." Still in a loose embrace, she banged her fist on his chest in a soft, steady beat. "She don't get outta here, Charlie, I'm gonna do something. I am. Something bad." She tipped her mascara streaked face to his. "And you best not be lying."

The angry way her eyes latched onto his made him regret suggesting she go even one inch closer to that .38. Not that he believed she could hurt anyone, but he'd check her purse when she came back.

CHAPTER THIRTY-SIX

LIKE AN AQUARIUM FISH, Charlie cruised the first floor non-stop while he waited for Desiree to get back from her short R&R. He even tried a quick inspection of the wine dungeon, but halfway down the stone stairs, static on the baby monitor he was carrying drowned out the sounds of Lauren's afternoon. TV, gargling, magazine pages turning, toilet flush, couple of boring phone calls. Only fun part was her singing off key and losing track of the lyrics, the way people did when they used earphones. Lots of times off-duty in Afghanistan, especially in the field, he sat near Marines who did that. Without knowing why exactly, he liked those people.

Hearing the garage door open was like he'd been let up for air. He hurried out of the great room, across the foyer, and into the kitchen, sporting a smile he hoped would be contagious. "Feeling better?"

She pointed to the monitor he was holding. "Surprised I'm not hearing you two going at it on that thing."

"That supposed to be funny?"

Thumping her purse onto the island, she handed him a Gander Mountain catalog. "That's all the mail, and I stopped by the post office to have them start forwarding. Gimme that." She ripped the monitor from him and set it on the counter, keeping her back to him. "Oh, and if you think the stink is gone from that oversized outhouse, think again. Damn near barfed up my frappuccino when I opened the door. Must be in the insulation or something. Never come out now."

Digging in her purse again, she twisted a small Walgreen's bag closed and tucked it under whatever else was in there. "Wasn't any propane, either. One damn chore and you let us run out. They're coming tomorrow at nine, COD, and we're getting an extra charge 'cause you're too dumb to keep one goddam thing—"

"That's enough!" Other than being called stupid, something else in what she said bothered him. "It's seventy degrees outside. How'd you find out we got no propane?"

Her hands slowed inside the purse. "I was gonna, y'know, use the burner to light a scented candle. Saw the pilot was out and checked the tank. Any more questions, officer?" She went back to fiddling in her purse. "Charlie," she said, losing the vinegar in her tone, "our little princess, she look sick to you this morning? Thought she looked a little off when I brought her lunch."

"All wrapped up like she is, who could tell?"

"Too busy checking her fake tits?"

No way they were fake. "Getting pretty tired of this. And I got a flash for you. Every pretty woman on this earth stirs me a little. That's how God made men, and every woman knows it. Quit pretending to be shocked."

"Knowing don't make it okay, sugar." She hobbled to him and hooked her arms around his neck. "Miss Vivien and her highness, they in their rooms?"

"Both sleeping, pretty sure."

One quick smooch and she slid her hands to his waist. "Going up to drop my stuff and change." She rolled her hips against him. "How about you get the last bag from the truck and join me?"

"Girl, you are plumb crazy."

"Maybe a good crazy." She bounced her eyebrows. "C'mon up and find out."

"And that's it? Just that easy?"

"Only one way to find out. I'll be upstairs."

At the truck, he wondered if her wild swings were part of "the change." If so, he'd ride it out. If not, now and forever could turn into one mighty long haul.

LYING IN BED, Vivien was awake enough to hear someone climb the front staircase. Desiree's cadence, without question. Same with her progress down the hall.

Vivien heard her say something just before a door clicked shut. Sounded like, "Get ready, bitch." Ears pricked, she propped against an upright pillow.

Charlie's soft-footed ascension followed soon after. Their bedroom door closed. A few clunks and bumps, and then quiet. She closed her eyes again.

A woman's "Oh" whispered through the back wall of her closet. Another "Oh," this time louder. "Oh's," one after the other, the spacing unmistakable. "Oh, Charlie," followed. "Oh, God's" mixed with "Oh, Charlie's." With Lauren's room next to the lovers, Vivien knew her daughter had to be hearing this as well.

The sound of pounding on the hallway side of Desiree's door confirmed it.

"Hey!" Lauren shouted, loud enough that it must have hurt her jaw. "Stick it in her mouth, for crissake."

"Shh," Charlie said to Desiree through a covered chuckle.

Hands on his chest, she sat high on his hips, rolling and popping like he was a mechanical bull. "Love me, Charlie?" she said, panting.

"Hush," he whispered, grabbing her hands.

She yanked them free, leaned back, and braced her arms on his thighs, keeping the rhythm steady. "Say it again. Tell me again."

"Not so loud," he said.

"Hey!" Lauren hammered harder on the door.

"Sorry," he called toward the door.

Desiree fell forward, her fingernails digging into his chest. "Shut your mouth," she growled in his face. She sat tall again, went back to snapping her hips backward and forward, so hard it felt like she was trying to knock his pecker clean off. "Tell me again, Charlie. Say it."

"Godammit!" Lauren hollered.

Was like Desiree was having a seizure or something. He lifted under her good knee and tossed her off him. "Sorry," he yelled toward the door.

Desiree scrambled back at him. Slaps and punches poured in, stinging his cheek and tender nose. A grunt or strangled shriek leaked out of her with each windmill swing.

He grabbed her wrists, steered his arms away from her bared teeth. Her head slammed into anything he left unguarded. One good heave launched her to the top of the mattress. Looking like she was fixing to charge again, he stuck the flat of his foot on her stomach and shoved. She pitched against the headboard with a thud.

Before he could get to her, she hopped off the bed. Hands covering squeaky sobs, she darted into the bathroom and locked the door.

Vivien had made it into the hall in time to hear someone or something bang against a wall in Desiree's room. Clutching her robe shut with one hand, she hurried toward the commotion.

Lauren stared toward her, arms wide. "Do you believe her?" she said. "How fake was that?"

"You promised," she whispered to Lauren. "And lower your voice."

"Promised? What are you talking about?"

"You. Why are you out here?"

"You're joking. Are you deaf?"

"Husbands and wives make love."

"Omigod, this happens all the time? And you listen? Mother, that's uh," she coughed on a laugh, "a little kinky if you ask me."

"I knew this wouldn't work. Though I am surprised you couldn't last a single day."

"Mother, wait." Lauren backed toward her room. "I thought they were, y'know, disturbing you. But now. Totally, totally sorry." She felt for the door handle, turned it, and disappeared into her room.

Knuckle poised to tap on Desiree's door, Vivien heard a bang like a dresser drawer being slammed. The quiet afterward lasted long enough that if there had been trouble, it was over. She was also certain that Charlie, unlike the vermin Lauren cultivated, would never strike Desiree. On tiptoe, she returned to her room. Apologizing for Lauren's intrusion could wait until later, when she and Desiree had tea.

CHARLIE'S STOMP into the dresser had knocked something loose. Sounded like a small piece of metal had hit a side or back panel of the drawer. "Dammit," he said under his breath. His temper had already cost them a mailbox, and now he'd have to fix this, too. Only good news was that he hadn't split the wood. Might have been nothing more than a cheap piece of hardware.

Figuring it would be better if he had some clothes on when Desiree came out of the bathroom, he put his skivvies back on. Sobs from the bathroom told him he still had some time, so he rolled out the top drawer of the broken dresser as far as the stops allowed. Careful not to let any arm scratches touch anything, he poked through Desiree's underwear, expecting to find a small screw or a busted flange. Instead, he came up with what looked like a diamond stud earring.

Holding it to the light, he rolled the post in his fingers, unsure if colorful glitter like that could come from plain glass. He reached inside again, this time slow and careful, like the drawer was full of cobras. Something dangling from the roof brushed the back of his hand. Turned out to be a piece of tape with the earring's mate stuck to the end.

CHAPTER THIRTY-SEVEN

CHARLIE SAT on the bedroom floor, legs out straight, his back flat against the dresser front. While Desiree's crying wound down in the bathroom, he waited, rolling the earrings in his hand like a pair of dice. Still hadn't put two proper words together when the bathroom went quiet and she opened the door.

Huddled in a towel, she stood in the doorway, hair poking every which way, smudged makeup ringing her eyes like a zombie. "Charlie," was all she got out before sniffles and squeaks started again.

She couldn't lash out or play him from over there, so he stayed put.

"What's happening?" she said.

"Wow." He scratched his head. "That one's getting tougher by the minute. How 'bout we jump right over you being crazy and start with this?" He held up one of the earrings.

Quick as a finger snap her wide eyes shrank back to normal size. "What is that?"

He wiggled the earring at her. "These real diamonds?"

"That an earring?"

He nodded. "Yours?"

"Where'd you find it?" She wrapped the towel tighter.

"Two questions and no answers. Not a good start."

"Can I see?" She edged closer. "Oh those. Got those at a yard sale in Dublin while you was in Key West."

"I guess that's why I don't remember them." He turned away from her and held the earring up to the light. "Not that I know anything, but they sure look real."

"Right." She snorted and beckoned with her fingers. "Real diamonds for six bucks. Give it here. Where's the other?"

"Why tape fakes to the top of the drawer?"

"Well," her eyes drifted away from his, "got no jewelry box, and that keeps 'em together." Smiling, she reached again. "Want to see how they look on me?"

"Why haven't you shown me before?"

"Gonna do that right now." She bounced her open hand.

Felt like she was lying, but if she was, he'd never trip her up. Only one way to learn the truth. "Know what?" He lifted his jeans from the floor and slipped the earrings into a front pocket.

"Gimme those," she said, rushing at him.

He nudged her away and stepped into the pants. "You may have come across a real treasure here. I'm gonna get these appraised."

"I'll do it." She yanked at the hand he'd kept in his pocket.

"Hang on," he said, swiping her hand away, "you're busy, and I'm not." He headed for the dresser. "Back before you know it."

"Okay," she called after him. "They're real."

Fists at his side, he started back to her. "Where'd you really get 'em?"

She glanced at his balled up hands and raised her chin. "First you cheat on me. Now what? Gonna beat me up?"

"Desiree," he said, stopping far enough away she'd know she was safe, "answer my questions, the way I ask them, or you and me are done." Her nod turned down his anger a bit. "Good. Now, where'd you get them?"

"Volker's Jewelry, up here in Oconee."

"How much?"

She winced and tucked smaller. "Three thousand."

Lightheaded, he dropped his butt onto a cushioned bench at the foot of the bed.

"But I had a reason." She inched to the bench and sat on a corner. "See, the letter about the taxes came, and I could see we was cooked. Figured the charge card companies would find out and cancel—"

"Hold it. What charge cards?"

She picked at a button in the cushion. "I know we agreed, but a body can't function these days without a charge card or two, so I just, y'know, kept the ones I had before we was married."

Being home most days, he got the mail, and he opened every envelope. "How is it I never saw any bills?"

"They go to, um, my post office box." Her face bunched up like she was braced for an injection. "Same with the tax bills."

He stared at her, waiting for the swirl of words in his mind to link up. "Box?" was all that came out.

"At the post office. See, when I moved here from Spartanburg, I took a furnished room. Knew I'd never stay in that awful place, so I got me a box. Still got it."

"I want to see the bills. Now."

"Can't. I open them right there, mail a money order for the minimum, and throw everything out." She edged near enough to swirl a finger next to his thigh. "Charlie, it's okay." Her voice was low and soft, like soothing a frightened animal. "We can pay for 'em now, but if things worked out different, and we couldn't, they're pretty smart if you think about it. Wouldn't have to pay if we went bankrupt, and we'd have something good to hock."

Seemed like each day she lost more camouflage. "That's stealing, and you know it."

"If it is, whole damn country'd be locked up."

"Okay then. How about just plain wrong?"

She shut her eyes, tightened her fists so hard they shook. "Don't know how to make you understand. I am sick to *death* of being me."

"A home, a husband who loves you, and a job. What's wrong with that?"

Her sigh and shaking head gave him the bad answer. "Charlie, that blue dress? The one got me fired? Had that on for, I dunno, a minute maybe. Know how long I'm gonna remember? Forever. Same with them earrings." She held out her open hand. "Let me show you how good they look on me."

221

"Oh, man," he said, fitting a few puzzle pieces together. "When I got home a day early from Key West. The sexy underwear. Face all made up. That's why you were covering your ears. Who'd you see in that little mirror, a high-price hooker?"

Gazing past him, she shook her head slowly. "Can't really say. Every time I have 'em on, it's me, but not me. A better me. I love that me."

He could tell from the softening around her mouth and eyes she was reliving a mirror moment.

"Real diamonds, Charlie. Woman in real diamonds gives the orders. Not some loser having a bargain-table life." Her head fell back. Smile got a little bigger. "And so elegant. Even the way I smoke." A vee of fingers floated near her lips, wrist tilted just so. She let her eyelids droop shut. "Times I wore them with my black underwear, I'd pretend I was just back from a nice restaurant or something. Theater maybe. Changing for bed. Making him wait."

"Making who wait?" His stomach fluttered.

"Nobody," she said with a shrug. "Anybody. It's just pretend." Eyes still closed, she slid fingers down the skinny leg as far as her knee, crossed the good leg over it. Angling toward him, she blinked a few times and held out an open hand. "C'mon. Let me show you."

"They're going back."

"No." She lunged at him. "They'll be paid for over time. Most likely. No shame if they're paid for." Both her hands tried to pull out the hand he kept in his pocket. "Please. If you just let me show you."

"Stop." He twisted free of her, jumped to his feet, and backed out of reach. "You look fine right now, and I'm gonna like you even more when all this is a bad memory."

"Charlie," she said, begging arms stretched toward him, "please. We both done something bad. Let's forgive and move on. C'mon."

Took a stiff effort not to wrap his hands around her and shake her until she woke up. "Last time in my life I'm saying this. I didn't do anything. And now I'm gonna undo what you did."

Hands covering her eyes, she lowered her head and started rocking. "Not going backward. I'm not. Can't make me." Rocking speeded up. "Killing me!" she screamed into shaking hands. "Got no right. They're mine." Head shaking hard, she kept rocking. "It's here, fool. All of it. Open your damn eyes."

"Leave with me, Baby Girl. C'mon. Right now."

"Make me sick, Charlie." Fingertips rubbed her forehead. "Just dead. How can you not want anything?" She tucked tighter and smaller. "I mean *want*. The way I—" She froze, peeked up at him. "What about her?"

He couldn't find any meaning that let him answer.

Eyes drifting every which way, she took to rocking again. "I mean, you done her. I know you did." She shrugged, her busy glances not finding him anymore. "Be okay with it. Pretty sure. And I keep the earrings."

No mistaking what she meant anymore. "We're done." Palm pushing at her, he grabbed his shoes from next to the bed and headed for the dresser. Socks and sweatshirt in hand, he left her sitting on the bench, her eyes squeezed shut, both hands clapped over her mouth.

...stones can't be unthrown, and words can't be unsaid...

"Tell her, not me," he said to GranDelia as he rumbled down the front stairs. Marriages picked up dents over the years. He knew that. Theirs just hit a bridge abutment.

QUICK, HEAVY FOOT strikes on the staircase told Vivien that Charlie had just rushed down the front staircase. Still in a robe, she eased into the hall and stepped quietly to Desiree's door. Following a fingertip knock, she opened it a crack. "May I come in, dear?"

"Not a good time," Desiree said, her voice choked.

"You poor child," she said, entering anyway.

Wrapped in a towel and lying on the button-tufted bench, Desiree repositioned from fetal to sitting, hands brushing her cheeks. "Miss Vivien, please."

"I'm sending her away. I just wanted you to know."

Desiree slumped forward and sobbed into her hands.

The towel exposed enough for Vivien to discover the size difference in Desiree's legs. Nature's cruel slipup, plus whatever else was torturing the poor girl, brought Vivien close to tears as well. She crept to the bench and sat. One hand touched lightly on Desiree's shoulder and pulled until the she fell against her breasts. "Ssh," she said, closing the embrace and swaying gently. "It's alright, darling." She brushed her lips against Desiree's floral-scented hair, returned the tightening hug, and rested a cheek on her head. "It's alright."

CHAPTER THIRTY-EIGHT

FIVE HUNDRED DOLLARS was the most Charlie could get from the drive-thru ATM, but that would be more than enough to cover tomorrow's propane fill-up. While he counted through the stack of twenties, a beep from the cash machine drew his eye to a tongue of white paper flapping at him. He yanked it from the slot and stared at the bottom line for so long the car behind him tapped the horn.

Pulling around to the front of the bank, he parked and took a last look at the receipt. Didn't want to go in and raise a fuss just to find out he was reading it wrong.

Current balance $2,200.00.

His arithmetic came up with *$2,700.00.* They'd kept a hundred out of the original ten thousand, paid Greensboro sixty-seven hundred, and he just took five hundred. Either Desiree hit the account, or someone hacked into it. He wasn't sure which would be worse.

A short visit with an account rep inside the bank confirmed there'd been an ATM withdrawal yesterday at 1:14 pm. Desiree for sure.

Soon as he got back inside his truck, the day took on his mood by spitting down rain. Running away skipped across his mind, but Volker's Jewelry waited only three doors away. He patted the tiny bumps in his front pocket.

"Afternoon," a slim, white-haired man said as Charlie pushed open the front door. Dressed in shirt and tie, the man had a tiny telescope hanging from a string around neck. Had a terrific smile, too, an old friend smile. "Be right with you, sir," the jeweler said to someone who ducked in right behind Charlie. "Anything special I can help you find, young fella?"

"Could take a while," Charlie said. "Maybe this gentleman should go first." He pointed to the second man, who was standing with his back to them, stooped over a display counter.

"I'm in no hurry," the man said. Hands clasped behind his back, he side-stepped to another glass case.

"Bernie Volker." The jeweler offered Charlie an open hand.

"Charlie Woods." Hand shaking done with, he reached into his jeans for the earrings. They felt too dinky to be worth anything, or to be causing so much trouble. "Actually, sir."

"Bernie."

"Okay," he said, holding out the earrings in his palm. "Want to return these, Bernie."

"These look familiar," Bernie's eyes moved from the earrings to Charlie's face, "but you don't."

"My wife bought them. Last week some time."

Bernie checked over both of Charlie's shoulders. "Is she maybe in the car? I'm very good with faces."

"No, sir. Truth be told. She's not happy about me bringing them back."

"Oh, sorry to hear that. How about a receipt? Got that?"

Charlie slapped himself on the forehead. "Course not. Why would I do something sensible? I'll be back in a few minutes." As he turned to leave, a sign on the rear wall caught his eye.

NO CASH RETURNS.
STORE CREDIT ONLY.

"Is that right?" He pointed to the sign. "I don't get my three thousand back?"

Bernie shook his head. "I'm sorry."

"But that's not fair."

"Charlie, it is. Think about it. If I give people their money back, what happens? They buy on Friday, wear on Saturday, and return on Monday. Who can stay in business like that?"

Getting rid of those earrings felt important, like a luck changer. "Can't you make an exception? Just this once?"

"I'm sorry."

"You must buy stuff. How about buying them from me?"

Bernie wrinkled his nose. "You come back with the receipt, and we can talk. But I'll tell you right now, you won't be happy."

Charlie slipped the earrings into his pocket. "Sorry to bother you."

"Wish I could help, but I'm sure you understand." Bernie pointed to the door. "I'll walk you out."

As they headed for the exit, the man who'd been waiting pulled the door open and left without turning or holding it for Charlie.

"New York manners," Bernie said. "Thirty-two years I'm out of there, and if I never see it again, hooray. My sister wants to see me? She can come here. Have a terrific day."

Behind the wheel of the pickup, Charlie pressed both hands flat on his head to keep it from exploding.

CHAPTER THIRTY-NINE

VIVIEN HAD SPENT the better part of nap time sitting by her window or pacing, weighing pros and cons, but her choice was clear. Tensions between her daughter and Desiree would only escalate, and risking Desiree held far more peril than inviting Lauren to depart. Bathed and dressed for tea, she glanced in the full-length mirror. "Helmet on, old girl," she said to the reflection before heading to Lauren's room. She knocked twice and entered without waiting for a response.

Parked in the cushioned bay window, clad in a snug turtleneck and jeans, Lauren glanced up from her hand-held computer. "One second, Mother ... Texting a friend. She's on *The Real Housewives of Atlanta*. Blond, of course. Huge boobs. Lips were a mistake. Tiffany, if you ever watch it."

"No hurry, darling," she said, easing onto the chair by the bed, more nervous than she expected.

Lauren closed the cover and tossed the device onto a cushion. "Not something *I'd* put in writing if I wanted to stay married." She stood, spread her feet, and stretched. "So, what's up?"

"Actually, darling, your welcome."

"I'm welcome for what," she said, elbows out, twisting side to side.

"I want you to leave. Now."

Lauren's arms dropped to her side. Inside the scarf, her eyes grew large. "What is this? I said I was sorry."

"You don't need to be here. I see that now. If not your apartment, call Ward or Sophia."

"Mother, what's going on? I mean really." She pointed to Desiree's room. "Is this about that whack job?"

Vivian would never divulge Desiree's jealousy. Years of observing Lauren had taught that she could stab and twist the slightest advantage into gaping cruelty. "Turmoil finds you, darling. I won't live in chaos. I can't." She stood. "Phone a car service and go. Whatever you don't get packed I'll have sent tomorrow."

"Ward is right," Lauren said. "You're fucking nuts."

"You will not speak that way." Marshall would have slapped the foul-mouthed tramp to the floor.

"And, you know where else he's right?" Lauren sashayed closer. "Charlie and his little cripple. They're going to take you big time."

Each syllable out of her daughter's mouth reinforced the rightness of her decision. "How sad for you, dear. Industry, generosity, affection. You see them as tactics. I've failed you, and I'm sorry."

"Good God, and I'm the drama queen." Lauren opened the door to the room's walk-in closet. "Go away. I have to pack. Or do you want to stay and watch so I don't steal anything?"

"Don't make this more than it is," she said as Lauren rolled an empty suitcase into the room and flung it onto the bed. "You're not being cast out. Well, actually you are, but it's not a disowning. I love you dearly, just not in the same orbit. Try to understand."

"If Justin hurts me again, it's on your head." Hand covering her nose, Lauren disappeared into the bathroom.

"*Gawd*, spare me." Vivien headed for the kitchen and the promise of a pleasant afternoon tea.

Clinks of dishes and the scent of cinnamon greeted her when the elevator doors opened on the ground floor. "That's new," she said to Desiree, trying to sound blasé after their tender encounter earlier. "Toast or muffins?"

"Just about to call you. They're cookies. Right out of the oven. Don't they smell awesome?" Her tone was breezy, but the lack of eye contact betrayed a shared awkwardness. "They'll be cool by the time I tote everything inside." She picked up a silver tray holding a plate of cookies and china tea service. Steam curled from the spout of the pot. "Solarium?"

"After you." Following behind, she marveled at Desiree's ability to steady the tray. Long-short strides rocked her shoulders without once rattling the cups on the saucers. Oddly touching. Almost heroic.

Desiree arranged two settings on the bistro table by the glass wall. "Raining," she said, pouring the teas while she waited for Vivien to catch up, "but even that's pretty from here. Cozy-like." After she'd settled Vivien in her seat, Desiree sat and spread a napkin on her lap. Her gaze stayed down. "Miss Vivien, want to tell you something, and please let me finish before saying anything." She glanced up.

"About upstairs?"

Nodding, Desiree dropped her eyes again. "Being so kind to me and everything, hard to tell you how much that meant. Was like I was little again, and my momma—God keep her—had hold of me during a bad patch. Same words even. 'It's alright.' Recalled her so clear my heart broke even more, but in a good way, if that makes any sense. See, being held like that, and those two words, got me through a pretty rough childhood." Twisting a corner of the napkin, Desiree peeked up. "Last thing I want is to make things strange 'tween us, but what I really want to say is, I love you." She shrugged, her attention remaining on the napkin. "And that's it."

Memories hurtled back years without Vivien locating anyone who'd professed affection. She tingled from the refreshed pleasure of it. "That is so sweet, darling."

"Besides my folks and Charlie, I never said that to another soul."

"We have formed a special bond. I feel it, too. You've become the best part of my day." Since adolescence, she'd found it impossible to parrot back anyone's *I love you*, even Marshall's. The words couldn't be delivered without the vacuity of a congregation response. And these days, the declaration meant even less. Every parting or phone conversation ended with a robotic, "love you." Manufactured, obligatory sentimentality. Nauseating. She raised a cup to her beaming maid. "Cheers."

"Cheers." Desiree winced from the steamy sip and set the cup down. "Can I ask you something?"

"Not 'can I', darling. It's may I. And of course you may."

"Do all husbands cheat?"

"Oh dear." A no-man's-land topic. Were Vivien not curious if Charlie had precipitated the upstairs spat by confessing to a tryst with Lauren, the matter would have gone no farther. "Meaning your own?"

"The other day," Desiree said, her finger ticking back and forth between them, "we promised to be honest with one another. That still on?"

"Absolutely."

Desiree's thumb bobbed at the ceiling. "She spent the night in my Charlie's room. Y'all know that?"

Uneasy about possibly fanning the flames, Vivien fulfilled her promise nonetheless and nodded. "Charlie assured me nothing happened, and before you ask why I never said anything, it's not my place to doubt him or create gossip."

"He gimme the same story, but how's that possible? Don't like saying nothing against your kin, but that woman's got a 'Who's next?' sign on her. And my Charlie," she said, head shaking, eyes wide and blinking, "that boy's plenty healthy, I promise you."

"Bit of advice, darling. Believe him. Your only other option is torment. Utterly pointless."

Slapping flip-flops approached. "Ah, finally." Lauren sauntered into the solarium. "Looking all over hell for you. Where's Charlie? I need him to carry my bag." She'd changed into a white, bare-midriff turtleneck and low-riding, Carolina blue sweat pants. With her head and face veiled in white, her appearance evoked a harem dancer.

"I'm afraid he's out," Vivien said, "You'll just have to manage." She couldn't decide if Desiree shrinking into the chair signified withdrawal or coiled aggression.

"I'm not supposed to lift anything over ten pounds." Lauren pointed to Desiree. "Have her do it."

"Laurie, the suitcase has a handle and wheels. You won't die."

"It's on the bed, and it's heavy. You," she said, her chin bobbing toward Desiree, "when does he get back?"

Brow wrinkled, Desiree glanced from Vivien, to Lauren, and back to Vivien.

"Having trouble with English, sweetie? When. Does. Charlie. Get. Back?"

"Don't know," Desiree said. "And I'd appreciate it if you didn't talk to me like that."

"Well, listen to you." Lauren said, rocking her hips and shoulders. "Snuggled yourself in all nice and comfortable, haven't you? And I know it was you, toots. I'm out of here because of you."

"Didn't do nothing," Desiree said, tilting away.

Lauren squirmed as she ran fondling hands over herself. "Oh God. Oh Charlie. Love me, Charlie? Oh God. Harder, Charlie. Har—"

"Laurie!" Ridicule for the passion of a wife for her husband. Even if the blow was intended for Desiree, she felt the slam, as well.

"How pathetic, Mother. As if that performance would get me out of his mind."

"I won't tell you again."

Lauren shoved her palm at Vivien and stepped closer to Desiree. "Honey, he won't ever forget me."

"You do not shush me in my home." Vivien nudged her chair back from the table.

Desiree folded her arms and raised her chin toward Lauren. "Already know about you parading naked in his room."

"And you think that was it?" Lauren bent nearer. "Ask him how he liked the taste of my tongue?" She twisted her hips and slapped her backside. "And I wouldn't dust this for prints." Fingers caressed high inside her thighs. "Have him describe what he found here."

"Be quiet!" Vivien struggled to her feet, horrified by her impotence, both in the moment and what it foretold about her future.

Eyes still on Desiree, Lauren folded her arms. "I am *not* lifting that suitcase."

"Then have the driver do it when he comes. Did you even phone?"

"He said ten minutes." Lauren stabbed a finger at Desiree. "Nothing better happen to me, you fucking skank."

"Leave this house!"

"It's alright, Miss Vivien." Desiree lounged back in her chair. "I'm used to people calling me names. Her included. All the things she's called me the last few days?" She shrugged. "'Fucking skank' ain't nothin'."

"Oh, Ward is right," Lauren said, nodding and pointing as she shuffled backward out of the solarium. "Right about both of you."

Vivien relaxed a bit more with every inch of the retreat. "Bravo," she said after the hallway went quiet. Still applauding lightly, she turned to find Desiree staring into the rain, tears dripping to her jaw. "Oh, darling don't. Why on earth would you believe her?"

"Knew I could never keep him," Desiree said as if speaking to herself. "Shouldn't have let him go to Key West."

"Poppycock. That trip was a gift from heaven. You wouldn't be here otherwise." She could tell from Desiree's faraway stare those words of encouragement were having the impact of elevator music.

Desiree rubbed her skinny thigh. "Y'know, I had me pretty much a sidelines life. Lots of time to watch people. Most aren't good. Aren't bad. Just sorta tumble every way a breeze sends 'em. But Charlie," she said, head shaking. "Man like Charlie loves a person, says something special about 'em. Something maybe even they can't see. But if he's hollow too, nothing means nothing. Not one damn thing in this life." Immobile as a wax figure, she stared out into the rain.

Vivien sat and leaned closer. "Darling, listen ... Desiree!" Her slap to the table captured big-eyed attention. "Let me explain Laurie to you. You see, there are those in this world who see a magnificent stained glass window and are thrilled by the beauty. But others, the thrill for them would be to smash it. Laurie's always been the latter. No doubt a psychiatrist would lay that at my feet. Based on my stable of failures, that's probably right, but at this point, I no longer care. My point is, trust Charlie over Lauren, darling, and above all, be thankful you have no children, at least none like mine."

"Baby coulda saved us." New tears dropped.

"You have to stop this. Nothing needs saving."

"Baby makes you need each other more."

Children had been nothing but wedges between her and Marshall. All their happiest times were spent on childless holidays and business boondoggles. "Romantic flapdoodle."

"Then how come you had so many?"

She'd asked herself that question so often, the answer no longer required reflection. "Aside from careless passion, the simple answer is pregnancy. I absolutely adored being pregnant. Rather mystical, really. The link-to-all-existence sort of thing, I suppose. And of course, being lavished with attention never hurt. Best, though, was the delightful suspense. Months to wonder, and worry, and hope. But then a child arrived."

"You're just saying that."

"Poor Devon paid the heaviest price." She sipped tea, aghast at the blurted revelation. "I do go on sometimes."

"Charlie's momma was a heroin addict. That's what killed her. He ever tell you that?"

The spotlight moving elsewhere was a relief. "He told me his grandmother raised him, but not why. How awful."

"Must've been a little like you. His momma, that is."

"Excuse me?"

"Way I heard it, soon as she found out about being pregnant, she cleaned herself up. No hospital or nothing. Just her and her mother, going through hell in the same dump me and him got right now. Two months after Charlie? Dead from an overdose."

"And somehow, dear, you see similarity?"

Doorbell chimes announced the arrival of Lauren's car service.

"Suppose I should get that." Desiree stood and tapped a napkin to her eyes and nose. "Okay if I do this in a bit?" she said, swirling a finger at the tea setup. "Got some private thinking to do."

"Certainly. But my advice is to let things alone. Sleep on it. Tomorrow you'll wake to a house with no Laurie. A whole new beginning."

Only Desiree's lips smiled. "Miss Vivien, want to thank you. This helped so much." She pointed toward the front door. "Better go."

"One second. That parallel you suggested between me and Charlie's mother. I don't quite see it."

"It's like you said. Being a mother, and being a momma. Not the same thing." She wobbled toward the front door.

A barb might still have been imbedded in there somewhere, but not enough to douse the rekindled glow of being loved.

WARD HAD ALMOST reached his home in Buckhead when the hands-free in his Mercedes rang. Dash display showed *Unknown*. Usually a marketer who merited three seconds or less. He pushed the answer button on the steering wheel, finger poised for a quick disconnect. "Dr. Granville speaking."

"Doctor, this is Tobias Gray. Gardner Culpepper hired me for your situation."

"The private detective?"

"I prefer investigator, but yes. Anyway, I followed the male subject to a Lake Oconee jewelry store this afternoon, and I may have some interesting news for you."

CHAPTER FORTY

SOMETHING ELSE must have blown up while Charlie was gone. As he pulled his pickup into Miss Vivien's driveway, a yellow cab passed on the way out. The veiled head and sunglasses in the back seat had to be Lauren.

Inside the house, he dropped his truck keys on the kitchen counter and made for the foyer, eyes and ears on the hunt for Desiree. Glancing into the great room, he spotted Miss Vivien stepping cautiously across the floor, hand at the ready to latch onto whatever came within reach.

"Ah, you're back." She lowered onto a nearby sofa and patted the cushion next to her.

"Was that Lauren I saw leaving?"

"She's decided to convalesce at home." Miss Vivien folded her hands in her lap. "Charlie, I think you should know, Laurie refuted your version of the night you spent together, in rather sordid detail and in front of poor Desiree, I'm afraid."

"She upstairs?"

"Have you been lying?"

"Told you once," he said, heading for the foyer, "I'm done talking about that." Careful not to let heavy feet announce his approach, he climbed the front staircase. Aware of noises coming from Lauren's room, he eased into their bedroom and spotted Desiree's purse on a desk chair. Inside the pocketbook, he had to flip a small Walgreen's bag out of the way each time he poked around in a new section. No gun, and another happy discovery, four hundred eighty-seven dollars tucked inside a zippered side pocket.

He stuffed the cash back and was about to snap the purse closed, but the pharmacy bag had him curious. Spreading the twisted paper open, he read the label on a small bottle. *Ipecac Syrup*. Never heard of it, but a quick check of the label said it was to induce vomiting. One more thing to ask her about. He took off his shoes and waited on the bed for her to finish whatever she was doing in Lauren's old room.

"Oh." She paused in the doorway when their eyes met. Stepping inside, she clicked the door shut and leaned against it. Her head bobbed toward Lauren's room. "That was me in there, case you heard something. She's gone. Permanent."

"So," he said, "you been to the bank. Was I ever gonna know?"

"I ain't the one with secrets, sugar." She folded her arms. "Told you the propane was coming C.O.D. The 'C' stands for 'cash'. Thought even you'd know that."

Feeling like a jackass didn't mean he had to sit for being called one. "I came back to talk. Don't want to do that? Tell me now. I'm done fighting."

"Just tell me the truth. Don't have to be a fight."

Hands raised in surrender, he dropped his feet to the floor, stepped into his shoes, and stood.

The house phone rang.

"I should get that," Desiree said. As she opened the door, the third ring ended short, like someone answered or the caller hung up. She waited a bit more and eased the door closed again. Nervous eyes searched his face. "Going to her?"

"God almighty." He sat on the bed and flopped onto his back. "Don't even know where to start with you anymore," he said, hands covering his face. In the dark quiet he heard the hum of the elevator, Miss Vivien's slow steps in the hallway, and a knock on their door.

He sat up and glanced at Desiree, still staring at him. "C'mon in," he called toward the door.

Miss Vivien pushed it open, but stayed in the hallway. "Charlie, I want to see the earrings you tried to sell this afternoon."

Standing slowly, he fished the diamonds from his front pocket and walked them to her. "How the heck do you know about that?"

"Never you mind." She reached into the room and picked one from his hand. After a brief, squinting examination, she dropped the earring back into his palm. "He's an idiot."

"What's going on?" Charlie said.

"Omigod," Desiree said, hand clapped over her mouth. "You thought those are yours?"

"Not me, darling. That nettlesome son of mine. Seems Ward has an investigator trailing you." She pointed to Desiree. "Apparently, the man linked your shoplifting arrests with the diamonds."

"Your what?" he said to Desiree.

"Oops." Miss Vivien pressed fingertips to her lips.

Desiree's face scrunched tight. "It's nothing, sugar. So long ago." She lowered her head and peeked at him. "Still, probably should've told you."

He wondered how much else he didn't know. "Arrests don't matter? And more than one?"

Her eyes flicked between him and Miss Vivien's blank expression. "About, I dunno, a lot of years back, me and a friend thought it would be a kick to swipe some clothes from Dillard's. Course, we got caught. When nothing happened to us, we did it again. Stupid, I know. Got community service for the second one. Scared me off that stunt for good."

Hell it did! he wanted to scream at her.

"Well, children are prone to mischief," Miss Vivien said. "And those earrings certainly are not mine. Ward needs to mind his own business. Tomorrow, I'll see if my lawyers can stop him."

"Miss Vivien," Charlie said, "I don't mean to be rude." He started to walk the door shut. "But we're still kinda sorting some things through here."

Nose crinkled, she wiggled her fingers in goodbye. "Of course. See you at dinner. Bath time."

Hand still on the knob, forehead resting against cool white paint, he waited for the clunk of Miss Vivien's door before facing

Desiree. "Now and forever, Baby Girl," he said as calmly as he could. "I don't say what I don't mean."

Eyes big and shiny, she limped toward him, arms open.

He bent and wrapped her slight body against him. "Past is past."

"I forgive you, too," she said.

Felt like snapping her neck, but he kissed her hair instead. Someone had to be the first to lay down their weapons.

CHAPTER FORTY-ONE

"SISTER DEAR," Ward shouted at the dashboard when Laurie answered his call, "we got 'em." Grinning, he banged a fist on the steering wheel. "The morons stole some of Mother's jewelry and tried to sell it. I'm on my way there now to throw them out."

"Wow. When was this?"

"Today. I phoned Mother right away so she could steer clear of them until I get there."

"How'd you get that three-legged Chihuahua to put the call through?"

"For some reason Mother answered. And Laurie, same advice for you. Don't let on to either of them. Not until I get there."

"Ward, I'm home. Crazy old witch gave me the heave-ho."

He didn't need Lauren inciting unrest any longer, but her eviction did whet his curiosity. "Was it because of anything, shall we say, indelicate with that idiot chauffeur?" A pornographic slideshow cascaded across his mind.

"Pure as new snow, brother dear. And, Ward, I should have listened to you. They've snookered Mother but good. That little gimp for sure."

"Details, sister dear."

Lauren laughed. "The bastards! They're killing her with kindness. It's so hard to watch."

"Well, they're still done. I am a little disappointed you won't be there to see them go down. By the way, how are you?"

"Pain's not bad anymore. Now I'm just scared. Justin's still out there somewhere."

"Cops are useless. Do you keep a gun?"

"Oh, I feel *sooo* much better now."

"Just a thought. Alright, call you afterward."

Driving through Security at Reynold's Plantation, he considered having them come along, but advancing behind a phalanx of geriatric rent-a-cops would look weenie. If the private detective's suspicions proved correct, and he had to enlist Lake Oconee's real police, that would be another matter entirely. He parked under his mother's portico, exited the Mercedes, and waited an unnerving amount of time for Desiree to answer the bell.

"Well I'll be." She stayed between him and the foyer. "You allowed to be here?"

"Let me by, or I call the police."

"If you want your momma," she said, smiling and backing away, "she's helping me make the dinner."

Approaching the kitchen, he wondered who was working for whom. His mother stood at the sink, rinsing greens. "Mother, what are you doing?"

She flinched and turned wide eyes to him. "Why on earth are you here?"

"That thing I told you about on the phone?" He flicked his earlobe. "Remember?"

"Ah." She leaned toward the breakfast table where Charlie was watching TV. "Charlie, Desiree, over here, darlings."

Took a second for "darlings" to register. His mother scattered "dears" without intending affection, and sometimes as the exclamation point on a skewering, but never "darling." He kept one eye on Charlie's approach as his mother dried her hands and smiled. More like a triumphant smirk.

"Gather, my chicks," she said, rolling her arms to all present. "Ward has something to say to you both."

Pinned between the sink and the center island, with the enemy tightening its circle, Ward swallowed away some dryness. "You two have five minutes to get out," he said, as calmly as he could.

"No," his mother said, finger raised, "that's not it, dear. You're going to apologize."

"What?" Without question, the woman had lost her mind.

She pushed her open hand at his face. "For harassing them with private detectives, who then falsely accuse them of stealing."

"Mother, I told you I'd take care of this. What's wrong with you?" If these cons discovered they'd been found out, they could have silenced her and been long gone, but he wasn't about to repeat that now, possibly even plant a dangerous seed.

Arms folded, his mother glanced at Desiree and Charlie. "We're waiting."

"How do you know they didn't do it?" Ward said.

"I saw the earrings," she said. "They're not mine." Her gaze drifted to the ceiling. "Still waiting," she sing-songed.

"Maybe they're not yours, but that doesn't mean they're not stolen. What are dirtbags like them doing with diamonds?"

"Hey!" Charlie pointed at him from the edge of the island.

The only fearless response Ward could think of was to point back. "He told the jeweler they're worth thousands. How'd they ever afford that? And they're working, so why would he want to sell them?" His mother's dancing eyes told him he'd given her food for thought.

"That," she said after a brief pause, "is none of my business." She tilted toward him. "Nor yours. Apologize or leave. In fact, apologize *and* leave. Oh, and call off the hounds or we're suing you."

"We?" These two chiggers had set themselves deeper than he imagined.

"Obstinate as always." She faced the sink again and turned the water back on. "You're interrupting our dinner. Drive carefully."

Satisfied faces on the hired help infuriated him. "He has a receipt, Mother. He told the jeweler that. Have him produce it, and I'll go."

"Charlie?" his mother said with a shrug.

Charlie shook his head slowly.

"Good for you, sugar." Desiree twitched her nose at Charlie and smiled.

"Well," his mother said, "there you have it. Goodnight." She resumed rinsing the vegetable.

Charlie's refusal strengthened Ward's suspicions. "Only a thief or a liar would refuse."

"That's it." Jaw set, Charlie started toward him.

Adrenaline buzzed Ward's head and neck, stood his body hair on end. There'd be no surprising Charlie this time. Had to get to open space. His speed needed maneuvering room. He skated backward toward the expansive foyer. "Don't make me," he said, stabbing a finger at Charlie. "You know I can."

Hands and feet expertly positioned, Charlie tracked him. Silent. Stone faced.

Lethal chess. Periodontist against experienced killer. What speed advantage? Madness. Limbs taut and trembling, Ward stood frozen in the middle of the foyer, the arena. Warmth, then chill, spread down his thigh.

Charlie stopped his advance and dropped his hands. "G'won, git." He jabbed a thumb over his shoulder at the women's approaching footsteps. "They don't have to know."

Tears had already started down Ward's face by the time he slammed the front door. Humiliation swelled in his throat on the sprint to the car. Puffs and yelps burst through his lips as he fumbled the seatbelt. Shaky fingers started the engine. Safely out of the driveway, he pulled to a curb, slammed the lever to Park, and screamed so loud his ears rang even after the rage ebbed. Spent, he rubbed the damp blotch in his slacks. Mother still needed saving, but destruction of those rednecks had risen to equal importance.

CHAPTER FORTY-TWO

NEITHER WOMAN acted the way Charlie expected after Ward sped off. He figured Desiree would be strutting like a boxer after a knockout, but Miss Vivien was the one wired up. Soon as she'd reached the foyer and saw him standing alone, she shook loose of Desiree's arm and tottered to him. Both hands on his cheeks, she pulled his head down for a humming smooch on the forehead. "The man of the house," she said, her pink face beaming up at him. "Yet again, I thank you."

Standing behind Miss Vivien, Desiree flashed him a canary-eating smile. "If y'all are still hungry after that ruckus," she said, "should be about ready."

"Charlie, darling?" Miss Vivien held out an elbow to him.

Assisting her to the dining room reminded him of a date. Every few steps she'd squeeze or pat his arm, tap her head against his shoulder. Kinda creepy, especially with Desiree adding an approving grin every time she'd turn to check their progress.

Dinner went pretty much the same. Miss Vivien and Desiree yammered between themselves like usual, but this evening they included him now and then, laying on uncomfortable compliments about him being handsome, or "sturdy," or some such. Made sure he had enough of this or that. Smiles for everyone and everything. The grins for each other were like they were in on something he wasn't. End of that meal came none too quick.

Stacking dishes at the table was a Miss Vivien no-no, so even three people at a meal meant a bunch of trips to the kitchen. "I got it, sugar," Desiree told him when he stood to help clear. "Stay and keep Miss Vivien company. Be right back with your tea," she said to Miss Vivien after taking her plate.

The door to the butler's pantry had barely swung shut when Miss Vivien leaned in his direction and patted the table. "I didn't want to alarm Desiree," she said in a hushed voice, "but I know Ward. He's wounded, not vanquished."

No surprise in that news. "Seen a few Marines like him. Smaller and skinnier they were—no offense—the meaner. Great in a fight, but no barrel of monkeys around camp."

"He can be quite single-minded. The only one of my children who ever stuck with anything." Fingers fluttering, she shook her head. "And of course that's not right. Luke's genius soars in so many directions he only appears flighty. I want you two to be friends once he's well."

Based on the little he'd heard about Luke, it'd be unlikely for that man to get well in eighty-one years, much less eighty-one days. "Unless Dr. Granville plans on coming back with a gun," Charlie said, "what can he do?"

"More lawyers and detectives, I suppose." Uneven footsteps drew Miss Vivien's eye to the butler's pantry door. She wrinkled her nose at him and tapped a finger to her lips.

"Awful quiet in here," Desiree said, pushing into the dining room. "If y'all were talking about how smart and pretty I am, just keep on going. I can take it."

"Oh, you were listening." Smiling, Miss Vivien wagged a finger at her. "Thought I'd broken you of that."

The women getting on so well should have pleased him, but during the spats he and the wife were getting into lately, he caught hints that Desiree's side of the affection had some play-acting in it. Like sizing up a stranger, he watched Desiree set a steamy tea in front of Miss Vivien and trail fingers across the old woman's shoulders on the way back to her chair.

"Okay if I get the rest after your tea?" Desiree sat without waiting for an answer. "Hip's been acting up." Her eyes found his and jumped away. "Got to thinking in the kitchen just now," she said.

"I'm glad about Dr. Granville coming here, making us air out some laundry, 'specially the earrings part. See, they're my second favorite thing in this world." She twisted more toward Miss Vivien. "Charlie, though, he acts like I'm trying be up-town and fancy. Y'know, too good to be a maid. But now," she reached an open hand to him, "we don't gotta hide 'em anymore." She crooked a finger. "Give 'em here, sugar. I want to show Miss Vivien how they look on me."

Pretty clever way to get her paws on those diamonds. "Think I'm just gonna hang on a bit longer," he said.

"Oh, for pity sake, Charlie," Miss Vivien said, "let her show me. They're lovely, and the perfect size for her features."

"Well, that may be," he said, "but we had us a time deciding to sell them. Don't want to pull that tooth a second time."

"Sugar, we don't gotta sell now. C'mon." She stretched her hand closer to him.

"None of my business, mind you," Miss Vivien said, "but why *are* you selling them? If you need money, just tell me how much."

"That a fact?" he said, flopping back in his chair. "Okay, we need sixty-seven hundred dollars."

"Charlie!" Desiree poked a finger at his face.

"Sixty-seven hundred," he said, leaning toward Miss Vivien, "so we can buy out our last two months here." Saying a plain truth for the first time in a while felt great, for about a second.

Miss Vivien's head sagged forward. Her glassy gaze dropped from his face to the tea. "I thought we were past that," she said, soft and sad.

"Charlie, why?" Desiree threw her napkin at him. She rushed to the side of Miss Vivien's chair and stooped to wrap her arms around the woman's shoulders. "We are past it. Way past. It's just, he gets mad at me about them earrings, for I don't know why. No reason to take it out on you." She rested her cheek on Miss Vivien's fine, silver hair and pulled the hug tighter. "Not going anywhere. Now or ever. Tell her, Charlie."

He stood, dug the earrings from his pocket, and set them on the table. "Don't know when I'll be back."

The instant Charlie disappeared through the swinging door, Vivien gripped at Desiree's waist and shook her. "Go after him."

"He's fine." Smiling, Desiree circled to the earrings side of the table and stood in front of the bits of sparkle. Her fingers hovered over them. "So beautiful." She pinched one from the table to examine it against the light of a candle. Easing the clasp off, she pulled on her earlobe and sighed when the post penetrated. Same for the other ear. "Well?" she said, presenting each in turn, a dreamy smile telegraphing she didn't need affirmation.

"Truly lovely, darling, but I think you should go after your husband." She only needed Desiree, but a marital schism could jeopardize everything. "I think I heard the garage door come down. At least phone him."

"Told you, he's fine. My husband, now and forever." She wobbled to a gilt-edged mirror behind a long server and exchanged a smile with the vision in the glass. "And when he does get home, that boy's gonna be plenty happy he gimme these back."

Desiree risking a rare find like Charlie smacked of reckless ingratitude, especially for a woman with physical disadvantages. "You know him better than I, but still."

"Miss Vivien," she said, continuing to admire her reflection, "be okay to take a bottle of wine from downstairs? Tonight feels like a celebration."

"*Gawd*, I'd forgotten about the cellar. Of course you may. I told you, if it's here, it's yours. None for me, though. You and Charlie enjoy it." She coughed into a fist. "And anything that might come afterward."

Still smiling, Desiree returned to the table and wrapped her in another hug. "You are just the kindest person I ever did know." She nuzzled a cheek against Vivien's temple. "Gonna take care of you forever."

To her astonishment, she clutched at Desiree, unable to hold back a trickle of tears.

CHARLIE SAT behind the wheel in his own driveway, engine idling, those damn earrings picking at him like they'd done the whole ride. Should have thrown them into Lake Oconee.

He killed the engine and made himself get out of the truck. Careful steps in the darkness carried him along the scattered squares of concrete they called a front walk. Weeds in the gaps brushed his ankles, making him twitch and slap at his cuffs. Wood stairs bellied under his weight. The front doorknob wobbled in the assembly when he stuck in the key. Insides of the house still stunk like old garbage.

Wandering around the cramped single-wide, hand over his nose, he had to admit Desiree was right about it being a dump. Made him angrier. Never was a dump until her. Except they'd had good times, too, before she took to stealing, and lying, and going back on promises. That's what he was smelling. Spoiled honor.

...let he who is without sin cast the first stone...

"Why's it just me all the time?" he shouted to the saggy ceiling in their bedroom. One good kick knocked the mattress off center on the box spring. He stomped to the window. Hands on the skinny sill, he rolled his forehead on the cool glass. Breath clouds grew and shrank on the pane, slower and smaller as the anger mostly left him.

Grabbing a corner of the mattress, he bounced it back to square on the box spring. From where he stood, Desiree's .38 slept not five feet away. At least he hoped so. There was that one afternoon she had the pickup, and she did come back with the mail, so he knew she'd been there. Down on one knee, he slid a hand underneath and fanned it side to side until his thumb bumped the barrel. Last time he confirmed the pistol was there, he took it as a sign she hadn't stopped thinking of their single-wide as home. This time he wondered if it meant she felt safe at Miss Vivien's, but not here anymore.

CHAPTER FORTY-THREE

CHARLIE ROLLED OUT of the driveway intending to go back to Reynolds Plantation. His pickup must not have agreed because it drove into Greensboro and parked in front of The Yesterday Café, a place he hadn't been since forever. Bad memories maybe. GranDelia, sick as she was, took him and Spuv there for dinner after graduation. Never really got out of bed again.

Locals sure loved it, at least tonight. He shook some hands on his way to a corner table. Lots of familiar faces saying, "Where you been?" or "When ya' coming back to the Fire Company?" or "No Desiree?" The Armisteads, and then the Hamptons, tried to get him to join them, but they would have asked about his life. All he wanted was a slab of buttermilk pie, a cup of black coffee, and a comfortable place to reconnect with what he loved about his town. He lingered through a second refill without feeling what he'd hoped.

"Saw you come in." The cashier smiled pretty at him as he approached the register to pay.

"Hey, Janelle." The two of them had kept company for a time after GranDelia died. Even spent a night or two with her. But he did that with a bunch of girls back then. Eighteen, a house of his own, and no one to answer to. He was one popular buck until the night GranDelia reminded him his life needed to mean more than beer and sex. Joined the Marines the very next morning.

"That'll be six-fifty-eight, baby." Janelle slapped his bill onto a spike. "So, still married?"

"Course," he said, handing her the money and forcing a grin. "What kind of question is that?" He wondered if Brandi or Spuv had been blabbing about Desiree being drunk and getting yanked out of Brandi's cousin car.

Janelle pulled a big plastic clip off her thick sandy hair. "Never see you by yourself, is all." Leaning her head backward, she gathered, twisted, and re-clipped her beautiful hair. "Nobody does."

He had no idea how women learned how to keep so much in place with one clip.

"Me and Carla," she said, wiggling a long, sparkly fingernail toward the street, "we was talking about that the other night at Bingo." Both hands went back to patting and shaping her hairdo. "Carla said the two of you are stuck together like a pair of them Chinese twins. So, where is what's-her-name tonight?"

"I believe you know it's Desiree, and she's working. I'll tell her you said hey."

She shrugged and turned away to fuss with a display rack of Tic-Tacs. "Don't be a stranger, honey," she said, soft and dangerous.

Waiting to back into light traffic, he thought about Janelle not liking Desiree and not caring if he knew. Old-times jealousy probably, but maybe she knew something he didn't, or saw something he was blind to. Maybe they all did. "Quit it," he said to his reflection in the rearview. Plain stupid to let doubts run loose. "Now and forever, son." He stabbed a finger at the mirror. "So get your sorry butt home."

But it wasn't home.

PAST 9:30 by the time he got back to Miss Vivien's. Before he'd even shut the inside door from the garage, Desiree appeared at the kitchen end of the hallway. Had on her long white robe, the one she always put on after a bath. Shouldn't have, but he let the robe remind him of Lauren Granville, and how different each woman looked without it.

She set a glass of red wine on a counter and held her arms open to him. "Startin' to get scared," she said, hugging him tight once he reached her, "but now here y'are." She rolled her cheek on his chest. Arms still hooked around his waist, she tipped back and wobbled for balance. "You got some catching up to do," she said, a big smile on her face. "Let go and I'll get another glass."

"Don't much care for wine, and I'd say you had enough for both of us."

Nose crinkled, she wriggled out of their hug and flipped a hand at him. "Not spoiling this for me, GranCharlie." She sipped the wine, set it down, and faced him. "Ain't said nothing about how I look." She pivoted her head and tapped behind each ear. "So?"

All made up like she was, she did look great, and he wouldn't admit it, but those damn earrings added something. Might have been nothing more than confidence, but something. Whatever, he was sorrier than ever for letting her have them. "Take 'em off and you go from pretty to beautiful."

"Wrong answer, sugar. Women know better, and the man who understands that?" Smiling, she nodded slowly. "Good things happen for that man." She pointed to the half empty bottle of red. "Sure I can't get you some? How about a beer?" She limped toward the fridge. "Don't want to celebrate alone."

"Got nothing to celebrate." He started for the foyer, but heard her uneven footsteps rushing behind him.

She latched onto his belt "Charlie, wait," she said, pulling his arm until he faced her. "Everything's good now. All good. Gonna see how good, I promise." Her pleading eyes roamed his face. "C'mon. Be happy with me."

"Okay. I'm happy. Know when I'm gonna be even happier?"

"Here we go." She cupped her hands over her ears. "Blah, blah, blah."

"Desiree, listen, dammit."

"Blah, blee, blah, blah," she said even louder, Shrinking away from his try for a grab, she stumbled toward her glass of wine. "Blah, blah, goddam stupid fuckin' blah!" Her fists slammed the countertop.

First f-bomb he ever heard from her. "Going upstairs," he said.

"Charlie, c'mon." She thumped the counter again, softer this time. "Talk to me. Just, y'know, talk."

"Alright." He leaned his hips against the center island and folded his arms. "Anything special?"

"Just, y'know, stuff. I dunno … married couple stuff." Her back stayed toward him. "Oh, while you was gone, know what me and Miss Vivien did?"

"How could I?"

She ran a finger under each eye. "Well, we put on sweaters and took a walk outside. Made it all the way to the pool and back. Her hanging onto my arm. Two of us jibber-jabbering about this and that. Me helping her on the steps, telling her how good she was doing."

Her stuffy voice told him she was crying.

"She asked could we do it again tomorrow. Daytime, so she could show me what flowers were gonna come up, and where. When I said we could, Charlie, that woman gimme the biggest smile." She wiped her cheeks again and took a sip of wine. "I know it's crazy, but being needed like that. Giving permission for a tiny nothing and seeing the happiness. Felt like a momma. Closest I'm ever comin'."

Like always, she got to him, made him ashamed he'd let Janelle drag a cloud over his deepest feelings. "Y'know," he said, "after getting done here, maybe we could check into adopting again." Mistake, and he knew it right off. They'd already been turned down, and things had only changed for the worse since then.

"Is that so?" she said. "You forgettin' how much …" Eyes big, jaw hanging, she turned slowly to him.

"Oh no," he said, reading her face. "No we are not."

"You heard her at dinner. Just tell her how much. Omigod." Hands walking along the counter, she scooted past the wine bottle and grabbed a glass from a cabinet. "Sure as hell got something to celebrate now, big boy."

"We could never pay her back."

The end of the pour splashed off the outside of his glass. "Oops.

Can't waste it." Long, slow licks swept droplets from the bowl and stem. She bounced her eyebrows. "You're next."

"We are *not* adding time here."

"Sugar, that subject's closed." She ran her tongue around her lips. "And I got a way better use for my head right now than ciphering."

Any other time, his pants would have been on the floor already, but not with her like this. Drunk. Earrings. Combination of both. Whatever the reason, he was dealing with a version of Desiree he could do without. On top of all that, he'd been boneheaded enough to bring up adoption. If he was lucky, come breakfast she wouldn't remember they even had this conversation. "I believe we'll leave all this for morning. G'night."

Still holding the wine glass, she jumped in front, blocking his way again. "For godsake, Charlie, you want to wait for everything. That's the old us. The us before here. Just stupid, 'specially for me. How much time you think I got?"

His stomach clenched. Except for being kinda drunk, she looked fine, but he'd learned from GranDelia's cancer the deadliest stuff always worked its evil in secret. "You trying to tell me something?"

She took his hand and pulled him toward the breakfast table. "Since I was little," she said, keeping hold of his hand after they sat, "I pretty much knew my life was going to be on the short side."

"Nobody can know that."

"Not true," she said, her head and finger sweeping slowly in opposite directions. "See, I think everybody's born with this, I dunno, death clock inside. More that's wrong with them at the start, quicker their time runs out."

"Desiree, you can't know that, and you sure as hell can't use it as an excuse."

"Sugar, when you're out there in the world, start paying attention. I mean, same as I done my whole life. Won't see any old cripples. I'm talking about the kind born that way, like me. And retarded people. See any of them get old? No, sir." She squeezed his hand. "Not complaining, really. Nature's way, is all." Her eyes took on a wet shine. "Charlie, there's my leg. And I can't have babies. Going through the change in my thirties. I know what's coming. What am I waiting for?" Took two tries to get her lips on the edge of her wine glass.

More talking wouldn't do any good tonight. "C'mon, let's get you to bed. How about I carry you? Would you like that?"

A quick nod sent a teardrop down her face. She finished what was in the glass and set it on the table. "May as well get mad now," she said, arms raised for the pickup. "Gonna ask her. I am. I mean, one question gets a baby? Well sir, that's it."

He scooped her from the chair. By the time they reached the front staircase, her head had dropped onto his shoulder.

"That woman loves me," she said, soft and drowsy. "Gonna get me a baby."

Thoughts tumbled during the slow climb. There was fear of a wider fight about staying at the mansion, plus going deeper into debt and all the chains that came with it. But a baby glowed underneath that mess, and he couldn't deny the wanting. The two of them, parents. Two lives not sliding toward a dead end anymore. A chance to add a person of honor to the world.

...nothing in this life is free...

"I know that," he said.

"Didn't say nothing," Desiree said. Snuggling closer, she scratched his neck with a diamond.

CHAPTER FORTY-FOUR

LAST NIGHT'S garden salad, plus the dessert of sliced pears and blueberries, proved to be the mistake Vivien feared. Arms shaky on the railings, she lowered into the bidet and gushed soothing water across her chafed bottom.

She wondered, as happened now with each episode, how much longer she could handle this unaided. The recurring parade of possibilities trooped through her mind. Would someone stand and watch, like walking a dog? Hold her hand or shoulders and make small talk until she'd finished? Discuss headlines as she turned the pages? Perhaps they'd put up a folding screen. Or fasten a seat belt. Give her a bell, and wait outside the door. Maybe some version of Lauren's baby monitor. And if she displeased whoever it was, would they do nothing? Let her flesh disintegrate in a soiled Depends for days?

These were questions for her doctors, were she willing to hear the answers. Aside from the icky nature of the topic, merely broaching the subject held the potential for medical concern, family consultations, and a shout-down of her objections.

"Well, not yet, old girl." She stood and patted dry with a bath towel. Today wasn't the day, but it was closer by one. Only the prospect of Desiree being her future attendant lifted the pall, and she'd continue the miraculous progress of that campaign in a few minutes, at breakfast.

The sight of Desiree at the kitchen sink, wearing blue jeans, red flannel shirt, and diamond earrings brought a smile that Vivien cleared with a manufactured cough.

"Mornin', Miss Vivien. Didn't hear the elevator. Sleep good?" Smiling with less than her usual wattage, Desiree shut off the water and hobbled toward her. "Tea water's ready. Let's get you to the table, and I'll bring a cup."

"I'm perfectly capable of maneuvering, you know," she said, pausing at the hallway opening, one hand braced against the wall.

A grimace waxed and waned on Desiree's face as she approached.

Vivien offered an elbow. "Are you assisting me, darling? Or vice versa. You appear ill."

"That obvious, huh? Thought good wine wasn't supposed to cause hangovers."

As they reached the center island, Charlie rose from his spot at the breakfast table. "Mornin'," he said, pulling out a chair for her.

"Such a dear. Thank you." She sat and smiled up at him, struck once again by his matinee idol looks. "And you, dear boy? Revenge of the grape as well?"

He shook his head. "The party had mostly wound down by the time I got back."

When neither he nor Desiree took his comment as a reason to eyeball the other, Vivien regarded the tiff at last night's dinner as minor and closed. "You're a lamb," she said as Desiree set a pill dispenser and glass of water in front of her, "and if you can bear the sight, darling, I'd adore a scrambled egg this morning. Wheat toast. Dry." Staying alert for subsurface hostility between the couple, she flipped open *Thursday* on the plastic pill holder.

Charlie paused a spoon over his corn flakes and bobbed his chin at the medications. "Eight every day. What do they do?"

A quick scan of the various sizes, shapes, and colors made her laugh. "Actually, I have no idea. Provide extravagant lifestyles for my doctors, I suppose."

"What would happen if you forgot, or mixed 'em up?"

"Oh, the usual," she said. "Green tongue. Scales. Spontaneous combustion."

"What?" He appeared sincerely alarmed.

"I'm joking, darling, and I've already told you. I have no idea." That partial truth sounded another custodial siren. One of the pills controlled blood pressure. She could greet death with a shrug, but not incapacity. Next refill, she'd have to bring Desiree to the pharmacy for a primer on the proper assembly of her daily doses.

"Wasn't so tough," Desiree said, placing the egg and toast in front of her. "Over easy? Now *that* might have been a problem." Smiling, she set her bowl of dry Cheerios on the table and sat.

The three of them ate in atypical silence, Charlie and Desiree appearing studious about avoiding eye contact with each other.

"Miss Vivien." Desiree twisted toward her in the chair.

Head steady, Charlie locked eyes onto his wife's face.

"What would you think if me and Charlie had a baby?"

Jaw muscles flexing, breaths whooshed through his nose.

For Vivien, the only positive aspect of the shocking question was that Charlie seemed to share her lack of enthusiasm. "But I thought you couldn't. Is this an announcement?"

Desiree glanced at Charlie and shrugged. "Depends on if you meant what you said."

"She wants money," Charlie said, glaring at his wife. "Desiree, just say it. You want someone to pay for another thing we can't." He stood and snatched up his dishes. "We didn't save, or plan, or nothing. But you want it, and by God that's all it takes. G'won, tell her." He stomped to the sink. His bowl and spoon clanged into the stainless steel basin.

"Charlie and debt," Desiree said to Vivien in a stage whisper. "Slow suicide in his mind."

"I'm confused," Vivien said. "Are you having a baby, or buying one?" Either outcome could compromise the role she wanted Desiree to play in the rest of her life.

"Can't buy no baby," Desiree said, crinkling her nose. "We want to adopt."

"Same thing," Charlie called over from behind the center island.

257

"Darling," Vivien said, beckoning to him, "we're not vegetable mongers, dear. Please join us over here if you have something to contribute." His sulky shuffle bought her a bit more thinking time. A baby might not be a catastrophe, particularly a girl. Quieter, less rambunctious, possibly enchanting in the early years. And with both parents on site, it wasn't as if Vivien would have any responsibilities. During the times she'd need Desiree's services, Charlie could tend to the child. Her new grandchild, in a fashion. A child who would know no other home, who'd rebel against leaving it. Cast in that light, she found herself warming to the prospect.

"What my husband means," Desiree said, glaring at him as he sat in his place, "is that agencies charge like ten thousand dollars, which we, y'know, don't got right now."

"But you must be close," she said. "I gave you ten thousand only a week ago."

Charlie shook his head. "Ten days."

"Most of that went to pay off stuff," Desiree said. "We only got what, sugar, two thousand left?"

"Little more." His attention hadn't left Desiree's face since he sat.

Vivien imagined her late husband scrutinizing the goings-on. Money for nothing would have set his teeth grinding. There had to be a quid pro quo that fortified her position. She swallowed another pill and stumbled through possibilities. "Ah, what if I bought your trailer?"

Charlie's "Absolutely not!" and Desiree's "That's perfect!" collided above the breakfast table.

Vivien flinched at the shouted reactions. "Well, there's' two counties heard from. Perhaps you should discuss it in private and get back to me."

"No need." Charlie folded his arms and fell back in the chair. "Not happening. Period."

"Sugar, please?" Desiree stretched an open hand to him. "Talking don't have to mean doing. But a baby. What's worth more than a baby? Sure as heck not that tool shed," she said, laughing.

Charlie's muscles tightened. Desiree had no business letting Miss Vivien know how she felt about their home, no matter how much of a wreck it was at the moment. "That house," he said, touching her fingers even though he didn't want to, "is where a baby would grow up. Nobody's giving us a baby if we got nowhere to live."

"Here." Desiree patted fast on the table. "Right here." She turned her face to Miss Vivien. "Isn't that what you meant? Family'd live here?"

"Naturally."

"Forever?" he said. "Look, we're getting a little nuts here. Still got eighty—"

"Sell it!" Desiree slammed her open hand on the table.

The outburst popped Vivien back in her chair.

"Sorry, Miss Vivien," Desiree said, head tipped down, hands curled into fists. "It's just, me and him already had this conversation. Too many times. Never going back there, and Einstein here should have figured that out by now."

"Wife belongs with her husband," he said, "and that's where I'm gonna be."

"That so?" Desiree said. "Well I say a husband belongs with his wife, and I'm staying here, for as long as Miss Vivien can stand me."

The two women exchanging little smiles made him feel like this whole thing had been rehearsed in secret.

"Charlie, I don't want to fight." Desiree reached for him again. "We just never been this close to a baby before. I want us to have it, to be a family. Why does it matter where?"

Vivien saw she needed to steer the discussion away from location, and back to baby. "Let's put our heads together," she said. "There must be some sort of compromise." Her fingers drummed the table. "What if? What if? What if? Ah, how about this?" She rested her folded hands on the table. "I lend you the money, with the trailer as collateral."

"Like a mortgage?" he said.

"I suppose it would be, yes. I give you a mortgage, with the proviso the proceeds can only be disbursed to an adoption agency."

"You can do that?" Desiree said, her eyes flicking between Vivien and Charlie.

"Lawyers will be the ones who say yes or no, but I don't see why not."

"Charlie?" Desiree pressed praying hands to her lips.

"You're a generous person," he said to Vivien, "and I thank you, but we couldn't pay it off. Be no different than selling." He shrugged at Desiree.

Vivien wiggled fingers at him. "Oh, pish. You'll work it off, same as now."

"Three more months?" he said. Last thing he wanted was a longer sentence, but the Lauren problem had mostly ended, and he'd sent Ward slinking off into the night. Other than Desiree falling deeper in love with a life they'd never have, he couldn't latch onto why he shouldn't jump at the chance. "I don't think I like that."

"Charlie," Desiree whispered, "a baby, and you still got the house. Three months for a baby. Not earrings, sugar. A baby."

A tiny silhouette slipped into his mind, and it was calling to him, along with a future he thought had passed them by. "Can I think on it?" he said.

"That means yes!" Desiree jumped from her chair. She stumbled around the table and locked a hug onto Miss Vivien.

The smiling old lady's arms flapped every which way as she tried to stay steady in her chair. She accepted Desiree's swarm of "thank you" kisses like a person tolerating dog licks. "You're choking me, darling."

Whatever crazy setup Desiree was dreaming right now didn't bother him. They'd bring the child up in Greensboro, in their own house, the way a kid needed it. Regular work, even if they both had to do it, would pay the bills, including a mortgage if it came to that. He stood for his turn to be thanked.

Desiree leapt, her arms and legs wrapping around him. "Knew you still loved me."

"Oh my." Smiling, Miss Vivien raised her eyebrows and turned away.

"Now and forever, Baby Girl." If all this happened, Desiree was in for a new nickname.

CHAPTER FORTY-FIVE

WARD SAT FORWARD in the desk chair of his home office, the room lit only by a computer screen. Clicking the mouse launched another video. One more enthusiastic nymphet acquiring a taste for semen. His nightly entertainment, especially on Philippa's three-times-a-week yoga evenings. He peeked at the clock in the screen's lower corner. 9:48. She'd be home any minute, and yoga nights nearly always ended with one of her *that-should-hold-you* handjobs.

Two years of this minimal satisfaction had turned his libido bi-polar. Near obsession for the unavailable, and teeth-gritting tolerance for anything Philippa. Videos helped bridge that widening chasm. They not only ginned up his interest, but provided substitute fantasies who weren't Lauren. Tonight, his dutiful wife would be the giggly redhead he'd already replayed four times.

A closing door announced Philippa's arrival. "Ward?" Keys clattered on a kitchen counter.

Laptop shut, he darted on tiptoe to the wall switch and flipped it on. "In here," he said, stepping into the great room. From there he could see the lighted kitchen and shadows of her movements. "You going up?" he said, ready to fall in line behind her on the stairs.

"Can you come in here?" Sounded like she'd spotted a silverfish or a leak.

He found her sitting at the breakfast table dressed in the usual warm-up suit, but still wearing her pink Braves cap.

"Take off your hat and stay awhile," he said.

"I'm not doing that." Eyes forward, she picked at her fingers. "Staying, that is."

"Pretty late for an errand. Want me to go?"

"That's funny," she said without a smile. "Actually, it's me. I'm going. I'm leaving. Tonight."

Stomach in his throat, he searched for sense in her words. "Pardon?"

"There's someone else, Ward. I'm sorry." Not a scintilla of remorse in tone or expression. She glanced at a wall clock and returned to staring beyond his shoulder.

He pictured her twitching on the floor, purple dent in her neck from a spin kick. Trembling, he slumped into a chair across from her. How anyone found her starved androgyny desirable was stunning in itself. "How could ... Who?"

"My yoga instructor, Marty."

"Well, I'll be godamned." He'd paid for two years of cheating.

"I'll take a few things now," she said. "While you're at the office tomorrow, I'll come for the rest." Her distant staring continued.

"Marty." He snorted and shook his head. "A name on a bowling shirt." Her pain from intercourse had begun right after starting those yoga classes. "Holy Christ. Did you stop fucking me because of him?"

"My life has changed. Leave it at that. We have to move on."

"No no no. After thirty years, I'm entitled to details. Is he getting my blowjobs?"

She winced and began to stand. "This is pointless."

"Sit down!"

Face tight, she lowered back onto the chair.

Whether fear or anger, at least he'd provoked an emotion. "Talk to me," he said, trying to sound composed. "Do you love him? Love both of us, but you're just so *fucking* confused?" He slammed a fist on the table.

"I should have left you a note." She stood and backed toward her purse on the counter.

"Phil," he said, both palms raised, "let's talk. I can fix this."

"You can't. You're negative energy. Always have been. Fortunately, Marty recognized my suffering, my yearning."

He burst out laughing. "And now I get clichés from a Hallmark special?"

"I nearly let you suck the last of my *prana*, my *chi*." She shook her head slowly, patted blindly on the counter until she located her purse. "But no more. There's a joyful path for me, and I'm taking it."

"What about Tyler? You think he's going to understand his mother taking off?"

"He's fine with it."

"Oh, is he now? And exactly when did he become 'fine with it'?" Clichés were piling up. He really was the last to know.

"I called him from Devon's funeral, and," her face ticked, "as I said, he understands completely."

"Get out of here before I kill you." He rose from the chair, arms and legs prepped for battle orders from his brain. "Wait. Who else knew before me?"

"You're right. I should go." Her hand found the car keys as she backed toward the door to the garage.

"I'm not going to hurt you," he said, enjoying the restlessness in her eyes. "C'mon, spill. Who else?" Small steps meandered in her direction. "My dear sister, Sophia?" He guessed Sophia because their last every-Sunday phone chat had been even more arduous than usual, too solicitous and syrupy.

Chin high, Philippa pulled back her shoulders. "I thought it important you have at least one caring relative after we separated."

"So considerate." He paced in front of her, one hand rubbing his forehead and smooth scalp. "Considerate to a fault."

"She thought you might move in with her after, you know, tonight."

No Marty was going to move into his house and screw his praying mantis wife, in his bed. He poked knuckles just below her sternum. Precise, not hard.

She jackknifed, thrust out her tongue. Arms curled around

her middle. Her keys and purse dropped to the floor. Eyes bulging, she collapsed to her knees and toppled onto her side.

Liberated by full-bloomed hatred, he dragged a kitchen chair next to her fetal writhing. "I know what you're thinking," he said as he sat.

Tears and saliva dripped down Philippa's contorted face.

"You think I'm going to be arrested for that." He crossed his legs. "Of course, you can try, but that love tap won't leave a mark. You say I did. I say I didn't."

Whimpers and coughs said her solar plexus was beginning to permit inhales. Slowly, her arms and legs repositioned until she'd risen to her hands and knees. Unblinking eyes trained on him, she swiped a warm-up sleeve across her face and gathered her purse and keys from the floor. She rose to her feet in slow motion, as if trying not to awaken the man staring back at her.

"One more thing," he said. "If you think you're breaking the pre-nup, wrong again. Sophia's ex found that out."

Blank face pointed his way, one hand rubbing her stomach, she shuffled backward down the hallway until she bumped into the door to the garage. Reaching behind, she turned the knob, disappeared into the dark, and closed the door with barely a sound.

Her departure rid the house of raw sewage. How could two people, he wondered, coexist in such mutual loathing for so long. He was almost sorry for Marty, and did regret punching Philippa. He should have thanked her. If she hadn't acted, the corral fence would have remained shut forever. Now he'd been released to experience life before it was too late. Modern women, like Lauren and the galaxy of Internet performers.

"Sayonara, you waste of oxygen." He strolled back to his laptop. If she could turn the page, so could he. Already primed for the evening, he typed "upscale escort services in Atlanta" in the search box and hit Enter.

CHAPTER FORTY-SIX

VIVIEN RARELY VISITED her home office. The resident aura of her late husband sapped her will to go on alone. She restricted usage of the room to financial or legal matters. This morning involved both.

Finished with the call to her financial manager, she lingered behind Marshall's modest desk, the one he'd used his entire working life. Most of his financial triumphs had been transacted across that very surface. Sitting there fed her sense of history, and appreciation, and loss. Within safe limits, she tilted the chair back and swiveled, swung her feet, rubbed hands on the worn leather arms and sniffed them for imagined traces of Old Spice. Shrunken as she'd become, she wouldn't have been surprised if a near-sighted observer mistook her for an awestruck daughter, rather than nostalgic spouse.

The chair also offered an ideal vantage to his collection of pictures. Wonderful pictures, walls of them chronicling their life together. Forty-six country stamps on her passports. Ocean liners, wild beasts, glaciers, motorcycles, beaches, the Great Wall and Eiffel Tower. Giddy smiles for the camera. Marshall, cigarette ever-present, embracing her in most shots. Unabashed affection, even after their hair had silvered. A truly great man and his treasured lady.

A ringing phone breached her peace.

"Miss Vivien?" Desiree hollered from somewhere distant. "Mind gettin' that? I'm kinda in the middle of—Thank you."

"Hello," she said. The receiver was still warm from the last call.

"Ah, Vivien, good morning. It's Bartram Winfield. I just got off the phone with David Miller about this mortgage idea of yours."

She detected disapproval. "Should I have spoken to you first, Bartram? I wasn't sure."

"David is, shall we say, *troubled* by your plan, as am I. You barely know these people, Vivien. Don't you think twenty thousand dollars in less than two weeks is peculiar? I'm sure if Ward found out he'd color it that way."

"I don't understand, Bartram. Mr. and Mrs. Woods are personally contracted for three months, and I'll have collateral for the rest. Where's my peril, dear?" She imagined a wink and nod from Marshall.

"It's the appearance. Ammunition for Ward. Be careful is all I'm saying. And if I may be so bold, why are you even considering this?"

"You've had a brilliant career, Bartram. What was your favorite part? I mean, when were you happiest?"

"I'm not following."

"Admit it, Bartram. It was the rising years, when you divined how to actually achieve your dream."

"I'll accept that. Your point?"

"I can help two very fine people take their first steps up the ladder. It excites me. What's wrong with that?" In the process, if she piggybacked along as a cherished obligation, all the better.

"Just doing my job, Vivien. So you're sure about this?"

"Absolutely, and I'm confident you'll protect me with the proper mumbo-jumbo, particularly the adoption agency restriction. Please have someone deliver the documents when they're ready."

"No reason you can't have them tomorrow, I suppose, if you're committed."

"Poor choice of words, old friend," she said with a laugh.

CHARLIE'S MORNING had started early. First he had to be in Greensboro by 9:00 AM for the C.O.D propane delivery, and then he had to swing by the pharmacy for another refill of Miss Vivien's prescriptions.

He pulled the BMW into the garage. On the way into the house, he made sure to keep hold of the Walgreen's bag that contained a small bottle. That would remind him. He tracked the hum of a vacuum cleaner until he found Desiree in the library.

His tap on her shoulder made her flinch. She smiled and clicked the OFF switch on the vacuum's chrome handle. "Scared me," she said. "What's up?"

"Sorry." He leaned in for a short kiss, but she slipped her hand onto the back of his head and held their lips together well beyond a peck. "Wow," he said. "What's that all about?"

"Just happy."

"Before you make me forget, been meaning to ask." He wiggled the pharmacy bag at her. "Found a bottle of something called ipecac syrup in your purse the other day. What'd you buy that for?"

"My purse?" Her gaze darted everywhere but his face. "You are a bad, bad boy," she said, mugging a scowl. "Don't be going in my purse. Now, g'won out of here. Let me finish up." She turned away and clicked the ON switch.

He reached around her, took the wand, and powered the machine off. "Why can't you ever answer a question?"

Eyes to the ceiling, she puffed out breaths and shifted foot to foot. "Guess it don't matter now," she said. "I wanted that bitch to get sick. She got sick, she'd have to leave. That's it." She flashed a flat smile and pointed to the vacuum. "You mind?"

"Mouth wired shut like that, barfing could've killed her."

Desiree folded her arms. "Oh, and wouldn't that have been too damn bad. Poor world, having to get by with one less whore."

"So, you did know it was dangerous." Lately, each peel off the Desiree onion showed a new bit of spoilage.

"Aw, worried about her, sugar?" She kissed the air at him.

He knew all his muscles had gone tight, but didn't realize he'd raised the chrome tube until Desiree covered her head and shrank away. Scared him enough that he tossed the wand onto a sofa and turned to walk out.

"I knew it." She hooked his elbow and stuck her face close to his. "Well, you can relax, lover boy. Ain't nothing gonna kill that she-devil. Those shakes I made her? Pee'd in the first two, and that didn't do nothing."

"You what?" Couldn't have heard that right.

"Just what I said."

"You did no such thing." He frowned just picturing the mechanics.

"Hell I didn't. When that didn't work, I got the ipecac, but she got herself kicked out first."

He pried her hand off his elbow. "I'm outta here. Last chance to come with me."

"Charlie, I wanted her gone, and she is." Her eyes searched his face. "And that's all in the past. Don't let's do this. I'm sorry. About everything. C'mon." She held open arms to him. "Be nice."

"Coming apart, Baby Girl." He made no move toward her.

"Not apart," she said, excitement lighting her face. "Together. It's all coming together." She limped toward him, arms still out. "Take the ride with me, sugar."

He caught her in a loose hug. "How do we fix you?"

"It's done. Look ahead, not back. Same as I'm doing. A baby, Charlie. That's what's gonna—Oh, oh," she said, breaking out of the hug and clapping, "Miss Vivien set it all rolling today. Heard her tell the lawyer to get the papers over here tomorrow." She jumped her arms around his neck and kissed his cheek. "It's happening, sugar. Got us some baby shopping to do."

He wasn't sure if she meant the actual baby or stuff for a baby, but it didn't matter. Things had to change before he'd be part of bringing an innocent life into this situation. "Want you to listen." He grabbed her wrists, pulled her hands to the front, and kissed her fingers. "I'm not doing this. Not now, and not here."

He kept hold of her hands but couldn't dodge every kick. "Desiree, stop! C'mon now, quit it."

Looking ready to spit in his face, she gave up. "Okay, I stopped. Let go." Hands freed, she picked up the vacuum wand. "I don't need your permission. Fact is, nowadays I don't even need a damn husband. And a fool at that." Turning away, she flipped on the noise and went back to housekeeping.

ONE SIDE TRIP to the Eatonton Walmart and Charlie had what he needed, at least for the short run. Everything he bought made sense except the nineteen dollar sleeping bag, a cheesy piece of goods he'd never use again after Desiree came home—if she came home. But nights were still pretty chilly, and the bag cost less than a set of bed linens.

A mile or so from home, he called Desiree's cell. She should know what was going on first. He'd call Miss Vivien after.

"What," she said as her hello.

He waited for more, but nothing came. "I'm on my way home. For good. That's it. Just wanted to make sure you understood."

"Free country."

Again, him staying quiet didn't loosen her tongue. "The way you been up there, Desiree, that's not you."

"Maybe the way I been down there, *that's* not me. Ever think of that?"

"Was for three years."

"How do I get through?" she said softly. "Charlie, you're killing us, and I don't know why. Got two simple choices. A beautiful, comfortable future, with a baby, or we go under slow and sad, disappear under that shabby shack you can't seem to give up. Ain't me that's gone crazy."

"Desiree, I keep trying to explain. We're short-timers. Whatever days God's got planned for Miss Vivien, ours run out with hers. Then what?"

"See, here's where I want to bounce a bullet off that concrete head of yours. Think I don't know that? Got me a whole plan going here, Charlie. That woman loves me. And I mean *loves* me. I listen for as long as she wants. Let her correct my talking. Help her see the faults in her kids. Course, her being sweet on you don't hurt neither."

"That's foolishness."

"Not blind, sugar. Just another Granville hoochie after my man."

Mad as he was, her laugh made him want to go back to Reynolds, work on things face to face. "So she loves you. That means she can't get sick? Or, God forbid, die?"

"Today's what, the fifth? Charlie, come May first, that old woman's gonna be begging to adopt us."

He twitched at the thought of being brother to Lauren and Ward. "And why would she do that?"

"Only way she's safe is if we're safe. Only way we're safe is to have power. Legal power, equal to the ones dogging her. She's gonna adopt us. You just wait."

"You best think through that one again. She starts down that road, and Ward's gonna have her declared nuts. Y'ain't even gonna get your eighty more days."

"Oh, it's gonna happen. She lives long enough, gonna be set for life."

"As what? Ticks on a hound? Not interested."

"As folks with possibilities, Charlie. And a new baby."

"Stop doing that!"

"Doin' what?"

"You know damn well. Dangling that poor baby like an apple to a mule." She never was like this before. Working angles on him, working Miss Vivien, like both were too stupid to see. "Not going back there, Desiree. Y'hear me?"

"Oh, I think you will. First, Miss Vivien still got time she's paid for. No chance you'd walk out on that."

"Not walking. Changing. Gonna call her soon as you and me are done. We'll work something out."

"Let me explain this so even you can grab it. She don't turn her phone on. Never. And who picks up the house phone? Me.

You wanna talk to her, you're gonna have to do it in person. Stop struggling, Charlie. Y'ain't getting out of either web. Now or forever." She hung up.

His pledge words, thrown back at him like a cup of acid. He slammed a fist into the roof of the truck. "Richer or poorer!" he screamed. "Good times and bad! Sickness and health!" Each set of words ended with another smash of his fist into the truck's ceiling. All his might went into the blast for, "Till death do us part!" Licking drops of blood from his torn skin, he glanced up and saw red smears across the tan fabric. One more mess to clean up.

He could chalk off "stupid" as angry talk, something she could apologize for later. Mocking the vows was different. He recalled saying and hearing them at the ceremony. Each one was an updraft, raising him out of a so-what life. Noble promises he was proud to make and humbled to receive. Dignity and support during rough patches. Generosity, given when needed most. Belonging. A special someone too precious to hurt or disappoint. But mostly he remembered being grateful that Providence, or pure dumb luck, had provided such an opportunity at all.

He thought she felt the same. Never saw a happier person than on her wedding day. Afterward, nothing went as perfect as it should have, but that was why the vows covered both sides of the coin. You're in, the promises said, so suck it up. But he could no longer recognize Desiree as the woman next to him at the altar.

...lie down with dogs, you get fleas...

Wasn't happy about GranDelia's choice of words, but he'd done all he could for Desiree without picking up an itch. Until something happened to open her eyes, he was stuck with the vow, but not her.

CHAPTER FORTY-SEVEN

SEATED ALONE at the breakfast table, Vivien felt like the lone guest at an off-season hotel. Outside her windows, puddles on the walkways popped with rain. Fog curtained off the lake and nearby hills, confining her universe to the silent house. She'd spent years beginning days this way, but today's solitude included a twinge of abandonment. First morning since she hired Desiree and Charlie that they hadn't been in the kitchen to greet and tend to her.

Through the mist and spindly hedges, she caught sight of motion down by the pool. Pulse quickening, she stood and shuffled to the glass.

From beneath the overhang of the pool house, puffs of smoke rose into the murk at intervals suggesting a cigarette.

"Charlie?" she called over her shoulder before remembering he wasn't there. At dinner last night, Desiree stumbled through an explanation about him feeling a cold coming on, possibly sleeping in Greensboro for a night or two so as not to be contagious.

Puffs from the pool house ceased. An umbrella opened and bobbed along the edge of the lower terrace. Its metronomic sway while ascending the steps told her who was approaching. She returned to her chair and waited.

Clip-clops wended through the solarium, great room, foyer, and hallway. In the kitchen, still sporting her diamond earrings, Desiree scrubbed her hands and face at the sink. Drying them with a dish towel, she turned and stutter-stepped at seeing Vivien seated at the breakfast table. "Hey, g'morning. Down early today. Don't even have the tea water on yet."

"Yes or no." Vivien tilted her head toward the outdoors. "Were you smoking out there?" She hoped folding her arms telegraphed that she already knew the answer.

"Was just the one," Desiree said toward the floor.

"I will not be liberal about this. My husband died because of that filthy habit, and I refuse to lose anyone else to it. Are we clear?"

"I'm sorry." Tears dripped down Desiree's cheeks when she nodded.

"Oh, don't." Vivien smiled and held her arms out, quite touched that Desiree could become so unhinged at displeasing her.

Desiree wiped her cheeks on her way to the waiting hug. "He's gone. What I told you about him coming down with something. Wasn't true. We had us a bad fight about the adoption."

"I am sorry, darling." She gripped lightly at Desiree's waist. "Was it the money? The mortgage? I must say, he did seem agitated by that."

"Some of that, but mostly here. This place. Can't seem to get him to understand. Me and him, and the adoption if we can pull it off, we belong here now, with you."

Erasing a baby from the script suited Vivien. "Perhaps you rushed things, darling. Crawl, walk, run as they say."

"I dunno." She dabbed a sleeve of her sweatshirt to each eye. "He's kinda got a stone head sometimes. Most times, in fact."

"Why don't we do this? You and I will know the financing is available when the time is right, but give poor Charlie a chance to digest at his pace." She patted Desiree's hips. "Go on, call him. I think once he hears you're reconsidering this whole adoption thing, he'll be here in two shakes of a lamb's tail."

Desiree laid her hands on top of Vivien's and caressed them. "Can I adopt you?" Tears filled her eyes again.

A little girl's question. Innocent, and foolish, and lovely. "It's 'may I', darling." She smiled and slipped her hands free.

PROPPED ON AN ELBOW in his king-sized bed, Ward stared at the pillow next to him, careful to maintain a respectful silence. He was in the presence of greatness. Adrianna, the second woman of his life. Surrounded by sweeps of auburn hair, plump lips slightly parted, her exquisite face glowed in spite of the rainy morning gloom.

Released after thirty hungry and uninitiated years, he ached to thank her, to bury his face between her perfect breasts and hug so tightly she couldn't doubt his sincerity. Aside from being pathetic, the gesture would have awakened her and officially ended the arrangement.

Three thousand for the night. A bargain compared to the banquet Adrianna spread before him in one miraculous, exhausting night, a night that relegated Philippa, that cadaver, to a cringing memory, replaced by skillful, obedient beauty. Pleasure whenever the whim struck. An emperor's life, with no need to behead the mistakes. Only two million to liquidate the pre-nup. Laughable. Quick arithmetic told him he had nearly seven hundred fantasy romps in the offing before reaching break-even.

Just thinking of the feasts to come jacked his pulse, fired his imagination. Adrianna again? Perhaps. She had been able to coax a third helping, despite the embarrassment of a lengthy failure to launch. This afternoon, he'd call his urologist for some chemical assistance. He was in the big leagues now, and all the top players juiced.

Adrianna. The name breezed through his mind like a sweep on harp strings. His inaugural foray into extreme pleasure began with the letter "A." Possibly a stroke of luck, but perhaps a sign he should debauch his way through the alphabet. At these prices, the escort service would surely accommodate. If so, lady "L" would require meticulous detail. And what woman's name began with "X," he wondered. Masks for that night might be a fun twist.

"Thank you, Philippa," he mouthed, unwilling to risk a whisper.

THE ONE little window in their bedroom never did let in much light, and rain this morning made the paneled room downright dismal. Perfect atmosphere if this turned out to be the start of life without Desiree.

Tough night. Aside from having trouble turning his brain off, Charlie forgot to buy a pillow to go with the sleeping bag. The few times he did drop off, the smallest rollover zapped him in the neck so bad it woke him. Took until nearly daybreak before he thought of using a rolled up bath towel. A Marine shouldn't have forgotten how to sleep, no matter where. One more part of his old life slipping away.

He kicked out of the scratchy cocoon, sat on the edge of the bed in his underwear, and sniffed. A whole afternoon and evening of Mr. Clean and Lysol had done the trick, mostly. Still caught a trace of rotten trash in the pine smell, but nothing like when he got there yesterday. Another can or two, sprayed smack onto the carpet and curtains, and he'd call it done.

"And then what?" he said, scratching his backside on the way to the bathroom. Being away from Miss Vivien's shiny trap and Desiree's scheming was a start, but a start of what, he wondered.

…trouble can run faster than you…

"Not now," he said to the ceiling.

Fifteen minutes of pacing and drinking coffee produced exactly zero ideas. He checked the time on his phone. 8:37. Pretty early to call Spuv, especially if the big man was coming off a successful Friday night, but he needed to talk.

"Charlie dense Woods," Spuv boomed into the phone, "what can I do you out of, son?" Saying "dense" meant he was alone.

"Sound awful bushy-tailed for this hour, Spuv. Working today?"

"Already headed to my second appointment, buddy. C'mon, you know Comcast'd crater without Spencer Upton Vaughn, Jr."

"Always thought you should be a senator or something with that handle. Anyway, calling because I was hoping you'd be up for a little fishing. Y'know, go on up to Dukes Creek."

"You serious? She gave you a hall pass?"

"Shaking things up some. Could even go tonight and camp if you got no plans."

"Damn. Just full of surprises. Fishing, huh? Man, I would most definitely enjoy that. Might have to … By damn, let's do it. I'll reserve us a site, and you pick up the food and beer. Holy shit, can we go in that bodacious Beemer?"

"I'm, uh, kinda done with that. Calling you from the house, actually. You come on by when you're done, and we'll go up in my truck."

"Desiree can't drive stick. Gonna leave her with no wheels?"

"Not a problem. It's just me."

"Hmm," Spuv said after some quiet. "Is there more to this?"

"I'll see you when you get here."

"Dude, friends for life and everything, but if we're going up there to dump a body, I'm gonna pass."

"Y'know, man as funny as you should be on the damn TV. Catch you later." Probably should have told Spuv about splitting with Desiree, if that's how everything was going to turn out, but he wasn't ready for told-you-so's. That is, assuming Spuv might have been thinking along those lines.

Using a ballpoint he found in the kitchen, he wrote "beer, food, pillow" on his palm. "Could still happen," he said, adding an "s" to pillow.

CHAPTER FORTY-EIGHT

DUKES CREEK was nearly dark when Charlie pulled his pickup into the driveway of a cabin, instead of a campsite. "Gave me the wrong site number, doofus," he said to Spuv.

"Hell I did. This is us." Spuv climbed out and grabbed two duffel bags from the truck bed. "I know you're used to a maid, buddy, but that ain't me. Haul your ass out here."

"Spuv, I brought a tent." he said, stepping onto the dusty gravel. "Why we wasting money on this?" He stacked two tackle boxes on a cooler. "Should've known something was up when you picked up an envelope at the ranger office. Hey, hold that door."

"Here to fish, son, not to get rain on my face and centipedes up my nose. Just say, 'thank you, Massa Spuv', and shut your cake hole. Speaking of fishing," he said, dropping the duffels by a set of bunk beds, "fish me out a cold one." He pointed to a door in the corner. "And check this out, buddy. Got us an inside shithouse, with a shower."

"Wish you would've said something." This morning, he'd only taken a hundred from the ATM. The sixty-five he had left would never cover his share. "How much am I stuck for this?"

"You're too righteous for me to say 'nothing." Spuv held out his hand. "Gimme a buck—American—and we'll call it square."

"C'mon. That's not right."

"Knew I'd never see that dollar, you cheap shit." Spuv flipped him the bird. "Okay, let's do this then. You got the next one." He headed back outside. "More to do, Lance Corporal."

"I made sergeant, and you know it." Not that it was something to brag on. Getting stuck at that rank was what killed his reenlistment.

"Call yourself a damn general for all I care. Just move. And by the way," Spuv said without turning, "I took this for three nights, so we can use the cupboard for the stuff."

"What's going on?" Charlie said, following close behind.

Spuv grabbed their fishing rods. "Charlie, I know you since before I knew what knowing was. You're the one with something going on." His palm popped up. "And it's more than okay if you don't want to talk. Last thing I want is hearing relationship bullshit. But if you *absolutely* have to talk, I got ears. And if there's something you need to puzzle through, this here's the best place for it."

"Coulda puzzled just as good in a tent."

"Course, you being the careful thinker that you are," Spuv said, his fingers hooked through the plastic loops of all the Publix bags, "might take more than a day. Now you got three." He hefted the sacks. "G'won, get the door. And dammit, did I, or did I not, designate you the beer fetcher?"

"What killed your last servant?" Charlie held the door wide.

"Sass."

Been like this forever. The two of them, all easy breezy. At least until they sprouted whiskers. Once that happened, stirring in even one female had a tendency to spoil the soup. One casual swing of her hips, as if there was such a thing. Maybe a sideways glance and smile, or a toss of her hair. Any of those was enough to scramble the loyalty zone in Spuv's brain. Turned a friend, even a best friend, into an opportunity to draw girls into huddles and giggles, and sometimes a whole lot more. Step on one heart to trifle with another.

But today wasn't that, and he was enjoying a boyhood feeling for the first time in too long. Just the tonic for a man whose trip through life may have come to a river he couldn't cross.

BURGERS EATEN and dishes done, Charlie dragged a chair near the wood-burning stove. He'd made dinner at the cooktop and done the dishes. Spuv built the fire. The cabin came supplied with split hardwood, so it wasn't tough to see who'd been slickered. But busy was better, and the blaze did overwhelm the stink of mildew and damp, half-charred wood.

Spuv sat by the stove, warming his bare feet and sucking down another beer. Had to be his sixth in two hours. "Bring me a couple more." He tossed Charlie the empty before he could sit. "That last one cleared off a good bit of confusion. Buddy, I just figured out how to fix your damn life. Be quick now," he said, slapping his fuzzy scalp. "Sometimes these flashes of genius disappear fast as they come."

Charlie would have been fine staying quiet about his situation, but now and again Spuv did put his intelligence to matters other than poking women. "Slow down on these," he said, handing Spuv two sweating cans. "Only bought a case, and I'm not about to go for more tonight." He sat and pried his shoes off. "Okay, Spuv the Great, commence fixing."

"Real simple." Spuv set one beer on the floor, slid his hips forward in the Adirondack chair, and crossed his ankles. "See, in this life," he popped the beer top, "you got your givers and your takers. Your leaders and your followers. You? You're a giving follower. Good soldier to the death." One eye lowered, he bounced a finger at Charlie. "And now here's the fix. You ready?"

"Lay it on me."

"Stop being that." Spuv turned a smile to him and hoisted the can. "You're welcome."

"Now how could I have been so blind? Thank you so much for that."

"Hang on. Think it through." Spuv twisted toward him. "Raised by your grandma." He lifted a hand like taking an oath. "Not a word against her, but all you ever knew was that woman telling you what to do. She died, and then what? You joined the Marines. More people telling you what to do. They muster you out, and in, I dunno, ten minutes, you latch onto Desiree. Older than you. Personality's a touch on the strong side." He sipped his beer and shrugged. "Same hymn, different church."

"How does that 'fix' my life?"

"Can't solve a problem 'til you know you got one. The rest? That's up to you."

Wanting and not wanting to confide about his Desiree situation reminded him of trying not to puke. Words kept pushing to the edge of his lips, but drew back. "I left her," popped out without him planning it. Sounded wrong, like a boast about a hurtful act, or sucking up to get a slap on the back for finally seeing women the right way.

"Whoa." Spuv wrinkled his brow and whistled out a long breath. "That's big." He leaned toward Charlie and reached out a fist. "Sorry, man."

He tapped knuckles with Spuv and nodded.

"Fight, or for good?" Spuv said. "If it's just a fight, blow it off. They'll always take you back. I hope you know that."

Sure felt like for good, and based on what he'd come to learn in recent days, he couldn't see wanting to be taken back. She'd turned into a sickness, threatening pretty much everything that felt right in his life. Still, he'd taken a vow and didn't want to hear "for good" spoken out loud. Best answer he could give was a shrug.

…where there's life, there's hope…

He wanted to ask GranDelia how that squared with *…lie down with dogs, you get fleas.…*

"Don't want to talk about it?" Spuv said, easing back into his chair.

Eyes forward, Charlie shook his head. Should've come alone. True grieving could only be done in private.

CHAPTER FORTY-NINE

GRANTING PERMISSION for Desiree to have wine with dinner might have been a mistake. A glassful of chardonnay, plus a top-off or two, had washed down one small bite of a chicken breast. "Darling, enough," she said as Desiree reached for another splash. "No point adding a hangover to your misery."

Eyes down, Desiree nodded. Her knife nudged a tiny boiled potato around the uneaten chicken and broccoli.

"Perhaps you should clear the table," Vivien said, interrupting a second lap for the potato.

"Sorry." Desiree laid the silver cutlery gently onto her plate. "Not thinking real good right now."

Charlie's brief absence had doubled gravity in the house. Spirits flattened. Paces slowed. Conversations required determination and endurance. "Darling," Vivien said, "I was married for decades. These things have to talked out. Phone him."

"He left." Desiree trained a blank stare on her food. "Been coming, and now it's here."

"You can't fix things if you don't speak. Be generous. Make the first move."

"Miss Vivien, I'm not being prideful. Done what I could. More than I shoulda probably. There's things …" She shook her head, more a shudder than a shake. "Me being here. It's like God rescued me, and not just from the bad. Got a chance for all the good now, too. Things I wanted, but he didn't. Taking care of you. Having a baby. Bringing it up here to know the love of an awesome grandmother."

Hearing that a baby might still be in the offing brought a crease to Vivien's brow.

Desiree fell back in the chair and twisted her napkin. "It's done. That's it." After a quick glance, she dropped her eyes again. "Biggest scare now is Charlie joining up with y'all's family to get me kicked out. 'Cause after me, we both know who'd be next."

"But that's absurd. Why would he?"

"People get mad enough, sometimes they do things." Desiree pushed her plate away and leaned closer. "That's mostly what's been on my mind. Trying to figure if he, y'know, *did* turn on us like that, how do we make it so they couldn't win. Sorry to say, I come up empty so far."

"Get Charlie back, and all that becomes moot. Would it help if I phoned him?"

"Miss Vivien, please stop. I mean about calling him. Not that easy." Dew glistened in her eyes. "One call? That's gonna mean years of trouble never happened?" She dabbed at her moist eyes with the napkin. "No way you could know." She dropped her face into a tent of fingers. "What's the use? He fools everyone."

"Are you saying he abused you?" Unfathomable. Yet, he had hurt Lauren in Key West.

"Miss Vivien, past is past. All I got is the here and now and what's to come. Only terror left is getting kicked out of here."

"No, we mustn't ..." Turning her head away, Vivien raced through the unbroken string of Charlie's gentle, protective gestures in their brief history. That he could have been so clever and duplicitous magnified the horror.

"Him teaming up with the family. That's what could sink us."

"You mean Ward."

"Uh-uh," Desiree said, head shaking in long sweeps. "Lauren, too, pretty sure."

That possibility flamed Vivien's old suspicion of Charlie and Lauren pairing up in Key West. Lauren's escalation of hostilities, including that outrageous manhandling, traced back only as far as Charlie's involvement in their lives. "Do you know something I don't?"

"If I had to guess, that's where he's been the last two nights." Lips quivering, Desiree turned her shiny eyes to Vivien. "What we gonna do?"

"Rely on my attorneys, I suppose." The protection she'd been engineering sat in ashes, reduced to a pair of impaired women, defended by milquetoasts wielding Montblanc pens.

"How do lawyers stop lies?" Desiree said. "With Charlie backing them up, your kids can say anything. Won't matter if they get found out later. I'll already be gone. You too. Even if they lose, they win. Gotta be something." The fleshy part of her fist bumped a steady beat on the table. "Y'know, too bad I'm not your daughter. I was? They couldn't touch me. Couldn't touch neither of us."

"I don't follow." Accepting Charlie's villainy continued to occupy her, along with a warm ache in her head.

"Well, I'm just saying. Daughters at home with their mommas. Two generations helping each other. Nothing strange there. If things was that way?" she said, flapping a hand. "We'd be safe 'til the crack of doom." She slumped against the chair's back and closed her eyes. "Course, if wishes was horses, beggars would ride."

Snippets of Desiree's explanation coalesced and displaced Charlie from her thoughts. "You're not suggesting ..." She studied Desiree's face, waiting for the woman to finish her thought without coaching.

"Huh?" Desiree squinted at her. "I mean, pardon?"

"Never mind." Dizziness had joined the dull ache. She turned her focus to stilling a tremor in her hand.

"Wait." Eyes wide, Desiree pointed at herself and smiled. "You thought I meant me *becoming* your daughter? Like, adopted?"

"I don't know what I'm thinking at the moment." She gripped and released the fingers of her shaky hand, but was unable to quell the trembling.

"No. I was only saying a daughter's got the same rights as a son." A smile popped onto Desiree's face. "Oh, that's funny. Adopted at my age. Imagine? Thank you for that." She reached toward Vivien. "Kinda starved for giggles right now. My goodness," she said when their fingers touched. "Hand's freezing. Can I get you a sweater?"

"Bed, I think." She held out both arms. "Would you mind?" Hip motion as she stood disclosed the need for fresh underwear, but dotty as she felt, executing a bath was out of the question. "Thank you," she said, unsteady on her feet. "Lead on."

Desiree held firm to Vivien's arm on their way to the elevator. "Gonna get you settled and bring up a nice cup of tea."

If Desiree was ever to graduate to all-encompassing caregiver, this moment had to come eventually. "You're being quite a good soldier, darling, all things considered. I hope my next request doesn't spark a desertion."

"Can't imagine what could do that."

"I need help." The pain in her head, niggling when she left the table, grew large enough to require a pause.

"Y'okay?" Desiree held her tighter.

"It's nothing." Her headache wasn't all that surprising based on household tensions and the humiliation that lurked only seconds away. Pressure behind her eyes eased enough to continue. "Back to my needing help." Warmth rushed to her face. "I'm speaking of bathroom assistance. Right now, for instance."

"That all?" Desiree patted her on the arm. "I'm here for whatever. Thought you knew that by now."

Relief at leaping that hurdle so easily didn't produce the drop in discomfort she'd hoped. "You really are a treasure," she said, eager to lie down. "I wish I *had* produced such a daughter."

"One call to the lawyer is all it takes," Desiree said, laughing. "Oh, wouldn't that be something? It'd fix everything, but World War Three would bust out for sure."

They entered the master bedroom. "Okay, we're here," Desiree said. "Tell me what I'm supposed to do. And don't fret about *nothing*."

Her first assisted potty stop in eighty plus years. Wobbly of leg and head pounding, Vivien pointed to the master bath door. "Water closet is to the left. We'll start there."

"Alrighty then," Desiree said as they stood in front of the toilet. "Now what?"

Vivien grabbed handfuls of her dress to lift it, but staggered and grasped Desiree's ready hands.

"Pretty unsteady tonight," Desiree said. "Felt it on the way up. So, let's do this." She turned Vivien by the shoulders and guided her hands to the wall. "If I lift the dress, can you hold onto it?"

Positioned for an execution, she felt equally resigned. "If you have a weapon, please use it."

"Oh, y'all are making too much outta this. Treat it like sex. First time's the only awkward one."

Vivien wanted to smile, but couldn't. Coolness on her legs climbed along with the hem of her dress.

"Now, you hang onto this." Desiree tucked dress fabric into Vivien's fingers. "Probably should get the legs a little wider, too. Okay then, let's get this party started."

As the disposable fell away, chill covered where panties used to. The faint odor that escaped at the lifting of her dress intensified, a degrading fist to the nose.

"Need to sit?" Desiree said. "I mean, don't want to do this twice. Right?"

Vivien shook her head, spreading pain temple to temple.

"Stay put now," Desiree said, "and mind that pretty dress. Gonna get a wash rag. Maybe a couple."

"No need." She fanned a hand toward the bidet. "Help me to it."

"Really? Seen these things, but I got no idea how they work. Gonna have to teach me."

Cautious with the dress, Vivien offered her elbow and shuffled on jelly legs to the bidet. Bending to turn on the water amplified the misery in her head, now accompanied by nausea. Both receded after she stood up again. With Desiree's arms hooked under her shoulders, the two staggered in an embrace until her bottom lowered into the refreshing stream.

Satisfied she was properly cleansed, Vivien turned off the water. "And now, darling," she said, hands clasped at the junction of her thighs, "a towel if you wouldn't mind." Perspiration chilled her lip and forehead.

"Probably should get some powder, or cream, or something." Desiree draped a terry bath towel across Vivien's lap. "Pretty raw down there."

"On the counter by the sinks, and darling," she said, causing Desiree to pause in the doorway, "Tylenol and a cup of water. Thank you." She wanted to add more words of gratitude, but speaking increased the agony building in her skull.

Sounds of Desiree rummaging in cabinets suggested that bed might be light-years off, and she needed to lie down. Gripping the handrails around the bidet, she tested her strength, rising several inches with minimal strain on two attempts. Feet wide, dress bunched forward on her lap, she counted to three and stood.

Lightning scorched behind her eyes. Floating in black ended with a painless blow to the head, like a whack from a pillow. Ears rang. Eyes refused to open. Smell and taste of blood.

"Miss Vivien!" reverberated in the water closet. "Omigod," echoed still closer. "Why'd—Jesus in heaven, not now!"

A hand scooped under her neck and lowered her throbbing head onto a soft cloth.

"Be right back." The limp rushed off. "Why now?"

Far-off moans. Wind in a night storm. Weak vibrations in her chest told Vivien the groans were her own. Feeble, abject. Sounds from someone perhaps dying. Hopefully dying. No point being saved just to die again. And Marshall so near now.

Desiree's clip-clop approached. "They're coming." She slipped Vivien's powerless hand into both of hers. "Please hang on, Miss Vivien." She stroked the flaccid fingers against her cheek. "Don't do this. Not now."

"Ssh," she said, desperate for silence and the end of pain.

CHAPTER FIFTY

SPUV'S SNORING was the first Charlie had to sleep through since Afghanistan. Seeing as dawn had broken, and he hadn't slept twenty minutes all night, he must have forgotten how. Except he knew Spuv's sputtering chainsaw wasn't the problem. All night he'd stared at the dark ceiling, reviewing the big turns in his life, especially these past couple weeks. Unhappy as he was about it, everything looped back to Spuv being right about him needing a ring through his nose.

Pale morning had brightened enough he could go for a hike and burn off some energy without breaking his neck. He flipped the covers off and vaulted from the top bunk. His feet thumped hard on the floor but didn't even cause a twitch from the hulk in the lower. Bumps and clunks while he dressed didn't affect Spuv, either. He knew it was small-minded, but he slammed the door on his way out.

Took a few minutes of kicking through underbrush and slapping away spider webs, but he began to feel some peacefulness. He stopped at a mossy log and sat. Sounds replaced noise. Trees clicked and creaked in the light breeze. Dew slapped onto last year's leaves and pine needles. Birds twittered overhead or chased down breakfast in the thick clusters of laurel. Another small step back from the world, and it felt right, same as yesterday when he turned off his phone.

The sun had risen full over the horizon, doing a fine job of melting off the chill. Even so, he slipped his butt to the cool ground and tightened the windbreaker around his sweatshirt.

...trouble can run faster than you...

"You keep saying that," he said to GranDelia, "but I'm thinking, not hiding."

...bad things can happen to good people...

"Meaning who? Me? Desiree? Every dang person that ever lived?" He knew GranDelia was trying to show love and support, but he got angry anyway. Same way he used to get when homework mystified him. Caring but useless, she'd find reasons to pass by the kitchen chair now and then, bring him a sweet tea, kiss him on the hair, or rub his back when he'd start to cry.

...nobody can do better than their best...

"A loser's excuse," he called up to her. The Marines made him see that nobody knew "their best" until something from outside made them dig deeper. *Quitters quit. Pain is weakness leaving the body.* Those weren't just words for t-shirts. Best he ever felt about himself was as a Marine. Honor and purpose. A calling, not a job.

Being a husband should have been that, too, but like when the Marines denied him promotion to Staff Sergeant, he found himself on the outside. Two commitments he'd seen as forever, gone. And now here he was, over thirty, no job, pretty much no money, a sketchy stranger for a wife, falling-down house, no living kin, huddled in the woods, and having a pity party.

Only thing he could deal with right then was that last part. He pushed to his feet and swatted leaves off the seat of his pants. "Least I got my health," he shouted to the treetops. Didn't know why, but that made him laugh. He started back toward the cabin. "And God loves me," he hollered through cupped hands. "Can't take that from me."

...no shame getting knocked down. Shame is not getting back up...

"There you go," he said, clapping his hands and adding pep to his step. "Now you're talking."

Back at the cabin, snores came grinding through the front door from twenty feet away. On the off chance he'd knocked Spuv awake by slamming the door earlier, he decided to go out and buy

289

a peace offering. Last night, they'd passed a Dunkin' Donuts just outside the park entrance. Dropping a box of Munchkins on the cabin table, along with a couple of large coffees would do the trick. With any luck afterward, he'd have a day so peaceful he might even stumble onto an idea or two about his next step.

CHAPTER FIFTY-ONE

LAST NIGHT, after Oconee Regional Medical Center contacted Ward about his mother's catastrophic stroke, he'd sped down from Atlanta with her living will and medical proxies. Even armed with those papers, he had to enlist that pompous gasbag Bartram Winfield to prevent the hospital from installing IV's and a feeding tube. After ensuring Mother's peaceful death—if dying from thirst could be considered peaceful—he'd phoned Lauren and asked her to contact the rest of the siblings.

Filial duty done, his last in their labored relationship, he stood beside Mother's bed and girded for rushes of sorrow or nostalgia. Minutes stretched, but her expressionless, cement-colored face elicited little. Events in their shared life replayed, but without a sense of involvement. She and his father had lived in an orbit above all of them, dipping dramatically close now and then, like a wolf moon, but always too briefly to be anything but a fear-inspiring presence. He ran fingers across her cool forehead. Tears dribbled down his cheeks. Not for the ashen face on the pillow, but for the foreclosure on the possibility of a mother. Without grasping what she'd withheld, he knew it was going to the grave with her in its original wrapper.

He'd slept in a chair in Mother's private room, partly to be there if she jumped the schedule, and partly to be there for Lauren and Sophia if they ignored his discouragement and drove from Atlanta in the middle of the night. They had not. They'd arrived together that morning a few minutes past nine, and the threesome shared a pro forma bedside visit to their vegetative parent. If and when brothers Luke and Archer would show up, even if only for the funeral, was anyone's guess.

After what he considered an appropriate few minutes for the sisters, he advised them about Mother's doomed prognosis. Lauren held up as expected, but Sophia's hysteria, and her remonstrations on his barbarity, drove him not just from the room, but out of the building.

Pacing under the canopied entry, clicking through complications he'd have to deal with when Mother officially died, he froze. There would be no complications. Her incapacity triggered his conservatorship. No more discussions needed. No more consensus building. Tasks of a more pleasant nature lined up in his mind. Dropping the axe on Bartram Winfield would require more time than he had at that moment, but another was only ten minutes away. His first official act would be to evict Charlie Woods and his smirky bitch of a wife from Reynolds Plantation.

Eager as he was for the victory, that was no excuse for recklessness. Before pulling under Mother's portico, he circled to the garages. No pickup truck. He returned to the entrance, trotted to the front door, and rang the bell.

Bleary-eyed, Desiree cracked the door and stared at him.

"Do you mind?" He nudged the door into her until she backed up.

"Please don't tell me she's gone." Desiree dabbed a wad of paper towels to her eyes and nose.

"No." He eased into the foyer, eyes and ears on Charlie alert. Passing Desiree, he picked up a whiff she'd been drinking. "Where's your husband. This concerns both of you."

"Friend of his said he's gone fishing."

It took a second before he caught the import of her phrasing. "What does that mean, 'friend of his said'? You don't know where he is?"

"Me and him …" She dabbed her eyes again. "Please tell me about Miss Vivien. Ain't slept a lick since they took her."

"She's stable, but back to your husband. Are you saying you

two split up? He's gone?" Reborn as a devout hedonist, he ticked a check mark next to Desiree on the possibilities list. A novelty act and rather pretty, in a peculiar way.

"Rough patch, is all," she said. "Did they say when she can come home?"

"This 'rough patch', is that why you're drinking at ten in the morning?"

Her face compressed deeper into sadness. Tears wiggled past the wad of paper she pressed to her nose.

"Aw, don't do that." An opportunity to plant a seed, he wondered? Arm extended, he eased toward her. She didn't recoil from his hand on her shoulder, but did when he let it slide down her slender back. "So," he said, forcing a smile, "which of Mother's wines are we drinking?"

She jumped backward, eyes big, head shaking. "I didn't steal nothing. I swear. She said I could."

"Desiree, it's alright," he said in his gentlest voice. "In fact, I'll join you. C'mon." He offered his elbow. "Doctor's orders."

Suspicion displaced the fear on her face. "Why you being nice?" She reached for his arm like testing for a hot stove.

"My problem is with your husband, not you. Kitchen?" he said, pointing toward the hall.

She nodded and wobbled toward it without taking his arm.

"It might surprise you," he said, hurrying to catch up, "but you and I are sharing parallel setbacks right now. There's Mother's stroke, of course, but my significant other took off as well." No harm making Desiree aware of his availability.

"Kinda guessed it was a stroke." Desiree paused in front of the refrigerator. "Poor woman was in so much pain. Then she just, I dunno, went all sleepy. Thought she died. Died with me holding her hand." She opened the fridge and presented an uncorked bottle of white wine.

He nodded. "She's comfortable. I promise you." The dimwit had glided right past what he confided about his marriage. Cuckolding Charlie would have been tasty, but he scratched her off the list.

"Goddam sister of yours." Desiree's open hand shot up. "No offense, but she cussed me out and hung up when I called the hospital room this morning." She poured the wines and brought his over. "One foul-mouthed woman, and that's a fact."

"She is a bit earthy. Ah well, cheers. To Mother." He held his glass out.

"Got any idea how long it's gonna be?" she said, after the clink and a big sip.

"None, which brings me to my visit." He set his glass down and leaned back, his arms propped on the center island. "I'm in charge of Mother's affairs now, and soon as you finish that, you're out of here. Permanently."

"What? No." Desiree's head shook like she had Parkinson's. "No sir. You can't. We been paid. I gotta—Place has to be nice for when she comes back. I do that. That's my job."

"Oh, that's right," he said, crossing his ankles. "You have been paid."

"Through June. Yes, sir." Hope brightened her expression.

"Well, there's no one to take care of anymore. And now your husband's disappeared. Half of what she paid for isn't even here. Classic breach of contract." He smiled and pointed to the side of her face. "You may have to sell those earrings after all."

She shrank into her clothes. The hand without the wine glass shot to her ear and rubbed as if he'd cuffed her. Frightened eyes kept finding and losing his face.

"We're done here" he said. "Offense completely intended, I'm joining you upstairs to oversee the packing."

"No. Please. Dr. Granville, I got nowhere to go."

"Ridiculous. Go where you were going at the end of June."

"Here." She jabbed a finger toward the floor. "I was gonna be here. It was all planned. And she's gonna need me more than ever now." She set her wine on the counter and clasped her hands in prayer. "Doctor, you just need to see how good we are together. I love that woman like we was kin. Please. I belong here. Me and her agreed. I gave up everything. Please."

294

"I didn't see the truck. Will you need a ride to wherever it is you're going?"

She crumbled to the floor on her knees. Hands covering her face, she sagged forward until her forehead rested on the floor. "This isn't happening," she said, her voice a grating, sobbing squeal.

"I don't need the police do I? Get up."

Grimacing as she labored to her feet, she glared at him. "Granvilles," she said in a rough whisper. "Somebody oughta put a bullet through each one of y'all. And oooh," she said, fist cocked and shaking, "I would just *love* to be the one who did you."

He checked his Rolex. "It's ten-twenty. If you're not in my car by ten forty-five, with," he said, finger raised, "a specific destination, I'll have you arrested for trespassing." He dropped the raised finger like a flag at Indy. "Go."

Five minutes beyond the deadline and lugging two battered suitcases, Desiree hobbled down the porch steps and weaved toward where he sat in the car. She'd changed clothes. Sweatshirt was now a white knit blouse opened to the bottom button, low enough to show meager cleavage and a good amount of black bra. Jeans had been replaced by a pale yellow skirt that rode loose around the hips.

He waited for her to get close to the car before pushing the trunk release button.

Eyes rolling, she detoured to the back of the Mercedes, pitched the bags in, and slammed the lid. "Thought you was brought up better than that." She climbed into the passenger seat and clicked her seat belt. As the car rolled around the front circle, she dug what looked like a plastic water bottle from her purse. She unscrewed the cap and sipped the light amber contents.

"Where to?" he said. "And if that's wine, dump it. I'm not getting a DWI because of you."

She raised the bottle to her lips, downed a hefty gulp, and flipped it out the window.

"This is a promise," he said. "If you vomit in here, I will boot you from the car while it's still moving. Now, tell me where I'm going."

"Greensboro, I guess. South on Lake Oconee Parkway." After some fussing with her clothes and purse, she twisted toward him in the seat, tucked her legs underneath, and nestled her head against the seatback. "Mind if I ask a question?"

He glanced her way and shrugged.

"Why you so mad all the time?" she said. "Something's missing, and I can't imagine what."

"Great," he said, turning the Mercedes out of the driveway, "store-front psychoanalysis from a drunk."

"Not all that drunk. Yet. And I'd really like to know. Y'all got everything, far as I can see. So what is it y'ain't getting? I mean, what do you *really* want?"

"At the risk of prolonging this, what are you talking about?"

"Well, a hundred people couldn't spend what you got. Not in ten lifetimes. But there still has to be something makes you want to get up every day. Everybody wants something. Love, money, power. Something."

"I'm fine." He slowed for a slow-lifting gate at the Reynolds Plantation exit.

"That so? Then why'd your missus take off?"

So she had heard him. He laughed. "She did me a huge favor, and I will be eternally grateful."

"Bull. Bet she caught you with your dick in another woman. All men cheat."

"Not that it's any of your business, but she was the one who cheated."

"Hmm … How about that." She unclicked her seat belt. Tugging the neckline of her clingy blouse wider, she wriggled closer to him. "Feels bad, don't it. I mean, when someone cheats." She reached a hand onto the top of his leg, drew figure eights with a fingertip. "Wanna pay her back?"

"Oh my God. Let me make sure I have this right. Twenty minutes ago you wanted to shoot me, and now you want to fuck me?" He glanced at her.

"I dunno. Might could be persuaded." She raised her eyebrows, shrugged and smiled. "Kinda cute. Always been attracted to powerful men. And I been drinking. Some women, makes 'em silly. Me? Horny as a teenage rabbit." Her hand slid to his knee and dipped between his thighs. "So maybe sex is what you really want. I take care of that? And I get what I want? Fair bargain, way I see it."

"And that would be you staying at my mother's?"

"Bingo." She walked her fingers to his fly and massaged him.

Pure serendipity. Jumping her bones offered a perfect test drive for the daily-dose Cialis he'd started yesterday. "Are you good? I mean, at everything?"

"Sugar, y'all turn this car around and come upstairs with me?" She continued to rub and squeeze. "I'll suck this so good you'll be screaming in tongues."

Choosing between a quick sex break and standing vigil over his sinking mother was a no-brainer—except for the specter of Charlie. If that cretin resurfaced unexpectedly, he could trap them on the second floor. Her house in Greensboro also presented danger. While he was considering options, a passing billboard caught his eye.

The Lodge on Lake Oconee, two miles ahead.

"Not that I doubt your abilities," he said, pointing to the sign, "but I believe I'd like you to audition."

"Uh-uh. No hotels." Checking out the windows in all directions, she grabbed at his zipper "You just keep driving."

"Absolutely not." He twisted his hips and slapped her hands away. "And I'm not pulling into a parking lot, either."

"My house is only a couple more miles." Her hand crept back onto his fly. "Can't leave you like this now, can we?"

"And Charlie just will stand at the foot of the bed and applaud?"

"Told you. He's fishing in the mountains 'til Monday. Got nothing to worry about." She ramped up the squeezes and rubs. "C'mon, sugar. Day's young, and I can go long as you can."

He pushed her away. "Alright, but leave me alone until we get there." She was going to raise a powerful stink when he pumped and dumped her, but it would be worth it. Sex with a cripple. Not a lot of men had done that. And he'd find out how Cialis worked under game conditions. Seemed to be doing a wonderful job so far.

Everything was breaking his way. A few seconds of shooting inside Desiree, and a lifetime of knowing he'd done Charlie's wife, in his own bed. Even more fun would be making sure Charlie knew it. He patted a front pocket in his slacks to confirm he had his iPhone.

CHAPTER FIFTY-TWO

WARD PEERED around the edge of Desiree's front window. His poor Mercedes, in plain sight on the driveway of this grim trailer, cringing beside a yahoo's Corvette.

"Beer?" Desiree said from behind him.

"And then what? We get to know each other?" He undid his belt and pulled down his fly. "Bedroom?" he said, pointing to the vinyl accordion door.

She nodded, tipped a long drink from the bottle, and did a poor job of covering a belch. "Sorry. Potty stop first," she said, falling in behind him. "Seems like you're in a hurry, so get them clothes off, and I'll be right in."

Other than two pillows on the bed, the room was bare, a depressing visual made worse by a smell evocative of wet dog. He used her time in the bathroom to set his iPhone to *Video* and secret it under a pillow. Waiting at the edge of the stained mattress, he scanned the droopy ceiling and wood-paneled walls. Only one decoration in the whole room, a framed photograph visible from the bed. A chubby older woman. Mother or grandmother, most likely.

"Oh," Desiree said, exiting the bathroom topless, but still wearing the skirt, "thought you'd be naked."

He pointed to the picture. "Your mother?"

"Charlie's grandmother." Her first step toward the bed was more of a stagger. "Believe I've had enough." She braced an arm against a wall and giggled.

"Lose the skirt." he said, undoing his pants. "Lose all of it." He wanted the whole of her unique body. See it, touch it, possess it.

"Me?" she said, crawling onto the bed. "Nah. I'm, y'know, kinda shy about my leg."

"I said all of it." He stepped out of his slacks and boxers. Unstimulating as she was so far, he credited his serious erection to Cialis.

"Whoa. Someone's ready." She crawled across the bed and reached for his stiff penis.

He snatched her arms and spun her off the bed, reversing their positions. Now sitting on the edge of the mattress, he held her upright as she struggled for balance. "Skirt, panties, everything. Do you understand?"

"C'mon. Don't gotta be mean," she said, grimacing and trying to steady her footing. "Let me make you happy. I know what I'm doing."

"Naked, or the deal's off." He popped up a thumb. "One." Index finger. "Two."

"Alright." She let out a long breath. "Alright," she said again, nearly lost in a sigh. Staring over his head, she unbuttoned and unzipped the skirt, tugged it down over her hips, and let it fall to the floor. Thumbs under the elastic, she peeled the black thong to her thighs. Resting a hand on top of his head, she nudged the panties down one leg at a time until they slipped to the floor. She stepped out of the black swatch and kicked it away with her good leg.

"Spread your feet a little," he said, fascinated by the angled hips and mismatched legs. Fingers rubbed and probed her trimmed, damp vulva. Woman scent built inches from his face. "Seems I'm not the only one ready. Turn around."

Limbs rigid, she dropped her hand from his head and tottered in a half circle. "Lemme just do you." She stopped swaying by bracing a hand on the window sash.

"You're auditioning, remember? How about a little enthusiasm?" He pressed his palm against the inside of her good thigh. "Wider." His hands swirled around and between her improbable lower half. Knees to butt, front to back, each round trip firing his need a notch higher. He slapped her bigger cheek. "Turn around."

Wobbling a half turn, she rested her fingers on his shoulders. Trails shone on her cheeks.

He was more than ready, but this would be his only shot at her. His fingers got busy again. Occasional upward glances caught her, stoic and trancelike, an occasional droplet slithering to her jaw and down her neck. The utter submission bumped his excitement to the red line. "Okay." He scrambled backward on the mattress until his head rested on the pillow. "In the mouth," he said, disappointed to be missing the cripple experience, but this was the only way he could sneak the video, "and do not look at me. Is that clear?"

Nodding and wiping her cheeks, she crawled between his legs and went directly to her assignment.

"Oh," rushed out of him on the first hot down-stroke. Whether her skill or the Cialis, this would be brief. He reached under the pillow and found the iPhone. Watching the viewer and aiming with both hands, he trained it on her bobbing head. Unsure if the phone made a noise when he tapped the start icon, he groaned a loud, "God almighty."

She never broke rhythm.

"Desiree, you're amazing. Charlie's an idiot to leave this." He panned to the old woman in the framed picture, held the shot briefly, and returned to taping his pleasure until the electric moment.

Gagging, she popped her head off him. She stretched across his leg, spit onto the mattress, and wiped the back of a hand across her mouth.

"Smile pretty," he said, still panting, "you stupid whore."

Motionless, she gawked into the shot. Quick as a snake strike, she snatched the iPhone. Prize in hand, she wriggled toward the edge of the bed.

He yanked her backward by the hair. From behind, his arms and legs imprisoned everything from the head down. He buried his face in her neck to avoid frantic tries to smash her skull into his face.

Resigned or exhausted, or both, she stopped struggling.

Prying the camera from her fingers met little resistance. Wary of a head butt to the mouth, he shoved her away. Slight as she was, the push pitched her off the bed. Scrambling to the edge, he peered over to see if she was preparing a counterattack.

Unsteady, she rose to all fours and rolled to a sitting position, her back pressed flat against the wall. A red abrasion glowed above her eye. "My head," she whispered, her face tight with pain, fingers dabbing next to the scrape.

He could see the fight was out of her. "Not that I'm a connoisseur yet," he said, still heaving breaths, "but I'd say your head is world class." He crawled to the foot of the bed and sat. Hunched over the iPhone, he set the video to *Play*. "In fact, let's review your performance."

"What are you gonna do with that?"

"I'm going to make you an Internet sensation." Engrossed in the video, he waved a hand over his shoulder. "Don't thank me."

"Can I see?" she said from close behind.

"No harm, I suppose." He held the screen toward her, but kept a shielding arm at the ready.

"Aw, Jesus," she said softly. "Gran—You gotta erase that."

"Isn't that a great shot?" he said, smiling at her. "I don't imagine you'd be willing to give me Charlie's email address."

Fingertips rubbed her creased brow. "Not doing this to him. You're not." She didn't look at him, but shook a finger of warning. "That ain't leaving here. Count on it."

"Oh, but it is, and I have another bulletin for you." He pushed *Play* again. "My mother will be dead in a day or two, and I'm selling the house. You just sucked me off in front of Charlie—so to speak—for nothing."

"Not letting you do this. I'm not. That's it."

He peeked up from the screen to watch the uneven pacing, her busy eyes never landing on anything. "In point of fact," he said, refocused on the video, "you can't stop me."

"Don't make me."

"You're pathetic." He eyeballed the end of the clip again, awed by knowing Australians would be able to see this within the hour. "What's your email address? You should have a copy, too."

"So, this is it." Slowly, she staggered past him toward the kitchen. After rummaging in some drawers, she returned with a thick candle and box of matches. Swaying in front of the open closet, she lit the candle and set it on the shelf.

"What are you doing?" he said as she pulled the sliding door closed.

"This is it," she said again. Eyes forward, she stumbled past him and rounded the corner of the bed. Near the headboard, she dropped to her knees, turned her back to him, and laid her cheek on the mattress.

"Ah, prayers before night-night. How sweet. Guess it is time to go. One more replay, and then I'll leave you in peace." He heard her stand and hobble toward him. Glancing to the side, he watched as she inched around the foot of the bed carrying a pillow in front of her middle.

"Little man," she said, trembling, "you're giving me that phone." Unsteady steps crept closer to him. "Last chance."

Knowing it would raise false hope, he wrinkled his nose and rocked his head. "Mmm … I don't think so." He pointed to the pillow. "And if you're planning on suffocating me with that, I believe the instructions say to do it from the front." Poor thing looked so forsaken. Pity she had to suffer on Charlie's account.

"We're going to hell, you and me."

"Even after those nice prayers?" He sniffed the air and craned his neck for a peek toward the kitchen. "I think your pilot's gone out."

A cold metal cylinder touched his temple.

CHAPTER FIFTY-THREE

CHARLIE PREFERRED fishing by himself, but invited Spuv along because he needed to tie his life preserver to something in a lost moment.

Having company was a useful distraction, but he'd forgotten how poorly Spuv fished. Without a boat, they had to cast from spots along the shore. More times than not, Spuv's tosses never reached the water. Overhead casts caught tree limbs. Side-arming snagged bushes. Even when his line found water, it often made two splashes, one where the hook landed, the other where the bait hit. Longer Spuv's troubles went on, worse his attitude got, and his language, and his ability to stay quiet.

"Big man," he called to where Spuv sat on a sloped patch of red clay, grumbling and ripping knotted line from his reel. "I'm gonna try yonder."

"Where the hell is 'yonder'?" Spuv's eyes stayed on the bird's nest of monofilament in his hand. "Damn redneck." He may have thought he said that last part under his breath, but nothing took the boom out of his voice, and the water acted like a loudspeaker.

"Cut that line, doofus," he said to Spuv. "This your first time?"

"How 'bout you kiss my ass. Oh, and before you head 'yonder', turn your goddam phone on. Desiree called mine while you were gone this morning. Woke my ass up."

"What'd she want?"

"Dude, I ain't Mister Lonely Hearts." He snapped nail clippers at the tangled line. "Wanna find out? Turn your damn phone on and call her."

"Soon." He closed and latched his tackle box. "Catch you later. And that'll be your only catch today."

Spuv leaned a butt cheek toward him and slapped it. "Right here, buddy."

Charlie began trekking the well-beaten path along the shoreline, now and then passing lone fishermen. Some waved or nodded. Most didn't. Nothing unfriendly, just that fishing was a solitary pleasure.

The spot he found after about ten minutes was so good he couldn't believe it was available. A sandy flat at the water's edge. Fish magnets everywhere he looked. Small island sitting near enough to reach with a good cast, trees on it throwing plenty of shade on the water. Took only two casts to hook his first. Five for the next. De-gouging the hook from that one, he heard voices getting closer. A massive pin oak blocked his view of whoever it was coming along the shore, but Spuv was definitely one of them.

He recognized the first person to crest a knob of earth at the base of the oak. "J.D. Potts for heaven sake," he said to his old schoolmate, now a Greensboro police officer. "What's with the uniform? Here to catch trout or arrest them?"

Hands behind his back, Spuv followed J.D. over the rise. A Georgia state trooper brought up the rear. Not a smile in the group and the State cop had a ready hand on his Glock 9mm.

"What's going on?" Charlie said, scanning the three faces.

Eyes wide, Spuv shrugged and turned sideways to show a pair of skinny plastic handcuffs.

"Charlie," J.D. said, "got State Trooper Earlie with me. He's the one tracked your truck here." J.D. pointed to the tree. "Now, I'm gonna need you to put your hands high on that and spread your feet."

"Tracking my vehicle? What for?" Charlie took the position he'd been told.

The officer started at the sleeves of Charlie's sweatshirt and worked his way down.

"What's going on, J.D.?" He wondered if Spuv might have been fighting again and hurt someone good this time.

J.D. finished at Charlie's ankles and stood. "Okay. Hands behind your back."

"C'mon, J.D., what's this all about?" Thin plastic bands secured his wrists, tight enough that they stung with every motion.   .

"Okay to turn around now," J.D. said. He slipped his hat off. "No good way to say this, Charlie, but your wife's dead."

He shuddered, then steadied himself. "Can't be."

"I'm afraid it is," J.D. said.

The shock on Spuv's face said he'd just learned, too.

Charlie didn't know why, but suicide was the first reason to pop into his mind. Guilt piled onto the shock. "What happened?"

"We can talk in the squad car on the way back to Greensboro," J.D. said, pointing down the path. "I'm parked at your cabin. Trooper Earlie's gonna bring Spuv."

"What about his truck?" Spuv poked his chin toward Charlie.

"Truck's gonna be trailered back," the trooper said.

"Aw, no." Charlie's body tingled. State and local cops tracking him. Frisking and cuffs. Impounding the truck. Separating him and Spuv. Could only mean one thing. "Someone killed her," he said. "That's it, isn't it?"

J.D. shrugged. "I was just told to deliver the news and bring you in." He pointed to Spuv. "And anyone who might be with you."

"This is bullshit, J.D.," Spuv said, advancing at the officer.

Legs wide, hand on his weapon, Trooper Earlie dropped to a crouch and pointed at Spuv. "Not another step."

"Spuv," Charlie said, "leave it go."

"Jesus Christ, J.D." Spuv said. "He kills his wife, and then goes fishing?"

"I didn't say that," the officer said, palm raised. "Just need to sort some things through is all. Now here's how it is. We got the right to bring you in, and that's what I'm doing."

"Tell him, Charlie," Spuv said, looking scared for the first time he could remember. "We been here two solid days."

"I gotta know," Charlie said, "and it looks like J.D. can't tell me. Let's just go quiet."

During the silent ride back to Greensboro, Charlie played back his short life with Desiree. Maybe it took her being gone, but he could see the steady slide toward what he'd walked out on. Like a painting someone took a rag to, rubbing the surface and finding a new picture underneath. And then again, and again. Each new version a little uglier than the one before. Still, he wished he had another chance with her, to blow on that ember of sweetness until it flamed on its own again. The woman who cried on his neck when they danced in the coatroom.

Station house activities flew past in a quick blur. Cuffs off. Pockets emptied and written on a list. As a Marine he'd already been fingerprinted, so J.D. passed that by and brought him to a small interrogation room. Sitting on a folding chair, elbows on a cool metal table, he stared at the two-way mirror. Too many thoughts jumbled in his head to fix on one. The door behind him opened. Detective Rupert, a man he'd known since forever, came in.

"Thanks, J.D.," the detective said, "I'll take it from here." He eased the door shut after J.D. left and reached out an open hand. "I'm real sorry about Desiree, son."

"Thank you, sir." He stood and shook hands. "You the one gonna tell me what happened?"

"Take a seat, Charlie. Get you anything? Coffee? Something cold maybe?"

"No, sir." He sat back down. "Just information."

The detective sat next to Charlie and turned his chair so he could face him. "Funny life sometimes," he said, leaning forward, elbows resting on his knees. "Who could ever think when they're coaching Little League that one day a favorite player, one of the finest kids ever, would be sitting where you are right now, talking about something terrible, something heartbreaking."

"Please stop doing this, Mr. Rupert. I need to know what happened to Desiree."

The man clasped his hands and tapped them to his lips.

"Charlie, we know Spuv rented that cabin two days ago. How is it you were there?"

"Fishing. We was fishing. I bought the food, he got the cabin. Why shouldn't I be there?"

Detective Rupert nodded. "How'd blood get on the ceiling of your truck?"

"It's mine," he said, showing the scabs on his knuckles. "Couple days ago I lost my temper."

"Lose your temper anywhere else lately? Home maybe?"

"Mr. Rupert, please tell me what happened to Desiree."

"When's the last time you saw her?"

"Friday, at Mrs. Granville's house in Reynolds Plantation, but I spent Friday night at my house in Greensboro. That's where Spuv picked me up on Saturday."

Detective Rupert nodded again. "Ranger did confirm Spuv got there Saturday evening. Either of you leave the grounds after that?"

"No, sir. Not for—Wait. I did. This morning I got some Dunkin Donuts."

"Remember where?"

"Wasn't more than a few hundred feet from the park entrance."

"How about the time? Recall that?"

"I don't carry a watch. Probably nine something?"

"Get a receipt?"

He patted his pockets and remembered they took all his stuff. "Might be with my money. Not sure."

The detective left and returned holding a stub of white paper. "Charlie, could take us a while to check this. If you want something, need to use the restroom, anything like that, just stick your head out the door and holler for me. We'll get this over soon as we can."

"Mr. Rupert, please. What happened to my wife?"

"Just need to clear this one thing."

No clock in the interrogation room, but an hour or more must have passed before the door opened.

Detective Rupert came in waving the little white stub. "A man can't be two places at once. Officer Potts checked the surveillance tape at Dunkin Donuts, and you were an hour's drive away at the time your wife was killed."

His breath caught like hearing about her death for the first time again.

"I never figured you could do it, Charlie." Detective Rupert patted him on the shoulder. "I'm real sorry for putting you through this, but your prints are on the gun, and Trooper Earlie saw the blood in your truck."

Only gun his prints could have been on was Desiree's, and last time he checked, that was under the mattress in Greensboro. "The .38?"

The detective nodded.

"She shoot herself?" He did and didn't want that to be the reason.

"Well," Detective Rupert said, scratching behind an ear, "there's the mystery. See, there was another person killed with her. Dr. Ward Granville from Atlanta. Know him?"

Charlie felt like he wasn't living his own life anymore. First picture to flash in his mind was two bodies in Miss Vivien's foyer, but Detective Rupert said it was Desiree's .38, and he knew that was still under the mattress. "Wait. Where'd all this happen?"

"Your house. That's another part of the problem."

"Aw Jesus." He covered his eyes and flopped back in the chair.

"Charlie, did you know him or not?"

"I did," he said, hand still covering his eyes. "Desiree and I worked for his mother at Reynolds Plantation."

"Hate asking, but I need a motive. Any chance they were having an affair?"

The question got him angry, like Mr. Rupert was calling Desiree a slut and him a fool. He sat tall and looked the detective dead in the eye. "No way they could have been together that way. And sure as heck not at my house."

"Son, that's obviously not so. We haven't made sense of the pieces yet, but it's pretty clear both of them died there. Shot point blank. Desiree through the heart, and. Dr. Granville through the head. Dr. Granville's prints are on the gun, and there's residue on his hand, so he fired it. Based on that, looks like he committed a murder/suicide." The detective stood and walked slowly toward the mirror. "But your wife had the same residue on her hands. So, who shot who? You, uh, hundred percent sure there was nothing going on between them?"

"She couldn't stand him, and that's a fact." Except that didn't explain them being together at the house. Even dead she was full of bad surprises.

"Charlie, I been at this a long time." Detective Rupert paused and flicked at the end of his nose. "Doesn't smell right. Anyway," he said resuming his stroll, "we may never know. What we do know is that whoever did the killing blew up the house."

Sound in the room hollowed. "My home's gone, too?"

"Afraid so. The volunteer boys got there real fast, but the place was pretty much flattened. Was them who found the bodies, out on the lawn. They figured both were killed in the explosion because some of the blood was still wet. The Medical Examiner was the one who found they'd been shot." He glanced at Charlie. "I'm sorry. Would you rather not go through all this right now? We can pick it up again tomorrow."

"No. Once and move on. Best way to get past anything."

"It gets rougher."

"Keep going."

"Okay, but you can say 'stop' whenever you want." He went back to pacing in front of the big mirror. "I asked about the affair because both were found nude. Don't know yet if anything happened between them. Medical Examiner's report will tell us more about that."

"Would it say if he raped her?"

"If that happened, yes. Those folks are pretty damn sharp, I promise you. By the way, did your wife own an iPhone?"

"No, sir. Flip phone, like me."

"Probably Dr. Granville's then. His prints and your wife's are on it, so we weren't sure. Anyway, someone put a bullet through it." He shrugged and resumed wandering. "Too bad. Hard to imagine anyone doing that unless it had something to do with the killings."

No idea if the iPhone meant anything, but Charlie was pretty sure he knew who did what. Blowing up the house was as good as a signed confession. What he'd never know was if it was a final spit in his face or something else. "Think I'd like to stop now, Mr. Rupert. Can I have my truck?"

"It's right here in the impound yard. So's the Vette Spuv left in your driveway. His took a couple of dings in the passenger door, but nothing major."

"He still here?"

"Last I saw he was waiting for you at J.D.'s desk." Detective Rupert strode toward him as Charlie rose from the chair. "Can't tell you how relieved I am you were on that surveillance tape. Just suspecting you made me sick." He opened the door and patted Charlie's shoulder on his way out.

He shook hands and headed toward where Detective Rupert was pointing.

"Dude," was all Spuv said to him as he approached J.D.'s desk. He hugged Charlie around the shoulder, grabbed his neck, and rocked it gently as they left the station house.

"Spuv," he said once they got into the sunny spring afternoon, "did J.D. tell you I got no house anymore either?" Tears swelled in his eyes. Not for Desiree or himself, but for losing what GranDelia spent her life trying to preserve, for making it the only real home in his life.

"Sucks ass, man. You're gonna stay with me."

"No," came out too strong. "I mean, thanks, but no. I gotta bury my wife and then spend some time thinking. Probably going back to Dukes for a few days after, y'know." He slapped Spuv's arm and forced a smile. "You don't need a fifth wheel."

"Friends over bitches, dude. You know that. Seriously, door's open, any time, day or night. And turn on your damn phone now. Nothing bad out there anymore."

He waited for Spuv's Vette to leave the impound lot so he could go in the other direction. Luckily, that left him the road toward the Microtel, where he planned on going all along. The isolation of a motel appealed to him right now. Some private time. A chance to grieve, remember, wonder, and cry it out if it came to that. Be done with it.

As he drove, the past seemed to get smaller with each glance in the rearview. Shock and sadness held most of his thoughts, but buried under that, long-building pressures were already bleeding off. He had a history of being wrong, a lot, but just maybe he'd settled onto the bottom of his life, the place he'd rise from.

CHAPTER FIFTY-FOUR

A WEALTHY DENTIST from Atlanta and a poor local woman, found naked and dead in her blown up trailer. In sleepy Greensboro, Georgia of all places. That combo had reporters looking under rocks in every corner of town.

Took them almost a full day to find Charlie at the Microtel, and even after he was located, being in the room was sort of okay because he could leave the phone off the hook and ignore knocks on the door. Only trouble was, he couldn't arrange the funeral or get proper clothes without going outside a few times.

First time he left his room reporters horrified him with their questions. *Did you kill them? How long were your wife and Dr. Granville lovers? Did you know they were lovers? How did you feel when you got the news?* His struggle to come up with answers only primed the pump for more, until he stumbled onto a response that knocked them off their game. "You got any decency?" he said to one of the vultures, and it made her flinch. From then on, if he said nothing but that, kept his eyes forward, and walked fast, they gave up.

He also learned that news gets old in a hurry. Killings happened on Monday, and by Thursday, they'd dropped off page one, even in Greensboro's local paper. Fine with him because Thursday night was Desiree's wake. He was still plenty angry with her, but she didn't deserve a circus sendoff into eternity.

Same way Mr. McCommons had done for GranDelia's wake, the funeral director set aside private time for him before public viewing hours. Arriving at 6:30 sharp, Charlie knelt at the open casket and said a prayer for the pretty little stranger. Lying there like a sleeping child, nothing to trouble her anymore, she touched him in the old way, the first-meeting way. But no tears.

Checking over each shoulder, he stood and bent to kiss her, but his eyes kept going to her diamond earrings. Poison tipped darts far as he was concerned. He regretted letting Mr. McCommons talk him into dressing her in her favorite things. Burying them with her crossed his mind, but the trip to heaven—hopefully heaven—would be hard enough without dragging those boulders. He kissed his fingers and touched her lips, or what used to be lips.

Still had twenty-three minutes until visitors. Charlie stood at ease next to the casket and tried to think of what each mourner might say, and what he should say back. Hard as he tried not to hate her, each glance at the peaceful body picked at another scab. Lying, breaking promises, stealing, cheating on him, murder, blowing up GranDelia's house. And him a chump through it all. She even nicked him after death. He couldn't afford a plot, so she got his. Now GranDelia would be flanked forever by a drug addict and a murderer.

Public hours started promptly at 7:00. For more than two hours, with Spuv standing next to him like they were brothers, he shook hands and returned hugs from what seemed like the whole county. Condolences, offers of a place to stay, invites to meals. Everyone had something kind to say and offered generosity that near broke his heart.

Wasn't until the river of friends and neighbors dried to a trickle around 9:15 that he realized not one person had told him something caring about Desiree. *Tragic loss. Terrible. Horrible. Too young to die.* All of that, but not how much they loved her and would miss her, or how they admired this or that about her. Not one person. Was like they'd heard he'd lost a favorite cousin in Seattle.

While he gnawed on that sad fact, a curvy woman in dark glasses and a white head scarf slipped into the room. Lauren Granville, for sure. She didn't get on the short line, but took a seat far in the corner and crossed her legs. Only when Mr. McCommons' son announced they were closing did she stand and approach.

"Whoa," Spuv whispered as she drew nearer.

"Charlie," she said, hand extended, "I am so sorry."

"Same here." He could see some bruising along the cheek-edge of the scarf.

Still holding his hand, she leaned in and kissed his cheek. "I know you can't mean that, but thank you."

A hand tugged at the sleeve of his jacket.

"Oh. Lauren Granville, this here's my friend, Spuv."

Spuv knocked Charlie off balance shooting his meaty hand out for a shake. "Real sorry for your loss, ma'am."

"Losses," she said, facing Charlie and ignoring Spuv's hand. "You don't answer your phone. Mother died today. I thought you might want to know."

"Aw no. That one I really am sorry about." Miss Vivien had created powerful memories of almost every second they shared, good and bad. Smart, a touch mischievous, ladylike, ornery, but never boring. "Pretty cool woman. What happened?"

"According to my sister Sophia, Ward murdered her, but actually it was a stroke. She suffered it last Sunday, died today. Very peaceful." Fingers of her free hand ran gently down his sleeve. "Are you hungry?"

"I sure am," Spuv said.

"Well then," she said, never turning her eyes from Charlie, "you should run along and get something."

"Oh, okay." Spuv backed toward the exit. "Tell you what. I'll get us a table at Yesterday Café. You show up, you show up. Nice meeting you, Lauren, and again, real sorry for your losses."

Charlie watched until Spuv left. "Usually isn't my way," he said, "but I'm afraid Spuv got a pretty good description of your, um, body art. Sorry."

"So it does pay to advertise." Her small smile showed the wires still tying her broken jaw together. "Any good spots near here, other than Yesterday Café?"

She scared him. Wrong as the moment was, wrong as the woman was, he felt the old attraction. "What do you want?" he said, unhappy it came out so whiny.

Tears dripped from under her sunglasses. She let go of his hand, dug a tissue from her tiny purse, and tapped it to her nose and cheeks. "I left Ward's wake, my own brother's wake, to come here."

"I'm sorry."

"I've lost half of my family in a month, Charlie. Half. The rest of them ..." Her head shook like she was trying to get rid of the thought. "I can't possibly explain my sister. Then there's an alcoholic brother who'll miss two more funerals. Another who seems pleased to attend and wouldn't mind more." Head still shaking, she shrugged. "And you have to ask what I want?"

No question she was hurting, but he had no idea how he could help, and wanted nothing more to do with Granvilles. He stayed quiet.

"You and I, Charlie," she said, linking her fingers together, "we're the ones left standing. I needed to reach out, to be, I don't know, tender with you. About everything. The way Mother trapped you. What Ward did. The trouble I caused. All of it."

If anyone should have reached out, it was him. His best guess still had Desiree doing the shooting.

"You're the most decent person I know," she said. "I need that right now, to spend a little time with a good person, to know I'm not just a Granville." She pulled at the cuff of his blazer. "Coffee, a drink, anything. Please?"

CHARLIE HAD NEVER driven a Ferrari, or anything like it. Amazing vehicle. Required so much concentration, he forgot his awful situation for a few minutes. He'd also never gone through the front door of the Ritz Carlton Lodge, but Lauren convinced him this would be the safest place to have their drink without being seen or pestered.

316

Trying not to gawk, he walked through the lobby arm-in-arm with her. Stone floors, overstuffed leather furniture on fancy rugs, carved beams across the high ceiling, fireplace big enough to roast a whole deer. Pretty easy to see how Desiree got dazzled.

"This way," she said, tugging him toward the Lobby Lounge sign.

They slid into a dimly lit booth, ordered, and sat in silence until after the waitress brought him a beer and her a sour apple martini.

She set her dark glasses on the table and raised her glass. "Should we drink to something?"

"No." He sipped his beer before she had a chance to change his mind about that, too.

"So, I'm curious." She tipped half of the martini into her mouth. "With your house gone, where are you living? With that Spuv person?"

"He offered, but, y'know, sharing's hard."

"And alone isn't?" She tossed down the rest of her drink. "Don't think you have to keep up." She raised and wiggled the empty until their waitress nodded.

"Not sure I'd be trying to drive that car after two drinks."

"I don't plan to." She leaned toward him. "You know, I was thinking on my way down here, if you need a place to stay, you can have Mother's house."

"Oooh no." He pressed back against the cushion.

"Don't be stupid. You need a place. It's there, and I'm in charge now. With Ward gone, I'm the conservator." Her mouth and eyes popped wide open. "Omigod, no I'm not. I'm the executrix. They'll be on me like a rash. Forever." She blinked her eyes and jostled her head. "Anyway, you should stay there until your house is rebuilt."

"Well, since that won't be happening, let's find something else to talk about." He lifted his beer to her and took a small sip.

"Don't tell me." Her head and shoulders slumped. "No insurance?"

He shrugged.

"Wait. I've got it." She spread her arms, "I'll rebuild it. I mean pay for it."

"You're not doing that."

"Charlie," she said, touching his hand, "my brother did this. Let me fix it." She sat back and pressed her fingertips to her heart. "God, this feels awesome. And it's *exactly* what Mother would have done."

Checking for nearby ears, he leaned close enough to speak low. "Listen to me." He waited until their foreheads almost touched. "Your brother didn't kill Desiree. Didn't blow up my house, either. Was the other way around, so you don't owe me a thing."

Brow creased, she pulled away, but still in whisper range. "Are you telling me you were there?"

"Course not. I just know, is all."

"The police aren't sure. How are you?"

"Over time, a man gets to know how his wife works."

"That's it?" she said. "Your knowledge of women is how you know?"

He waited for the waitress to leave after bringing Lauren's second martini. "Sure as we're setting here right now," he said, patting the table.

"Maybe this'll change your mind. Do you know Ward's wife walked out on him only days before the shootings?" She raised her eyebrows as she sipped her drink.

"So what?"

"Don't you think he might have been a little pissed off?"

He shrugged.

She dropped her eyes to the table. "Haven't you wondered why he was with your wife? At your house?"

"Don't know, and neither do you." He gripped the beer bottle so hard he was afraid it might shatter.

"Of course I do. Sex. I just don't know—"

"No!" He couldn't come up with a different reason, but there might have been one, and that's where he was going to leave it.

"Had to be," Lauren said, "and something went wrong. Maybe she didn't realize, or changed her mind. What else?"

Hands clamped over his ears, he rested his elbows on the table.

She pulled one of his hands away. "Do you think I want to believe he did it?"

He tugged free of her hand but kept staring at the table. "Blowing up the house. That was her. She couldn't have done that if he wasn't already dead." He crossed his forearms and laid his head on them. "Stop talking."

"Okay," she said, stroking his hair. "And what does it matter now, anyway? What does matter is I can help you, and I want to. Please let me."

Sitting tall, he slid sideways out of the booth, stood, and fished the Ferrari fob out of his pocket. "Got a long, bad day ahead of me tomorrow. All set?"

"Leave that on the table." She lounged back in the booth. "I believe I'm going to have another, or three, and stay here tonight." She dug a twenty dollar bill from her purse. "This should get you back to wherever it is you're staying. G'night."

He snatched the twenty. "You are some piece of work." Angry and dazed by how easily she got over on him, he started for the lobby.

"Charlie, wait. Your friend, Spuv. What's his real name?"

"Spenser Vaughn."

She smiled and wiggled her fingers in goodbye.

The idea she might try to get Spuv up there for some knocking boots, at a time like this in her life, doused the tiny spark of respect she'd earned by being open and generous. Ducking her for the rest of his life would only make it better.

CHAPTER FIFTY-FIVE

IF DR. GRANVILLE and Miss Vivien had been buried separately, or in different cemeteries, Charlie would have gone to Miss Vivien's service. Instead, he spent the two days after Desiree's funeral holed up in his Microtel room, sleeping in short bursts, eating Domino's pizza, watching TV, and avoiding Spuv's phone calls. Not that he was mad at Spuv, just wasn't ready for aggressive cheering up.

A knock hit the door in the middle of an ESPN recap. "Must be a slow night," he said on the way to the door. He'd called in his pizza order no more than ten minutes ago.

"Gotcha." Spuv angled his size fourteen boot against the doorjamb.

"Go away." Back at the bed, Charlie fell onto it, propped pillows behind his head, and trained his eyes on the TV.

"Dude," Spuv said, kicking the mattress in a slow rhythm, "answer your damn phone once in a while." His voice was too big for most spaces, and definitely for this matchbox room.

"Big man, say your piece and git. And quit your damn kicking."

"Got an invitation for you." His boot kept up the steady beat.

"Go away."

"Tomorrow night." Kick. "Fire house." Kick. "Six o'clock." Kick. "And you're going." Kick. "Even if it's in a body cast." Kick.

"Quit it!" He sprang from the bed. "Look, I'm not going anywhere. Just leave me the hell alone."

"Wrong. Boys at the firehouse are running a fundraiser to rebuild your house, and you're going." He shook a fist in Charlie's face. "Understand?"

"Call it off. They got no money."

"Ain't just them, dumbass. It's everyone. The whole town. The whole damn county." His arms whirled in wide circles. "All of America, for crissake. Sea to shining friggin' sea. They're calling it Dense-Aid. Willie Nelson's flying in. Got one of them contribution thermometers set up by the street and everything. Whadaya say now?"

"Very funny, but I'm not taking money from people who got none." He turned to crawl back onto the bed, but Spuv yanked him backward by the belt and slammed him face first against the door.

"Why's everything such a righteous goddam toothache with you?" His giant forearms pinned Charlie to the cool metal. "It's done, fool. Money's already raised. Twenty grand. Just show the hell up and smile."

"What are you talking about," he said, squirming against the pressure without any success. "How can twenty—Oh no. Give it back to her."

"Listen!" Spuv's arms pushed the air out of Charlie. "She wired it to my account. For you. Either take it, or I will."

"Can't breathe," he gasped.

The pressure relaxed, but only a little.

"No sin in accepting a kindness, jackass." Spuv shoved away from the door.

Learning why Lauren wanted to know Spuv's Christian name made him ashamed about thinking she was a soulless tramp, trolling for a quick jump between funerals. Unless that's what actually happened. "Did you go to her at the Ritz?" He twisted and rolled his achy back.

"I wish. Did everything over the phone." He bounced his eyebrows. "But I got her number now."

"Well good for you. Couple of pigs like—" He launched backward onto the bed to get away from Spuv's rush.

"You got no call insulting people."

"I called you a pig before."

"Not me. Her. And remember, you damn fool, she did this

with a truckload of shit on her head. If nothing else, take it so she don't have to eat another kick in the teeth right now."

He bought time by grimacing and rolling his head. More than once now he'd judged Lauren wrong.

"Woods," Spuv said, finger jabbing at him, "you don't show up tomorrow night, I promise you, I will beat the everlovin' shit outta you."

"Spuv?"

"Dude, I'm serious," Spuv said, fist cocked.

"It's my privilege to know you."

CHAPTER FIFTY-SIX

FELT LIKE a year, but just five days had ticked past since the fund raiser. A touch over twenty-two thousand, raised at a party that started in hushed voices but broke into a carnival after the announcement of a big, anonymous donation.

Charlie was grateful to Spuv for making him go. The party-hearty crowd booted him out of his brooding, out of his dead-end anger at Desiree. And catching so many people in a good deed pushed her a little farther back in his thoughts. Allowed the life ahead of him to take more shape.

It would be a life without a twenty thousand dollar head start. He only pretended to accept it so Spuv wouldn't be tempted to keep it, but he also flat-out knew it was Desiree, not Ward Granville, who blew up his home. Keeping that money would have been no different than Desiree keeping those damn earrings.

The fund raiser hadn't just helped his attitude. It was bigger. Reminded him of a graduation, the end and start of something at the same time. That very night began long stretches of peaceful sleep. Each day, bigger bits of normal crept back into his life, so fast he wondered if it was decent. A dead wife should have been at least a standing eight-count, but that supposed a wife who'd held up her end.

Decent or not, today he was ready. One week, and he was ready. Just past 9:00 AM, he shoveled a bowlful of Cheerios into his face, jumped into the pickup, and headed south. Hadn't been to Hunger and Hardship Creek in a lot of years, but there wasn't a more appropriate spot on the planet for his mission.

Forty-five minutes of easy driving got him to Dublin. He parked along the roadside and high-stepped through a weedy lot. Used to be a roadhouse there when he was a kid, but only a cracked concrete slab survived. Spring rains had added enough to the little creek that he heard it before reaching the edge of the steep bank. He patted his front pocket one last time, scrabbled halfway down the slope, and sat on a flat rock. Dumping the earrings was why he came, but first he called the number Spuv gave him.

"Hello?' a sleepy-sounding woman said after two rings.

"Sorry if I woke you. It's Charlie Woods."

"Who?"

He was afraid Spuv gave him some other honey's number by mistake. "Charlie Woods. This isn't Lauren Granville?"

"Oh, Charlie. The last name threw me. Hang on." She rustled around, probably sitting up. "Why are you calling me before dawn?"

"It's comin' onto 10:00."

"What do you want?"

"The money. I know it was you. Just wanted to thank you."

"You're welcome," she said through a yawn.

"And to tell you I can't keep it."

"Don't be stupid. Of course you can."

That damn word again, but this time he was glad to hear it. Anything that helped push him away from her. "No, I can't. How do I get it back to you?"

"My first generosity. Why are you spoiling this?"

"I'm fit and able. Go find someone else who—" The perfect choice smacked him. "I got it. If you're still in the giving mood, give it to Wounded Warriors."

Her next yawn ended like a winding down siren. "Fine. Send it to them. Makes it deductible. Good plan."

"Serious? I can do that?"

"Why not? Say it's from me and get a tax receipt. You can give it to me next time you're in Atlanta. We'll have a drink or something. Maybe finish our morning in Key West." She laughed, one of those husky, sexy laughs some women have, especially after a good night.

Much as he'd enjoy it, making that visit would be like getting a tattoo, something to regret for the rest of his life. "I just buried my wife, for heaven sake."

"Charlie, relax. I'm kidding ... sorta. You're a born husband. But the next wife? No rescue dog. Find a pretty young thing at church, fuck her full of babies, and be insanely happy."

"Y'know, you can throw off on me all you want, but that's exactly what I'm gonna do."

"Do it. You deserve it. See you in heaven." She hung up.

He stared at the phone. Typical Granville conversation. He wasn't sure if he'd been slammed. Was "rescue dog" an insult, or a way of saying Desiree was special and deserved someone more capable than him? Either way, Wounded Warriors wasn't going to care, and cursed as the money might be, Granville cash couldn't hurt those boys any worse than they already were.

Only one more thing to do, the reason he'd driven to the creek. He stood, fished Desiree's earrings out of his pocket, and wiggled them in his palm. Two tainted bits of glitter that cost him way too much. Arm cocked to toss them into the current, he stopped. Desiree was dead. What good could come from ditching them now? He sat on the rock again. More he thought on it, more he realized they weren't his to throw away. The real owner was the charge card company. Didn't have a clue which one she used, so he decided the best he could do was give them back to Bernie, the jeweler, and hope the man was honorable enough to cancel the sale.

The walk back to his truck felt lighter, like he'd broken the last chain. Nothing more from the past to tidy up, and the curtain lifting on what was ahead filled him with a panicky excitement. Lauren's suggestion to find another wife and start a family kept repeating in his head. He'd only snapped an answer back to shut her up, but she was right, and he couldn't see any reason to wait. Problem was, coming so quick on the heels of Desiree killing herself, folks in Greensboro might not see things the same way. That left one option, and the only person he could tell was Spuv. He dug out his phone.

"Dude," boomed into the phone.

"Big man, I have to come over. If you got anyone there, send her on an errand."

"Shit. How much time I got?"

He still had to return the earrings and clear out of the Microtel. "Couple hours."

"You in trouble, son?"

"Just the opposite."

CHAPTER FIFTY-SEVEN

IT'D WORKED for Candy when she wanted to tranquilize Spuv, so Charlie showed up at the big man's house with a steamer pack of Krystals sliders.

"What the hell?" Spuv hollered when he opened his front door. Grinning, he stepped to the side and pointed toward the living room. "You! Get your damn self in here, and bring that ugly Marine with you." He snatched the carrier and nuzzled his cheek on it as he headed for the kitchen. "I will not be gentle, darlin'."

First time he'd been in Spuv's home in years. Same as he remembered it. Clothes everywhere. Dishes, cans, and bottles setting on two small tables and the TV. Smelled like old cooking grease and Italian leftovers. "How can women stand this place?" he said, trailing Spuv into the ranch house's tiny kitchen, also a mess.

"Who the hell knows? Must bring out the mother in 'em. Any of these burgers for you?" Spuv reached into a plastic bag of paper plates sitting on top of a brown-streaked toaster oven. "Fine with me if they're not." He cracked open one of the Krystal boxes and stuffed a mini-burger in his mouth.

"Spuv, I'm here to say goodbye. I'm leaving."

"Bullshit." Another slider disappeared.

"The heck I'm not. My stuff's all packed up outside. Figure to drive until someplace feels right. Or I'm outta money. Or the truck says it's had enough." He snapped his fingers. "Oh, and I had my mail forwarded here for now. Hope that's okay."

"Dude, chill." Spuv piled a second paper plate with Krystals boxes. "Here, eat these. We'll get you so busy fighting heartburn, you'll forget about running off." He bobbed his chin toward the fridge. "Grab us a couple beers. We'll down these rascals out back."

"Not running off. Running to. It's out there, waiting. Longer I stay here, less time I'll have to find it."

Holding a mounded plateful in each hand, Spuv tapped his boot against the back door. "How 'bout you bore me with this out in the sunshine."

"Best friend I ever had, big man." He stuck out his hand.

"Son of a bitch, you're serious." Spuv set the plates on the counter, rubbed his palms on his sweatpants, and gripped Charlie's hand. "Don't do this, man. Least give it a month. What's a damn month?"

"Got one last favor. The donations for my house have to go back." He slipped a check from his shirt pocket and held it out.

"Can't go insulting those good people, jackass. What's wrong with you?"

"I gave hers back, and the rest—"

"You what?" Spuv rose taller and leaned at him.

"Don't ask me to explain, 'cause I can't. I just know things'd go bad for me if I kept it."

"And what about all the others? How the hell would you feel?"

"Spuv, without her part, the rest wouldn't get me a carport. Way I see it, it'd be more of an insult to keep their money but do nothing with it." He pushed the check closer. "C'mon, take it. Sweet talker like you should be able to spin it right."

Looking stunned, Spuv took the slip of paper.

"Made it payable to you. Every penny. If there's any you can't give back to the folks, send it to Wounded Warriors. Can I count on you?"

Spuv glanced at the check and set it down. "You ain't, uh, fixing to do something," his eyes jumped to Charlie's, "y'know, crazy."

"C'mon now," he said, smiling.

"Then what the hell's going on in there?" Spuv bonked the heel of his hand against Charlie's forehead.

Still smiling, Charlie shrugged. "Got a question for you. I figured the answer today, but I want to see if you know. Ready?"

"Wait. *You* know the answer? Shit, I better not miss this." Spuv slapped himself on both cheeks, rolled his head, and jogged a couple of steps in place. "Okay. Go."

"Alright. If all of us owe something to each other, what is it? I mean, what's the best thing a person can do with their life?"

"Whoa!" Spuv pointed to the oven clock. "Is that the time? Dude, you're gonna hit some nasty-ass traffic if you don't hightail it."

"Gonna tell you anyway, doofus," he said, laughing. "We have to leave behind better people than we were. I don't mean richer, though that's fine too. Just better. And that's what I'm hoping to do."

"Gonna be a damn preacher?"

He shook his head. "Nope. A daddy, and I think I'll be good at it." He jabbed a thumb toward the street. "There's someone out there, Spuv. A good woman who wants kids, maybe already has some, and I'm gonna find her."

Spuv dropped his gaze to the floor. "Might be out of line saying this, but you didn't do so good with the last one."

Again, he wondered if Spuv knew more than he'd ever tell. "No shame getting knocked down, big man. Shame is not getting back up."

"So get back up in Greensboro."

"You're a fisherman. When a spot gets played out, you move."

"Dude, you haven't thrown in a line around here for a lot of damn years. How do you know they're not biting? Which, by the way," he said, socking Charlie's shoulder, "ain't as bad as it sounds. C'mon, buddy, we just got you back. All of us. Give it a chance. This is your home."

No way he'd be able to explain why that wasn't true anymore. "I'll keep my piece of ground just in case. Least I'm gonna try. Only got about two thousand left, but I'm not really worried. There's always work for the willing, and my truck's comfortable enough."

Spuv let out a laugh, but without a smile. "Gonna live in your damn truck?"

"Just 'til I find something."

"Sure you thought this through? You're gonna hit every town looking and smelling like Hobo Joe."

Hadn't occurred to him staying presentable would be important. That meant motels at least some of the time, and his puny nest egg would disappear that much faster. He needed to get out of there before Spuv poked another hole in his life raft. "Might be right. Two weeks from now you may have a new roommate. All I know is, my life was here, and now it's not. Could be a sign to start over someplace else, and I'm gonna find out." He took a Dr. Pepper from the fridge. "Highway's calling."

Spuv walked him to the truck and held out a paper plate of Krystals as Charlie got settled behind the wheel.

Lowering the driver's window, he took the food and set it on the passenger seat with his Dr. Pepper. "Wish me luck."

One of Spuv's jumbo hands reached inside and shook him by the neck. "Last crack at rolling that pea brain of yours back into place."

Charlie elbowed the hand away, smiled a goodbye, and dropped the pickup into reverse. "Call you when I get somewhere." As he rolled down toward the street, his eyes bounced between the empty road and Spuv, his friend's waving hand never getting above chest high.

Leaving didn't feel sad as he thought it would. All the quiet time he'd had in recent days got him to see he'd really been gone since he became a husband. Was like saying "I will" had shrink-wrapped his old life, with him on the outside of everything he'd known and been. He could see through the cover but never break back in. Nothing more to do but slide it behind him and get on with the new.

Only had one rule for the drive: avoid interstates. He wanted towns. Get out at cafes, churches, VFW's, and firehouses. Talk to folks. See what kind of work might be available. The first outbound road he came to headed east. Good as any.

Hardly a mile out of town, the two lane county road rose

enough that he could see some of Greensboro in his mirrors. He pulled to the shoulder, grabbed his Krystals and Dr. Pepper, and sat on the tailgate. In every direction, endless green rolled along the horizon. Chewing burgers and sipping pop, he took guesses where things were, pictured them as pins on a map. One for his used-to-be house. Another for Spuv's. The firehouse, high school, and Antioch Baptist church. The final pins were packed in a tight cluster. GranDelia, his mother, and Desiree, side by side in the only ground anyone owns forever, waiting for the end of time.

He finished lunch but didn't shove off. Not one vehicle had cruised east the whole time he'd been setting there. "Mistake?" he said toward puffs of white drifting across the sky.

GranDelia stayed quiet, like she'd done since Desiree died.

Smiling with only half his mouth, he hopped off the tailgate and shuffled to the driver's door. One last look at the countryside and heavens before he climbed in. "Not real good at goodbyes, are we?" he said out the window. Re-adjusting the mirrors, he fired up the engine and eased onto the road going somewhere.

BOOK CLUB DISCUSSION TOPICS:

1. Did the opening have a good hook?

2. Are the characters introduced logically and naturally? Are they authentic? Does each have a distinctive voice that reinforces characterization?

3. Do settings serve as characters and help create the proper mood and tone for each scene?

4. Is the plot plausible, and did it hold your interest throughout?

5. Do GranDelia's cameo appearances help or hurt the book?

6. Could any scenes have been eliminated?

7. Was the sex more graphic than necessary?

8. Is pornography a catalyst for any outcomes?

9. Why are war terms used so frequently by the characters?

10. Are minor characters more than interruptions in the tension?

11. Was the end satisfying?

12. Did the title make sense after finishing the book?